EXPOSED

Also by Lisa Scottoline

Rosato & DiNunzio Novels
Damaged
Corrupted
Betrayed
Accused

Rosato & Associates Novels
Think Twice
Lady Killer
Killer Smile
Dead Ringer
Courting Trouble
The Vendetta Defense
Moment of Truth
Mistaken Identity
Rough Justice
Legal Tender
Everywhere That Mary Went

Other Novels
One Perfect Lie
Most Wanted
Every Fifteen Minutes
Keep Quiet
Don't Go
Come Home
Save Me
Look Again
Daddy's Girl
Dirty Blonde
Devil's Corner
Running from the Law
Final Appeal

Nonfiction (with Francesca Serritella)
I Need a Lifeguard Everywhere but the Pool
I've Got Sand in All the Wrong Places
Does This Beach Make Me Look Fat?
Have a Nice Guilt Trip
Meet Me at Emotional Baggage Claim
Best Friends, Occasional Enemies
My Nest Isn't Empty, It Just Has More Closet Space
Why My Third Husband Will Be a Dog

EXPOSED

A Rosato & DiNunzio Novel

Lisa Scottoline

ST. MARTIN'S PRESS ❧ NEW YORK

This is a work of fiction. All of the characters, organizations, and events portrayed in this novel are either products of the author's imagination or are used fictitiously.

www.stmartins.com

Library of Congress Cataloging-in-Publication Data

Names: Scottoline, Lisa, author.
Title: Exposed / Lisa Scottoline.
Description: First edition. | New York : St. Martin's Press, 2017. | Series:
    A Rosato & Dinunzio novel ; 5
Identifiers: LCCN 2017016193| ISBN 9781250099716 (hardcover) |
    ISBN 9781250151032 (signed edition) | ISBN 9781250099730 (ebook)
Subjects: LCSH: Rosato & Associates (Imaginary organization)—Fiction. |
    Women lawyers—Fiction. | BISAC: FICTION / Mystery &
    Detective / Women Sleuths. | GSAFD: Mystery fiction. | Legal stories.
Classification: LCC PS3569.C725 E95 2017 | DDC 813/.54—dc23
LC record available at https://lccn.loc.gov/2017016193

Our books may be purchased in bulk for promotional, educational, or business use. Please contact your local bookseller or the Macmillan Corporate and Premium Sales Department at 1-800-221-7945, extension 5442, or by email at MacmillanSpecialMarkets@macmillan.com.

First Edition: August 2017

10 9 8 7 6 5 4 3 2 1

This book is dedicated to the physicians, nurses, and staff of the Children's Hospital of Philadelphia.

"Hell is empty, and all the devils are here!"

—William Shakespeare, *The Tempest*

EXPOSED

CHAPTER ONE

Mary DiNunzio stepped off the elevator, worried. Her father and his friends looked over from the reception area, their lined faces stricken. They'd called her to say they needed a lawyer but until now, she hadn't been overly concerned. Their last lawsuit was against the Frank Sinatra Social Society of South Philly on behalf of the Dean Martin Fan Club of South Philly. Luckily Mary had been able to settle the matter without involving Tony Bennett.

"Hi, Pop." Mary crossed the lobby, which was otherwise empty. Marshall, their receptionist, wasn't at her desk, though she must've already gotten in. The aroma of fresh coffee filled the air, since Marshall knew that Mary's father and his fellow octogenarians ran on caffeine and Coumadin.

"HIYA, HONEY!" her father shouted, despite his hearing aids. Everyone was used to Mariano "Matty" DiNunzio talking loudly, which came off as enthusiastic rather than angry. On the table next to him sat a white box of pastries, as the DiNunzios didn't go anywhere empty-handed, even to a law firm. The box hadn't been opened, so whatever was bothering him was something even saturated fats couldn't cure.

"Hey, Mare!" "Hi, Mary!" "*Buongiorno, Maria!*" said his

friends The Three Tonys, like a Greek—or more accurately Roman—chorus. They got up to greet her, rising slowly on replacement knees, like hammers on a piano with sticky keys. Her father had grown up with The Tonys; Tony "From-Down-The-Block" LoMonaco, "Pigeon" Tony Lucia, and Tony "Two Feet" Pensiera, which got shortened to "Feet," so even his nickname had a nickname. It went without saying that naming traditions in South Philly were *sui generis,* which was Latin for completely insane. The Tonys went everywhere with her father and sometimes helped her on her cases, which was like having a secret weapon or a traveling nightmare.

"Good morning, Pop." Mary reached her father and gave him a big hug. He smelled the way he always did, of hard soap from a morning shave and the mothballs that clung to his clothes. He and The Tonys were dressed in basically the same outfit—a white short-sleeved shirt, baggy Bermuda shorts, and black-socks-with-sandals—like a barbershop quartet gone horribly wrong.

"THANKS FOR SEEIN' US, HONEY." Her father hugged her back, and Mary loved the solidity of his chubby belly. She would move mountains for him, but it still wouldn't be enough to thank him for being such a wonderful father. Both of her parents loved her to the marrow, though her mother could be as protective as a mother bear, if not a mother Tyrannosaurus rex.

"No problem." Mary released him, but he looked away, which was unlike him. "You okay, Pop?"

"SURE, SURE." Her father waved her off with an arthritic hand, but Mary was concerned. His eyes were a milky brown behind his bifocals, but troubled.

"What is it?"

"YOU'LL SEE. YOUR MOTHER SAYS HI."

Just then Feet raised his slack arms, pulled Mary close to his chest, and hugged her so hard that he jostled his Mr. Potatohead glasses. He, too, seemed agitated, if affectionate. "Mare, thank you for making the time for us."

"Of course, I'm happy to see you."

"I appreciate it. You're such a good kid." Feet righted his thick trifocals, repaired with Scotch tape at one corner. His round eyes were hooded, his nose was bulbous, and he was completely bald, with worry lines that began at his eyebrows and looked more worried than usual.

"Mary!" Tony-From-Down-The-Block reached for her with typical vigor, the youngest of the group, at eighty-three. He worked out, doing a chair-exercise class at the senior center, and was dating again, as evidenced by his hair's suspicious shade of reddish-brown, like oxblood shoe polish. He gave her a hug, and Mary breathed in his Paco Rabanne and BenGay, a surprisingly fragrant combination.

"Good to see you." Mary let him go and moved on to hug Pigeon Tony, an Italian immigrant with a stringy neck, who not only raised homing pigeons but looked like one. Pigeon Tony was barely five feet tall and bird-thin, with a smooth bald head and round brown-black eyes divided by a nose shaped like a beak. In other words, adorable.

"*Come stai, Maria?*" Pigeon Tony released her with a sad smile, and Mary tried to remember her Italian.

"*Va bene, grazie. E tu?*"

"*Cosi, cosi,*" Pigeon Tony answered, though he'd never before said anything but *bene*. You didn't have to speak Italian to know there was a problem, and Mary turned to address the foursome.

"So what's going on, guys? How can I help you?"

"IT'S NOT ABOUT US," her father answered gravely.

Feet nodded, downcast. "It's about Simon."

"Oh no, what's up?" Mary loved Feet's son Simon, who was her unofficial cousin, since The Tonys were her unofficial uncles.

"He's not so good."

"What's the matter? Is it Rachel?" Mary felt a pang of fear. Simon's wife, Ellen, died four years ago of an aneurysm, and Simon had become a single father of an infant, Rachel. When Rachel turned three, she was diagnosed with leukemia but was in remission.

"Simon will explain it. Oh, here he comes now!" Feet turned to the elevator just as the doors opened and Simon stepped out, looking around to orient himself.

"Hey, honey!" Mary called to him, hiding her dismay. He looked tired, with premature gray threaded through his dark curly hair, and though he had his father's stocky build, he'd lost weight. His navy sport jacket hung on him and his jeans were too big. She hadn't seen him in a while, since he was busy with Rachel, though they'd kept in touch by email.

"Hi, Mary!" Simon strode toward her, and Mary reached him with a hug, since she could only imagine what he'd been going through, not only with the baby, but losing Ellen. Mary herself had been widowed young, after the murder of her first husband, Mike. Even though she was happily remarried, Mike was a part of her and always would be, which suited her and her new husband, Anthony, just fine.

"It's so good to see you, honey." Mary released him, and Simon brightened.

"This office is so nice, with your name on the sign."

"Believe me, I'm as surprised as you are." Mary could see Simon was happy for her and felt a new rush of affection for him. "How's the baby?"

"I'll fill you in later." Simon's smile stiffened. "I just moved her to CHOP."

Mary wondered why Rachel had been moved, but it wasn't the time to ask. CHOP was the Children's Hospital of Philadelphia, one of the best in the country. Mary's heart went out to him. "I'm praying for her, and so is my mother. She's got the novenas on overdrive."

"I know, and she sends me Mass cards, God bless her." Simon's smile returned. "I tell our rabbi, I'll take all the help I can get."

"Exactly. She prayed for me to make partner."

"Ha! Anyway, thanks for seeing me on such short notice. Are you sure you have the time?"

"Totally. My first appointment isn't until ten thirty." Mary motioned him out of the reception area. "Let's go to the conference room."

"Okay." Simon fell into step beside her, followed by her father, The Tonys, and the pastry box, which gave Mary pause. Simon was a potential client, and she wouldn't ordinarily have a client consultation with an audience, blood-related or not.

"Simon, did you want to talk alone?" she asked him, stopping in the hallway. "What we say is confidential, and it's your call whether your dad or anybody else comes in with us. They can wait in—"

Feet interrupted, "No, I wanna be there, Mare. I know what he's gonna tell you, we all do."

Tony-From-Down-The-Block snorted. "Of course we'll be there. Feet's his father, and I taught him how to ride a bike."

"I CHANGED HIS DIAPERS!"

Mary looked over, skeptically. "When, Pop?"

"THAT ONE TIME, I FORGET." Her father held up the pastry box by its cotton string. "PLUS I GOT BREAKFAST."

Pigeon Tony kept his own counsel, his dark gaze darting from Simon to Mary, and she suspected that he understood more than he let on, regardless of the language.

Simon smiled crookedly. "Mary, you didn't think we were going to shake them, did you? It's okay. They can come with us."

"THIS WAY, I KNOW WHERE IT IS!" Her father lumbered off, down the hallway.

"Of course, we're all going!" Feet said, at his heels. "We're family. We're all family!"

"*Andiamo!*" said Pigeon Tony.

Mary led them down the hallway and into the conference room, where Thomas Eakins's rowing prints lined the warm white walls and fresh coffee had been set up on the credenza. The far side of the room was glass, showing an impressive view of the Philadelphia skyline thick with humidity. July was a bad-hair month in Philly, and Mary was already damp under her linen dress.

She closed the conference-room door, glancing at Simon, who perched unhappily on the edge of his chair. He'd always been one of the smartest and nicest kids in the neighborhood, affable enough to make friends even though he was one of the few who didn't go to parochial school. He'd gone to Central High, and the Pensieras were Italian Jews, but the religious distinction made no difference as far as the neighborhood was concerned. The common denominator was homemade tomato sauce.

"Simon, would you like coffee?" Mary set down her purse and messenger bag while her father and The Tonys surged to the credenza.

"No, thanks. Let's get started." Simon sat down catty-corner to the head of the table.

"Agree." Mary took the seat, slid her laptop from her bag, and powered it up while her father and The Tonys yakked away, pouring coffee and digging into the pastry box.

"MARE, YOU TWO START WITHOUT US. DON'T WAIT ON US."

Mary pulled her laptop from her bag, fired it up, and opened a file, turning to Simon. "So, tell me what's going on."

"Okay." Simon paused, collecting his thoughts. "Well, you remember, I'm in sales at OpenSpace, and we make office cubicles. We have different designs and price points, though we also customize. We did $9 million in sales last fiscal year and we have forty-five employees, including manufacturing and administrative, in Horsham."

"How long have you worked for them, again?"

"Twelve years, almost since I graduated Temple, and—" Simon flushed, licking lips that had gone suddenly dry. "Well, I just got fired."

"Oh, no," Mary said, surprised. Simon was smart and hard-working, a success from the get-go. "When did this happen?"

"Two days ago, Tuesday. July 11."

"Why?" Mary caught Feet's stricken expression, and her father and the others had gone quiet.

"They said it was my performance. But I don't think that's the real reason."

"What do you think?" Mary's mind was already flipping through the possible illegal reasons, which weren't many. Pennsylvania was a right-to-work state, which meant that an employee could be fired at will, for any or no reason, as long as it wasn't discriminatory.

"Honestly, my performance is great. I'm one of the top reps. I've gotten great reviews and bonuses for years. Things started to go south after Rachel was diagnosed. The final straw for them was—" Simon hesitated, and Feet came over and placed a hand on his shoulder.

"Son, the baby's going to be fine. We're all praying, and she's got good doctors. *Great* doctors."

"Thanks, Dad." Simon returned his attention to Mary, her gaze newly agonized. "I didn't let people know, but Rachel relapsed and she has to have a bone marrow transplant. That's why she got moved to CHOP."

"Oh no, I'm sorry to hear that." Mary felt her chest tighten with emotion, but she didn't want to open any floodgates, especially with Feet, her father, and the others. Now she understood why they'd been so upset. Simon was in dire straits, with Rachel so ill and now him out of a job.

"Obviously, I wish the chemo had worked, but I feel great about the BMT Team at CHOP. They specialize in ALL." Simon caught himself. "Sorry about the lingo. BMT stands for Blood and Marrow Transplant Team and ALL is acute lymphoblastic leukemia, which is what she has."

"I can't imagine how hard this is to go through, for all of you."

"We're doing the best we can. My dad's there all the time, so it helps when I have to work." Simon managed a shaky smile. "It's just that as a father, you feel so helpless. I mean, it sounds cliché, but it's true. I know, I *live* it. You have hope, but no control. None at all. Well, you get it. You know, you see. She has to be okay."

"She will be," Feet said quietly, and Mary's father, Pigeon Tony, and Tony-From-Down-The-Block walked over, their lined faces masks of sorrow and fear. They stood motionless behind him, having forgotten about the coffee and pastries.

"SIMON, WE'LL HELP ANY WAY WE CAN. WON'T WE, MARE?"

"Yes, we will," Mary answered, meaning it. She patted Simon's hand again.

Tony-From-Down-The-Block chimed in, "We're going to get through this together." He gestured at Pigeon Tony. "He's gonna make some baked ziti for you, Simon. He's an excellent cook, like, gourmet. All you gotta do is put it in the microwave."

"Thanks, guys." Simon turned around, then faced Mary. "Anyway, I think that's the reason why they fired me."

Mary blinked. "How so?"

"Well, when Rachel was first diagnosed, my boss, Todd, was really nice about it. I have decent benefits and they covered Rachel. I took out a second mortgage to cover what it doesn't. The meds are astronomical." Simon leaned over, urgent. "But OpenSpace is self-insured up to $250,000, which means that their insurance policy doesn't reimburse them until their employee medical expenses reach that amount. They have to pay out of pocket until then."

"Understood. It's like a deductible." Mary knew the basics of employment benefits.

"Exactly." Simon nodded. "But Rachel's bills alone are so high that the insurance company was going to raise the premiums."

"I see, and are the premiums going up?"

"I don't know, but I'm getting ahead of myself. After Rachel's first round of chemo, my boss, Todd, kept asking me how Rachel was. I thought he was interested, like, being nice. He has a ten-year-old daughter. But then he made comments about the bills when I submitted them. And then when the first bills for chemo came in, for seven grand, he reduced my territory from three states—Jersey, Pennsylvania, and Delaware—to just Delaware."

Mary didn't understand something. "What does it matter that your territory was reduced?"

"A reduction in my territory means I can't make my sales quotas. Not only that, but the territory he gave me was more residential and had less businesses, so there was no way I could ever make quota." Simon flushed. "I tried, but no matter what I did, I was only selling a fraction of the units. For the first time in twelve years, I didn't make quota."

Mary put it together. "So your sales go down and your performance suffers."

"Right." Simon nodded. "Todd was trying to force me out, hoping that I would quit, but I didn't. I love my accounts, my reps, and my job, and I need the job."

"Of course."

"So when Rachel's pediatric oncologist told me she needed the transplant and referred me to CHOP, I told Todd and he asked how much it was going to cost. At the time, I didn't know the costs of the transplant, but the donor search alone cost like $60,000 to $100,000, and I told him that."

"To search for a match? Why does that cost so much? It

didn't cost that much when we tried before, did it?" Mary was referring to a previous time, when Rachel had been considered for a bone marrow transplant and they had all registered as donors, by giving cheek swabs to collect DNA. None of them had been matches.

"It's not the costs of donating, it's the costs of finding a donor. The hospital has to contact the Bone Marrow Donor Registry to get a list of potential matches, but they have to test at least six potential donors to get one that's a perfect match. Each test costs six to nine grand. It adds up fast."

"Oh, man." Mary hadn't realized.

"Luckily, CHOP found us a match, changed Rachel's chemo protocol, and got her into remission. You have to be in remission to do the transplant."

"That's sounds like a Catch-22."

"I know, but it isn't. I'll fill you in another time. Anyway, when I told Todd that Rachel needed the transplant, he fired me the next week, supposedly because I didn't make quota—for one month. The first time in twelve years."

"So it was a pretext because they didn't want to pay for Rachel's expenses? And they didn't want their premiums to go up?"

"I think so."

"That's heartless." Mary felt a surge of anger, the kind she always felt when somebody had been wronged. But here, it had happened to someone she knew and loved. Simon. And Rachel.

Feet shook his head. "They're bastards!"

"WHAT KINDA PEOPLE FIRE YOU BECAUSE YOU GOT A SICK KID? THEY SHOULD BURN IN HELL!"

"*Disgrazia!*"

Simon shook his head. "The irony is that OpenSpace wouldn't have had to pay another penny. CHOP worked with me and Aetna, and since I'm a Pennsylvania resident and the illness is life-threatening, I can use secondary insurance like the

CAT fund and Medicaid. They cover the costs of the transplant, which is astronomical."

"How much does a bone marrow transplant cost?"

"A million bucks."

"Whoa, are you kidding?" Mary said, shocked.

"No, start to finish, it's almost a year-long process, and you can't imagine the expertise and care it takes."

"I bet." Mary got back on track. "Do you remember the comment your boss, Todd, made to you, about how much it was costing?"

"Yes, and I even have proof. I wrote down every time Todd said something to me about her bills. I didn't want to write it on my phone because it's company-issued." Simon reached into his sport jacket, pulled out a Moleskine notebook, and set it down. "I can show you right here, when and where."

"Great." Mary picked up the notebook, opened it, and glanced at Simon's characteristically neat writing, with dates and times noted. "Simon, what's your boss's full name?"

"Todd Eddington."

Mary made a note. "How long has he been your boss and what's his job title?"

"He's sales manager. I've reported to him for twelve years." Simon swallowed hard. "I thought we were friends. I know his ex-wife, Cheryl. They were both good to Ellen." Simon's voice trailed off, but Mary wanted to keep him on the case.

"So did Todd make the decision or did somebody else?"

"He does. He makes a recommendation upstairs, to hire or fire, and it gets rubber-stamped by the president, Mike Bashir."

Mary made a note of the name.

"So is it legal, what they did?" Simon leaned over. "It seems so wrong to me. I understand that a transplant costs a lot, but they're going gangbusters and I worked for them for twelve years. Can they get away with this?"

"Not in my book. We can sue them for this, and we should,

right away." Mary knew disability law as a result of her grow-ing special-education practice and she was already drafting a complaint in her mind. She loved it when the law actually did justice, which happened less frequently than God intended.

"So it's illegal?" Simon leaned forward, newly urgent.

"Yes. There's a federal law, the Americans with Disabilities Act, and it prevents discrimination in employment based on disability or illness. So for example, you can't fire somebody because they have cancer—"

"But how does that apply to me? I'm not the one with can-cer, Rachel is."

"I know, but the law has a special provision that applies here, though it's not well-known. In fact, there's very little case law on it, but it applies to us." Mary started searching online for the statute. "It's called the 'association provision' and it forbids employment discrimination on the basis of an illness contracted by people who are *associated* with the insured employee, like their family."

"Really?" Simon's eyes widened with hope.

"Yes, under the ADA, an employer is prohibited from"—Mary found the statute and started reading aloud—" 'exclud-ing or otherwise denying equal jobs or benefits to a qualified individual because of the known disability of an individual with whom the qualified individual is known to have a rela-tionship or association.' "

"MARE, WE DON'T GET THE LEGALESE!"

Mary explained, "It means Simon is a qualified individual under the law and he is associated with Rachel. In other words, Simon's company can't fire him because she got sick and her medical expenses are going to cost them. I have to research the cases and get more facts from you, but I think we have an ex-cellent case here."

"That's great!" Simon threw his hands in the air.

"Thank God!" Feet cheered, and Tony-From-Down-The-Block, Pigeon Tony, and Mary's father burst into chatter, all at once. *"Bravissima, Maria!"* "Way to go, Mare! Go get 'em!"

"MARE, I KNEW YOU'D KNOW WHAT TO DO! I'M SO PROUD A YOU!" Her father shuffled over and kissed the top of her head. "THANK GOD YOU'RE SO SMART! AND BEAUTIFUL!"

"Aw, Pop." Mary flushed, relieved. She couldn't have lived with herself if she couldn't help Simon and Rachel, fighting for her life. If there was any reason she had become a lawyer, this was it. To help families, children, and the community as a whole. She felt as if she had finally found her niche in special-education and disability law and lately she'd come to work happier than ever before.

Simon beamed. "Mary, that's so amazing. How does that work? Do you think I could get my job back? I really need to work."

"Okay, hold on." Mary put up her hand. "I have to study your notebook and do my research before I can answer any of these questions for sure. And the procedure under the law is that before we go to court, we have to file a complaint with the EEOC, the Equal Employment Opportunity Commission, first. Then they give us a right-to-sue letter and we can go to court. As far as remedy, I don't know if you can get your job back, but why would you want it? Do you have an employment contract or a non-compete?"

"Yes, for two years, and it covers the mid-Atlantic states. So now I can't work in sales in the area but I can't move out of the area because of Rachel being at CHOP."

Mary saw his dilemma. "Okay, we'll see what we can do. We might be able to get a decent settlement, then you can stay home with Rachel during her treatment."

"But what about her medical expenses?"

"You buy COBRA with the settlement money. That covers you both for eighteen months and you'll find another job when you free up more."

"That would be best of all! I don't know how to thank you, Mary." Simon broke into a huge smile.

Her father grinned. "HOW MUCH CAN YOU GET HIM, MARE?"

Feet chimed in, "Yeah, how much?"

Mary waved them off. "Don't get ahead of yourselves. I need to know more before we make a settlement demand and I want to see the notebook, so I understand exactly what happened."

Simon nodded, excited. "So you'll take my case, Mary? Do you have the time?"

"Of course." Mary mentally cleared her calendar. She didn't have anything as pressing as this. This was for family.

"Thank you so much!" Simon squeezed her hand. "And I just want to say up front that I'm paying you for this. I'm not expecting you to represent me for free."

"YOUR MONEY'S NO GOOD HERE. YOU KNOW THAT."

"Simon, my father's right," Mary said, meaning it. She'd have to tell her partner, Bennie Rosato, but the days were over when she'd have to ask for permission.

"What do we do next?" Simon checked his watch. "I should get over to the hospital."

Feet nodded. "Simon sleeps there, and we trade off. We like to be there when she's up."

Tony-From-Down-The-Block added, "So she knows she's not alone."

"OF COURSE SHE'S NOT ALONE!" Mary's father said, and she saw his eyes begin to glisten, so she rose.

"Okay, then. Let me get started so we can get a demand letter out right away. See if we can get this settled without having to file suit."

"Think we can?" Simon stood up, his entire demeanor improved. He held his head higher and squared his shoulders.

"I can't guarantee it, but I feel good." Mary gave him a reassuring hug and gathered him, Feet, her father, the remaining Tonys, and the untouched pastry while they all exchanged "good-byes, "thank-yous," and "love-yous." Then she ushered them out of the conference room, down the hall, and into the elevator, giving her father one final hug.

"Mary, thanks so much!" Simon called to her.

"BYE, HONEY! LOVE YOU!"

"Love you, too!" Mary glimpsed her father's eyes begin to glisten as the elevator doors slid closed. Something was still bothering him, but she didn't know what or why. The doors had sealed shut and the elevator rattled downward, leaving her to her own thoughts. She felt so good that she could help him and Rachel, but so awful that the baby needed the transplant. Only four years old, and her young life had been a series of tests and chemo, needle pricks and IV ports. It couldn't be possible that children suffered so much, yet she knew it happened every day, in every hospital in the country.

The other elevator doors slid open, and inside was Bennie Rosato, whose appearance never failed to intimidate Mary. Maybe it was because Bennie was her former boss and a super-lawyer with a national reputation, or the fact that Bennie was six feet tall and towered over Mary, or the fact that Bennie always wore a khaki power suit, or that her curly blonde hair was always in an unruly topknot, proof that she was far too sensible to care about anything as dumb as hair.

"Good morning," Mary said, as Bennie flashed a confident smile, which was the only kind she had.

"Hey, DiNunzio. I mean, Mary. What are you doing, standing here?"

"I just met with a new client," Mary answered, faking a smile.

"Tough case? You look upset." Bennie strode toward the

reception desk, and Mary fell in step beside her, telling herself not to be nervous around her own partner, for no reason. Or maybe for four reasons, as above.

"Yes, tough case." Mary was thinking of Rachel.

"Tough on the law?"

"No, it's just sad. On the law, it's a winner. A sales rep got fired because his daughter needs a bone marrow transplant." Mary summarized it like a legal headnote since Bennie was in a hurry.

"Ouch." Bennie grimaced as she walked. "Go get 'em, tiger."

"It's totally illegal under the association provision of the ADA. I'm hoping for a quick settlement."

"Who's the defendant?"

"Some cubicle manufacturer."

"Not OpenSpace." Bennie stopped, frowning under the gleaming Rosato & DiNunzio plaque.

"Yes, why? How did you know?"

"OpenSpace is the biggest cubicle manufacturer in the area, and you can't sue them. I represent their parent company."

"I don't understand." Mary's mouth went dry.

"You're conflicted out of the case, and I didn't hear what I just heard. Decline the representation."

CHAPTER TWO

Bennie Rosato didn't understand why Mary looked so upset. It was a very simple statement. The only thing she could do was repeat it. "Mary, you can't take the case. I represent the parent company of OpenSpace, which is Dumbarton Industries."

"But I want to take the case," Mary said, stricken.

"Well, you can't. You can't sue OpenSpace because I represent Dumbarton. You have a conflict of interest. I'm sorry," Bennie added, because she was trying to improve her interpersonal relations, especially where DiNunzio was concerned. For example, she'd reminded herself to call her new partner by her first name, Mary. It was a regular lovefest.

"But I didn't know you represented Dumbarton."

"Now you do. They've been a house client since I started the firm, way back when."

"But I never represented Dumbarton."

"That's legally irrelevant. If I represent Dumbarton, *we* represent Dumbarton. I've worked on many of their matters over time and I've known the CEO since law school. Nate Lence. He deals with me personally. They have a solid in-house legal department, and what they can't handle, they farm out to us and other firms. In fact, if the case is too big for us, Nate consults me on whom else to hire."

"Bennie, I don't know the first thing about Dumbarton."

"Haven't you seen their name on the new-matter sheets?" Bennie was referring to the system by which lawyers in the firm notified each other that they were taking on a new matter. Every law firm was required to have such a system, so conflicts of interest could be caught before the representation went too far down the line. Luckily, it sounded as if this one could be nipped in the bud.

"Sure, yes, but I've never seen OpenSpace on the new-matter sheets. Have you ever represented OpenSpace?"

"No, but I represented Dumbarton and several of the other subs. You have to decline the representation." Bennie noticed red blotches appearing on Mary's neck, a nervous tell. Bennie made a mental note to mention it to her before she stood in front of her next jury.

"Even though I never represented the parent? Only you did?"

"Yes. How can I make this any clearer? A client of mine is a client of yours under the Rules." Bennie was referring to the Rules of Professional Conduct, which governed the ethics of lawyers, at least those who allegedly had them.

"Because we're partners?"

"No, because we're members of the same firm. Even if you were still an associate, the result would be the same." Bennie glanced at her watch. It was eight fifteen, and she had a deposition starting at ten, for which she needed to prepare. If they were going to keep talking, she had to get moving. She headed for the reception desk, and Mary followed.

"Are you sure that Dumbarton owns OpenSpace?"

"Absolutely."

"Wholly owned or partially owned?"

"Wholly, and it's a private company." Bennie reached the reception desk, which was empty. Marshall must be in the bathroom but she had already sorted the morning's mail and placed it in its holders. Bennie grabbed her mail, a thick packet of correspondence and court orders with pink phone messages on top. She channeled most of her calls through the firm and rarely gave her cell number to clients. She didn't like to be too available.

"How do you know they're wholly owned?"

"I read the papers. Morgan Lewis did the deal. I recommended them to Nate." Bennie left the reception area, and Mary walked beside her, hurrying to keep up, since she was a short girl with a short stride.

"You did?"

"Yes." Bennie strode down the hallway, which was lined with associates' offices. She noted with disapproval that they were empty even though it was after eight o'clock, then remembered that two of the associates, Anne Murphy and John Foxman, were on a securities fraud case in Atlanta. That meant only Judy Carrier was late, but that child marched to the beat of a different drummer. "Mary, let me fill you in. Dumbarton is headquartered in King of Prussia and owns twenty-six subsidiaries, among them OpenSpace, which they acquired recently."

"I didn't know!" Mary was getting more upset, which even Bennie could see, since the girl wore her emotions on her sleeve. As well as her arms, her legs, and her face. And neck.

"Understood. So I get why you took the meeting—"

"—of course, I would—"

"—and it's too bad that you learned something Dumbarton would be interested to know, namely that one of their subs is about to be—"

"You're not going to tell them, are you?" Mary interrupted

again, like she always did when she got excited, which Bennie let go. Her office was at the end of the hall, and she beelined for it like a finish line.

"No, I think I can keep it to myself consistent with my obligations. But don't tell me another thing about the case. Decline the representation by letter." Bennie stopped outside her office, hoping they'd spoken the last word. Her deposition today was critical, in a securities fraud case in which she was going after the CFO of a Fortune 500 accounting firm.

"I can't decline the representation. It matters to me, and I really want to take it."

"Why? You're already so busy." Bennie didn't get it. Mary represented every mom-and-pop business in South Philly, and her practice of small-matter, state-court cases complemented Bennie's own big-matter, federal-court practice. It was why Bennie had made Mary a named partner, as hard as it was to give up control, her favorite thing in the world.

"It's personal."

"This is business."

"Business and personal can be mixed."

"No, they can't."

"They can for me," Mary shot back, more firmly. "The plaintiff is one of my oldest friends from the neighborhood. I can't *not* represent him. I already accepted."

"So withdraw. It was an honest mistake. You didn't know you had a conflict." Bennie noticed Mary's jaw tilt upward in a determined way, which could be a problem.

"I don't know anything about Dumbarton and have never worked for them. It's not unethical."

"Of course it is. Read the rules. I don't make them."

"But think about it. You said they have twenty-six subs. Are we conflicted out of all of them?"

"Yes."

"That can't be." Mary frowned more deeply. "Are we conflicted out of all of the subs of all of our clients?"

"Yes." Bennie was pretty sure she was right, but she'd double-check later.

"But as applied to Dumbarton and OpenSpace, it's a technicality."

"Mary, we're lawyers. Technicalities are our business." Bennie would have laughed if she had time. "How can I make this any clearer? Dumbarton and OpenSpace are in the same corporate family."

"But this isn't about a corporate family, this is about a *real* family. My family."

"Are you saying that this plaintiff is a family member? Although that wouldn't cure your conflict of interest." *As a technical matter*, Bennie wanted to add, but didn't.

"We're not blood-related, but I know his family and he knows mine. We couldn't be any closer as families. My father was even in the meeting, and so was his father."

"Your father was in a consultation with a new client?" Bennie had never heard of such a thing, but didn't criticize, since she wasn't supposed to do that anymore. On the contrary, she had to hand it to Mary, who practiced law her own way. You couldn't argue with success. Up to a limit. Then Bennie noticed Judy Carrier coming down the hallway toward them with her big smile and spiky pink hair.

"Morning, guys!" Judy waved as she approached. "I made muffins!"

"Good morning," Bennie and Mary said politely, a split second apart.

Mary returned her attention to Bennie. "That's my point. It's not weird that my father was here. I grew up with the plaintiff and went to his wedding. I went to his wife's funeral and—"

"Hey guys!" Carrier interrupted, arriving. "Did you *not* hear that I made muffins? Actual banana-nut muffins! I'm like a housewife without the house and the wife!"

Bennie and Mary fell suddenly silent, but Judy bubbled over.

"Also look at my new jeans skirt! How cute am I?" Judy spun around with her arms outstretched. She had on a hot pink T-shirt that matched her hair and a faded jeans skirt with an embroidered peace sign.

Mary managed a smile. "Very cute."

Bennie did a double-take. "I owned a skirt exactly like that. I made it from my bellbottoms. It had a white peace sign, too. Where did you get that?"

"At a vintage shop on Pine Street."

"Vintage?" Bennie looked at the skirt more closely. "My God, I think that's *my* skirt!"

"Seriously?" Judy's eyes flew open, an incredulous blue.

Mary burst into laughter. "How funny is that?"

"Not funny at all," Bennie said, but it was a little funny, so she forced a chuckle. She didn't mind getting older. She was happy with her life and viewed herself as an elder of their tribe. The only problem was that the young-uns didn't always listen.

Judy must've picked up their mood. "Are Mommy and Daddy having a fight? Please tell me that you still love me and it's not my fault."

Mary interjected, "We're not fighting."

Bennie nodded. "Yes we are. Over an ethical question."

Judy cocked her head. "What is it? I wrote a comment on ethics in law school. I'll be the judge. Hey, that makes me Judge Judy!"

Bennie didn't smile. "Here's the issue. Can a partner in a law firm sue a subsidiary when another partner in the same firm represents the parent?"

Judy wrinkled her nose. "Please tell me this is a hypo."

"Is it against the rules?" Bennie asked again, since Judy was a legal scholar, despite appearances.

Judy looked from Mary to Bennie. "I had to research that issue last year. Believe it or not, it's not a settled question."

"Terrific!" Mary practically cheered.

"I don't have time for this," Bennie said, leaving for her office.

CHAPTER THREE

Mary grabbed Judy, and they hustled into her office, her hopes soaring. The morning sun poured through the window behind her desk, casting a soft light on the pretty antique quilt hung next to her diplomas like a display of girl self-esteem. Mary felt so much better after what Judy had said, but she still wanted to talk it over like they always did. They had worked together since day one, though Mary had made partner while Judy remained an associate, but that didn't matter. There was nothing better than working with your best friend, even if you had subsequently become her boss. Technically.

"So it's not against the rules?" Mary asked, closing the door behind her.

"I didn't say that. I assume you represent the sub?"

"Yes, how do you know?"

"Because Bennie represents everybody and you look vaguely hysterical." Judy set her backpack on the floor, zipped it open, and slid out a Tupperware container.

"It's been a long morning, and when I tell you about this case, it will break your heart." Mary stowed her purse in the bottom drawer and set her laptop on her desk, which she kept orderly. Case files were stacked on the left and correspondence on the right. At the front of the desk were pictures of her wedding, her parents, and her twin sister, Angie, who was a nun on her umpteenth mission in Africa. Mary respected her sister's decision to save the world but she missed her every day, since they had shared a room, and a womb.

"Get out your copy of the *Model Rules of Professional Conduct.*" Judy sat down in one of the chairs opposite Mary's desk.

"I have one of those?"

"Yes. We got them the first day of school. With a pencil case and a protractor." Judy pried the lid off the Tupperware container, releasing a fattening smell. "My God, it's like perfume. Do you want a muffin?"

"No, I'm too excited to eat." Mary started digging through her bookshelves.

"I'm too excited *not* to eat." Judy gazed in delight at the homemade muffins on a bed of tinfoil, their golden brown tops studded with nuts. "I take it back, I *am* a housewife. I'm going to marry myself. I'm ready to make the commitment."

"Here we go." Mary located her copy of the model rules and pulled the book off the shelf. It was a maroon paperback, never opened. Still, she considered herself ethical since she knew the basics and went to church every Sunday, which should count for something.

"Go to Rule 1.7, Conflicts of Interest." Judy took a big bite of the muffin. "Yum, this is so delicious. I *do*!"

Mary found the rule and read aloud: " '(a) Except as provided in paragraph (b), a lawyer shall not represent a client if the representation involves a concurrent conflict of interest.' "

"Thanks for nothing, guys." Judy chomped away. "Wow, this is so moist I don't even need coffee. I'm incredible."

" 'A concurrent conflict of interest exists if: (1) the representation of one client will be directly adverse to another client—' "

Judy interrupted, "An interesting issue is the meaning of 'directly adverse.' How much adversity is *direct*? How much is *indirect*?"

"Okay." Mary could hear Judy going into lecture mode. You could take the girl out of Law Review, but you couldn't take Law Review out of the girl.

"Keep reading." Judy came over, spilling crumbs on her T-shirt.

" 'Or if there is significant risk that the representation of one or more clients will be materially limited by the lawyer's responsibility to another client, a former client or third person or by personal interest of the lawyer.' " Mary thought a minute. "What's that mean?"

"Not applicable here." Judy took another bite, and another crumb dropped on her chest. In a minute, she'd be wearing the muffin.

Mary wondered if the "personal interest" part might be relevant, since she was personally interested in representing Simon, but she wasn't sure that was what the rule meant.

"Skip ahead. Comment Thirty-Four speaks specifically to the situation."

Mary flipped to the comment. " 'A lawyer who represents a corporation or other organization does not, by virtue of that representation, necessarily represent any constituent or affiliated organization, such as a parent or subsidiary.' " She looked up, delighted. "Bingo! That's me! I can take the case!"

"You would think so, but read the next line."

Mary looked down. " 'Thus, the lawyer for an organization is not barred from accepting representation adverse to an affiliate in an unrelated matter unless the circumstances are such that the affiliate should also be considered a client of the lawyer . . .' "

"Stop there."

"But that begs the question, doesn't it? The whole issue is if the affiliate is considered a client of the lawyer."

"Precisely, it's unclear. It could go either way." Judy popped the last of the muffin into her mouth, wiped her fingers on her skirt, then opened Mary's laptop and started searching online as she spoke. "So I worked backward and researched how Rule 1.7 was drafted, like a legislative history. I thought that would shed some light on the subject."

"Good idea."

"I know. And I can bake too. I wonder what I'll get myself for a wedding present." Judy searched online. "Anyway, I did research into the ABA Opinions, because there's a Committee on Ethics and Professional Responsibility that issues formal opinions on ethical matters, decided in panels just like judges."

"Oh." Mary had no idea. She read over Judy's shoulder.

"And I found this old panel decision that was completely on point, number 390. See?" Judy pointed to the screen. " 'The Committee has been asked whether a lawyer who represents a corporate client may undertake a representation that is adverse to a corporate affiliate of the client in an unrelated matter, without obtaining the client's consent.' "

"That's us. Nobody's talking about consent." Mary made a mental note.

"The majority says that this is a problem created by the growth and consolidation of modern corporations—"

"That's what *I* said!" Mary felt validated. "We can't be conflicted out of representing every sub of our parent companies. And what did the Committee decide?"

Judy checked the screen. "The majority allowed the representation, but it held that whether a lawyer may represent a corporate affiliate of his client 'doesn't depend on any clear-cut rule *per se* but rather on the particular circumstances.' "

"So you look to the 'particular circumstances,' whatever that means?"

"Yes, and the dissent said—"

"There was a dissent? On an ABA panel?"

"These are lawyers, remember? Everybody has to pee on the hydrant. We're just terriers with J.D.s." Judy rolled her eyes. "The dissent would not have allowed it, saying that 'the opinion opens a Pandora's box of unintended consequences which most assuredly will return to vex us in the future.' And here we are, being vexed."

Mary couldn't smile. "We're worse than vexed."

Judy straightened up. "This Opinion led to Rule 1.7, which is what we started out with. In other words, in typical lawyerly fashion, there is no clear answer. It depends on the circumstances. The totality. The context."

"So the ethics rules offer no clear-cut guidance. Bennie is wrong that it's against the rules."

Judy smiled crookedly. "But she's also right that it's against the rules. It depends on the situation."

"Why was she so sure the rules go her way?"

"She's old-school. The rules provide that a lawyer has a hundred percent duty of loyalty and confidentiality to a client. So it follows from that, logically, that if a parent company has a sub, which is part of the same legal entity, then the lawyer should have the same duty of loyalty and confidentiality to the sub."

"Right." Mary mulled it over.

"And Bennie's also right that a client of one lawyer in a firm is a client of every lawyer in the firm. That's been true since forever." Judy cocked her head. "Who's her client?"

"Dumbarton."

"Oh man, you're kidding, right?" Judy moaned. "They've been a house client for a long time. She's buddy-buddy with the CEO. They have a small in-house department and they farm out the major cases to big firms like Dechert and Morgan Lewis. He takes her advice on whom to hire. She even reviews their bills."

"How did I not know this?" Mary blurted out, but she knew how. She had her own client base and so did Bennie. They worked in the same firm, but independently, and the twain never met.

"I've done work for Dumbarton, too." Judy frowned.

"You have?" Mary asked, dismayed, if not surprised. Judy had clerked at the federal appellate level and was their resident genius, with impeccable academic credentials, Stanford and Boalt Law School. She could have taught anywhere or clerked for the Supremes.

"Bennie sends me a contract question now and then, and I look over any appellate brief that outside counsel files in the big cases."

"For the parent or for one of the subs?" Mary should have realized it because Judy worked on many of Bennie's cases.

"For most of the subs."

"OpenSpace?"

"No," Judy answered, then her blue eyes widened slightly. "Yikes. You want to sue OpenSpace?"

"Yes." Mary didn't reveal that Simon was the plaintiff because it would put Judy in a terrible position. Judy had met Simon plenty of times and she knew Feet very well. Mary had told her all about Rachel's cancer, and she knew Judy would feel as compelled as she was about Simon's case.

"Then I guess this means we can't talk about the facts."

"I guess it does." Mary recoiled, momentarily stumped. She talked to Judy about everything, and they always bounced ideas off of each other on cases. "But I think we can talk about whether or not I can represent the sub without discussing the facts or merits. Right?"

"Yes, we can."

"For example, under the rules, the test is the totality of the circumstances. If you look at them as a whole, I can take the case."

"How so?" Judy folded her arms, leaning back against the desk.

"I never did any work for Dumbarton, OpenSpace, or any of the other subs. I don't even know what they do."

"That doesn't matter under Rule 1.10, the imputation rule. Each lawyer in a firm is charged with having the knowledge of any lawyer."

Mary groaned.

"Let me get you up to speed on Dumbarton. It's a commercial construction company, building offices and hospitals. They've grown like crazy and are integrating vertically."

"Which means what?" Mary was forgetting her antitrust law.

"They buy companies that make what they need. Some of its subs are associated with construction. WallCo makes drywall, MetalLabs fabricates metal, and PowerPlus makes electrical wiring. OpenSpace makes modular furniture cubicles, and to do so, it buys drywall from WallCo, wiring from PowerPlus, and metal frames from MetalLabs. It keeps it in the corporate family."

"When did corporations become families?"

Judy didn't smile.

"Look, I've never worked for OpenSpace, Dumbarton, or any of its subsidiaries. I was completely unaware that we represent them—" Mary caught herself. "Rather, that Bennie does. I'm not privy to any trade secrets or confidential business information of theirs, in the least."

"It's a wholly owned subsidiary, Mare."

"I know, but we just read the rule, and when you look at it in context, I don't see how it's unethical, as applied to me."

Mary threw up her hands. "I get that *you* couldn't represent this client against OpenSpace, but I can. Those are different circumstances. I'm one step removed."

"True." Judy frowned. "But it would put you in direct opposition to Bennie. Your partner. What if she takes the case herself?"

"Oh God no." Mary's mouth went dry. She didn't relish the prospect for personal reasons, not to mention the fact that Bennie was the best lawyer she ever met, or maybe that ever lived. Then she thought again. "She's got a big trial next month, with Sam. She wouldn't take it herself. Plus, like you said, Dumbarton farms out the work. They'll send it to one of the big firms."

"Even if it's not literally her case, it pits you against her, politically."

"I know but I can't help that." Mary thought of Simon and Rachel, in such dire straits. It was a matter of life or death. A child's life was more important than a business relationship, especially when the child was Rachel.

"But won't it be weird between you two?"

"I can deal with it, if she can," Mary said, meaning it. "I'm friends with opposing counsel in my cases. And Bennie's the one who always says that business isn't personal."

"Why don't you give the case to somebody else? Refer it out?" Judy's blonde eyebrows sloped down with concern.

"I can't, I have to do it myself." Mary felt a wrench in her chest at the thought of sending Simon away. "Nobody will care about this plaintiff the way I do. It's kind of, for family. And not corporate family."

"It's somebody from the neighborhood, isn't it?" Judy met her eye sympathetically, and Mary knew that she would understand. Judy was like an honorary daughter to Mary's parents and she adored The Tonys, too.

"Simon."

"Oh no." Judy sighed. "Then get him somebody *awesome*. You do so many favors that somebody has to owe you one. It doesn't have to be you."

"But I wasn't going to charge him. He doesn't have that much money." Mary brought her up to date about the bone marrow transplant, since Judy already knew about Rachel's cancer.

"Maybe you can get Simon a discount, out of professional courtesy?"

"Nowadays?"

"I can try and call some of my friends."

"And piss Bennie off? I don't want to put you in that position."

"Mare, this sucks. But you shouldn't take this case." Judy touched her arm. "Tell Simon why. He'll understand."

"No, he wouldn't, and even if he did, Feet wouldn't. Neither would my father." Mary couldn't imagine telling Simon she was referring him out, much less Feet, The Tonys, or her father. The word would spread. She couldn't let the entire neighborhood down.

"So what are you gonna do?"

"I don't know," Mary said, though she did. Her chest went suddenly tight. She felt as if a curtain had fallen between them. "I'm just surprised you would take her side."

"I'm not taking her side," Judy shot back, pained. "But I don't want to see you get in trouble with Bennie—"

"I won't get in trouble with her. She's not my boss anymore, she's my partner. And we used to get in trouble with her all the time. We were a united front."

"Okay, then I meant square off against her. Cross swords with her. You know how tough she is." Judy recoiled, stung. "Besides, we're still best friends. We're united. We just disagree."

"Is that possible?"

"Of course," Judy answered, finding a reassuring smile. "Don't get all *Godfather* on me. I'm your bestie. I love you."

"I know." Mary felt torn. "Sorry I snapped."

"You need an emergency muffin."

"I need to look at that rulebook again," Mary said, getting an idea.

CHAPTER FOUR

Bennie sat at her desk and stared at her notes without really seeing them. She usually felt jazzed before a deposition because it was the first time she would encounter her adversary. Plenty of lawyers played nice, warming up the witness only to work him over at trial, but she wasn't built that way. Her litigation strategy was to assert her dominance from the outset and never let up. There was a reason she had a coffee mug that read I CAN SMELL FEAR. Actually, she had two of them. One was a gift, and she'd bought the other one in case the first one broke.

But this morning, Bennie didn't feel jazzed. She tried again to concentrate on her notes, which she'd handwritten on yellow legal pads with a ballpoint pen that made satisfyingly bumpy ridges on the paper. She loved computers as much as everybody else, but there was something about a fresh legal pad that got her juices going. Bennie Rosato loved everything about being a lawyer and she was born with what lawyers called a "justice bone," which ached whenever somebody was being treated unfairly. For that reason, she'd been looking forward to her deposition today, but her mind kept wandering. Her fight with Mary gnawed at the edges of her brain.

Bennie's gaze strayed around her office, with its messy bookshelves stuffed with binders, legal cases, clipped articles, and textbooks from law school, which looked older than usual, perhaps because she herself was vintage. Whatever. Across from her desk were two patterned chairs, and all four walls were covered with awards, citations, and certificates she'd gotten from public-interest law groups all over the country, and the American Bar Association. Acrylic and glass awards filled the entire shelf, and her gaze stopped on one of them, given for exemplifying ethics in the practice of law.

Believe it or not, it's not a settled question.

Bennie got up from her desk in frustration. She crossed to her bookshelves and started digging through all the crap until she found a copy of the model rules, then flipped to the provisions regarding conflicts of interest and read aloud: " 'A lawyer who represents a corporation or other organization does not, by virtue of that representation, necessarily represent any constituent or affiliated organization, such as a parent or subsidiary—' "

Bennie stopped, surprised. This wasn't the way she remembered the rule, but it must've been amended. She kept reading, ". . . 'the lawyer for an organization is not barred . . . unless the circumstances are such that the affiliate should also be considered a client of the lawyer . . .' "

"Aha!" Bennie got the gist, reassured. Maybe the rule wasn't as black-and-white as it used to be, but bottom line, each case had to be analyzed in its individual circumstances. So Bennie was right, and circumstances clearly prohibited Mary from representing OpenSpace against Dumbarton. It was good to be right, and Bennie never tired of it. She closed the book with a satisfying slap and slid it back onto the shelf, just as there was a knock on the door.

"Come in, Sam!" Bennie was expecting her old friend Sam Freminet, who'd sent her the client she was representing this morning.

"Good morning, honey!" Sam entered the office and kissed her on the cheek, and Bennie breathed in his spicy aftershave, since he always smelled better than she did. He looked better, too, his reddish hair in a short feathery cut, his small blue eyes bright behind his rimless glasses with earpieces of tan plastic, and a tan-patterned silk tie and tan suit of light wool, undoubtedly custom-tailored. Sam was one of the most prosperous bankruptcy lawyers in the city and he always dressed expensively, an irony that wasn't lost on him.

"Good morning, Sam."

"Why are you so frowny? Getting ready to destroy the enemy?"

"No, then I'd be smiling." Bennie went around the desk and sat down, while Sam took a seat opposite her, crossing his slim legs.

"Then is it because of the skirt?"

"What skirt? You mean my jeans skirt?"

"Marshall told me." Sam laughed wickedly. "Honey, please. So what, she bought your skirt. You should be ashamed that you owned a skirt like that in the first place."

"I was young."

"Were you also high? I mean, constantly? Or at least when you bought the thing?"

"I made it."

"Then you were temporarily insane." Sam chuckled at his own joke. "Anyway, I'm surprised it bothers you. You know you're old. I know I'm old. We're old now."

"We're in our forties."

"Like I said. I may be forty-five, but that's ninety-two in gay years. It's like dog years. Who cares anyway?" Sam waved her off. "The day I didn't want to go to clubs anymore, I knew it was over. Now I sit happily at home with Paul. We put on our jammies and watch British crime shows on Netflix. You and Declan never go out either, do you?"

"We don't get to see each other that much, so no." Bennie was crazy about Declan Mitchell, a lawyer she'd met on a recent case, but they had a long-distance relationship, since he had a home and a general practice law firm in York. They took turns driving, and Declan was the kind of man worth driving three hours for. She'd never been so happy in her life, but the Mary thing was still bugging her. "Pop quiz. Can Mary DiNunzio represent a sub of a client of mine and sue my parent?"

"Possible," Sam answered without hesitation.

"What are you talking about? We're partners. I represent the parent and she wants to sue the sub."

"But the new rules say it depends on the circumstances."

"How do you know that?" Bennie didn't understand how everybody in the world knew this and she didn't.

"I deal with that issue all the time. The world is changing, girl. The more consolidation, the more headaches. We're crazy with the parents and subs, constantly running pre-conflicts checks and conflicts checks." Sam rolled his eyes. "Nobody wants to turn down work. We all parse the circumstances to keep the client. In your case, who's the parent and sub?"

"The parent is Dumbarton. The sub is OpenSpace."

"Dumbarton?" Sam's eyebrows flew upward behind his cool glasses. "Big-time. Nate's company."

"Right." Bennie, Sam, and Nate were all in the same class at Penn Law.

"So you have to deal with Richie Rich."

"Yes." Bennie smiled at Sam's old nickname for Nate. "Don't hate. He came from nothing. He did it all himself."

"I know. He's a self-made asshole."

Bennie let it go. "Anyway, I think Mary is conflicted out of the representation."

"Not necessarily. It could go either way, but in this case, it's okay."

"What? Why?"

"You want me to tell you she can't take the case."

"Of course I do. You're my friend."

"You're shameless."

"I'm loyal."

"You're too loyal." Sam leaned over, warming to his topic. "Dumbarton is a 143-million-dollar company with twenty-six subsidiaries. I only know because Nate reminds me at every frigging reunion. Size matters to those who don't know better."

"But OpenSpace is wholly owned, in the same corporate family."

"A very large corporate family. Like those Duggars. There's way too many of them. Give it a rest, people!"

Bennie stayed on track. "Why should it be a different answer if it's twenty-six subs or two? What difference does that make, in principle?"

"That's different circumstances, right there. And the subs are spread across the country, aren't they?"

"Yes," Bennie had to concede. "And he's about to acquire two more in the Midwest."

"I collect watches, he collects companies." Sam sniffed.

"Your point?"

"Are the board and the officers the same?"

"There is no board. They're not public companies."

"Oh, right, of course. Mr. Total Control loves total control."

"Not like you and me."

"But we're fun and he's not."

"That's true." Bennie smiled.

"How do they handle the legal work for the subs? Do they handle it all in house at Dumbarton?"

"No, it depends on the size of the sub. Some of the bigger subs have their own legal department on the premises, even if it's one man. OpenSpace is a small sub, so they handle it at Dumbarton."

"That cuts in your favor." Sam thought a minute. "Who's general counsel these days? It's not Nate, is it?"

"No, he stopped about three years ago. The general counsel is Leo Magid and he runs their department like a law firm, with lawyers grouped according to specialty. He's got about ten guys in house, at Dumbarton headquarters in King of Prussia."

"Who do you deal with in house?"

"Not many of them, only Nate."

"So Nate takes time from his insanely busy schedule to deal with you? That's the *lamest* excuse I ever heard to hit on somebody." Sam snorted. "I bet he prays that people slip and fall so he can call you. If I know him, he'll be dropping banana peels."

Bennie let it go. "He likes to keep his hand in."

"I bet he does."

Bennie let that go, too. "He doesn't hit on me anymore."

"Only because he knows you'd hit him back." Sam burst into laughter, and Bennie had to smile.

"Puns are beneath you."

"Evidently they're not. Okay so back to business." Sam thought a minute. "Another factor is if the subs are in the same business, but his aren't, are they? The subs he currently owns aren't all in construction, are they?"

"No. Some are, some aren't. He just bought a coat company that donates one-for-one to the homeless, like Tom's Shoes but in the U.S."

"He has no social conscience. He's just trying to get in your pants." Sam smiled slyly. "You friend-zoned him, but he won't stay there. He's *that* guy."

"What guy?" Bennie asked, amused.

"The guy who nobody says no to, so he wants whoever said no."

"Still, no. Please, get back to the ethical question."

"When we analyze those conflict questions at my firm, we

also look at the financial impact the putative litigation could have on the parent. For example, what's the case about?"

"It's an ADA action on behalf of a sales rep who was fired. The facts are sympathetic. If Mary can prove it, it's a winner."

"So they should settle it." Sam spread open his palms in appeal. "If it's little, it makes sense to settle. If it were bigger, I'd be on your side. I'd be more inclined to say that Mary should take it. But it's not anything with enough exposure to impact the bottom line of Dumbarton."

"True." Bennie didn't like the way this was going.

"So, it's an individual case with some measure of damages that affect the bottom line of Dumbarton. It's not even worth litigating, and OpenSpace is insured for the loss. What's the big deal?"

"It's the principle of the thing."

"What principle?"

"The duty of loyalty to the client. I knew Nate when Dumbarton had two subs, then six, then twenty. I watched it grow."

"So what? It's a business, not an embryo." Sam lifted an eyebrow. "Wait, what? Are you getting maternal on me?"

"God, no," Bennie answered quickly. She knew she had a justice bone, but she wasn't sure she had a maternal bone in her body. She loved dogs, but she was pretty sure it wasn't the same thing.

"Then what's bothering you?"

"I'm not proud of what she's doing and I don't think it's right, so I don't even feel that I could defend it to Nate."

"But it's a judgment call under the rules."

"He'll never see it that way. He'll feel betrayed, and he's a major client."

"Pssh." Sam waved her off. "You're not going to lose him over it. He loves you."

"He loves my *work*."

"Keep telling yourself that. And more importantly, what

about Mary? Aren't you trying to play nice with her? She's your partner now. Where's your loyalty to her?"

"What about her loyalty to the firm?"

"Not the point. She didn't know. She's trying to be a good lawyer."

"So am I."

Sam frowned. "Bennie, compromise. You should try to work with her."

"I'm trying."

"Try harder, girl. You're her partner. Act like one."

"Okay, whatever." Bennie checked the clock. She had only a half hour before the deposition. "Let's move on. We have more important things to talk about."

"What do you know?" Sam snorted. "You made a skirt out of pants. I've lost all respect."

CHAPTER FIVE

Mary sat at her desk behind her laptop, working faster than she had ever before. She'd already formulated a litigation strategy around her new idea and gotten a thumbs-up from Simon. The EEOC complaint was just a form, but the complaint took more work. She tapped away on a draft complaint, mindful of her main task. Under the ADA, it was unlawful for OpenSpace to fire Simon because it didn't want their insurance premiums raised because of Rachel's medical expenses, but it was lawful to fire him for cause, like falling sales quotas. She had to prove that the medical expenses were the real reason he was fired, not his performance. It was a commonsense task to show a causal relationship between the medical expenses and the termination, and in that regard, Simon's notebook was extraordinarily helpful because the temporal relation between the two was clear.

Mary took the facts directly from Simon's notes, and there were three different occasions on which Eddington had made comments about Rachel's medical expenses, and Mary made each one into a specific allegation of facts to support her theory of the causal connection. She typed:

On Wednesday, October 20, after the plaintiff's daughter's first round of chemotherapy started, plaintiff submitted a bill to Todd Eddington, whereupon Eddington stated, "I hope this works, for her sake and for ours. These expenses are going to mount up, and we met our deductible already. Our premiums are going to go up."

Mary shook her head with disgust. She could only imagine how betrayed Simon must have felt by Eddington, who'd been so callous in the face of Rachel's life-or-death struggle. Mary understood that business wasn't always warm and fuzzy, but she also knew that corporations purchased insurance policies for a reason. Medical expenses for employees were a cost of doing business, and this situation was exactly the type that the Americans with Disabilities Act had been legislated to prevent.

She kept typing, detailing the second incident:

On Thursday, January 5, plaintiff submitted a bill for his daughter's chemotherapy to Todd Eddington, who said, "This is the beginning of a new quarter and a new fiscal year. Do you think this is going to be as expensive as the last round?"

Mary typed the quote with grim satisfaction. She wouldn't usually be so detailed in the complaint, but she had strong facts and believed that if she highlighted them, the other side would see she had a winning case and be convinced to settle more quickly. It was part-and-parcel of her new plan. The only problem was Bennie.

Mary kept writing:

On Thursday, March 30, plaintiff informed Todd Eddington that his daughter would require a bone marrow transplant, and Eddington asked how much the transplant would cost. Plaintiff didn't know at the time, but told Eddington that the search charges to find a donor would cost approximately $60,00 to $100,000. Eddington stated, "These expenses are going to kill us this quarter. We can't keep this up. They're going to raise our rates."

Mary knew it didn't get any better than that in terms of proof. Eddington was practically admitting that he was going to find a way to cut Rachel's medical expenses, which was homerun evidence for their case. She was always surprised at how many supervisors, bosses, and middle managers made statements that were completely unlawful, merely because they either didn't know the law—or didn't care. But not on her watch.

She wrote the next allegation in a more argumentative style to drive home the point:

It is no coincidence that the very next day, on March 31, Todd Eddington informed plaintiff by email that his region was being decreased from three mid-Atlantic states to just one, the smallest, Delaware. This employment decision was essentially a demotion and virtually assured that plaintiff would not be able to meet his sales quotas because . . .

Mary kept writing, detailing her facts, laying out the legal portion of the complaint, and finally arriving at the damages, which she left boilerplate, "in excess of $50,000," since that was the minimum for federal-court actions. She would leave the amount open-ended until after she had studied the bills, which Simon had already emailed her but she hadn't had a chance to review yet. Obviously, she wanted to get as much money as possible for Simon, but her strategy in settling cases was to start at a reasonable number, because it signaled that she was willing to settle.

The sun moved across the sky behind her, shifting a shaft of sunlight from her correspondence to her laptop, but she barely noticed. She ate lunch while she worked, a small garden salad brought to her by Judy, which made her feel better. She spent the rest of the afternoon finishing the draft complaint, writing a cover letter, and crunching the numbers for a settlement demand. It took her until the end of the day and she printed out the complaint, checking the hallway to see when Bennie came out of her deposition, which was in the conference room across the hall.

There was a commotion outside, and Mary grabbed the complaint and hurried out of her office. The deposition was over, and a weary court reporter, a few men in suits, Bennie's friend Sam, and finally Bennie left the conference room, saying good-bye to Sam with a sheaf of exhibits in her hand.

"Bennie, got a minute?" Mary intercepted her, right outside the door.

"Just about," Bennie answered, heading for her office.

"I won't take long." Mary had a plan, and this was the time to execute it. She followed Bennie into her office and closed the door behind her, while Bennie sat down at her desk, plopping exhibits in the middle. The strain of the day showed in her face, and her topknot was askew, with a pencil stuck in the middle.

"Is this about OpenSpace? Because we discussed that already."

"But we're not finished yet." Mary stood her ground, literally and figuratively. "I looked at the rules, and it's not as clear-cut as you might've thought."

"I know that already and—"

"I really think that the circumstances allow me to take the case."

"We have to agree to disagree for now." Bennie met her gaze evenly, her eyes flashing a sharp blue. "I have work to do."

"Unfortunately, we can't agree to disagree because impasse won't work in this situation. We have to find a middle ground."

"There isn't one." Bennie's mouth set in a grim line, and to Mary it looked as if her lips were chiseled in stone, but Mary told herself not to be intimidated.

"Yes, there is. I checked the rules, and if the client consents to my undertaking the representation, then the conflict is waived."

"I know that too."

"So that may be a way to break the impasse."

"I know Nate very well, and he'll be furious if I ask him to consent. I can't imagine a worse move for client relations. He'll take it as a breach of my duty of loyalty to him and to Dumbarton."

"But he'd be wrong. We know that now. You can explain that under the rules, it's perfectly ethical for me to take the case."

"He's a lawyer. He can read the rules as well as we can. He won't see the circumstances the way you do. It's a judgment call at best."

"Here's my plan. Here's the complaint and demand letter I've drafted in this matter, which I would file if I were to represent the plaintiff." Mary set the complaint on Bennie's desk. "This case is so open-and-shut that I think we should proceed informally, maybe even less adversarially, which will work for us both."

"How can litigation not be adversarial? That's the fun part."

Mary let it go. Bennie was weird sometimes. "But this case is so sympathetic and OpenSpace was clearly in the wrong.

I have the facts, including contemporaneous notes by the plaintiff that are very convincing, and I detailed that in the complaint."

"So?" Bennie glanced at the complaint with a frown.

"I say that we call Nate together, tell him about the complaint, and even that we disagree on the representation. Let's put the cards on the table and see if we can settle this case, informally, because all of our interests are aligned."

"How are Dumbarton's interests aligned with somebody suing its subsidiary? And if anybody calls Nate, I will. Alone."

"Because when this complaint becomes public record, or if it came to light in a newspaper, it would be terrible publicity—"

"Is that a threat?" Bennie recoiled.

"No, it's a fact," Mary answered, though it was a threat, kind of. And Bennie was the one who had taught her to use the media to her advantage in a case. "It's a case that they're going to want to settle, if they have any sense at all. I have no doubt that when you read this complaint, with their interests in mind, you'll feel the same way, and I'm willing to be reasonable in my settlement demand."

Bennie didn't say anything.

"Tell Nate you're doing him a favor, in a way."

"How am I doing him a favor, when my firm is suing his sub?"

"Because you got him in at the ground floor. If the plaintiff had gone to anyone else, you wouldn't have known about it. We're giving him a chance to make this go away before it gets bigger, and I'm not charging any fee. That saves him thirty percent, right there."

"You're doing it for no fee?"

"Of course. I told you, they're family. I love this little girl. Her father, and her grandfather. I love them all."

Bennie rubbed her face, leaving a reddish mark on her fair skin. "Mary, I'm trying to compromise, but you're not understanding this from a business point of view. *Our* business. Nate has his pick of law firms in the city, but he's been loyal to me, even as he's outgrown—"

"I know but—"

"Wait, hold on. Don't disregard that. I will tell you, as someone who's been running a law firm longer than you have, that no business prospers by ignoring its client base."

"You're right, but I have the same problem. This is a case that comes to me out of the neighborhood. It's very high-profile in South Philly, and everybody knows Rachel. The school, the synagogue, and the church have held bake sales and fundraisers for her since the day she got sick. I even organized one at my old high school."

Bennie fell suddenly silent, so Mary kept going.

"I have a client base too, and even if my heart weren't on the side of taking this case, then my client base is. Everybody in South Philly will know if I turn them away, *everybody*. It could hurt my reputation, even ruin it. And frankly I could never live with myself. I'm begging you. Please call Nate, OpenSpace, or whoever, and try to settle it informally."

"I couldn't go forward without investigating it myself, you know."

"Then please, investigate. Do whatever you have to do. It's all in the complaint."

"Okay, enough." Bennie picked up the complaint. "Tell you what. I'll read this and decide."

"Great, thanks!" Mary's hopes soared.

"I'm doing this for you, partner to partner. I'm compromising."

"I appreciate that," Mary said, meaning it. "When will you let me know your decision?"

"As soon as possible."

"Tonight?"

Bennie shot her a warning glance. "We'll see."

"Okay, thanks." Mary started edging backwards toward the door. Every lawyer knew that when you win, get out of the courtroom. She opened the door and fled before Bennie changed her mind.

CHAPTER SIX

Bennie entered the restaurant, relieved to step into air-conditioning after the walk from the office. She'd emailed Nate to talk to him about Mary's case, but he was in the city and suggested they do it over drinks. She'd agreed, only because she could pitch it better in person, so she hadn't sent him the complaint. She could only hope he wouldn't throw a fit, but Vetri's was one of the city's best restaurants. The air smelled like fresh basil and expense accounts.

The maître d' wasn't at the front, but she spotted Nate waving to her from the right, so she threaded her way through the tables, which were filled. The dining room was small but had a cozy Italian country vibe with sunflower-yellow walls and rustic tables. She had no idea how Nate had gotten the reservation so quickly, but that was a perk of being the CEO of a company that owned twenty-six subs that occasionally made bad decisions.

Bennie organized her thoughts as she approached the table. She had read Mary's complaint, and the case was a loser with considerable exposure, which was why she had agreed to this folly. It was hardly the way she would have done business, but she was also thinking about what Sam had said, that she had to try and get along with her new partner. Still, compromising didn't come naturally to her and she had no idea how people did it. But then again, that's probably why she had few friends and never married. She used to think of herself as undefeated, but lately she was less sure.

"Hey, Nate," Bennie said, sitting down opposite him. Nate was tall and handsome in a rich-guy way, with a costly layered haircut that minimized the length of his face, regular grooming that kept his eyebrows separate, and an unshaven look intended to make him look rugged when he was anything but. His best feature was his intense green-blue eyes, and he usually wore either green or blue to set them off. Like tonight, he had on a light blue linen jacket with a cream colored T-shirt and jeans. He never had problems getting women, just keeping them.

"So good to see you, Bennie. I ordered you a Tanqueray and tonic."

"Thanks." Bennie wasn't surprised that he remembered her drink. They'd dated briefly after his second divorce but she'd cut it off, since they weren't a good match and she needed a client more than a lover.

"I was surprised when you emailed. To what do I owe the honor?"

"It's a case that involves OpenSpace."

Nate mock-pouted. "Straight to business."

"You know me."

"So you're still seeing whatever his name is."

"Yes. Declan Mitchell."

"I stalked him online. Solo practitioner in Middle-of-Nowhere, Pennsylvania. Former state police officer, mounted division. Ruggedly handsome, married to his horse. He's not good enough for you."

"That's quite enough." Bennie didn't smile.

"You think I'm a snob."

"I know you are," Bennie shot back as the waiter came over, served her drink, then placed a wineglass in front of Nate, uncorked the bottle, and poured some.

"Thank you." Nate swirled the wine around the glass, sniffed it, then took a thoughtful sip, by which time Bennie was out of patience.

"Surprise, it's wine!"

"Do you always have to bust me?" Nate smiled crookedly, setting down the glass. A maroon stain covered part of his upper lip.

"Yes, because you make it so easy."

"I could educate you on this Beaujolais. I'd be happy to, and you might learn something."

The waiter interjected, "Mr. Lence knows his wines."

Bennie smiled. "Mr. Lence knows everything."

"On that we agree." Nate motioned to the waiter. "Please, pour the rest before she emasculates me completely. It won't be pretty."

"Certainly, Mr. Lence." The waiter poured generously, then made himself scarce.

Bennie leaned over the table. "Nate, take a big gulp because you're going to need it."

"What's up?"

"My partner, Mary DiNunzio, got a case this morning from a sales rep who was fired by the sales manager at OpenSpace. She took the meeting because she didn't know I represented Dumbarton."

"She took the meeting without a conflicts check?"

"Yes, and you can understand that. It was an honest mistake. That happens."

"She can't take the case." Nate blinked. "She doesn't think she can, does she?"

"Hold on." Bennie held up a palm. "Don't freak. She's not

filing anything yet, and you need to flip your thinking. There's a way we can turn this to your advantage."

"I can't believe I'm hearing this." Nate frowned. "Are you trying to tell me your partner is seriously considering suing my sub? She *can't*. Has she never heard of the code of ethics? Who the hell is your partner again? And since when do you have a partner anyway?"

"Relax." Bennie kept her hand up. "We checked the rules, and they don't offer clear guidance in a case like this."

"Then I will. Your partner is conflicted out of suing Open-Space or any other subsidiary of Dumbarton. I won't have it. I'm astounded you would."

"Obviously, my initial reaction was against it, but there is a way that we can turn it to our advantage." Bennie met his troubled gaze. "You have every right to be angry, and I would've been too. But she has a draft complaint that details the facts surrounding the termination, and after I read it, I realized that we'd be putting form over substance. We both know settlement makes sense, when called for. We have a chance to do that right now."

"Is this where you tell me that the Chinese symbol for crisis is also the symbol for opportunity?"

"No, I didn't know that." Bennie felt encouraged, since Nate was keeping a lid on his anger. "Here's the thing. I know you don't get involved with every little case that comes down the pike, but this is one that could get a lot of public attention and it would be terrible PR."

"Like what?" Nate glowered.

"It looks as if the rep was fired because of his daughter's medical expenses, which is unlawful under the Americans with Disabilities Act. The child has leukemia, and she's four years old."

"A cancer kid?"

Bennie cringed. "Not very sensitively put, but yes. If you're going to be absolutely cold-hearted about it, that means that you have a case that could attract negative attention and also have potentially broad exposure."

"So? It happens every day in the big city."

"Not like this, and not in this political climate. People are hurting with healthcare expenses. It's in the news every day. It's all over Facebook and social. This is a kid who needs a bone marrow transplant to live, and the boss made a number of statements that are really damning. One was an admission."

"Like what?"

"Like that 'these expenses can't keep up, our premiums will go up,' et cetera. He clearly had a discriminatory animus, and the plaintiff made contemporaneous notes of his comments, which occurred on four separate occasions. It's homerun evidence."

"But how do you know it's true?"

"I don't, but it seems credible. The plaintiff claims the boss explained the corporate deductible to him and that it's capped at 250K. I know that's true, and so do you. How would the plaintiff know that if he wasn't told it? Why would a boss be discussing that at all?"

"It means nothing."

"Really?" Bennie modulated her tone. "How big is your HR department at OpenSpace?"

"One person, I think. OpenSpace only has forty-five employees."

"My point. With how many managers, in the whole company? Sales? Operations? Administrative?"

"Whatever."

"And you have them trained on their responsibilities under the federal and state employment laws? Title VII? Age discrimination? Sexual harassment and the like?"

"We have somebody at one of the big firms to run seminars on that. Some labor jock at Dechert."

"But what about disability law? The ADA, the Rehabilitation Act? I bet you don't. I bet that's a footnote in the seminar, if that. Wanna make a wager?"

"You might be right," Nate said, after a moment.

"I bet your boss didn't even know that you can't fire somebody because you don't want to pay their kid's medical expenses. It's called the association provision of the ADA, and there haven't been many cases decided under it."

"I never heard of it."

"There you go, and that's how these things happen. No bad intent. Just ignorance of the law, which, unfortunately for us, is no excuse." Bennie saw his forehead relax, so she kept talking. "My partner attached the plaintiff's photocopied notes as exhibits to the complaint, which is very detailed. I can email it to you, and you can read for yourself. My partner is eager to settle and she's reasonable, unlike most of the thieves in the bar association. And because she's personally associated with the case, she's taking it for no fee, which saves you half."

"How is she related to the case?"

"The plaintiff is the grandson of a friend of her father's. Everybody in South Philly knows about the child. They've had fundraisers and articles in the local newspaper."

"South Philly has a newspaper?" Nate picked up his wineglass.

"Don't be a snob."

"It comes so naturally."

"Look. We should settle. We can just do this down and dirty. Simple dispute resolution, without bloodshed. We won't make a habit of it. One and done. It makes a lot of sense, Nate. It really does."

"I don't know—"

"If my partner doesn't take the case, another lawyer will." Bennie tried her last-ditch effort. "And that person might not play ball with you the way she would."

"That's blackmail."

"No, that's reality." Bennie lowered her voice. "Don't underestimate your downside risk, either. If another plaintiff's lawyer took the case, they could join Dumbarton as a defendant. I know *I* would. Then you and your deep pocket are on the hook, too."

Nate shook his head. "When did litigation become extortion?"

Bennie gathered it was rhetorical. "And what if they expand discovery to the ADA policies of your other subsidiaries? Your exposure can be very broad unless you nip this in the bud."

"Damn you." Nate's eyes flashed darkly.

"We should set up a meeting tomorrow at OpenSpace."

"Who would be there?"

"The plaintiff's boss and me, plus whoever we want. We're improvising. We won't invite my partner or the plaintiff. I know you wouldn't ordinarily sit in, but you could if you wanted to, or just send your in-house guy that deals with OpenSpace."

"What's the point of the meeting?"

"Factual investigation, like any case. I interview the boss and see what our defense would be. That would enable us to have a fuller analysis of the case before we went forward."

"This is so wrong." Nate took another sip of his wine, then another. "My own lawyer is suing me, and I'm consenting."

"You're a more nuanced thinker than that. Be creative. It's thinking outside the box."

"You're the only woman I know who has the balls to pitch me this way."

"Thank you."

"It wasn't a compliment."

"So you say." Bennie smiled. "Lighten up, Nate. You're not too old to rock 'n' roll, are you?"

"Please don't try and jolly me along." Nate glowered. "I expect you on my side, not theirs."

"I'm still on your side. If it turns out that you're not comfortable with my partner taking the case, even informally, then we don't go forward. Or if you don't want to settle or your in-house guy doesn't, then we don't go forward. We'll have lost nothing. And we could be averting disaster, like if the plaintiff goes to a different lawyer."

"I can't believe you're talking me into this."

"Me neither." Bennie smiled, inwardly relieved.

"Only you." Nate smiled back.

"It's in Dumbarton's best interests, and OpenSpace's, too."

Nate met her eye, arching an eyebrow. "Why shouldn't I fire you?"

"You're too smart to do that."

Nate burst into laughter. "Good answer!"

"That's why I make the big bucks."

Nate's eyes glittered. "Bennie, come on. Ditch the cop, whatever his name is."

"It's Declan, and he's a lawyer."

"I bought a coat company for you. Would he do that?"

"I can buy my own coat," Bennie answered, smiling.

CHAPTER SEVEN

A hazy dusk streaked the sky a copper-tinged blue, as if the sky itself were rusting, and Mary got out of the cab on 34th Street, hoisted her purse and messenger bag to her shoulder, and scanned the ultramodern building, with its curved glass façade. White electrified letters on top read The Children's Hospital of Philadelphia, in the colonial script favored by the University of Pennsylvania, on whose campus the hospital was situated. Mary had gone to Penn for undergrad and law school, but she had never been to the Children's Hospital before now.

She beelined for the entrance, crowded with families, visitors, and staff wearing scrubs, their blue ID lanyards flying. She went through the doors, showed ID at the front desk, and entered a cheery, bright atrium that looked ten stories high, hung with colorful mobiles. The floor tile was covered with stars, planets, and circles, like a whimsical solar system, and the lobby was more like a playground than a hospital. Children pulled levers on a funky modern playset and banged on a piano in a glass-walled music area with real instruments. More than one toddler wore a surgical mask, and Mary felt a wrench in her chest as she passed them.

She joined the crowd at the elevator bank and rode up in

an elevator packed with staff, families, visitors, and both sick and well children. She couldn't fight the sensation that she was entering a world that she had never been a part of before. She had grown up so healthily, but she knew from talking with Simon that Rachel lived an entirely different life as a child. Simon never complained, always mindful that Rachel was the patient, and he hid the toll that her illness took on him. He lived every day since her diagnosis with the strain of her up-and-down white cell count, her sudden rashes and mouth sores from chemo, and the fear of sudden or unexplained fevers. Mary sent up a silent prayer for Rachel and every other child at CHOP, fighting a daily battle for something that so many adults and children took for granted. Life itself.

She got off on Oncology, then kept going until she reached the special wing with bright green doors that read **Blood & Marrow Transplant Unit,** next to a Purell stanchion with a red sign, VISITORS: PLEASE DO NOT VISIT IF YOU ARE FEELING SICK. Mary knew from Simon that she was entering one of the most private areas of the hospital, since its young patients had so little resistance to disease, even less than other cancer patients. In fact, Mary had learned that in order to be able to accept a blood or marrow transplant, the child's immune system had to be essentially destroyed so that it wouldn't reject the marrow.

It would be a three-hundred-day countdown to transplant day, and before that would be an endless series of blood tests, a spinal tap to make sure that there were no leukemic cells, three days of total body irradiation followed by three days of chemotherapy using Thiotepa, which required that Rachel be showered every six hours and go to the bathroom every two. Transplant Day would be Day Zero, and Rachel was only on day 278, so the trick would be keeping her in remission and without infection so that she could maintain her eligibility for the transplant. Even so, Mary had been surprised to learn that CHOP's BMT Unit didn't require surgical masks unless the patient was in isolation. CHOP wanted to keep its atmosphere as friendly and upbeat as possible, and the nurses and doctors wore street clothes. Visitors weren't restricted unless the patient was in isolation, which Rachel wasn't.

Mary used the sanitizer, went through the doors, and walked to the nurses' station, a curved wooden counter with a colorful mosaic of ducks, butterflies, and flowers. "I'm going to visit Rachel Pensiera in 3E46A," Mary said, and they gestured to the right. She followed the curve around the desk, and along a path of pretty stripes on the floor matching the mosaic. Children's pictures hung on the wall, and a homemade bulletin board with a baseball hat that read WE ARE THE ONCO TEAM, THANKS FOR BEING A TEAM PLAYER!! Underneath were homemade baseballs and on each one was a crayoned thank-you to a nurse, a doctor, or a fellow patient.

She passed a painted mural of Ronald McDonald holding a teapot in one hand and a tray of muffins and flowers in the other, which was mounted above a glass door next to a sign, FAMILY LOUNGE. She hadn't realized that McDonald's sponsored a lounge here, though her parish church cooked Christmas meals for Ronald McDonald House in West Philly, which was a large home that the company maintained for out-of-town families who needed a place to stay during their children's hospitalization at CHOP. She turned the corner and kept going until she got to Rachel's room, easily identifiable because of its cutout of her beloved Horton, the elephant from Dr. Seuss.

Mary peeked through the window and could see Simon sitting next to Rachel's hospital bed, reading her a book. Rachel looked more pale than she had been, with her eyes closed like half-moons and her little bald head to the side, grasping a plush purple elephant under one arm. The light in the room was gentle, shed by a pink elephant lamp that must have been brought from home. A crayoned sign taped to the head of the bed read RACHEL, and red, white, and blue streamers were woven through its slats, decorations that a healthy child would have put on bicycle spokes.

The room had a window on the far side, overlooking the atrium, and in the middle was Rachel's hospital bed with its vital signs monitors, computer monitor on a standing desk, and IV stalk to the left, next to a rolling night table with a pink-plastic pitcher, a yellow tub of Magic Markers, and board books. On the far side of the bed was a blue chair, a counter with a video game console, and a long purple couch with a bed pillow and an elephant print coverlet, under which Feet slept soundly in his clothes. His Mr. Potatohead glasses lay folded on top of his stomach, rising up and down as he snored.

Mary swallowed hard, touched. She admired the way Feet and Simon had stepped into the vacuum created by the sudden death of Rachel's mother, Ellen, which broke everyone's heart. The aneurysm had struck Ellen when she'd been shopping with the baby at Toys R Us, a story so remarkable that it made the local news. In the aftermath, they'd all been left reeling, they'd thought Ellen's death was the worst thing that could happen. Rachel grew into a happy, precocious toddler who loved to babble away, and Mary would take her to the library to give Simon a break. They'd pick out some books and snuggle into the denim beanbag chair, and Mary had loved every minute, breathing in the sweet smells of Rachel's dark curls and reading her whichever books she chose. The one book Rachel always wanted was *Horton Hatches the Egg.*

Mary forced herself to keep her emotions at bay, thinking of it now. She used to wonder how much Rachel remembered of her mother and Mary sensed that Rachel knew that her mother was gone and that she herself was their collective egg. And after Rachel's dreadful diagnosis, Mary never stopped taking her to the library, reading *Horton* to her and fulfilling a silent vow to always be faithful to the little girl, one hundred percent, in Ellen's memory.

Mary came out of her reverie when suddenly Rachel's eyes fluttered, her dark-eyed gaze unfocused until it found Mary. A slow smile spread across Rachel's face, and she gave a wave with her free hand. Mary waved back, and Simon turned around to see who had arrived.

"Hi, Mary!" Simon called out. "Look who came to visit you, Rach. It's Aunt Mary. Come in, Aunt Mary!"

"Okay." Mary opened the door, reminding herself of something Simon always said. *See the child, not the cancer. Then you'll be happy when you visit, not sad.*

"Mary!" Rachel raised her arms for a hug. "Hi!"

"Hi, honey! I'm so happy to see you!" Mary put her belongings down, went to Rachel's bedside, and kissed her on the cheek. The child smelled like Jolly Ranchers and antiseptic wipes.

"I ate my *whole* dinner."

"Good for you."

"Horton helped." Rachel smiled sleepily.

"Good for him. What do elephants eat?"

"What Daddy says."

"Right." Mary smiled.

Simon smiled, too. "Everybody does whatever Daddy says. All the time. Ha!"

Rachel's eyelids started to droop. "Horton hatched the egg."

"I know," Mary said, more quietly. "Because Mayzie flew away to Palm Beach."

"Pom Beach."

"Right." Mary stroked Rachel's head, remembering her hair, which used to be so rich and thick. "I think it might be your bedtime."

"I'm not tired." Rachel closed her eyes.

"Good night now, sweetie. I love you. I'll see you again soon." Mary kissed her on the cheek, backed away from the bed, and got her stuff. She went out into the hallway as Simon gave

Rachel a kiss and left the room, shutting the door quietly behind him.

"Thanks for coming," Simon said tiredly. "She saw you right away, didn't she? That made me happy. I like that she wasn't snowed under. Sometimes these drugs, they just put her out."

"I bet."

"She loves you." Simon's gaze met hers, and they both knew what they were feeling, so neither of them had to say anything.

"I love her, too. Anyway, I have good news."

"Tell me. Let's go sit there, I want to be nearby if she wakes up. My dad needs the rest." Simon motioned to a line of blue bucket chairs outside a playroom, with a sign on the door: **For the safety of our BMT patients, the playroom is open only to patients and parents/caregivers. When leaving, patients must put dirty toys in the dirty toy bin. Thanks!**

"Here's what's going on." Mary took a seat and told him everything, including the conflict-of-interest issue, which concerned him.

"I'm sorry if I'm making life difficult for you," Simon said, after she had finished.

"You're not. It's a judgment call, and I'm making a judgment. And in any event, it looks like it's form over substance."

"So what's the next move?"

"We wait and see how they respond to the complaint and our settlement demand. I'm optimistic, I really am." Mary's gaze shifted to the room, where Rachel had fallen asleep in an identical posture with Feet, their heads off to the left. "Look at those two. You think they're related?"

Simon turned around, then burst into a grin. "Oh, I would say so."

"Your dad must be exhausted."

"He is. Yours, too."

"What do you mean?" Mary asked, surprised. "Is my father here?"

"Yes, in the family lounge."

"The McDonald's one? I didn't look in when I passed."

"He's in there. I tried to get him to go home, but he wouldn't listen. He never does."

"This is typical?" Mary didn't get it. It wasn't as if her father had so much else to do, but he wouldn't ordinarily stay out all day.

"Completely typical. He stays, even after Pigeon Tony and Tony From-Down-The-Block go home. Why don't you persuade him to go? Maybe he'll listen to you. I sleep here, but if he goes home, he can take my dad."

"Oh boy." Mary rose, hoisting her bags to her shoulder. "You need somebody to wrangle senior citizens."

"Exactly." Simon chuckled.

"Let me go see what I can do." Mary headed down the hallway toward the lounge, then spotted her father shuffling toward her from the opposite end of the hallway. His head was downcast so that his bald head shone in the bright overhead lights. She stood at the lounge door until he had almost reached her, looking up with a startled smile.

"MARE?" he said in a stage whisper, but that was still too loud, so she hustled him into the family lounge and closed the door behind them.

"Pop, what are you still doing here? You must be beat."

"I'M FINE, I'M GOOD. HOW YOU DOIN'?" Her father eased into a soft chair, and Mary sat down next to him. The lounge was remarkably homey, decorated with cheery print curtains, matching soft couches and chairs, and lined with popular hardbacks and other books. The far side held a cozy kitchen outfitted with new appliances, directly across from a laundry room that held a washer-dryer, thrumming away. A flat-screen TV mounted in the corner played on mute.

"I'm good, but what's going on? Were you here all day?"

"SURE."

Mary felt worried about him. At home, he would have napped twice. "Is it because of Feet? I mean, that's very nice of you to support him, but all day?"

"HE LIKES THE COMPANY. SOMETIMES WE TAKE A WALK. OR WE HAVE A CUPPA COFFEE DOWN-STAIRS."

"I'm sure he wouldn't mind if you went home."

"I KNOW. IT'S NOT ON ACCOUNT OF HIM. NO, HE TELLS ME TO GO. SO DOES SIMON."

"Then why?"

"I STAY. I DON'T MIND. I LIKE IT."

"Are you serious?" Mary couldn't even wrap her mind around what he was saying. It seemed impossible to like it here. She thought to herself, *children died here,* a notion that unsettled her so deeply she couldn't even give it voice.

"I GOT THE TV. I GOT COFFEE. I GOT THE PAPER. I DO THE PUZZLE. I GOT ALL I NEED." Her father gestured to the newspaper, where he'd completed the Seek & Find. He wasn't a crossword-puzzle kind of guy.

"But you could be home, relaxing."

"I RELAX HERE."

"What about the things you were doing at home? The bath-room floor? You were going to regrout it." Mary liked that her father stayed active, doing projects around the house. He had been a tile setter his whole life, a fact in which he took great pride, saying his grout was like sugar. The only unfortunate re-sult was that tile covered almost every available surface of the house, of late.

"THAT JOB CAN WAIT. WHAT'S UP WITH SIMON'S CASE?"

"It's fine. What about Mom? She's home alone all day."

"SHE DON' MIND. SHE AIN'T HOME ANYWAY. SHE GOES TO CHURCH."

Mary let it go. His attention turned toward the TV, where

the local newscaster was reporting on a warehouse fire, and she watched her father squint at the closed captioning from behind his bifocals. "Can you read that, Pop?"

"YEAH. I LIKE DENISE NAKANO."

"Who?"

"THE CHINESE GIRL ON THE NEWS." Her father gestured at the TV, then his hand fell to his lap. "SHE'S GOOD. VERY PROFESSIONAL."

Mary smiled to herself. Denise Nakano was Japanese, but she let it go. Her father wasn't racist and he didn't need her to nag him.

"I CAN'T GIVE PLATELETS. I TRIED AGAIN. THEY SAID I'M TOO OLD."

"I know." Mary thought it came out of left field, but she felt for him. She knew it bothered him that he hadn't been able to give blood in any of the directed donations for Rachel. She had been able to give at regular intervals because she was CMV negative, which was a rarity, indicating the absence of a common virus.

"SOMETIMES WHEN I SIT HERE, I PRAY. CHURCH CAN BE ANYWHERE. LIKE, THIS IS CHURCH."

"Right," Mary said, softening her tone. They fell silent a moment, then her father looked away from the TV, but didn't turn his head to her, averting his eyes.

"I MEAN, SHE'S JUST A BABY. AND HERE I AM. AND FEET. WE'RE FINE AND SHE'S SICK. THAT AIN'T RIGHT."

"No, it isn't." Mary patted his arm, touched. She thought back to the time when she and her father had taken Feet to the emergency room for a sprained ankle. Her father had been upset there, too.

"FEET TOLE ME HE WOULD GIVE HIS LIFE FOR THAT KID. AND HE WOULD. ME TOO." Her father shook his head, shrugging, his heavy shoulders going up and down in his transparent white shirt. "I DO WHAT I CAN DO. I'M HERE. SAME WITH FEET. THAT'S ALL WE CAN DO. BE HERE."

"It's going to be okay, Pop."

"YOU DON'T KNOW THAT, MARE." Her father turned to her, and his brown eyes glistened behind his glasses, the irises rimmed with grayish cataracts like stormclouds. "NOT EVERYTHING TURNS OUT OKAY."

Mary masked her surprise. Her father was the person who always told her that everything would turn out okay. For the first time, she sensed that he was speaking to her as an equal, adult-to-adult, not father to child. And she wasn't sure she liked it. She wanted her rock to stay a rock. "Pop, I know but—"

"I THINK ABOUT YOU AND YOUR SISTER. IF ANYTHING HAPPENED TO YOU."

"Nothing's going to happen to me, Pop. Or Angie."

"WHAT ABOUT MY GRANDBABY?"

"You don't have a grandbaby. I'm not pregnant, Pop. And Angie's saving the world, so believe me, she's not pregnant either."

"THAT'S THE PROBLEM."

"That I'm not pregnant?" Mary swallowed hard, realizing that maybe he was wondering if he'd live long enough to see a grandchild.

"NO. WHAT IF I HAVE A GRANDDAUGHTER LIKE RACHEL? A LITTLE ANGEL LIKE THAT BABY? WHAT IF SHE GETS CANCER TOO? IT CAN HAPPEN." Her father shook his head, suddenly agitated. "HOW CAN GOD LET THIS HAPPEN? HOW CAN OLD MEN LIVE AND BABIES DIE?"

Mary got it finally. "I love you," she said, reaching over and putting her arms around him.

"Love you too, honey," her father whispered, then his tears started to flow, and Mary held him tight, heartbroken by his hoarse sobs and the way his shoulders shook, heaving each time. She had never seen her father cry and never wanted to again. She got him Kleenexes from a box on the end table, and in time he collected himself, mopped up his eyes under his glasses, blew his nose loudly, and apologized to her for getting so upset. She told him that it wasn't necessary but she couldn't convince him, and she realized that tonight, in a hospital lounge, something had changed between them as father and daughter.

She had become *his* rock.

Mary got home by nine o'clock, exhausted and drained as she closed the door behind her. She dropped her purse and messenger bag on the floor, ignored the mail stacked on the console table, kicked off her flats, and padded through the darkened living room to the kitchen in the back of the house. The light was on, which meant Anthony was home, and as she entered, he looked up from the kitchen island with a warm smile, which still made her heart skip a beat. Anthony Rotunno was still the sexiest man she'd ever seen, an Italian-American hunk just shy of six feet, with thick dark hair, a strong Roman nose, dark eyes the color of espresso beans, and an omnipresent smile, at least for her.

"Anthony, I had the worst day *ever*."

"Aw, poor thing." Anthony came toward her, opening his arms.

"I'm going to whine and whine. Be ready."

"I am." Anthony gave her a big hug, rocking her slightly, and Mary buried her head in his chest, which was warm and soft under his worn T-shirt, which he had on with a pair of khaki shorts and bare feet. "How's Rachel?"

"Not good, and my father's upset, and this case at work, it's a nightmare." Mary released him, and he gave her a quick kiss.

"So what's going on? Why is Rachel back in the hospital?"

Mary had texted him, but not filled him in. "Long story short, she needs a bone marrow transplant, and Simon got fired this week because his company didn't want to pay for it."

"Are you *serious*?" Anthony stepped back, appalled. "Is she going to be okay? That's high-risk. When did all this happen?"

"I found out today."

"Oh no." Anthony sighed, taking her hand. "Tell me about it over dinner. I hope you feel like eating. I waited when I got your text."

"Thanks, yes, I do. What are we having?"

"My incredible amazing seafood salad."

"Nice." Mary began to rally.

"Come with me." Anthony led her into the kitchen, which was spacious and pretty with black-granite counters and white cabinets, her favorite room in their new house. The island had been set with place settings, wineglasses, and a big wooden bowl of romaine and arugula mixed with fresh shrimp, seared scallops, and red pepper, topped with strips of fresh basil, which smelled delicious.

"Wow." Mary sat down on a stool at the kitchen island. "I'm loving the you-making-the-dinner thing."

"It's the least I can do until I get a job."

"Aw, don't worry, you will." Mary knew it bothered him that he was still out of work. Anthony had a Ph.D. in American History and had taught at Penn and Drexel, but there were no openings on the tenure track in the area. He'd been of-fered a tenured position at Stanford but had turned it down because Mary didn't want to leave Philadelphia.

"So you say." Anthony went into the refrigerator, pulled out a bottle of Lambrusco, and twisted off the wire around the neck.

"How was your day?"

"Good. Did some research. Found an article I hadn't before."

"Nice." Mary was proud of him, because he was using the

downtime to finish his book, a nonfiction account of anarchism in 1930s America. He would rather be teaching, but he never complained, and she made enough money to support them. It wasn't the way he wanted it, but she knew it was temporary.

"I worked here instead of the library. The air-conditioning's better." Anthony popped the cork, and Mary could smell the bouquet of the fruity Lambrusco.

"Ah, the perfect summer wine."

"You say that every time. Even in winter." Anthony smiled, pouring.

"So fill me in on what happened. That's so sad, about Rachel."

"I know." Mary told him the whole story, bringing him up to speed about everything, including Rachel's turn for the worse, her father at the hospital, and the fight over her representing Simon. They talked easily back and forth, as usual, and she finished by telling him about how she was waiting to hear whether Bennie would try to settle the lawsuit informally. "So I'm hopeful."

"You should be. It's common sense. Only lawyers see things adversarially all the time. It encourages conflict in a way. Peace is better than war. Communication can work wonders. Look at Yalta."

"Right." Mary got the gist, though half the time, she had no idea what he was talking about. And if she asked him to explain, they'd be up all night.

"It's so terrible about Rachel. Simon must be scared out of his mind. First you lose your wife, then maybe your daughter? *And* your job? Sheesh." Anthony pushed away his empty salad plate.

"I know, but he handles it all, somehow."

"Does he?" Anthony paused, his expression darkening. "Or maybe it just *looks* like he handles it."

Mary thought the way he said it made her wonder if he was talking about himself.

CHAPTER EIGHT

The next morning, Bennie parked in the visitors' lot at Open-Space, a boxy building of tan stone with an all-glass entrance on the left. To the right were the corporate offices, a tan façade interrupted by two strips of black smoked glass, and tucked behind was a seven-thousand-square-foot manufacturing facility of tan corrugated tin, plus loading docks. The employee parking lots flanked the building, and they were full because the first shift started two hours ago, at six o'clock.

Last night, Bennie had told Mary on the phone that she was going to give her idea a try and see if she could settle the case, so here she was, against better judgment. She got out of the car with her purse and messenger bag, ignoring the humidity, walked the concrete path to the entrance, and entered the building. It was insanely air-conditioned, so she was glad she had on her khaki blazer, which had become her uniform. She didn't like to worry about what she was going to wear every day, and it made getting ready easier. She strode to the reception area, shaped like a cubicle itself, with gray-paneled walls and functional gray seating around a glass-and-chrome table.

"Hello, may I help you?" asked the receptionist, a young brunette with short hair.

"I think I'll go to the hospital tomorrow. Check in

"That would be nice," Mary said, touched. She st

back. "Let's go upstairs."

"What about the dishes?"

"Leave the dishes."

"Whoa, now we're getting crazy." Anthony grinned

then, Mary's phone started ringing, a faint sound com

her purse, which she'd left in the entrance hall.

"Hold on, it might be Bennie!" Mary jumped up an

the entrance hall, but she reached it as the rings stop

dug inside her purse, found her phone, and checked th

The call had been from Bennie, who was still in Ma

tacts as Da Boss.

Mary pressed Redial, holding her breath.

"Yes, thank you." Bennie slid her driver's license out of her wallet as she introduced herself. "I have a meeting with Todd Eddington and Jason Worrall."

"And Ray Matewicz."

"Pardon?"

"Mr. Matewicz will be joining you as well, I believe. They're waiting for you. You can go right into the conference room. I'll buzz the door." The receptionist gestured to a door to the right.

"Thanks." Bennie went through, finding herself in a hallway lined with glossy ads for the company: Office Cubicles, Modular Furniture, Call Center Stations, Treadmill Workstations! Only the Finest Building Materials, Sourced from the World Over! We Build to YOUR Specifications and Price! She went to the only open door, reaching the threshold of a no-frills conference room containing three men sitting at a round Formica table.

"Good morning, gentlemen." Bennie introduced herself, closing the door behind her and setting her belongings on the table. The three men stood up instantly, led by Jason Worrall, a tall African-American lawyer with bright brown eyes behind horn-rimmed glasses and a studious smile typical of younger lawyers, who thought every case was a final exam. When in fact, it was a war.

"Bennie, good to see you again." Jason extended a hand. He had on a blue oxford shirt with no tie and a pair of dark slacks, the only man not dressed in a green polo with the white Open-Space logo. He gestured to the others, one older and one younger. "Meet Todd Eddington. He runs Sales."

"Great, hello." Bennie knew from the complaint that Todd was the one who had terminated Simon Pensiera.

"Hey, Bennie, good to meet you." Todd stepped forward, the younger man, with a strong handshake. He seemed about Bennie's age, also tall, with sandy-brown hair cut in costly layers, sharp blue eyes, a thin nose, and the broad smile of a salesman, though his teeth looked oddly bonded together. His arms were tan, but his hands weren't, so she guessed he was a golfer, which fit the profile.

"You too." Bennie turned to the older man. "And you are—"

"Ray Matewicz, VP and Operations manager." Ray was shorter and heavier than Todd, maybe in his fifties, with small hazel eyes behind wire-rimmed glasses that were almost the same color as his grayish hair, which he wore in a short practical cut. His build was stocky, with a belly paunch that contributed to an overall lack of vanity, which Bennie liked. Like most operations types, he came off as strictly business, so she didn't want to waste his time, since most of them thought that that was a lawyer's reason for existence.

"Nice to meet you all. Should we get started?" Bennie pulled out a swivel chair closest to her.

"Sure," Jason answered as they returned to their seats on the opposite side of the conference table, though he paused before he sat down. "Hey, I should have offered, you want coffee or anything?"

"No, thanks," Bennie said, since that was the right answer. It was morning for her, but it was almost lunchtime for them. She slid a pen and a fresh legal pad from her messenger bag, but left her laptop inside. She wanted to make eye contact while they spoke, not be looking down at a computer.

Suddenly, the door opened, and they all turned. Bennie twisted around, surprised to see Nate entering the room, dressed in a light blue sweater and jeans, with an easy grin. Bennie didn't need him here, but she hid her annoyance since she'd invited him, after all. "Nate, I didn't know you were coming."

"I wanted to drop in. Don't mind me. I won't say a word." Nate pulled a chair from the table, turning to Todd and Ray, who shook his hand in turn. "Good morning, gentlemen. I'm Nate Lence, with Dumbarton. Just thought I'd sit in."

Bennie assumed Nate finessed who he was so they wouldn't get nervous, which was a good call.

Todd shrugged. "Sure, whatever, I'm Todd Eddington, and this is Ray Matewicz, my boss."

"Great to meet you." Nate took a seat just as Jason popped up with a professional smile.

"Nate, good to see you."

"You, too. Proceed as if I'm not here." Nate waved his hand dismissively, and everyone sat back down.

Bennie turned away, getting down to business. "Well, folks, you're wondering what this is about. We need to discuss the termination of one of your reps, Simon Pensiera. But before we get into detail, let me understand a few things about your corporate structure." Bennie shifted her attention to Todd. "Do you report directly to Ray?"

"Yes, as VP."

Bennie turned to Ray. "And to whom do you report? The company president?"

"Yes. Mike Bashir."

Bennie recognized the name from another of Dumbarton's subsidiaries. "I know Mike Bashir from Joselton Ltd."

"Right. He came from there. They make kids' clothes."

"Who made the decision to terminate Simon Pensiera?"

"I did." Todd tensed.

"Is anybody required to approve that decision?"

"Mike Bashir. He rubber-stamps it."

"How about with anybody at Dumbarton?" Bennie held her breath.

"No."

"Do you keep anybody at Dumbarton informed of hiring and firing?"

"No."

"How about payroll? Where does that come from? You'd have to take Pensiera off the payroll."

"We do our own payroll and accounting."

Bennie breathed a relieved sigh. So far so good. She avoided looking over at Nate and put him out of her mind. "How big is the Sales department?"

"I have ten reps under me."

"And they all have different territories?"

"Yes, we're national."

"So you're spread thin."

"Understatement of the year."

"Do you have accounts, as manager?"

"Yes, I kept some of mine as I got promoted. It makes up for the lost commissions. I kept my bread-and-butter, mostly in the area. I got tired of being a road warrior and I have a lot more paperwork as manager."

"Okay, I'm here to try to understand the facts concerning Mr. Pensiera's termination. Let's start with—"

"Why?" Todd leaned forward, with a frown. "Why does this come up? What does this have to do with you, an outside lawyer?"

"Mr. Pensiera is claiming that you fired him to mitigate medical expenses for his daughter, Rachel, who has cancer."

"That's bull!" Todd raised his voice, his handsome face flushing under his fresh tan. "Are you serious? I mean, for real, what are you accusing me of?"

Jason interjected, "Todd, she's not accusing you of anything. She's here as our lawyer to tell us about the suit."

"There's a *lawsuit*?" Todd's blue eyes flew open, incredulous. "Simon is suing me? What law says that I have to keep a rep who doesn't do his job anymore?"

Bennie raised a hand, signaling for him to calm down. "I know this is unpleasant, but let's get the facts on the table, then we can sort it out. That's the quickest way to get us all back to work."

Jason nodded. "Todd, please listen to what Bennie has to say."

"Fine!" Todd lowered his voice, but a frown took up residence on his forehead, creasing his sunburn.

Ray said nothing, folding beefy arms over his paunch.

Bennie changed tacks. "Tell you what, Todd. Instead of me doing all the talking, why don't you tell me why you fired Pensiera?"

"Okay, good." Todd shifted forward in his chair, his anger controlled but obvious. "It was his performance. He was doing a bad job. His numbers were going down. They don't lie."

"Has that always been the case?"

"No. He's always been one of our top guys. Always made above quota. His accounts love him. He reports directly to me. We get along great. I gave him the biggest region. We're friends, for God's sake! We socialized, at least we used to. I can't believe he would do this to me!" Todd banged the table, but Bennie ignored the outburst.

"When did his performance start to change?"

"I would say about two years ago."

"How?"

"He wasn't as into work as he used to be. Ellen, his wife, died a few years ago, and he became a single father. He lost his edge. His priorities changed. He became more of a family guy. Then Rachel got sick and it got worse."

"Are you saying his performance was affected by his child's illness?" Bennie asked, a legally significant question. Last night, she had researched the case law under the Americans with Disabilities Act, and even if an employee was distracted because of the illness of a family member, it was still illegal to terminate that employee.

"No, not because she was sick. I think it was because his wife died and he had to take care of the kid. He made calls, but he didn't care anymore. His heart just wasn't in it. He wasn't closing as many deals. It's like his values changed. Like I say, he lost his edge."

Bennie listened critically, evaluating Todd's response as he spoke. If he were telling the truth, then it would have been a nuanced theory of the defense and even permissible under the ADA, as a performance-based termination.

"He turned touchy-feely. Warm and fuzzy. Seize the day, all that. I might get that way too, if I had a really sick kid. But I need reps who are committed. Sales is a brutal business, especially in this economy."

"How does the economy impact you?"

"Our market is the most competitive. We're the middle tier of cubicle manufacturers. We compete with Knoll and Kimball, plus remanufacturers and clone manufacturers from China."

"What's a clone manufacturer?"

"It's a copied system with a tried-and-true design. It's sourced from China using cheaper materials. Our business is growing but it's not easy. Nothing about this business is easy. You have to grind every day, every hour. That's why I reduced his territory."

"Why, exactly?"

"Because he wasn't paying attention. His numbers were slipping."

"Did he make quota?"

"No."

"For how long?"

"A month, and he was trending down. He made fewer calls each quarter. You could see it in his call logs and his POs, or purchase orders. He was falling asleep at the switch." Todd threw up his hands. "That's why I reduced him to Delaware and figured he could knock himself out."

"Did you ever fire another rep who didn't make quota after one month?"

Todd thought a minute. "Uh, no."

Jason made a note on a legal pad, but didn't interrupt.

"Did you warn him?"

"No."

"Why not?"

"I didn't think I was going to fire him. I thought reducing his territory would work. Most reps would see the writing on the wall and take it up a notch."

Bennie glanced at Jason. "Does OpenSpace have a termination procedure with any kind of warning system, written or no?"

Jason frowned. "Unsure."

"It should."

"We just acquired OpenSpace last year, so we're just coming up to speed. I'll get on that."

Bennie let it go, returning her attention to Todd. "When you reduce his territory, don't you ensure that he can't make quota?"

"Not necessarily. Well, er, wait." Todd held up a hand like a traffic cop. "Let me explain. We also adjust his quota, so he could've done very well."

"How, if it was a smaller territory? And I also understand that it contained fewer businesses." Bennie was referring to the complaint.

"True, but they tended to be high-end. We produce three lines of product—expensive, medium, and cheap. The businesses in the region that I gave him are very high-end. Businesses incorporate in Delaware because the state laws are favorable. They headquarter or keep an office in Wilmington and the subs. They have the money and they go for top-of-the-line construction." Todd leaned over again, warming to the topic. "Stainless-steel frame. Floor-to-ceiling. The best drywall. Real glass windows. Electrified under the counter, with LED lights. Some even have doors. Some are custom. I could go on but I won't bore you."

"I'm not bored."

"Anyway, you get the gist. Even if he had fewer accounts, he could make more money per account. I thought he could handle fewer accounts better than so many. I thought I was doing him a favor. No good deed." Todd sighed. "Anyway, I had good reason to fire him and I didn't like doing it, but I did it. I'm not a jerk. I'm a father, too. I know that his kid is sick. I know that he needs a job. But *I* need a *rep*. Because if I don't produce, then I get fired. So it's my family or his family."

Ray nodded, a newly determined set to his lips.

Bennie asked him, "Ray, did you discuss this decision with Todd?"

"The decision to fire Simon? Yes, I did."

"What did he tell you about why he wanted to let Simon go?"

"He said it was sales. Performance. Like he just told you."

Bennie kicked herself for having them both in the same meeting, because they were supporting each other's version of the facts. "When did you have this discussion with Todd?"

"The day before he fired Simon. Monday."

"Was that the first time you heard Todd was unhappy with Simon's performance?"

"Yes."

"You didn't discuss it before that?"

"No."

"Why?"

"Why would I? He runs his people, I run mine. We're busy. We talk twice a week, if that." Ray shrugged, arms still folded.

"How long have you worked here, Ray?"

"Twenty years, same as Todd."

"Do you socialize, play golf, have dinner?"

"Hell no." Ray chuckled, for the first time. "I'm not the social type."

Todd laughed with him. "He doesn't even drink. And if you don't drink, I got no time for you."

Everyone laughed, and Bennie took advantage of the moment to check her notes. "Todd, I just have a few more questions, but they're specific. Simon would submit medical expenses to you for his daughter, didn't he?"

"Yes."

"And what would you do with them?"

"Pass them on to accounting."

"Why would he submit them to you and not directly to accounting?"

"I'm his boss. That's how it works." Todd frowned again. "Why?"

"Did you ever make a remark to Simon about the amount of the expenses?"

"No."

Bennie kept a poker face. She had been hoping that Todd wouldn't deny it and that it was an honest mistake, ignorance of the law. "Did you ever say anything like offhand, well, 'that's a lot of money,' or anything like that?"

"No."

"Did you ever say anything like 'I hope this chemo works because it's pretty expensive'?"

"No," Todd answered firmly. "Did he say I did?"

"Yes, he does."

"That's a lie!" Todd slammed the table again, and Jason looked over with a frown, but didn't say anything. Ray unfolded his arms.

Bennie bore down. "Did you ever explain to him the fact that the company is self-insured up to $250,000?"

"No."

Bennie couldn't tell if Todd was lying or not, but this was shaping up to be a credibility contest. "You *never* discussed that with him?"

"No."

"Was anybody else ever around when he handed in expenses?"

"No, he brought them into my office."

"Was Ray ever present?"

"No, nobody was."

"How about your secretary?"

"Who has a secretary?" Todd snorted.

"Did he ever submit them by email?"

"He may have, I forget." Todd permitted himself a half-smile. "I would say yes."

"So would I," Ray interjected, with a wry smile.

"Why do you guys say that?" Bennie looked from one to the other.

Todd chuckled. "We call Simon the Mad Emailer. He emails about everything and he writes paragraphs and paragraphs. He writes *books*. I barely get through the first paragraph."

Bennie turned to Jason. "I'd like copies of Mr. Pensiera's emails for the past year, his personnel file, call logs, purchase orders, and his sales info. It has to show department-wide sales, so I can compare his performance to the other reps. Can you send that to my office before the weekend?"

"Sure, that's standard operating procedure." Jason turned to Ray. "Can you make that happen by the end of the day?"

"Yes," Ray answered. "Most of it's in the computer. I'll text Mona in HR so she can get started. She'll have to talk to our IT guy." He picked up his phone, texted a message, then set it down. "Thy will be done."

Bennie smiled. "Thanks. Todd, let me ask you a few final questions. Have either of you ever had any training in employment discrimination laws?"

Todd blinked. "They send us to a bullet-point slideshow for sexual harassment. We go to some law firm in town. You wouldn't believe the food. They put out a spread like a wedding."

"Ray, how about you?" Bennie asked, turning to him.

"Not always."

Todd interjected, "He cuts class. He's a bad boy."

"I have to work," Ray countered.

Bennie forced a smile, her mood circling the drain. "Do you remember getting any training in the law under the Americans with Disabilities Act, the Rehabilitation Act?"

Todd thought a minute, then shook his head. "No, not really."

Ray shook his head. "I don't either. I'm sure HR knows about that. But that's not my bailiwick."

Bennie had to get the truth, but she couldn't do it with an audience. She stood up, crossed to the door, and opened it with a smile. "Gentlemen, I'd like everyone except for Todd to leave the room."

Todd recoiled, bewildered. "For real?"

"Yes. I won't keep you long."

"Okay." Jason and Ray rose from the chairs and headed toward the door.

Only Nate didn't move, looking up at her with a mock-frown. "You can't mean me, too."

"Yes, I do," Bennie answered, opening the door wider.

CHAPTER NINE

Mary and Anthony threaded their way through the Children's Hospital lobby, which was bustling with early-morning activity. Doctors in scrubs and surgical caps, nurses with decorated stethoscopes and laminated IDs, and staff with colorful plastic carry-alls hurried this way and that, mixing in with the patients' families, the mothers and fathers bearing up under the strain, tugging toddlers and siblings by the hand.

Mary and Anthony fell silent as they climbed into the crowded elevator, and she knew that he felt the same way that she did inside. The elevator pinged on their floor, the door slid open, and they made their way out of the cab, down the hall, and into the BMT unit, where they Purelled their hands. They stopped at the lounge, taken aback at the crowd filling it to its glass walls.

"What's going on?" Mary wondered aloud, then did a double-take at the same moment that Anthony did, when they began to recognize faces from the neighborhood in the crowd.

"It's everybody. It's all of South Philly."

"You're right, and both our families. They didn't tell me they were coming." Mary's father, her mother, and The Tonys were there, and so was her mother-in-law, Anthony's mother, Elvira, whom Mary secretly called El Virus. They were talking with a group of Simon's cousins from the West Coast and Italy, whom Mary had met at Simon and Ellen's wedding, and sadly, at her funeral.

"Oh no," Anthony said under his breath. "You don't think anything bad happened, do you?"

"No, they'd be crying. There's a reason the best operas are Italian."

"We go hard on the waterworks."

"And why not, really?" Mary spotted her mother smiling and talking, the shortest one in the crowd, with thick glasses and white hair teased into a cumulus cloud to hide her bald spot. She had on her flowered housedress with her orthopedic shoes, which looked oddly great together. "How cute is my mother?"

"Cute. She gets it from you." Anthony chuckled, Mary joined him, and for a moment they stood outside the glass, watching their blood relatives as if they were strangely exotic fish in a fishbowl, which in a way, they were.

"Oh, look. There's Simon, so nothing terrible happened." Mary noticed Simon at the center of the crowd, being hugged and kissed by his cousins.

"You mean nothing worse."

"Right." Mary felt her stomach clench. "I think it's nice that his family came from Italy, don't you?"

"Yes, but it's also concerning. How long can she wait for a donor? This is awful. Such a sweet little girl."

"I know." Mary squeezed his hand. Anthony adored Rachel and had a special way with kids. Someday he'd be a wonderful father, and they'd both talked about having kids when the time was right. Until then, they loved spending time with Patrick O'Brien, a child whom Mary had met on her last big special-education case.

"Let's go." Anthony opened the door for Mary, and heads started turning as soon as she entered the lounge, with everybody reaching for her, trying to hug her, and calling to her.

"It's Mary!" "Hey, Mary!" "Look who it is!" "Come here, Mary!"

"Hi, everybody!" Mary called back, hugging everybody in sight, getting kissed on the cheek, and breathing in the smells of Aqua Velva, Aquanet hairspray, and aqua–everything else. They were treating her like an absolute rock star, and she realized that the word must've spread that she was representing Simon in his lawsuit.

"*Maria!*" her mother said, grabbing her cheeks and giving her a big smooch.

"HEY, MARE! I DIDN'T KNOW YOU WERE COMIN'."

"I just thought I'd check in before work." Mary hugged her father, who seemed back to his usual chipper self, flashing her a big grin as he let her go. She hugged and kissed Pigeon Tony and Tony-From-Down-The-Block, with Feet bringing up the rear, like a caboose with glasses.

"Mary, I'm so glad you're fighting for Simon. It's like we got Perry Mason on our side! Thank God!" Feet squeezed her tight, and Mary let him go as Simon reached her side.

"Mary, thanks for coming." Simon gave her a big hug, then gestured behind him. "You remember my cousins, Amelia, Adriana, and Elisa from Rome? They're the good-looking branch of the family, my Uncle Tullio's daughters."

"Of course, hello." Mary shook the manicured hands of a bevy of beautiful dark-haired women, all about her age, with similarly lovely cheekbones that had to be in the Pensiera DNA.

"Mary, it's wonderful to see you again," Amelia said in perfect English. "Thank you so much for helping Simon and Rachel."

"Mary, yes, thank you," said Adriana and Elisa, almost in unison, looking so chic in lovely sundresses and color-coordinated sandals. Their makeup was perfect, and it struck Mary that, in a way, everybody in the lounge was putting on a brave face, but underneath their lipsticked smiles, they were all worried sick about Rachel.

"I'm happy to be able to help," Mary told them, meaning it. She turned to Simon. "How's Rachel today?"

"Luckily, a little better. She just fell asleep, so I figured I'd come out and say hello. Plus this gang needed discipline." Simon winked. "I told them to keep it down to a low roar."

Mary smiled. "Are you even allowed to have this many visitors?"

"The nurses are cutting me some slack, but everybody has to stay in here. Anything new with the case?"

"I would've emailed you but I wanted to tell you in person. I didn't expect a crowd." Mary looked around worriedly, but Simon leaned closer.

"Go ahead, what's new?"

"So far, so good." Mary lowered her voice. "I don't want you to get too excited, but my partner Bennie agreed to go to OpenSpace and try to settle the case. She's there right now."

"That's awesome." Simon burst into a smile. "Do you think it will work?"

"It's a long shot, especially this early. We haven't even filed the suit papers. I drafted a complaint, and Bennie has it with her, so they know the facts. I'm hoping it will be persuasive enough that they counter-offer."

"So you can settle before we even file the lawsuit? I didn't know that. That's wonderful."

"Yes, but don't get your hopes up."

"But it's a good start. I can't tell you how much I appreciate this."

"No worries, fingers crossed."

"But I wanted to say thank you." Simon stepped back, raising his hands in the air. "Everybody, can I have your attention for a minute? Please, can everybody settle down?"

Mary didn't get it. She hoped Simon wasn't about to tell them about the settlement. "Simon, what I just told you is confidential—"

"I know that." Simon waved her off with a smile, and everybody settled down, all the faces turning to him. "Folks, I'm not going to say this loud, so I hope you changed the batteries on your hearing aids."

"WHAT?" Mary's father said, and everybody laughed.

Simon smiled. "I just wanted to say I'm very grateful to all of you for coming today. I didn't expect you, but here you are." The crowd chuckled, nodding. "But then again, I never called my mother before I went to visit her, and she told me I didn't have to. Family is family, and home is where they have to let you in." Everybody chuckled again, and Mary swallowed hard, remembering Simon's mother, who was a sweetheart.

Simon continued, "Anyway, I know you're here because we love Rachel and we support her. I showed her that picture that I took of you this morning, and she loved it. I'm going to print it and put it above her bed, since you can't go in there to see her yourself."

The crowd reacted instantly, murmuring their approval with, "Aw thank you!" "That's a great idea!" "That's so sweet!"

Simon turned to Mary. "I especially want to thank you, Mary. You, Anthony, and your family have been so great to me for so long, and now you're helping me get justice against my company."

Mary felt her face flush, as heads turned. Everyone called out to her, thanked her, or grinned at her, which suffused her with happiness and gratitude, just to be here among them. Everybody was standing together behind Simon and Rachel—family, friends, and neighbors alike—which was the essence of South Philly. She knew there were similar communities carved out of cities and towns all across the country, maybe even the world, and she knew how lucky she was to be a member of one.

"So Mary, I wanted you to have this token of appreciation from me and my family." Simon slipped a hand in his sport jacket and produced a small turquoise box, unmistakably from Tiffany's, then presented it to Mary. "Please, take this, with thanks from the Pensieras and the Dragottis."

"Simon, really?" Mary's hands flew reflexively to her face. "You didn't have to do that!"

"We're happy to. You've been such a good friend all my life, to my father, Ellen, and Rachel too." Simon's eyes glistened, his upper lip trembling, but he kept it together.

"Oh my, you are too sweet." Mary accepted the gift, tugged at the white satin ribbon, and took the lid off. Inside was a velveteen box nestled in white paper.

"I KNOW WHAT IT IS!" her father said, but her mother backhanded him in the arm. Everyone in the crowd came closer, craning their necks to see.

"HOLD IT UP, MARE!"

"I will!" Mary opened the box to find a small gold locket shaped like a heart, then held it up so the crowd could see it, to oohs and ahhs. "Thank you so much! This is so pretty!"

"It opens."

"Really?" Mary opened the locket to find a small picture of Rachel on one side and a little lock of her hair on the other. "Oh Simon, this is too much." Mary almost burst into tears, but she kept it under control.

Anthony didn't do as well, his eyes welling up. "Thanks, Simon," he said.

"You're welcome." Simon cleared his throat. "I know how much she means to you."

"Aw, thank you." Mary hugged him.

"We just want you to know how much we appreciate you doing what you're doing. You're helping save her life." Simon managed a smile. "Here's how I look at it. I'm doing everything I can do, and you're doing everything you can do, too. The rest is in God's hands."

"I agree, thank you so much for this." Mary closed up the jewelry case, put it back in the box, and put everything in her purse, including the pretty ribbon. She swore to herself that she'd give the case everything that she had.

She couldn't lose.

CHAPTER TEN

Bennie faced Todd across the table. "I'm going to give this to you straight. It's really important that I understand exactly what happened in any conversations you had with Simon Pensiera about his daughter's medical expenses."

"I told you, we didn't have any." Todd gestured at the closed door behind Bennie. "Why did you throw the others out?"

"Because you and I need to speak more frankly, not in front of your boss or anybody else."

Todd pursed his lips. "You think I'm lying."

"I need to know if you're lying."

"I'm not. I told you the truth. There's two sides to every story. You made up your mind before you even came in here."

Bennie had to admit to herself that it struck a chord, but only because the contemporaneous notes were such strong evidence. "You never once mentioned the daughter's expenses?"

"No, I didn't."

"Not even in passing? By way of commiserating? No words to the effect of, 'well, these medical bills are something, Simon'?"

"Nothing like that." Todd's tone remained firm.

"But you must have talked about her illness or her treatments."

"No, not that I recall."

"How is that so?" Bennie wasn't buying. "You're supposedly friends, and his daughter is very ill? You don't ever once ask him how she is?"

"Okay, whatever. Once or twice I probably said, 'I hope Rach gets better.' It went without saying. I didn't bring it up because I don't want him to get upset at work. You don't need that in your face all the time, I wouldn't like it. I felt sorry for him."

Bennie wasn't buying. "Todd, you need to come clean with me. If you were trying to save the company some money, there's no shame in that. You were between a rock and a hard place, feeling sorry for Simon but knowing that you were responsible for your bottom line."

"I never said anything like that to him."

"Did you ever *think* anything like that?" Bennie watched him carefully for signs to see if he was lying, but so far, she wasn't sure. "I mean, you knew that the company was paying those medical expenses out of pocket, since they were under the cap. In accounting, do those losses or expenses come out of your department?"

"Yes," Todd admitted, after a moment.

"So that can't be good for your bottom line."

"It's not."

"And it can't be good for you if your department causes the premiums to go up."

"No. But I never said anything to him about it."

"Did anybody ever say anything about that to you? Ray or Bashir?"

"No, never."

"Was it just understood?"

"No, I mean, I admit, I'll tell you, I worried about it. But I truly never said anything about that to Simon." Todd shifted in the seat.

"Just tell me, Todd. If you did, no harm, no foul. We can settle this case. It won't come back on you."

Todd shifted again. "You don't know that. You don't know anything about this business."

"True, but you don't know anything about my business, either. And this is about my business—litigation. If this suit gets filed, goes to court, and we lose, it will cost the company a lot more than if we settle. And the PR will be terrible. We can make it go away now, but only if you tell me the truth."

"I told you the truth!" Todd said, raising his voice. "Why do you think I'm lying? Why? You don't even know me!"

"Hold on." Bennie slipped her hand into her messenger bag and extracted Exhibit A, B, and C, the contemporaneous notes attached to the complaint, which she had photocopied. She turned them facedown on the table, watching Todd, who reacted instantly, shifting again in his chair and eyeing the sheets.

"What's that? Is this some kind of game?"

"No, I'm just trying to get you to level with me. If you're really telling the truth, then so be it. But I have to know, and this is what you're up against." Bennie turned over the top sheet, which was Exhibit A, showing Pensiera's careful script on a notebook page:

Wednesday, October 20, 11:45 a.m. Todd said: "I hope this next round works, for her sake and for ours. These expenses are going to mount up, and we met our deductible already. Our premiums are going to go up."

Bennie slid the piece of paper across the table and turned it around so that it faced Todd the right way. "Do you recognize that handwriting?"

"Yes, it's Simon's."

"Take a moment to read it." Bennie folded her hands,

watching Todd critically. He read the sheet quickly, then raked his hand through his hair, leaving lines in the expensive layers of his haircut.

"I don't know why he would write this. It's a total lie." Todd looked up, his face flushing with new anger. "He's trying to set me up. He's framing me. He made this whole thing up."

Bennie kept her expression impassive. "Just so we're clear, you're saying that you never said any of this."

"I never said any of this!"

"You remember that you did *not* say it."

"I remember that I did *not* say it," Todd repeated, mimicking her intonation.

"It has the date and the exact time."

"So what?"

Bennie changed tacks. "You wouldn't happen to remember where you were on October 20 of last year, would you?"

"Of course not."

"You keep a calendar?"

"Yes, of course."

"Is it in your phone?"

"Yes," Todd answered with a scowl. "You want me to check it?"

"Yes, if you don't mind."

"Fine." Todd leaned over, slid an iPhone from his back pocket, and started thumbing the screen.

"So, were you in the office on Wednesday, October 20 of last year?"

"Look." Todd held up the screen, showing it to Bennie. "No appointments out of the office. I wasn't calling on accounts that day. But that doesn't mean I was in or that we had a conversation like this. It doesn't prove anything."

"Let's move on." Bennie reached for Exhibit B. The fact that Todd was in the office and could have made the statement went against him. "This is the second instance in which Pensiera claims that you made comments about his daughter's medical expenses. Why don't you take a look at that and tell me what your reaction is?"

"I can't believe this!"

"Here we go." Bennie passed Exhibit B across the table to him, which read:

Thursday, January 5, 9:15 a.m. Todd said: "This is the beginning of a new quarter and a new year. Do you think this is going to be as expensive as the last round?"

Todd looked up, angrier. "I'm telling you, I never said anything like that. This never happened. When does he say this happened?"

"You can see for yourself. On January 5, nine fifteen, when he turned some bills in to you after her second round of chemo."

"I didn't say it!"

"Okay, please check your phone for me and let me know if you were in the office that day, around nine fifteen."

"This is so ridiculous." Todd scrolled through his phone. "This is like a search, an illegal search. I didn't say any of this stuff and even if I did, is it illegal? Is it illegal to ask questions? To *talk*?"

"No, but under the Americans with Disabilities Act, it's illegal to fire an employee to save the company from paying the medical expenses of the employee's family member. It's considered discrimination. If you said these things, they are direct evidence of discriminatory animus."

"What about my rights? Don't I have a First Amendment right to say what I want? Not that I said it, but I am asking you."

"No. Your First Amendment right is guaranteed as against abridgment by the government or a state actor, but that's it. In other words, you don't have a First Amendment right to say whatever you want, whenever you want to."

"Lawyers!" Todd scrolled angrily through his phone, then held it up. "Okay, again, so no appointments. I was probably in the office that day at nine fifteen. They pay me good money to come here, so I do. I don't remember meeting with Simon and I *know* that I did not say anything like that!"

"Okay, here's Simon's last note, but I want you to take a very careful look at this one because it matters most of all."

"This is unreal." Todd shook his head, fuming.

"Here." Bennie passed Exhibit C to him, which contained the admission:

Thursday, March 30, 10:15 a.m. Todd said: "These expenses are going to kill us this quarter. It's really too much. We can't keep this up. They're going to raise our rates."

Todd sent the paper sliding back to her, his mouth tight. "I didn't say anything like that. I didn't say it. He made this whole thing up."

"Why would he do that?"

"So he could start a lawsuit. Simon is a very smart guy. What if he had this planned? Back when Rachel got sick, like I told you, he lost interest in the job. He doesn't want to work but he still needs money. So he makes up this story. He takes fake notes on days he *knows* I'm in the office." Todd dismissed the exhibits with an angry wave. "This isn't proof of anything. He's trying to get the money for Rachel's transplant. He made the whole thing up from the get-go."

Bennie's ears pricked up. "What transplant?"

"The bone marrow transplant." Todd hesitated. "You said he's suing me because I talked about the costs of her transplant."

"No, I never used the term 'transplant.' Neither does he in

his contemporaneous notes. I said 'medical expenses.'" Bennie eyed him hard. "The need for the transplant was a recent development, and it hurts our case that it came so close to the termination, suggesting a causal link."

"Okay, whatever. It's semantics." Todd rolled his eyes. "Stop acting like you caught me in a lie, for God's sake. I knew she needed a transplant, we all knew. Word got around."

"Did you discuss the transplant with him, *per se?*"

"No!"

"Thank you." Bennie took the exhibits back. "Please check your calendar for me."

"Under protest, yes." Todd thumbed his phone, then held it up again. "Ooh, look! Guilty as charged. I was in the office at ten fifteen. Or at least I wasn't out of the office, because there's no appointment that morning."

"Thank you."

"I don't like being called a liar. I don't like being accused of things I didn't do. Those notes of his are BS." Todd stood up abruptly, pocketing his phone. "We're done here, right?"

"Yes, we're finished. Thank you very much." Bennie put the exhibits back into her messenger bag, slid a business card from the inside pocket, and passed it to him. "Please take my card. Feel free to contact me if you have any questions or any further thoughts."

"I don't need your business card." Todd reached the door and put his hand on the knob. "And I'll tell you one thing. Don't settle this case. I want my day in court. I want to clear my name."

"Understood," Bennie said, nodding. Though it was the worst thing she could have heard in the circumstances.

Bennie found Nate in the manufacturing part of the facility, standing high above the factory floor on a concrete ramp that was protected from the noise below by a Plexiglas wall. The ramp thrummed with the vibration of the heavy machinery below, and the air smelled warm and dusty. Nate smiled when he saw Bennie, gesturing to the factory below.

"Want to take a factory tour? I just had mine. I like to do it from time to time. It's educational."

"No thanks, I don't have time." Bennie was in no mood. After that interview with Todd, she had a big problem on her hands, and so did Mary.

"I could show you around. It's so awesome!"

"It's not a toy, Nate."

"You're right, it's a bottom line." Nate chuckled, turning to the factory floor. "It looks like they're making cubicles, but they're making money. For me."

Bennie humored him, scanning the scene below. Production lines of heavy machinery and industrial conveyor belts manned by workers in earplugs and safety goggles were attaching stainless-steel frames to a white piece of drywall. In other circumstances, she would've loved a factory tour, but not today.

"See that?" Nate pointed at the closest production line. "That's what Todd was talking about. That's the line that makes the high-end cubicles, where the components are the best. The drywall is made in the U.S. and so is the steel. None of it's outsourced at this price point."

"Nate, we need to talk."

"No, we don't." Nate swiveled his head toward her, his expression turning grim. "It looks to me that everything is pretty clear. We're not going to be able to settle this case like you thought. Todd didn't make any of those comments."

"I think he's lying."

"Disagree. It's a credibility contest. Nevertheless, he's not backing down, and neither is Ray. He just told me. They're on the same page. They want to fight this thing, so I'm not settling."

Bennie bore down. "I confronted Todd about the contemporaneous notes, and his reaction wasn't good. I don't think he'd be a good witness on the stand. I think he'd tank on cross."

"Are you saying that because your partner's on the other side?" Nate lifted an eyebrow.

"No, I came here with an open mind and I analyzed Todd's demeanor, as I would any witness. He's the decision maker, and his testimony is the most critical. He was tense in the meeting with you and he lost his temper with me."

"He's unjustly accused, and I'm not settling. Ray doesn't want to settle either. They both think that the plaintiff is in it for the money, for his kid. He made the whole thing up."

"Nate, I'm not going to quibble with you about whether that's likely or not. In my opinion, it's not." Bennie kept her cool, leveling with him. "But the fact is, it doesn't really matter. The plaintiff's case is extremely sympathetic. He has a child with cancer and he lost his wife a few years ago—"

"So what does that matter? You're a lawyer, not some bleeding heart who gives out money just because it's a company being sued. The plaintiff couldn't do the job and he deserved to be fired."

"You didn't let me finish. The plaintiff made his quota for almost twelve years and he fell off one month. Todd admitted that he's never fired anybody else who didn't make quota after one month. If you single one rep out, that's discrimination *per se*."

Nate didn't interrupt her again, so she kept talking.

"When the jury is looking around for a reason why Todd fired the plaintiff, they have an easy answer. Todd wanted to save the company money. The medical expenses and transplant affect his bottom line and reflect poorly on him to management. I would settle this case. You're in trouble."

"No, you're in trouble. Because you're going to defend this case and your partner is conflicted out."

"You expect me to sue my own partner?"

"Yes. Welcome to the NFL."

"If you're not going to settle, I'm not taking the case." Bennie had prepared for this possibility, at least mentally. "Farm it out to one of the big firms like you would have before."

"You're turning down the work?" Nate straightened up, with a new frown. "Why, if your partner is conflicted out?"

"Because I don't want any part of it, unless it's to settle it. I'm not going to war with a personal friend of hers. She regards the plaintiff as a family member. She loves the kid. I just won't do it."

Nate burst into laughter, without mirth. "Well, look at you! Sisterhood is powerful! Why?"

"I thought about it. I knew it was a possibility that Todd would deny everything, and now that I've interviewed him, I feel stronger than ever. I'm not taking this case. Send it to somebody else."

"I'm sending it to you."

"I'm not accepting it."

"Really." Nate's eyes flashed with anger. "Then I'm no longer your client. I'm not sending you any more work from Dumbarton or the other subs. Checkmate."

"So be it." Bennie didn't blink.

"What do you mean? You want to lose me? And *all* my business?"

"If that's the way you want it, that's the way it has to be." Bennie remained calm. In fact, she only got calmer in conflict, which was why she loved being a lawyer. When things went well, she didn't know what to do with herself.

"You're just saying that. You're calling my bluff. You don't think I'll fire you because were friends."

"No, *because* were friends, I think you'll fire me. I know you and I know how you think. You like getting your own way. You're used to it. But you can't make me take a case I don't want, and if you feel you have to fire me, I'm fine with it." Bennie had made her peace, last night. His business was considerable, but it wasn't everything.

"So you're serious."

"Totally."

Nate blinked, stepping backwards. "Hold on. Rewind. You should think this over."

"I already have."

"Reconsider. Slow down this transaction. Go back and crunch the numbers. Take a look at your billings. See how much of them come from Dumbarton and the subs. And consider our relationship, which evidently I value more than you do."

"I value our relationship too. But the fact is, I have a partner now, and her name is Mary DiNunzio. Not you or any other client. So take care, I have work to do back at the office." Bennie turned away, holding her head high.

"Call me and let me know your decision," Nate called after her, chuckling. "I'm giving you the second chance you won't give me!"

"Good-bye," Bennie called back, heading out the factory door.

CHAPTER ELEVEN

Mary looked up from her laptop to see Bennie arriving at the threshold of her office, her topknot messy and her skin vaguely flushed, probably from the heat. Bags weighed down her shoulder, and her lips formed a flat, uncharacteristically grim line. Mary felt a clenching in the pit of her stomach, since she knew Bennie had been at OpenSpace.

"DiNunzio, I mean Mary. I have bad news."

"Oh no." Mary gestured to the chair opposite her desk, then realized Bennie had never visited her in her office, it usually was the other way around. Still. "You can sit down if you want to."

"No thanks. I've been in the car for almost two hours. There was an accident on 611."

"Okay, so what's up?"

"The case isn't going to settle," Bennie answered, matter-of-factly. "I can't go into detail because the situation is ethically challenged, at best. Suffice it to say that I gave it the old college try, but it isn't happening."

"Are you sure?" Mary tried to absorb the information. She had hoped for the best and convinced herself it was actually going to happen, because she wanted it to happen, so much.

"Yes, I'm sure."

"Is there any chance of settlement down the line?"

"Not in the near future."

"Oh no." Mary considered the implications. That must've meant Todd Eddington denied making the statements. The case was a credibility contest, and the company was going to stonewall.

"I really did try, Mary," Bennie said, her tone softening, and the sunlight coming through Mary's window shone on her face and caught the blue of her eyes, making them look crystal-clear.

"I'm sure you did." Mary forced a smile, despite her disappointment. "Thank you. I really appreciate it."

"I was glad to do it. I know how much this case meant to you. It was the right thing to do, to try, but it didn't work."

"Was my settlement demand too high?" Mary was kicking herself. "I tried to keep it reasonable but we'd settle this for less. Simon just needs the money for Rachel."

"It wasn't the number. More than that I can't tell you. What I learned today is privileged between OpenSpace and me, and I shouldn't say any more."

"They're going to lose at trial, you know." Mary felt an ember of anger, hot in her chest. "They're in the wrong. The notes are such good corroboration, and the case is incredibly sympathetic. Simon has them dead to rights."

"There are two sides to every story, as they told me this morning, and they're going to tell theirs. As for you and me, we shouldn't talk about the merits anymore."

"But settling it is the right result."

"Agree, it's a case that should settle."

"It makes the most sense for everyone involved." Mary couldn't let go of her frustration. Her chest felt squeezed, like she had on the smallest sports bra of all time. "I know there are two sides and they're not horrible people. I'm sure the boss didn't know what he did was illegal. Every company tries to cut costs, and he probably felt duty-bound to do it."

Bennie opened her mouth to say something, then clamped her lips shut. "Understood."

"Did you pitch settling, can I ask?"

"Of course. I did pitch it, and they declined."

"Did you show them the complaint?"

"No, I didn't need to, and I didn't think it was wise to. I didn't want to open up a can of worms when they saw my firm name on the last page."

"I get it. Arg!" Mary groaned. "This is so *wrong*. This is just the wrong result."

"Mary, trust me, the thing that should happen doesn't always happen. Life isn't fair. Litigation is less so. You should know that by now." Bennie's tone turned worldly-wise. "The right result isn't always the result."

"I understand." Mary felt heartsick. Her hand went to the gold locket around her neck, which Simon had given her. It killed her that she wasn't able to settle this case. It could have eased his mind. It could have helped Rachel.

"I hope that your friend finds himself a great lawyer, and you should feel comfortable helping him do that. I even have some recommendations if you need one. And of course I wish his daughter a speedy recovery."

Mary didn't get it. "Thank you, but I'm still going to represent Simon."

Bennie blinked. "You are?"

"Yes, absolutely," Mary said, though her mouth went dry. "I thought you understood that."

"No, I didn't." Bennie frowned slightly. "I thought we were tabling the issue of the representation."

"Well, no."

"Yes, we are. I thought we were setting aside the issue and trying to see if we could sort it out, extra-legally."

"True, and we tried and it didn't work, so that means we go back to square one. I'm not conflicted out and I'm going to represent Simon. I'm still going to sue OpenSpace."

Bennie's lips parted. "I think you are conflicted out. I went through the factors—"

"—and it's a judgment call." Mary sat up straighter. "My judgment is that I'm not conflicted out under the rules. The circumstances say I'm not."

"The circumstances say you are, in my judgment." Bennie waited a beat. "What did Judy say?"

"She thinks I am."

"Bingo!" Bennie smiled. "There you have it."

"What did Sam say? I know you must've asked him."

Bennie's smile evaporated. "He thinks you're not."

"Bravo." Mary felt a surge of hope. "But I don't want to make it a headcount."

"Neither do I, but you're wrong."

"No, you are."

Suddenly they both looked over, as Judy popped her head into the doorway, standing next to Bennie. "What's going on? What am I missing? Don't taunt me. You know I have major FOMO."

"I don't even know what that means."

"Fear of missing out."

"OpenSpace isn't settling," Bennie answered, turning away. "I'll let Mary fill you in. I have to get to work."

"Bennie, hold on!" Marshall called out, coming down the hall. "I have something for you. This just came for you and Mary by hand-delivery."

"Thanks." Bennie held out her hand, and Marshall gave her a manila envelope, then gave one to Mary, too.

"Thanks," Bennie answered firmly, opening the envelope with her thumb. She slid out the piece of paper, which was a single sheet of correspondence on Dumbarton letterhead.

"What's this?" Mary asked with dismay, opening the envelope and pulling out a copy of the same letter, then reading aloud:

Nathaniel Lence, Esq.
President & CEO
One Dumbarton Drive
Horsham, PA

DUMBARTON ENTERPRISES

Dear Ms. DiNunzio:

It has come to my attention that you, a named partner in the law firm of Rosato & DiNunzio, seek to represent Simon Pensiera in a putative employment discrimination action against his former employer, OpenSpace. OpenSpace is a wholly owned subsidiary of Dumbarton Enterprises, and Dumbarton has been a long-standing client of your firm. Therefore, any such representation by you constitutes a conflict of interest in breach of Rule 1.7 of the Model Rules of Professional Conduct.

Please be advised that if you do not withdraw from the aforementioned representation forthwith, Dumbarton will file the attached Misconduct Complaint against you with the Disciplinary Board of the Bar Association of Pennsylvania and the American Bar Association Committee.

Best,
Nathaniel Lence, Esq.

cc: Bennie Rosato, Esq.

"Oh my God. Can he really do this?" Mary felt stricken. Seeing her name on a disciplinary action shook her to her very foundation. It was embarrassing, even shameful. She had never been before a disciplinary board. She'd been the quintessential Good Girl, until now.

"Yes," Bennie answered, tense. "It's hardball, but that's Nate. He didn't get to the top by playing nice. He's an excellent litigator. He attacks on all fronts, evidently even the lawyers."

Mary shuddered. "But this is out of bounds."

"To most lawyers, yes. Even I would never do this. But he doesn't think that way. He doesn't have bounds. He makes his own rules. He feels personally attacked, so he'll think this is self-defense. He signed it himself. He's not even using his in-house guy, Jason."

Judy practically growled. "I wanna kill him."

Bennie shot her a look. "And that's the test. If you consider homicide, he's an excellent litigator."

Mary flipped to the complaint, which was a single page long, offering no facts or argument. "Is this enough? It doesn't even say anything."

Judy frowned, reading over her shoulder. "Agree. Is this all it takes?"

"For starters." Bennie put her copy back in the envelope. "He's striking fast and furious. It's the most he could do in short order. He can amend it later. It commences the proceedings and gets the job done." Bennie eyed Mary hard. "Nate just upped the ante. Your ethical position is getting you called on the carpet. Granted, your position is a judgment call, but be aware that these bar association committees and disciplinary committees are old-school. If I were you, I would refer this case out."

"Mare," Judy said, urgently. "I know how you feel and that you want to help Simon, but I think you should refer it out, too. You're not the only lawyer in the city. I swear, we can get him somebody terrific."

"But I still don't think I'm in breach." Mary knew she was

doing the right thing. The factors were in her favor. She flashed on those faces at the hospital this morning, turning to her. She couldn't let them all down.

Judy touched Mary's shoulder. "Think of it this way. It doesn't help Simon's case if there's litigation over you. It might even prejudice the court against him."

Bennie nodded. "Mary, she's making a good point. Nate has put *your* credibility at issue, and this is a case where credibility is critical. You need a judge to credit Simon's allegations and testimony. Can he do that if he thinks Simon's lawyer has an ethical issue?"

Mary felt torn, her heart sinking. "But Simon wants me to represent him."

Judy interjected, "Are you sure, after this? He'd feel terrible if he knew what just happened. You need to ask him."

Bennie scoffed. "No, you don't," she snapped.

Mary looked over, surprised by Bennie's demeanor. "What do you mean?"

"No client tells us what to do. Neither friend nor foe." Bennie looked as if she were going to elaborate but stopped abruptly. "You're the lawyer, Mary. *You* decide, not your client. Now I have to get to work. Good luck."

Judy turned to Mary. "Honey, she's really right. Let the case go. You don't have any other option."

"Not necessarily," Mary blurted out. "There's one other option we haven't talked about, Bennie."

Bennie turned to her in the hallway, expectantly. "What other option?"

Judy cocked her head. "Yes, what?"

"It's a nuclear option." Mary swallowed hard, wishing she hadn't said anything, but needing to air it out. It had kept her up all last night. She'd known it was a possibility that Todd Eddington would deny everything, and there was only one way out that she could see, but she hated to pull the trigger.

Bennie fell silent, waiting.

Judy frowned, nervous. "Nuclear option? Mary, that sounds bad. What are you talking about?"

Mary heaved a sigh. "I'll tell you, just to talk about it, but I don't want everybody to get upset. I'm not wedded to it. It's just an idea."

"Now you're scaring me." Judy frowned more deeply. "What?"

"Well, the ethical problem is that the firm has represented Dumbarton." Mary braced herself. "His complaint is that nobody from this firm can represent OpenSpace against Dumbarton."

"Okay, yes, go on . . ." Judy motioned to Mary to keep talking.

"So, uh, we need to think outside of the box. The conflict is that I'm a partner in the firm. One option is to give up the case, and the other is to"—Mary braced herself—"the other is to consider taking some time away from the firm."

"*What?*" Judy asked, astonished.

"Listen," Mary rushed to explain, "if I did, the conflict would go away, since I never represented Dumbarton myself or was privy to any of its confidential information. So I was thinking, maybe I could take some time out to work on this case, like a sabbatical, or I would have to leave the firm."

"Are you *serious*?" Judy's eyes flew open. "Time out from the *firm*? *Leave the firm*? How can you say that? Your name is on the sign and letterhead. You just made partner! You can't go!"

"I don't want to." Mary felt guilty seeing Judy so upset and she could barely bring herself to look at Bennie, but now the words were out of her mouth. "I mean, I would never do it otherwise, but it's an option, a way out—"

"No it isn't!" Judy wailed. "It's *not* an option! You can't leave *me*!"

Mary saw Bennie looking aghast, which provoked a profound wave of guilt. She didn't want to leave the firm but she didn't see any other way. She had come to love Bennie, even though she was still intimidated by her from time to time. She had worked for her for almost ten years and had been amazed when she'd become Bennie's partner. They'd grown to be friends even though Bennie was hardly girlfriendy and they'd never socialized outside of work, even eaten out together. But working as partners had brought them closer, without Mary even knowing it. And she owed Bennie so much. Bennie had taught her that she was a better lawyer than she'd ever realized, and ironically, that she was strong enough to make it on her own.

Mary faced Bennie's pained eyes. "Bennie, I'm sorry. Believe me, I know this is hurtful, but I can't turn my back on Simon, Rachel, my family, and the whole entire community. If you had seen them at the hospital this morning, you would understand. It's no-win, either way."

"Mary." Bennie regained her composure, her lips forming a grim line. "You and I have a partnership agreement. It can be dissolved by written notice from either one of us, at any time. If you wish to dissolve the partnership agreement, please let me know. It's your decision."

"I don't *want* to do it, I just think I'm in a position where I have to do it." Mary felt heartsick. She had to make Bennie understand. There was no good answer. "I go way back with Simon and—"

"You needn't justify it to me or anybody else. No hard feelings. I understand. Make whatever decision you need to, but do it quickly."

"But I'm so sorry—"

"No need to apologize. You can't live your life to please other people, even me. Now I really do have to get to work." Bennie turned away and resumed walking toward her office. "Let me know your decision."

Judy grabbed Mary's arm, her expression agonized. "Mary, you can't mean this! You can't leave the firm! We've worked together forever! Two peas in a pod, best friends! You can't do this!"

"Judy, let's talk about it—"

"No, Mare, I don't want to talk about it! I don't want to even consider it! You're blowing up our law firm? Our friendship?"

"Nothing blows up our friendship," Mary said, speaking from the heart. "Let's go to lunch and talk it over."

"I can't, I'm too upset to eat!"

"Let's go." Mary took her hand, tugging her away.

CHAPTER TWELVE

Bennie stood at her office window, trying to collect her thoughts. Her view faced north, an orientation she favored because it was upward, onward, straight ahead. But she didn't feel that way right now. Things had happened so fast, and she didn't know how everything had come undone. In a single day, she had lost a partner—and a major client—but that didn't matter. Which, right there, was a revolution in her own priorities, turning them topsy-turvy.

Bennie's restless gaze flitted to the skyscrapers, all of them sleek monoliths of mirrors. If she looked hard enough, she wondered if she could see herself, a bewildered woman standing at a window. Her cell phone rang in her purse, but she let it go to voicemail. There were stacks of correspondence on the desk and email filing into her inbox. There were calls to return and briefs to write, but she had come to a total standstill. And suddenly she realized why.

She felt hurt. Loss. Bewilderment. She was having an emotional reaction at the office.

Bennie smiled to herself, since that was practically against federal law, or at the very least, the first time it had ever happened. Not that she was an android, because she had Actual

Human Emotions, but she tried to compartmentalize them at work. It was necessary when you were the boss, and she had to separate herself from the associates, way back when she had hired Mary and Judy. But since then they had worked so many cases together and gone on so many adventures, that she had come to feel closer to them, without realizing it until now.

Bennie swallowed hard. She didn't understand why Mary felt so strongly about keeping the case, but Mary was tied up with her family, her friends, and her community, connecting so easily to people that she could chat up a parking meter. Bennie was nothing like that, nor did she envy it; she was a loner, an only child raised by a single mother who suffered from depression. She never knew her father, had never even met him until it was far too late. She relied on herself and had made her life into what she wanted it to be, gloriously on her own.

She looked at the mirrored skyscrapers, her thoughts racing. No one but her knew how much hard work it had taken, how often she had acted unafraid when she was in fact afraid, how much fighting, kicking, and clawing the law could be, day after day, year after year. Her law firm had finally reached its pinnacle, and she'd earned her success, then she'd even found Declan, who was a great man even by her incredibly picky standards. But she had just been thrown for a loop.

Bennie wondered if she should have done anything differently with Mary, but she wouldn't have changed it. She could have told Mary that Dumbarton had fired her, but that would've only made Mary feel worse. The last thing Bennie wanted to do was guilt her into staying. Bennie couldn't control whether Mary stayed or left. If she thought about it—really thought about it *hard*—the only thing she really wanted was for Mary to do what was right for her.

It struck her as an epiphany, and it lightened Bennie's heart and gave her a sense of direction, if not northward, then close. Because she could help Mary get what she wanted, and that's what a friend would do. Evidently she had become Mary's friend, whether anybody knew it or not. And the only thing that stood in the way of Mary getting what she wanted was Nate.

Bennie turned around, went to her desk, and opened the envelope, sliding out the letter and skimming it again. Her gaze dropped to Nate's signature, noting that he had signed it as an original, pressing hard on the ballpoint pen, probably angry as hell. It didn't get more personal than that, and she knew he was trying to get back at her for not wanting to get involved with him again, even if he never acknowledged that to himself. This wasn't only about sex, this was about power, and even so, she had a job to do. It was overreaching for him to bring Mary before a disciplinary committee, and Bennie didn't want to take the chance that some crotchety judge would level sanctions against Mary, maybe even suspending her license to practice and leaving a lifetime blemish on her record.

Bennie still had one move left. She reached into her purse, dug at her phone, and just to confirm her suspicion, scrolled to missed calls. NATE LENCE, read the entry, which was what she had thought. He was playing a game, upping the ante. She had only one way to up the ante on him. She didn't know if it would work, but she had to try. She pressed Redial and waited for him to answer, standing at her desk.

"Are you mad at me?" Nate asked, his tone light.

"Withdraw that letter you sent to DiNunzio."

"Why?"

"Because it's a terrible thing to do to my partner."

"She made her own bed."

Bennie didn't think his choice of words was coincidental. "If you don't withdraw that letter, our friendship is over."

Nate fell silent a minute. "Oh, come on."

"I'm letting you know. Withdraw that letter or forget my name."

"I have a counter-offer. You don't have to take the case for OpenSpace and you can have all the Dumbarton work back. But I'm not withdrawing the letter."

"I was never going to take the case for OpenSpace and I don't want to work for Dumbarton any longer. The only thing that's on the table is our friendship, such as it is. And if you don't withdraw that letter, I'm gone for good."

"So you're making this personal."

"You made it personal. You attacked my partner to hurt me. You don't care about a small-stakes discrimination case in a sub. You showed up at OpenSpace to see me, or to fluster me. But no matter. Yes, I'm making it personal." Bennie kept her tone even, because she was speaking from strength, though oddly, she had almost no leverage. Except that leverage was a state of mind. So was power.

"You always say business is never personal."

"I was wrong." Bennie remembered she had said the same thing to Mary. "Are you going to withdraw the letter or not?"

"Come on, Bennie. You're making too much of this." Nate chuckled softly. "Why make such a big deal? This is litigation, that's all."

"This isn't litigation, this is life. Evidently, they intersect. I didn't realize how hollow you had become as a person. We both know that I'm the only person in your world who tells you the truth. Maybe because we go back, maybe because of who we are. That doesn't matter either. So keep me or let me go. Your choice, but on my terms. You haven't agreed to withdraw it, so good-bye."

"Wait—"

Bennie hung up and turned it off, because she didn't want to hear it ring and she didn't want to hear it not ring. She turned to her landline and buzzed the intercom button for Marshall. "Can you come in, please?"

"Sure. Be right there."

"Thanks." Bennie turned around to her credenza and started thumbing through the case files in their red accordions. She pulled out one case for Dumbarton, then another, and a third, stacking them on her chair. Then she went into the file cabinet underneath, pulled out the big drawer, and went through the files alphabetically until she got to D. She reached a block of Dumbarton files, yanked them out, and put them on the floor in a pile. When the file started to totter, she started another one. She was already starting to feel better.

"Bennie?" Marshall knocked on the door.

"Come in," Bennie called out, and Marshall entered the office, hesitantly.

"Bennie, is Mary leaving the firm? Is this really happening?" Marshall's blue eyes had gone round with worry, and her crow's-feet looked deeper than usual. She was their firm's Earth Mother, with simple, pretty features, a long brown braid, and a denim dress. She'd been with Bennie since forever and she was owed an answer.

"I don't know, Marshall, but we're not going to worry about that now. Close the door behind you, please."

"What do you need?" Marshall closed the door.

"I want to get all these Dumbarton files out of here and shipped back to corporate." Bennie gestured to the files on the door. "Then I want you to get all of the Dumbarton files that are in the file room and in the business archives, and I want you to ship them back to Dumbarton corporate too. Got that?"

"All of them?

"*All* of them. If Dumbarton is in the caption, send it back. It's going to be a lot of work because there's a lot of files. Hopefully most of them are at the business archive, so you can just make the phone call and they'll ship it over. I want it to happen today and I want it to be between us. Nobody else in the office needs to know what's happening. If anybody asks you, just say I'm cleaning out some old files in my office."

"Okay, I can do that."

"Thank you." Bennie reached for her phone and purse, then went to the door. "I'm going out and I won't be back today."

"Where are you going?"

"Between us, I'm not exactly sure," Bennie answered, then opened the door and left.

CHAPTER THIRTEEN

Mary brought Judy up to speed on everything as they walked along, and Judy became calmer, listening with her head down since she was so much taller than Mary, the two of them heading on autopilot toward Rittenhouse Square. They'd fallen into this routine in the almost-decade that they'd worked together, eating in the park when the weather was good, like everybody else who worked in Center City. It was just starting to be lunchtime, and officemates were walking around them in groups, excitedly talking away, happy to be free for the break, carrying plastic clamshells of take-out salads or reusable bags of lunches from home.

Mary noticed that they got one or two second looks from people passing, which she had gotten used to, not only because they were such different types of people and looked it; Mary in her prim Oxford shirtdress with low heels and Judy with cobalt-blue hair, the dye so fresh that it bled onto her forehead, dressed today in jeans shorts and a white T-shirt that read DON'T HASSLE ME I'M LOCAL, an outfit that would have been casual on the beach, but was vaguely criminal in a law firm. Plus their height disparity would draw wisecracks from old men, who would call them Mutt and Jeff, but nobody was in a joking mood today.

Mary told Judy everything, every detail of the first meeting with Simon, the complaint, the contemporaneous notes, her discussions with Bennie about the representation, the downturn in Rachel's health, and finally this morning at the hospital, the gift of the locket presented in front of most of South Philly. Judy knew all the players—Simon, Feet, Mary's parents, The Tonys, and El Virus—so those details didn't need to be filled in, but Mary told her about them anyway, gradually becoming aware that she was kitchen-sinking Judy with detail, talking for the sake of talking, her words almost like a prayer, soothing her. Because things had happened so fast that she needed to process them, and she didn't want to leave the firm either.

Mary finished, saying, "I know it's awful and strange, and I can't imagine leaving the firm, but Bennie and I have been at loggerheads about this case. We're at an impasse, and I'm pulled in a direction that I don't think she can understand. You can because you know everybody and you know what it's like."

"I can, I really can," Judy said, her head down, nodding. A breeze blew through her short, fine hair and the sunlight made it look even brighter, like a blue M&M.

"And it's not like I want to leave the firm, God, Judy, you know that, I mean, I love you, I love working in the same place as you, we always have!"

"I know, I know—"

"—and I just made partner, I'm established, I don't want to go—"

"—I know, I know, you can't, you can't—"

"—I know, but what am I going to do? How do I get out of this? I'm in a bind here. Now Nate, who's the biggest jerk on the planet, is hauling me before a disciplinary committee, which makes me sick to my stomach—"

"—of course, that's ridiculous, it's a judgment call, he's such a jerk—"

"—and come on, be real, I don't think it's even about the case." Mary became vaguely aware that they were interrupting each other almost constantly, but that's how close they were as friends, that they not only finished each other's sentences, but they never let the other one finish the sentence, which was true love.

"—I don't think it's about the case either, he's having some kind of power struggle with Bennie, and he has such a crush on her it's not even funny—"

"—so maybe she should just sleep with him and get it over with." Mary laughed, and Judy joined her.

"Yes, she should take one for the team. Get us out of this with her magical vagina."

Mary laughed, though it felt hollow. She couldn't believe it had come to a head so fast, that she was actually considering leaving a firm that she loved. They had been together forever, had tons of cases, adventures, and misadventures. Helped each other through major trials and love affairs. She didn't know if she could do it, but maybe she had to.

They reached the corner with the business crowd, suspended their conversation because everyone was in earshot, then crossed the street into Rittenhouse Square, a gloriously green block ringed with privet hedges, and they crossed the street into the park, walked along the pathways, and grabbed the first park bench that was available, because they filled up fast.

Mary flopped down, suddenly exhausted. "We forgot lunch."

"I can't eat anyway." Judy's face fell into crestfallen lines, and Mary's heart went out to her.

"Honey, I'm sorry. I feel horrible putting you through this."

"I know, and I feel horrible making you feel guilty when you're trying to figure this out. I know you're in a really hard spot. I get it. I really do." Judy sighed heavily, turning to her,

her head inclined. "Is it horrible if I say that I wish this case never came in in the first place?"

"No, that is definitely not horrible. That is what I thought about a million times. I wish they never fired him in the first place, just for my sake. It's all about me, right? Not my friend who lost his job and his wife. Not his daughter who has cancer."

"Right." Judy smiled wryly. "We're lawyers, so it's always about us."

"Exactly." Mary felt a wave of love for her friend, who understood everything about her, even her weird sense of humor. "We will *always* be friends."

Judy swallowed hard. "I know, but it's different when you don't work together."

"No it isn't," Mary said gently.

"Yes it is, you don't see each other as often. You don't go out for lunch together. You say you'll see each other but you don't."

"We will, we would."

"You say that."

"But it's true."

Judy sighed heavily. "So you're really considering leaving."

"I don't know, I guess I am. I guess I have to." Mary hurt inside, and the wrench in her chest was becoming familiar.

"What does Anthony think?"

Mary cringed. "I didn't talk to him about it yet. I only thought about it in the middle of the night, and he was asleep. I just thought to myself, 'what if the settlement doesn't work out,' 'what if push comes to shove,' and here we are."

Judy pushed her. "You would go out on your own then?"

Mary blinked, getting an idea. "Well, I wouldn't have to be completely on my own, now would I?"

"What do you mean?"

"Girl. Come with me."

"Ha!" Judy burst into laughter. "Are you serious?"

"Why not?" Mary said, trying to wrap her mind around

the idea. "I have tons of work, Judy. I have a very solid client base. If I have to go, you could come with me. It would be great."

"Wait, wait, wait," Judy said, putting up a restraining hand. "Mare, are you forgetting? We have been in business together, way back when. Remember when we tried to start a practice after we left Stalling & Webb?"

"Oh, right." Mary had forgotten, or more likely, blocked it out. "You mean, how our impulsive decision to flee our big firm led us to hang out our own shingle—"

"—and set up shop and wait for a phone to ring? Which it didn't?"

"Well, look at the bright side, we did a lot of pro bono work."

Judy grinned. "We could have saved the world. And also starved."

"Oh, that."

"Yes, that." Judy laughed.

Mary got serious. "But that was then and this is now. Times are different. I have business. I don't have to wait for a phone to ring anymore. In fact, there are days when I don't answer the phone because I don't want another case."

"Really?" Judy's eyes narrowed, a skeptical Delft blue.

"Honestly. You know how many cases I have, ongoing, right now? Take a guess."

"Well, twelve active cases is a lot," Judy began, thinking aloud. "And you need a base of about fifty ongoing cases, whether they are superactive or not."

"Agreed." Mary folded her arms, self-satisfied. "So guess."

"Sixty?"

"Try a hundred and twenty."

"*What?*" Judy's eyes rounded with amazement. "Are you serious? What are the billings?"

"About $1 million a year."

"That's as much as Bennie!"

"Tell me about it. It was more than her, last fiscal year." Mary had been astounded herself, when she realized how much her practice had grown. "And I'm already paying overhead because we split it, so that's payroll, rent, fixtures of about four hundred grand a year, so I take home three hundred grand after taxes."

"Wow, I make one hundred fifty."

"I'll give you a raise," Mary said, meaning it.

"You're serious?" Judy burst into laughter.

"Totally. That's why my client base is so important, that's what I tried to tell her. I don't get the big cases, but I get the volume and they keep coming. Everybody has contract disputes, wills drafted, construction disputes, slip and fall, basic med mal, and now special education, which is a wonderful practice."

"The stuff you're doing lately, for kids with special needs?"

"Yes, I love it, and you would too. These kids are not being served, getting the interventions they need, and you get to do some good."

"Really."

"You make a difference in a kid's life, just like Rachel. It's not a special needs case, but it's the same feeling for me, inside. You see the good you're doing. You actually effect change."

"Really," Judy repeated, though her tone turned positive, if not excited.

"Yes, and from a business point of view, it's awesome because in Pennsylvania, if you win a special-education case, your fees get reimbursed by the district. That's true for the Philadelphia School District and for the suburban school districts. You never have to worry about getting paid. And they pay your going rate. It's truly doing good and doing good."

"It sounds win-win."

"Exactly," Mary said, getting excited herself. "And how much better is that than no-win? Litigation can be *so* no-win. Even if you settle, both sides are unhappy; that's even the mark of a good settlement."

"Honestly, yes!" Judy brightened.

"Sometimes you get tired of banging your head against a wall, don't you? Bennie loves to fight, but I don't. I thought I didn't like being a lawyer, but that wasn't right. I just didn't like practicing the type of law I was practicing." Mary felt her heart lift, hearing herself say aloud something she'd been thinking for a long time. "And I'm happy now. I'm happy at work for the first time ever."

Judy's expression darkened. "So why blow it up?"

"I don't think of it that way."

"I know." Judy made a face. "But everyone else will. Bennie does, Marshall does. I told her, and she started crying. And wait'll Anne and John get back. They're going to freak."

"I know and I hate that." Mary felt the weight of guilt, but reminded herself of her purpose. "But I have to do what I have to do. Right?"

"Right. So what will I work on, if I came with you?"

"Well, the types of matters I said."

"How about the special-ed cases?"

"I don't have a lot of them yet because I'm just starting in the practice and that bar is pretty tight. But I'm starting to get referrals. I feel like in three to five years, that will be the majority of my practice, but it isn't yet."

"Are you ever in federal court?"

"Not really, no. There's more state-court issues, contract issues, or arbitration, and it's a lot of horse trading. In fact, I don't really get into court that much. In fact, I avoid it." Mary could see Judy's shoulders deflate. "Look, I admit, it's not really the kind of work you're used to. But you would like it."

"So there's no appellate work or anything like that."

"Federal appellate, no." Mary knew that Judy loved the intellectual rigor posed by federal questions that went up on appeal, like cutting-edge constitutional issues, but Mary's clients didn't present and couldn't afford that type of litigation. "But if you brought in that kind of work, that would be great."

Judy hesitated. "That's the kind of work that comes to Bennie, and she gives to me."

Mary shifted forward. "I know, but Judy, with your credentials, you could attract that kind of work."

Judy looked at her like she was crazy. "Mary, take a look at me. Do I look like the kind of person people want for a lawyer? I dress crazy and I like it. I don't want to change. And I'm not a business getter, I never have been. I don't like schmoozing people, going to the bar conferences and the cocktail parties. It's just not me."

Mary listened to her without interrupting, for once, because she had never heard Judy talk about herself this way.

"I finally found my niche, too. I wrote three briefs for the Supreme Court last year, a petition for certiorari, and two amicus briefs, which is probably more than any associate in any big firm. And the cases come from all over the country, on the sexiest legal issues ever. Important issues. Voting rights. Election funding. Intellectual property. Antitrust. Environmental cases."

"Wow," Mary said, because she hadn't realized, too busy with her own work.

"Right? It's great. I know I look great on paper. I'm the girl behind the scenes and I love that. I just want to be left alone to write and research." Judy smiled briefly. "I told Bennie she should think of me as her brain-in-a-jar. That's my niche."

"But I don't attract that kind of work. That's the problem, right?"

"It kind of is." Judy heaved a big sigh, then slumped against the wooden back of the bench. "I love what I do and I don't want to stop. And I know you love what you do, and believe me, I don't think one type of practice is better than the other—"

"—I know—"

"—I'm not a legal snob—"

"—I know you're not, it's not that—"

"Not at all." Judy's lower lip buckled. "But I don't know if I should go with you, if you leave. You also work more hours than I do and you have to go at a moment's notice, like you're on call all the time. I like my own schedule and I want time to paint—and guess what, I didn't even get to tell you, I bought a loom."

"A loom, like, for weaving things?" Mary smiled. Judy was so cute, always finding new things to do, like weaving things that you could buy already woven.

"Exactly, it's so much fun! There's so much to learn. It comes next week. The only bad thing is it's going to take up my whole bedroom. I'm never going to get another boyfriend. I don't have room for sex."

"So weave something. A blanket."

"A sex blanket!"

Mary smiled. "Or do it standing up."

"Whoa, Mare!" Judy's eyes flared in fake shock. "You're *married*."

"Hey, it happens."

"How often?"

"Once, until I fell down," Mary admitted, and they both laughed.

Judy's smile faded. "So I don't know if I'd be happy doing what you do. I don't know if I should come with you, if you go. Are you going?"

"I think so," Mary had to admit, though she couldn't believe it herself.

"Oh no." Judy's eyes glistened. "I'm not crying."

"Don't, or I will. We're still friends, that's the key thing. We can still see each other every day."

"Right." Judy wiped her eyes, flushing under her fair skin.

"Probably more than we do now. We'll make a point of it. Lunch, right here, like always."

"Totally." Judy nodded. "They say that after a divorce, the dad sees the kid more."

"Right." Mary forced a smile because Judy was trying to cheer them both up. "And you can always come with me, but no pressure."

"I know, thanks. I can always come with you, but I have to think about it. Can I think about it?"

"Of course." Mary felt heartbroken, and it was even worse to know that she had nobody but herself to blame. She was breaking her own heart. And Judy's.

Suddenly Mary's cell phone pinged with an incoming text, and she pulled it out of her bag and checked the screen. The text was from Simon, and it read:

Can you come to the hospital? No emergency but ASAP.

Mary rose instantly. "I'd better go," she said, concerned.

CHAPTER FOURTEEN

Bennie lowered the car window, traveling the winding roads through the proverbial rolling hills of Pennsylvania, which really existed, dense with woods and underbrush this time of year. She'd texted Declan that she was driving out to see him, and he'd texted her back a heart emoji because he'd turned into a big mushball, which she secretly loved.

Wind blew through the open window, messing up her hair and buffeting her eardrums, a not-entirely-pleasant sensation, but at least it was fresh air. It felt good to be outside in summer, not boxed in, climate-controlled, bounded by concrete and skyscrapers. She realized she hadn't had a vacation in years, and there were plenty of days at work when she never felt the sun, at either end of the day. Now it warmed the skin of her left forearm, resting on the side of the car, and she had to put down her visor, even with sunglasses.

She inhaled a lungful and smelled the heavy sweetness of wild honeysuckle mounded by the roadside, then brush roses that bordered people's front yards as she passed through one small town after the next, each with colonial clapboard houses set right at the curbside, having been constructed in an era when the only thing on the road was a horse and buggy.

An hour passed, and Bennie reached Voxburg, a former mining town that held a post office, a middle school, a medium-sized office park, and an enclave of old and new homes, including the converted Victorian in which Declan rented the first floor for his law firm. It was on the far side of town, set at the top of the hill, and she pulled off the road onto its gravel driveway and traveled upward, catching sight of the place, which was lovely.

The house was a true Painted Lady, three stories of crisp white clapboard, navy-blue curlicue trim on its eaves, and a slate roof with a pointed turret in one corner, which Declan took for his own office. Bennie's favorite feature of the house was its magnificent wraparound porch, with an old-fashioned porch swing. She reached the end of the driveway, parked next to a few other cars belonging to the dental offices on the other floors, then cut the ignition.

"Perfect timing!" Declan came through the screen door with a grin, holding two bottles of Rolling Rock by the necks.

Bennie got out of the car, her mood improving. Declan Mitchell was good-looking in a way that had never attracted her before; clean-cut with conventionally handsome features and dark hair that he kept unfashionably short. He was dressed as casually as he ever got, in a blue Oxford shirt with khakis and loafers with white socks. Declan had been a state trooper with the mounted division when she'd met him, on the other side of a case that had changed her life. They'd lost track of each other, then reconnected after he'd become a lawyer, but he still carried himself like a cop, coming off taller and less fun than he actually was. She'd fallen in love with him the first time she saw him kiss his horse.

Bennie walked to the porch. "Did you see me coming?"

"The advantage of the high ground." Declan grinned. "I was waiting for you. I sat at the window like a dog, panting and panting."

"Sure you were." Bennie crossed the crunchy gravel.

"How good to see you, babe!" Declan opened his arms, wrapped them around her, and gave her a big hug, and even though she felt the cold beer bottles on her back, she wasn't complaining.

"I missed you. It's been, what, three weeks?"

"Tell me about it. It's killing me." Declan leaned over, kissing her gently, once, then again. "Oh, man. I love you."

"I love you too." Bennie reached out and rubbed his back, feeling her world gradually fall back into place.

"Come sit down and have a cold beer. You look like you need it." Declan kept an arm around her, and they walked together to the porch swing, sitting down.

"I do. I'm glad you were here." Bennie accepted the Rolling Rock and took a quick sip, which tasted delicious. She scanned the bucolic setting, a hilltop surrounded by woods, and it felt cooler this high, with a gentle breeze. Declan moved his arm around the back of the porch swing, and she felt herself relax against it like a pillow, taking another sip of beer.

"I'm glad I was too. Harrisburg drives me up the wall. I'm glad that deal's over."

"How's the family?" Bennie asked, which used to be a touchy question. They had met on a criminal case, when she defended a man who had been charged with murdering Declan's ne'er-do-well nephew. Bennie had proved her client innocent, but Declan's attachment to his sister and her children were part of the reason their romance was long-distance.

"They're all doing well. My sister's clean and sober, and the kids are doing great. They're both at a daytime baseball camp, which is cute. I go to the games." Declan took a swig of beer. "So tell me what's going on. I'm happy to see you but I want to hear the deal."

"It's a long story."

"I got time, and the whole left side of my body feels good." Declan smiled down at her.

"Okay, here we go." Bennie filled him in, telling him the whole story from yesterday afternoon, since he'd been out of town and they kept missing each other, trying to connect on the phone, but failing.

"I hate to have her leave. It's been fun, and we all get along so well. It's actually the best situation."

"That's nice. Sorry you have to lose it."

"Me, too, but that's not the only problem."

"You can't afford to lose her, can you?" Declan cocked his head.

"No. To be precise, I have the fees coming in, but the problem is cash flow." Bennie hated to admit it. "I don't think she realizes that, but that's neither here nor there. It's my problem and I have to deal with it."

"Break it down for me." Declan rubbed her shoulder on the back of the swing.

"Right now, she pays half of the overhead. Payroll. Insurance, equipment rental, like the duplicating machines. Office supplies. All the other costs."

"Your payroll must be a killer. Four lawyers, the receptionist."

"It is." Bennie knew he would understand. He had a solo practice, like she used to. "I'll have to sit down with our accountant and go over the numbers, but I doubt I can stay in my offices if she leaves. I might have to move and start all over again."

Declan frowned slightly. "But you used to cover the overhead before by yourself. You just made her partner recently, right?"

"Yes."

"So what happened in the interim?"

"I shifted my practice. I assumed that we'd be together longer than a year, so I changed the cases I took." Bennie had thought it over on the way here, trying to sort it out. "Since I had help with the overhead, finally, I was able to take bigger cases that raise my profile—but they last longer. You know how litigation can be. The bigger the case, the longer it takes to get through the court system. Most are in the public interest, a lot of high-profile work on important issues."

"But it doesn't keep the lights turned on." Declan nodded. "You thought you had the backup."

"Exactly, and now I don't."

"It's like the rug gets pulled out from under you."

"Right." Bennie felt her heart ease. It made her feel better to be so completely understood, even if it didn't change the situation any. She had never really believed that could be true, but it was, happily. Love was a good thing.

"I'll tell you one thing. If I weren't so happy with you sitting here, I'd drive to Philly and open a can on that Nate character." Declan looked at her sideways. "But you wouldn't like that, would you?"

"On the contrary, not a bad idea," Bennie shot back, and they both laughed.

"How could you go for a guy like that? Temporary insanity?"

"Just about." Bennie smiled. "Anyway, that's not the point. The point is I don't know what to do."

"Well, you gotta make plans if Mary decides to go."

"Right." Bennie sighed, trying to resign herself to the next step. "I guess I have to call the accountant."

"If you want, we can crunch some numbers right now. I know you hate math. I'll help you. Do you keep those records in your laptop, like in Excel?"

"Yes, but I left without it."

"You left *without work*?" Declan's eyes flared open, comically.

"I know, I jumped in the car to see you. I was uncharacteristically spontaneous."

"Is that another word for horny?"

"Come to think of it, yes," Bennie answered, and they both laughed again.

"Hell, I'm done for the day if you want to go home. Or we can go upstairs and play with the laughing gas. The dentist tells me he does nitrous with the hygienist. Wanna give it a go?"

"Um, no." Bennie took another swig of beer, which tasted better and better. Or maybe she stopped tasting it altogether.

"Or, I have another proposition," Declan said, after a moment.

"What?" Bennie asked, enjoying herself.

"How about you and me go into business together?"

"Wait, what?" Bennie wasn't sure she'd heard him right.

"You heard me. Partners. You and me. It could happen."

"How can it happen?" Bennie asked, incredulous. "You're here and I'm there."

Declan's expression grew serious. "If we want to make it happen, we could make it happen. I could fill in the blank for you, the one that Mary's leaving. I could take on half of your overhead."

"Why, when your practice is here, almost three hours away? You can't move your practice. What about your client base?"

"Granted, I wouldn't move. But I could open a second office."

"You could?" Bennie tried to process the information. "Were you thinking about doing that?"

"I wasn't, not completely. But I was trying to think about ways to get together down the line. With you." Declan frowned. "This whole long-distance thing, it's hard. It gets old. I'd like to see you more than once a month. We play telephone ping-pong all the time, like last night."

"I know." Bennie felt the same way. She'd been trying to get in touch with him, but they kept missing each other.

"So maybe the time is right to take expansion more seriously. I practice state law. I can do that in Philadelphia."

"You, in the city? What about the farm?" Bennie knew Declan loved his horse farm, a pretty A-frame in the country with a barn for his two horses.

"I keep it. I live there. I'll get the kid down the street to take care of the horses when I'm away. When I come to visit you, I'll do a case, and maybe I'll use it as an excuse to come see you." Declan smiled at her, and Bennie smiled back, but felt uncertain.

"I'm just surprised. I didn't know you were thinking this."

"I was. I plan ahead, long-term."

"Could you afford it?"

"I'm pretty sure I could. I can ballpark your expenses. They're not that much different from mine, even accounting for a higher cost of living." Declan shrugged. "I've been practicing for almost ten years now. You know I live cheap. I've got a lot of capital. My overhead is unbelievably low. I don't even use a secretary anymore. I use an answering service."

"Hmm." Bennie mulled it over, but her doubts began to surface. "You wouldn't be doing this if Mary hadn't left, would you?"

"Well, no," Declan answered, after a moment.

"So you're just trying to help me."

"Well, yes of course. I can help you."

"I don't know, honey. It's a lot to ask, and I would never ask you to do that."

"You didn't, I offered it."

"But what if it's a burden? What if it doesn't work out, what if you don't want to practice in Philadelphia, what if we start fussing over money, or over space, or over Xerox machines?"

Declan smiled wryly. "I'd let you have the Xerox machine. You can have custody of the Xerox machine."

"I'm serious."

"I know."

"It would worry me. It's risky." Bennie knew from experience, but she wasn't about to fill him in. Many years ago, she'd been in business with a boyfriend, and mixing business and pleasure hadn't turned out to be a brilliant idea.

"I'm willing to take the risk. I think we can deal. We give it a shot. If it doesn't work, we undo it."

"I don't know, I'm not sure." Bennie used to think she was good at taking risk until she met Declan. "Let me think it over."

"That means no." Declan took another sip of beer.

"Not necessarily," Bennie told him, but deep inside, she knew it did. "Okay, you're right. It does mean no."

"Alternatively I could lend you the money. I can stake you for six months, even longer. You could ramp up in that time."

"Aw, thanks, but no. I would never take your money. I really appreciate your offering though." Bennie swallowed hard, feeling a rush of love for him. She rested her head back against his arm.

"I mean it. I'm not just saying it. You can pay it back when you want to. No rush."

"Thank you, but no." Bennie nudged his knee. "Finish that beer, will you?"

"Then what?" Declan smiled. "The laughing gas?"

"No," Bennie told him. "Home."

CHAPTER FIFTEEN

Mary sat waiting for Simon, who'd texted he'd be right in. The lounge was empty, so she assumed that her and Simon's families had either gone home or were downstairs in the cafeteria having lunch. If so, she hoped the hospital had enough baked ziti. She'd given up trying to read her email on her phone because she was too preoccupied. Suddenly she spotted Simon hurrying toward the lounge, and he caught her eye, tugging down his surgical mask to reveal a stricken expression.

Mary pocketed her phone and went to him as soon as he entered the room. "What's the matter?" she asked, hugging him briefly. "It's not Rachel, is it?"

"No, that's why I said 'no emergency' in the text. You're not going to believe this. Todd and OpenSpace are suing *me* now—for *two million dollars.*"

Mary couldn't believe what she was hearing. "What are you talking about?"

"They're saying I defamed him and the company. It's lies, total lies!" Simon's eyes were round with fear. "Mary, I don't know what to do. What do I do? Where am I going to get two million bucks?"

"How do you know this? What are you talking about?" Mary

hadn't even had a chance to tell him that settlement negotiations hadn't worked this morning.

"Look, here's the complaint. They just served it on me, here, like, an hour ago. Some guy told the nurses he was a visitor and when I came to see who it was, he handed me the papers and said, 'Mr. Pensiera, you've been served!'" Simon's words rushed out, driven by stress. "Mary, can they do this? Just lie about things I said?"

"They served you in the *hospital*?" Mary couldn't imagine the cruelty it took to serve him suit papers in the Children's Hospital. "Let me see the complaint. Do you have it?"

"Sure, yes, right, of course, I'm just so scattered, I mean, the doctors are saying that Rachel's white count just went up, and I just can't even think straight. Here's what the guy gave me." Simon reached into his back pocket, pulled out a sheaf of legal papers, and handed them to Mary. "I guess the settlement talks this morning didn't go so well, huh?"

"No, I'm sorry, and I was going to tell you after lunch. Bennie pitched them but she doesn't think they're going to settle." Mary skimmed the front page of the complaint, which had been filed in the Common Pleas Court of Philadelphia under the caption *Todd Eddington and OpenSpace v. Simon Pensiera*. The blanks for plaintiff's counsel were filled in by Coburn and Wright, LLC, so Dumbarton had farmed the case out. Coburn was one of the best boutique law firms in the city, specializing in defamation and related tort actions.

"Oh no, I was really hoping they would settle, it makes so much sense to settle, and they know they were in the wrong."

"I agree and I'm sorry, but we tried, and I will keep the pressure on toward getting a settlement down the line. A lot of people talk tough in the beginning, then they cave." Mary didn't update him on the fussing over the representation issue or the fact that she might leave the firm. Her personal problems were her own, and Simon had enough on his plate right now.

"Okay, listen, I really appreciate you trying and coming down here right now. I just don't know what to do. This is incredible!"

"You know why they're doing this, don't you? They're trying to intimidate us and back us down." Mary had seen so much of this lately. More and more, corporations were using litigation as a tool to threaten, bully, and even bankrupt the little guy, like Simon. She wasn't about to let that happen.

"Where the hell am I going to get two million dollars? We didn't ask anywhere *near* that in our complaint, I never would have, and they're a big company! I'm up to my ears in medical bills, with more on the way." Simon flailed his hand in the direction of Rachel's hospital room. "You should've heard what these doctors were telling me, the procedures she's going to need. Her white cells are through the roof. That's where my money should go, not to some ridiculous lawsuit! It's her life that's at stake!"

"Oh, Simon, I'm so sorry." Mary's heart went out to him, and she steadied him with her hand on his arm. "Don't worry, we're going to deal with this. Getting a complaint can be frightening, and that's what they're trying to do. It's like terrorism by litigation. But I'm glad you called me, and just know that I can handle it and we're going to stay the course."

"Okay, okay," Simon said, his forehead wrinkling under the strain. "I used to think I was good in an emergency, but things are really piling up, this is too much. My mother used to say, everybody has a breaking point, and today, I worried I was reaching mine. I thought I was helping Rachel by filing the lawsuit against OpenSpace but now I'm worried that I made everything worse."

"No, not at all." Mary felt terrible for him. "You did the right thing, *we* did the right thing in filing suit against them, and that's what lawyers are for, to handle the stress. In fact, they're not supposed to serve you with papers when they know you're represented by counsel. They're supposed to serve them on me. So much for the ethics police."

"I just feel so helpless. Like everywhere I turn, I can't do anything. With Rachel, with this litigation. I know it's a cliché, that you feel so helpless, but anybody who has a sick child, they know what it's like. Your kid's crying and there's nothing you can do, when they beg and they plead and they ask you to stop sticking them with needles and they want to go home. They ask, over and over, Rachel does, she asks me, she asks my father, 'Zayde, when can I go home?'" Simon's voice broke, but he held it together. "And there's nothing you can do."

"Aw, Simon." Mary hugged him again. "So why don't you sit down while I read this? Just try to collect your thoughts, or do you want a water or anything? I'm sure I can get you one."

"No thanks, I'm fine. I don't know how much time we have to talk, I might have to go in with Rachel. My dad and everybody are in the cafeteria, and I don't like to leave her alone." Simon flopped into a bucket chair and took a deep breath, exhaling slowly. "Ellen used to say, 'do your Lamaze breathing.'"

"Good idea. You keep breathing and let me take a quick look at this." Mary flipped through the complaint, which set forth two civil causes of action against Simon: first, that he was liable for slander because he had defamed Todd Eddington on two occasions, and secondly, that he had committed trade libel against OpenSpace. Coburn must be pulling out all the stops because trade libel was a relatively rare tort, similar to defamation of a company.

"Will you read that thing! It's ridiculous! He's claiming I said he didn't care about Rachel, that he was heartless, which I never ever said, I swear to you."

"I understand," Mary said, modulating her tone to calm him down, even though she was furious inside. She couldn't believe that OpenSpace was retaliating at Simon so viciously. It was an overreaction, and she suspected it had something to do with Nate's anger at her taking the representation, or something personal between him and Bennie. Or both.

Mary read the first set of factual allegations aloud:

> In a conversation on February 16, Defendant Simon Pensiera defamed Plaintiff Todd Eddington by stating to Raymond Matewicz, Operations Manager at OpenSpace, that: "Todd doesn't care about Rachel at all," "Todd has no heart and only cares about money," and "Todd is jealous of my abilities and all of the attention I'm getting because of Rachel's cancer."

Mary looked down at Simon. "Who is this Ray Matewicz and what do you have to do with him?"

"I don't have *anything* to do with him." Simon looked up plaintively, his chin in his hands. "Ray runs the plant, and I talk to him from time to time but we don't talk about Todd. I never said anything bad about Todd, not at all. Why would I badmouth my boss to a guy I hardly know? I'm not that stupid!" Simon raked a hand through his hair. "Besides I don't think Todd is jealous of me. The only thing I think is that he fired me to save the company Rachel's medical expenses, that's it! Otherwise I don't give him a second thought. I have enough to think about!"

"I believe you, I know." Mary turned the page, and there was another set of factual allegations in support of the defamation claim, which she read aloud again:

> In a conversation on March 22, Defendant Simon Pensiera defamed Plaintiff Todd Eddington by stating to Ernie Greeley, Director

of Security at OpenSpace, that, "Todd doesn't care if Rachel lives or dies. The only thing he cares about is the numbers."

Mary looked at Simon. "Tell me about this Ernie Greeley."

"Same deal," Simon said defensively, throwing his hands up in the air. "Ernie does plant security. Makes sure we're locked up at night. Makes sure there's no fighting on the floor. Sends somebody home if they come in drunk. I have nothing to do with him, either."

"Do you ever talk to him?"

"Rarely, the only time I ever talked to him was, like, one or two times when I smoked out back by the loading docks"— Simon looked up sheepishly—"I know, I know, I quit a long time ago for Ellen, but lately, there have been times when I really needed a cigarette."

"It's okay, Simon." Mary didn't smoke but she wasn't about to judge him, considering what he was going through. Anyway, carbohydrates were her chosen addiction.

"So Ernie would be out back grabbing a smoke, and we would talk about sports or whatever. But I swear to you, I never said anything about Todd."

"Understood, okay. Let me see what else this thing says." Mary returned her attention to the complaint, turned the page, and read ahead to the factual allegations to support the claim of trade libel, which she also read aloud, so he could respond:

In a conversation on April 19, Defendant Simon Pensiera stated to Raymond Matewicz and Ernie Greeley that he had told one of his accounts that, "The quality control had fallen off the table in OpenSpace's top-of-the-line

142 | Lisa Scottoline

cubicles and that OpenSpace was ripping off
its best customers," and defendant also told the
two men that the account, which he declined to
specify by name or location, had therefore failed
to order more cubicles.

Simon moaned. "I never said that either. I never said anything like that. Sometimes I worry about quality control and I
wrote an email to HR or Ray about that, but I've never said it
to a client and I never would. We have so much competition
and I'd never run down our product outside. I'm in sales, for
God's sake."

"Okay, I get it." Mary was sensing a pattern. "It sounds like
these false allegations contain a grain of truth, and that lends
them some credibility."

"They're still lies."

"I know, I hear you." Mary read the rest of the complaint
but there was nothing else of substance except for the damages
amount at the end, which really did read $2 million, which
meant that Dumbarton, Nate, OpenSpace, or whoever was
behind this lawsuit had just upped the ante even more, for
major stakes in federal court.

"So what does all this mean, the defamation and all? Can
you tell me what's going on?"

"Of course." Mary folded the complaint and sat down beside him. "Defamation means that you made a false statement
that disparaged someone or lowered their reputation in the
community. If you had made these statements, they would constitute defamation, in that they would tend to damage Todd's
reputation. You follow?"

"Yes, but I didn't make them."

"I know you didn't, but this is going to be a credibility contest, and the concerning thing to me about this—not that we
can't deal with it because we can—is that this complaint

suggests that both Raymond Matewicz and Ernie Greeley are going to lie for the company. My guess is there's no proof, no contemporaneous notes like you took, and there's probably no recording." Mary thought a minute. "Do you have security cameras on the loading dock or anywhere else?"

"I assume so."

Mary made a mental note. "Me too. So let's assume that they even have a video that will show you on these three dates, talking with Ray on these two dates and with the two of them on the final date."

"But that doesn't prove what I said, and I didn't say what they're saying."

"I know, and that's the most they can come up with, and that's not very persuasive. It's something but it's not a home run."

"Is it as good as my contemporaneous notes?"

"No," Mary answered firmly. "Now let me explain about the trade libel, which means that you said words that tended to disparage OpenSpace's business, which resulted in them losing money, and the statement that they allege, if true, would constitute trade libel."

"If I said it."

"Exactly, if you said it, but you didn't." Mary thought about how she had to phrase her next thought, because she didn't want to upset him. "I'm more concerned about the trade-libel allegation, because Ernie and Raymond will be able to corroborate each other. In other words, they are the proof that you said it."

"But they're lying!" Simon's eyes flew open, and up close, Mary could see how bloodshot they were and wondered if he had gotten any sleep last night.

"I understand that. But let me talk about the underlying facts. Do you have any concerns with the quality in Open-Space's top-of-the-line cubicles?"

"Sure, and I write about them internally, but I never expressed that to any account and I never would. I try to listen to what the account needs and meet their needs with whatever line we can sell them. I don't ever run down our own products to accounts."

"Okay." Mary processed the information. "Let's talk about Ray Matewicz and Ernie Greeley. Are they friends? Why would they back each other up? And if they are, are they friends with Todd Eddington?"

"Yes, and I do see them together. They're all department heads and they've been with the company from the beginning, longer than I have. They have management meetings with Bashir, so they must talk there."

"Do they socialize out of work?"

"I don't know, like I say, I'm calling on accounts, I'm on the road, or I'm at the hospital."

"Why would they lie for the company? Who would ask them to? Todd? The president, Bashir?"

"God knows." Simon raked his hands through his hair again. "I really thought Todd was my friend. I can't believe he fired me and I can't believe they're doing this now. I never say bad things about him, I have no time to gossip."

Mary touched his shoulder. "I understand, and please try to put this out of your mind, as hard as that may be. I will stay the course in the meantime. I'm going to send a complaint letter to the EEOC to start the ball rolling on our ADA case, and I'm going to draft an answer to this complaint." Mary thought a minute about legal strategy. "I haven't decided yet if I'm going to try to remove this case to federal court and combine it in the same action, so let me give that some thought. That would be hardball, which is the only thing these guys know."

"Thank you, really, I appreciate it." Simon straightened up, rallying with a shaky smile. "I never really thought of you as a hardball type before."

"Oh, you have no idea," Mary said, but truth to tell, she didn't either. She'd handled tough cases before, but never one like this, with Simon's future, her career, and Rachel's very life on the line.

She had to get busy.

CHAPTER SIXTEEN

Bennie woke up drowsily, with Declan's arms around her, his naked body curved to fit hers under the sheet. The late-day sun shone through the window, flooding the bedroom with dark gold light, burnished to bronze. A portable fan whirred on a nearby table and made a pleasant, if artificial, breeze across her skin. They had made love and fallen asleep, happy and satisfied, but as soon as her eyes came fully open and her consciousness caught up with her, her mood spiraled down. It had been fun to stave off reality in his arms, but she couldn't deny the fact that she was losing Mary and her firm was coming apart.

Bennie let herself wallow in self-pity for a little longer, a self-indulgent emotion she rarely allowed herself, but this was hitting her hard. She hadn't seen it coming and it happened much too fast. She already missed Mary, and the money was an issue. Declan had been sweet to offer to fill in the gap, but that wouldn't be wise and she would never accept a loan. She had to resign herself to Mary's leaving, plan her next moves, and mitigate the damage.

She felt struck by a horrible thought, one she probably would've had before if not for the beer, the man she loved, and this very soft bed beckoning to her. Mary and Judy were best friends, having worked together since they'd left Stalling & Webb as young associates. They'd only gotten closer over the years, and nobody would take Mary's leaving the firm harder than Judy. And Bennie realized suddenly that Judy might leave the firm with Mary, which would be a terrible prospect in every way. Bennie had come to really enjoy having Judy around, even though she was out there as a personality, and Bennie assigned her a ton of cases.

She shifted upward in bed, as the realization began to dawn on her. She was able to trust Judy with anything and kept her busy twenty-four/seven. More importantly, Judy had a brilliant legal mind that could analyze even the most sophisticated of legal issues, as well as the patience to research endlessly. Plus her legal writing skills were the perfect blend of analysis and language, and one of the amicus briefs that Judy had written had been quoted in a slew of law reviews, cited with approval.

Bennie couldn't lie around in bed feeling sorry for herself for another moment. It wasn't like her, and she was about to lose her entire firm. She looked around for her phone.

Declan stirred behind her. "You awake, babe?" he asked, his voice low.

"Yes." Bennie took her phone off the night table. "Sorry if I woke you."

"No worries. I can't believe how late it is. It's all your fault." Declan chuckled softly.

"I just realized I have to make a quick phone call. I'll be right back."

"You can do it here if you want to. I don't mind. I'm up." Declan shifted up in bed, resting his back on the headboard. "I want to catch the end of the ballgame. They played in the afternoon today. I watched it on mute. Make your call."

"Okay, thanks." Bennie shifted upward next to him, in no

hurry to get out of bed. She scrolled to Judy's number and pressed Call, just as Declan picked up the remote, aimed it at the TV on his bureau, and flipped the channels to the Phillies game. Bennie looked away from the TV so she could focus better on the call as the phone rang and rang.

Judy picked up. "Hello, Bennie," she asked, and Bennie could tell from the tone of her voice that she was upset too.

"Hi, I'm calling to talk to you about this situation with Mary. I guess she's really thinking about leaving the firm."

"I know," Judy said, but it came out like a moan. "It's just terrible. I mean, everything is so good and I think we're such a good firm. We all work so well together. I know that she's in a real bind, but I don't want her to go, I really don't want her to go. And I know you don't want her to go either."

"No, of course I don't." Bennie swallowed hard. She didn't want to get swept into some emotional tailspin, but emotional tailspins were Judy's and Mary's favorite things.

"I just can't believe that it would come to this. I mean, don't get me wrong, I understand her position completely, and I guess it can't be helped, and I know she hasn't really made her decision yet, and I know that's hard on you too."

"And I know it's hard on you," Bennie said, trying to stay patient and go with the flow.

"It is, *so* hard, it really is because I love her and I want her to be happy and I understand why she wants to take the case, why she has to help Simon, but I can't help it, I have to tell you it feels like you guys are getting divorced, that we're breaking up something that we've had together for so long—"

"I understand," Bennie interrupted, realizing that she wasn't as patient as she thought. Or maybe she didn't trust her own emotions if they went any further down that road. "But I'm calling you about your position with the firm."

"Mine?"

"Yes, I know that you and Mary are best friends and you might be thinking about going with her. I wanted to touch base with you and persuade you to stay at the firm. You know I think you're a terrific lawyer and you've become my right-hand man, er, woman." Bennie felt so awkward. "Anyway, you're irreplaceable to me, and I'm hoping that you will stay."

"That's so nice of you to say, and I really appreciate it." Judy sounded surprised, if troubled. "I've been thinking about it, and I am trying to decide what to do, to tell you the truth."

"Well, do you want to hash it out? We can hash it out together. I don't blame you, I totally get it. But I'd like to try to discuss it with you."

"Really?"

"Sure. There's no reason for anybody to be secretive. We care about each other and we want to make the best decision. It may feel like a divorce, but it's a friendly one." Bennie caught Declan's eye, and he winked.

"Sure, that would be great." Judy sounded relieved. "I mean, I guess it's okay if I tell you that Mary did ask me to go with her, and I told her that I had to think about it."

"Of course, I get that she would do that." Bennie hoped she hadn't lost any advantage by not talking to Judy first. She'd just been too thrown for a loop, even an old warhorse like her.

"And you know Mary and I are super close and I love her, and we've always practiced together. But I really love working for you, Bennie, and I love your cases. I think your practice and her practice are really two different things."

"That's true." Bennie took heart, straightening up in bed, and Declan took his smartphone from the night table and started tapping away.

"And like I told Mary, I really do love to work on your cases and I would lose that if I went to her. She totally understands that, too."

"Right, she can't give you that kind of work. And you and I have things worked out so well together, with me getting that work and bringing it in and you working on it, am I right?"

"Right, we do have it worked out but still, I feel really caught in the middle. Like that's already happening with the Dumbarton cases. I love working on those cases. I've gotten really friendly with Suzanne and Tom from MetalLabs, and they're a really great group. I never knew metal fabricators could be so nice, and they have really interesting issues. Now I'm in a tug-of-war, with Mary representing OpenSpace and you and me representing Dumbarton."

Bennie cringed inwardly. She considered not telling Judy that they'd been fired by Dumbarton, but it would be a material omission, which was lawyer speak for dishonest. "Judy, I do have some bad news. We're not going to be working on Dumbarton anymore."

"*What?* What the hell is going on?"

"They fired us, and I sent back all my files. You will have to too, when you get a chance."

"Just like that? But I'm in the middle of, like, five active matters."

"I know, but it's over." Bennie worried the conversation wasn't going the way she'd wanted.

"Why did they fire us? When did this happen?"

"This morning." Bennie didn't want to dwell on it. "Nate wanted me to represent OpenSpace against Mary, and I wouldn't do that."

"Oh no." Judy groaned. "So he pulled all his work?"

"Yes, but I have plenty of other clients, as you well know, and I don't want this blown out of proportion. And especially, you should not tell Mary."

"Why not? You did such a nice thing for her. She should know. She'd feel terrible."

"And that's why." Bennie switched tacks. "And besides, you

and I both agree that there's a conflict of interest, even if she disagrees. There can't be any further talk to her about our relationship to Dumbarton. It's divulging confidential client information, and we have to be a lot more observant of these boundaries, especially now."

"Oh man."

"It's even in her best interest. If Nate really goes forward with those disciplinary charges, the less Mary knows about Dumbarton, the better. Understood?"

"Yes, but this sucks," Judy said after a moment. "And I know she'll feel even worse, leaving the firm after you did that."

"Again, not a word."

"Not a word."

"Good." Bennie wanted to return to the subject. "So I hope you'll stay with the firm."

"I just need to think about it and try to make a decision. You don't mind if I take some time to think, do you?"

"No, of course not, you can take all the time you need to decide. You know the players and the practice, and you know what I have to offer you." Bennie felt Declan tap her on the arm and looked over to see him holding up his phone. He had written on it: **sweeten the deal. offer her something.**

Judy was saying, "That's really sweet of you, Bennie. I do appreciate it. I know this can't be easy for you."

"For you either." Bennie took Declan's suggestion. "But let me mention something else for you to consider. You know how you and I have talked in the past, and we decided that you would probably be making partner next year."

"Yes, I remember."

"Well, it occurred to me that we could accelerate that, if you wanted." Bennie caught Declan's eye again, and he grinned, shot her a thumbs-up, and went back to his ballgame.

"Really?" Judy said, sounding interested.

"Yes, to be perfectly transparent with you, I am probably going to have to downsize the offices if Mary goes. The overhead is too high for me to handle alone, given cash flow, but that's not the end of the world." Bennie put on a brave face, which was her version of makeup. "We'll have to reconfigure everything about the firm. Start fresh. This might be the perfect time for you to become a partner."

Judy fell silent a minute. "You don't have to do that, Bennie."

"I know, but I want to," Bennie said, meaning it. There was no reason to delay Judy's becoming a partner any longer, and Bennie knew it had been uncomfortable for Mary to become partner when her best friend had remained an associate.

"So what would that mean, financially?"

"It would mean that we split the profits. We're fifty-fifty partners in the billings. Your name goes on the plaque and letterhead instead of Mary's."

"I don't want that," Judy said quickly. "I don't need to be a named partner."

"Why not?" Bennie asked, sensing she had said the wrong thing.

"I don't want to replace Mary, nobody could replace Mary. I don't want the credit anyway, and that's really for people who want their name out there and want to get business. I don't want my name out there. I'm happy just to keep it going the way it has been, with me in the background and you getting the business."

"All right, that would be your choice. Whatever you want." Bennie understood, knowing Judy. Every lawyer in Creation wanted to be a named partner, but not Judy Carrier. She hated attention, even though she dyed her hair blue. It didn't make sense, but Bennie loved her for her quirks. She couldn't lose Judy, too.

"So I'll think about that," Judy said, brightening.

"Please do, and take your time. I want what's best for all of us, I really mean that."

"I know you do. Thanks a lot, and have a great weekend."

"You too," Bennie said, hanging up. She tried to rally, inhaling. "I hope that works. I'd hate to lose her. What if Anne and John went, too? I'd lose my whole law firm."

"Don't worry about it until you have to."

"I have to now."

"No, you don't. It's Friday. Come down here." Declan patted the bed, and Bennie tried to put it out of her mind, shifting down.

"Thanks for the assist on the phone."

"See? I'd make a great partner." Declan smiled.

"I know that." Bennie hoped he wasn't hurt, but he tended to roll with the punches, like her. Usually.

"Anyway it's a standing offer. You change your mind, you know where to find me."

"Thank you, really," Bennie said, kissing him on the cheek. She snuggled beside him and put her arm across his chest, which was broad and strong, with lean muscles earned from riding horses and pitching hay. She secretly liked his farmer's tan, typical of his lack of vanity, and he had the perfect amount of chest hair, dark and shot through with silvery strands. Just holding him calmed her down.

"Damn. The game's on rain delay."

"Aw, too bad. It's raining in Philly?"

"Yes, a big thunderstorm."

"It was fine when I left." Bennie glanced at the television, where the news was coming on, broadcast from Philadelphia. The lead story was weather, and she rested her head on his chest and watched the TV without really seeing it, replaying Judy's conversation in her mind. Suddenly a photo on the TV drew her attention, and she did a double-take.

"Declan, turn the sound on," Bennie said, getting up onto her elbow.

On the screen behind the anchorperson was a smiling photo of Todd Eddington from OpenSpace. A lurid red banner read **LOCAL MAN FOUND STABBED TO DEATH**.

Bennie reached for her phone.

CHAPTER SEVENTEEN

Mary's cell phone started ringing on her desk, and she felt a tingle of nervousness when she checked the screen and saw it was Bennie calling. Bennie's profile picture was a candid of her laughing, taken in happier days, and Mary felt a guilty wrench at the sight. She had been working all afternoon, drafting an answer to the defamation complaint and doing the research to see if she should move the case to federal court. The fact that she was leaving the firm, and the effect on Bennie and Judy, had been in the back of her mind the entire time.

She picked up the phone call. "Hi, Bennie, how—"

"Did you see the news? Are you near a TV or a laptop?"

"I'm at the office." Mary felt startled at the alarm in Bennie's voice. "What news?"

"Todd Eddington was murdered. I just saw it on TV."

"Oh my God." Mary got onto Google, typed in Todd's name, and a news story came up, a single paragraph:

Local Man Found Dead

Horsham resident Todd Eddington, 38, was found stabbed to death in his car today, at approximately 7:15

**p.m., in the parking lot of Tomahawk Country Club in Phil-
adelphia. Eddington was a member of the club and was
employed as a Sales Manager by OpenSpace, a cubicle
manufacturer in Horsham. Authorities say that Eddington's death was the result of a stab wound. It has not been
determined at this time whether it was self-inflicted.**

Mary couldn't process it quickly enough. "This is terrible!
This just happened? Didn't you interview him just this morning?"

"Yes," Bennie answered after a moment.

"Did he seem okay to you?" Mary's mind raced, and she had
a million questions at once. "Did he seem depressed or anything,
like he'd want to kill himself? Do you think he killed himself
because of the case?"

"I don't know. I shouldn't say more. We still have a conflict,
and I don't want to divulge privileged information. I shouldn't
have told you that I met with him."

"But this isn't about a case, this is about a person. He died,
maybe by suicide. Or he could have been *murdered.*"

"I understand, but this doesn't end our conflict. Whether it
ends your lawsuit is up to you."

"Right, that's true." Mary tried to collect her thoughts. "I
wonder if they'll continue the defamation case against Simon."

"Pardon me?"

"The defamation case against Simon." Mary repeated, her
jittery gaze traveling over her desk, which was cluttered with
Xeroxed cases on trade libel.

"I don't know anything about that."

"I didn't think you did," Mary said, relieved. "It's retaliation,
pure and simple, and I knew you wouldn't sanction them serv-
ing papers on him in Children's Hospital, especially when they
know that he's represented. That was shameful. I assume the
orders came from Nate, and you should tell him that—"

"Mary, I should really go. I wanted to let you know as, uh, a friend."

"Sure, right, thanks." Mary heard the hitch in Bennie's voice and realized she'd been about to say *partner*. That Bennie called her *friend* was enough. Mary tried to ignore the wound in her own chest, which was definitely self-inflicted. "Where are you?"

"Declan's."

"Good, that's good." Mary felt another wave of guilt. Declan usually came to Bennie because she was the busier of the two. Bennie must have been at an all-time low if she'd chucked work and made the drive out west.

"You okay?"

"Yes." Mary felt tears come into her eyes. She had betrayed Bennie and she deserved to feel terrible. There was no penance for this sin. "How are you, though?"

"I'm really okay, Mary. Don't feel bad about your decision. I understand. Take care. Stay well." Bennie hung up, and Mary swallowed the hard knot around her Adam's apple. It only made her feel worse that Bennie was being so nice, but Mary willed herself to get her head back in the game. She had to tell Simon what happened and he'd be beside himself. His talk about breaking points this morning worried her, and she knew he'd feel responsible for Todd's suicide, if it had in fact been a suicide.

Mary pressed in his phone number, listened to the phone ring, but then it went to voicemail. She cleared her throat and left him a message: "Simon, please call me when you get a chance, it's important." She pressed End, concerned. It was hard to reach him in the hospital because he was always busy, so she texted, **Please call when you get a chance. Important.**

Mary set the phone down, hopped back on the computer, and started reading through the stories about Todd Eddington, hoping for more details. There weren't many and none of them had any more details, since the big news was the thunderstorm raging outside. Rain pounded on the window behind her, and had been all afternoon. Still she would never understand why the weather got better coverage than human life, but that was a question for another day.

Mary rose, picking up her phone, and grabbing her purse and an umbrella before she left the office. She didn't want to wait for Simon to call back and, on second thought, it was better to deliver the news in person. She just wanted to get the jump on telling him, so he didn't find out on the TV, which was on all the time in Rachel's hospital room, though was usually turned to Nickelodeon unless Feet was there, watching the Phillies game.

She hurried out of her office and down the hall, past the empty reception desk, since she was the last one still at work. She crossed to the elevator bank, pressed the button, and found herself turning to face the brass plaque in the lobby, which read Rosato & DiNunzio. She looked at it for a long time and didn't turn away until the elevator finally came.

Mary hustled out of the building, opening the umbrella and hurrying to the curb to flag down a cab. Rain snarled the traffic, which was congested because it was rush hour, but she spotted a Yellow cab up the street and flagged him down. Businesspeople flowed around her on the sidewalk, their umbrellas bumping into one another as they hustled along, shouting on their phones to be heard above the downpour.

Mary waved at the cab frantically, and it flashed its lights at her, which calmed her down. She had to collect her thoughts because Simon would be full of questions about his lawsuits, once he got over the initial shock of Todd Eddington's death. Its effect on the lawsuits wasn't easy to figure out, and again, Mary felt the loss of not having somebody to bounce ideas off of. Not only didn't she have Bennie, but she didn't have Judy anymore, either, as a result of the conflict of interest.

She was completely on her own, which was undoubtedly the shape of things to come.

Be careful what you wish, came immediately to mind, but Mary shooed that thought away. She jumped into the cab as soon as it arrived, closing the door behind her and calling and texting Simon again as they lurched off into traffic. She left the same phone messages and texts, but they weren't returned even by the time the cab had reached Walnut Street and was heading west to the Penn campus.

The traffic lightened up once they left the expressway entrances behind, and Mary used the time to compose herself, focusing on the task at hand. Simon would need her to be calm, even if she felt inwardly jumbled. His problems were far worse than hers right now, and the only way she could lighten his load was to inspire trust in him. She squared her shoulders as she got out of the cab, hurrying under the canopy, keeping her umbrella closed.

She entered the hospital, which was even busier than usual, filled with families standing near the entrance waiting for rides, their babies in their arms, some with a child-sized plastic tube taped to their little cheeks. She hurried to the elevator bank, grabbed the first one, and had it mostly to herself, patting her hair into place and getting her act together as the elevator doors opened.

Mary stepped out of the elevator cab, but there was a crowd in the elevator lobby. Hospital security in white shirts mixed with uniformed Philadelphia police, talking among themselves, their walkie-talkies crackling. Raindrops dappled the heavy shoulders of the cops' uniforms, dotting their light blue shirts, and they had plastic covers on their hats, which were also wet. Mary had never seen security officers on the floor before, much less Philadelphia police, and the sight of their thick utility belts with retractable nightsticks, Tasers, and holstered Glocks seemed oddly out of place in a hospital dedicated to healing.

"What's the problem, Officers?" Mary asked, making her way through the crowd.

"Nothing to be concerned about," one of the cops answered, with a professional smile.

"Okay, well, thanks for what you do." Mary let it go, turned down the hallway, and headed for the nurses' station. She had almost reached it when a cadre of police and more hospital security turned the corner, coming toward them like a phalanx. In the middle of them walked Simon, who tugged down his surgical mask to reveal an expression numb with shock.

"Simon?" Mary called back, reeling. She couldn't imagine what the police wanted with him.

"Mary!" he called out, his eyes flaring with alarm. "Come with me!"

Mary hustled to the group, which closed ranks around Simon, behind the lead cop. "Officer, what's this about?"

"It's police business, ma'am," the lead cop answered, his expression grim under the bill of his cap. "Please, step aside."

Mary stood her ground, blocking the way. "Officer, my name is Mary DiNunzio, and I'm here to see him—"

"That's my lawyer, she's my lawyer!" Simon called out from the middle of the crowd. The nurses and a doctor at the nurses' station edged away, their expressions collectively shocked.

"Ma'am, please step aside," the cop repeated, his tone more conciliatory. "There's very sick children on this floor. We don't want to disturb them."

"I know, his daughter is one of them." Mary lowered her voice anyway. "Just tell me what's going on, please?"

"We're escorting him downtown for questioning."

"For *what*?" Mary asked, flabbergasted.

"In connection with the death of one Todd Eddington." The cop gestured over his shoulder at two men in suits, who had just turned the corner with a hospital-administrative type in a

CHOP lanyard. "You want details, ask them. They're the detectives."

Simon called out, "Mary, call my father."

"I will," Mary called back, her mind reeling.

"Ma'am," the cop said, sternly. "Now please, move aside."

CHAPTER EIGHTEEN

Bennie sat at Declan's kitchen table and hunched over his laptop, pressing Refresh to see if there had been any developments in the death of Todd Eddington. The police hadn't released any new details, so all she knew was that it was a result of a single stab wound to the chest, but her senses were on high alert. Authorities hadn't weighed in on whether it was suicide or murder, and she knew there would be no official statement until the medical examiner had officially completed the autopsy in a day or two. But Bennie had handled enough murder cases in her day to know that this one stunk to high heaven.

The undercounter TV was on next to her, and she checked the screen to see if there were any new developments, but a car commercial was on. She returned to the laptop and hit the Refresh button on autopilot, but there was nothing new, there either. Still, she kept trying to put two and two together from the facts she had, replaying her interview with Todd in her mind. She kept coming up with the same conclusion; he didn't strike her as someone who'd commit suicide. He was cocky, competent, and aggressive, the kind of man who turned his anger outward, not inward. And his last word as he had left the conference room today clearly suggested he was looking forward to the future.

I want my day in court. I want to clear my name.

"Babe, five minutes!" Declan called to her from the deck, where he was barbecuing burgers. An aromatic haze wafted through the screen of the sliding doors, and she hit the button for Refresh on autopilot, her thoughts churning. She felt vaguely stressed since her conversation with Mary and she couldn't help but feel sorry for the girl, who would have to figure out the effect of Todd's death on Simon's case against OpenSpace. Bennie thought it would improve Simon's case, since OpenSpace wouldn't be able to put Todd on the stand and have him testify that Simon's allegations were false, thus losing the chance for the jury to find him credible or even like him.

Bennie hit Refresh again, continuing her train of thought. And if Simon's case went as far as trial, Mary would still get the contemporaneous notes admitted into evidence, even over a hearsay objection, because they were coming in only to prove the fact that they were said, not that they were true. Legally, Todd's death could be good news for Mary's case, but Mary would never think about it that way. Mary cared about people more than cases, even her friend Simon's case, and she would nevertheless feel terrible that someone had murdered Todd.

"Babe, come out and get some fresh air!"

"In a minute!"

"You said that fifteen minutes ago!"

"But this time I mean it. That time I lied!" Bennie hit Refresh again, wondering about what Mary had said, that there was a defamation suit filed against Simon. It struck Bennie as an overreaction to an individual ADA case and she sensed Nate was taking out his anger at her on Mary and Simon. She couldn't imagine a basis for any suit against Simon, but she didn't have to guess.

"Babe! Come out, come out, wherever you are!"

"Okay, here I come!" Bennie logged on to the website for the Common Pleas Court, clicked on the magnifying glass for its searchable case index, and plugged in OpenSpace in the block for plaintiff's name and Simon Pensiera for the defendant's. In the next moment, a link popped onto the screen, and she clicked it, opening a complaint that had evidently been filed in the case today. She rose with the laptop as she read the allegations, walking outside into a cloud of barbecue smoke.

"You're like a kid with that thing." Declan flipped his hamburger, and Bennie crossed the small deck to a faded red canvas chair that matched the reddish trim on the A-frame house, which was surrounded by Declan's pastures in the middle of the country. His horses grazed near the fence, having been fed and turned out for the night, and the air felt cool and breezy as the sun slipped behind the jagged tree line.

"I'm reading a complaint that got filed today, in what can only be retaliation for Mary's suit against OpenSpace."

"Not a counterclaim, an entirely separate lawsuit?"

"Yes, for defamation, based on some comment Simon made about Eddington and also for trade libel based on quality control."

"Man." Declan waved the smoke away from his face. "Do you think your buddy Nate knows about that litigation?"

"I think so," Bennie answered, because she had been thinking the same thing. "He wouldn't normally, but this time, he's taking it personally."

"Because you're involved. Hell hath no fury like a lawyer scorned."

"You think he's doing it to get to me?"

"Yes." Declan nodded, matter-of-factly. "You know what convinced me? His bringing Mary in front of a disciplinary board. That's *way* out of line. You could ruin somebody's career. And for what? A judgment call?"

"I know, right? It's weird."

"Not weird, obvious. He knows you care about her, so he's going to hurt her. He's throwing everything he has at your girl." Declan picked up a spatula and a platter from the side of the grill.

"Hmm." Bennie scrolled to the complaint, skimming the statements that Simon was alleged to have made. "I don't believe a word of this. I think this Todd is a liar. *Was* a liar. I just don't know why they would do this. And I don't know what, if anything, either of these suits has to do with his murder."

"It was definitely murder," Declan said, with the confidence of a former cop. "Unless they find a note, not a suicide. And maybe even if they find a note. Not a suicide."

"I agree, but what makes you say that?"

"It's almost impossible to kill yourself by stabbing yourself in the chest. The sternum gets in the way. It's even hard to stab somebody *else* through the sternum." Declan took the food off the heat and set it on the table. "Dinnertime."

"Educate me," Bennie said, rising with the laptop. She came over to the picnic table, sat next to him, and set the laptop on her right so she could keep checking.

"The sternum is a big, thick breastbone that runs down the center of your chest. It's meant to protect the heart. It does a good job. I arrested a guy once, he broke a hunting knife on another guy's sternum." Declan picked up the ketchup and squirted it all over his burger, and Bennie tried not to imagine blood.

"Did the guy live?"

"Yes. The knife died." Declan grinned crookedly. "You have to pick the exact right spot. The ribs get in the way."

"But it's possible. If Todd didn't do it himself, then somebody did it to him."

"I didn't say it couldn't be done. I said he couldn't do it himself. Highly unlikely." Declan placed his hamburger bun on top of his burger, then mashed it down with the flat of his hand. Ketchup oozed out of the sides, and Bennie started to lose her appetite. She had been so preoccupied with the case that somehow, she had forgotten the fact that a human being had died.

"This is so awful, I don't know who would kill Todd Eddington. A sales manager at a cubicle manufacturer? Sitting in a parking lot at his country club?"

"You told me he drove a Porsche. Could've been a carjacking gone wrong. What about his wallet and watch?" Declan took a big bite of his burger, chewing away.

"I don't know. And they left the car."

"When the job goes wrong, they don't take the car."

"But a carjacking in broad daylight?"

"It's pouring in Philly. Visibility is low. Nobody's outside. Nobody's playing golf. The lot couldn't have been that full. Opportunity plus motive equals crime. I'm good at math." Declan chewed happily away, but Bennie had grown used to his gallows humor, having been around enough homicide detectives to know that it was a defense mechanism.

"But how random could it be? A country club is private property."

"I doubt they check your ID when you go in. We could find out in five minutes." Declan gestured at the computer. "Or it could be another member. Jealous husband. Has our boy been fooling around?"

"Possibly. He was divorced and not terrible looking."

"He had a big job. That's catnip."

"Don't be sexist." Bennie shot him a look. "I have a big job."

"Why do you think I'm sleeping with you?" Declan took another big bite of his burger, which was almost finished. "Aren't you going to eat your veggie burger? I cooked that barley to perfection."

"Thanks, in a minute." Bennie turned to the computer, refreshing Philly.com for the local news, but there was nothing new. "So much is going on, and I'm worried about Mary. She sounded shell-shocked when I called her."

"I agree, she's got a lot going on. ADA case. Ethics complaint. Defamation case." Declan smiled in a knowing way, reaching for his beer bottle. "Luckily, she's not your partner anymore. Or your problem. She's leaving your firm, remember?"

"I know." Bennie felt a pang. "She wouldn't if she didn't have to."

"I know that," Declan said with a smile, and Bennie knew he meant it because he liked Mary.

"Then what's your point?"

"She's leaving. You're going to have to let her go."

"I'm letting her go. I'm not stopping her." Bennie hit Refresh again.

"I mean figuratively. Let her go." Declan met her eye directly. "Her problems are not your problems anymore."

"But I still care about her."

"Try to detach."

"It's hard," Bennie blurted out, surprised to hear the words coming out of her own mouth. "It took me so long to get attached. I'm attached."

"She's not a puppy, babe."

"I know, but I'm worried about her. She won't have anybody if Carrier stays with me. She'll be completely on her own."

"Didn't I just hear you pitch Judy to stay with you?" Declan smiled slightly, his crow's-feet crinkling with amusement.

"I know." Bennie hit Refresh, and suddenly the screen changed, to a video feed in front of the Roundhouse. A new headline read **Man Questioned in Stabbing Death**. "Look, something's happening!"

"What?" Declan got up and came around Bennie's other side, watching the laptop over her shoulder.

"There's video!" Bennie clicked to play the video, which

showed a man being escorted into the revolving doors at the Roundhouse, which was the police administration building.

The voiceover said: "Police have brought in for questioning an unidentified male in connection with the death of Todd Eddington, the Horsham man found stabbed to death today. Authorities have not yet identified the man, who has not been arrested for the crime. He is considered a person of interest . . ."

Bennie eyed the man. "I wonder who he is."

"*That's* the perp? What is this, chess club?" Declan snorted, but Bennie fixated on the screen as the video showed the man disappearing inside the building, followed by a small woman whom she recognized instantly.

"That's *Mary*!" Bennie hit the button to freeze the video.

"Your partner?" Declan asked, incredulous.

"Yes!" Bennie rewound the video and played it over again, confirming her identification. She felt a bolt of surprise when she put two and two together. "The person of interest must be Simon!"

"Oh, whoa." Declan grimaced. "So the cops think Simon killed Eddington? Damn. Now that makes sense."

Bennie found herself on her feet. "Why? What would make you say that? You don't know any of these people."

"Common sense." Declan shrugged. "Eddington fired Simon. And when Simon sued him for it, Eddington sued him back. That's motive."

"Poor Mary." Bennie edged backwards, suddenly restless. "I need to get back to the city. She's got a murder case on her hands. She hasn't done that many of them."

"Hold on. Think this through." Declan rose, holding up a hand. "Like I just said, she's not your problem. She's a lawyer. She knows what she's doing. Let her do it."

"I can help. I'll be backup, I won't interfere, just let her know I'm there if she needs me. It's not like we're in conflict anymore.

This isn't a civil case, and Dumbarton isn't on the other side. The Commonwealth is."

"I know. But that's not your problem." Declan came toward her, touching her arm. "Babe. You can stay here. Relax for the weekend."

"She's got a tiger by the tail."

"She didn't call you."

"She probably didn't feel she could. Or she didn't have the time." Bennie thought a minute. "Just like you, when you offered me the loan. I didn't ask for it, but you offered it. That was just kind. I appreciate that. I want to be kind to Mary. If she needs me, I'll be there. I have to go."

Declan sighed. "Okay. I understand. Good thing we had sex first."

Bennie burst into laughter and gave him a big hug and a kiss. "I agree," she said, meaning it.

"Take your veggie burger," Declan said, kissing her again.

CHAPTER NINETEEN

Mary followed the detectives, the remaining cops, and Simon, bringing up the rear as the group funneled into the narrow corridor that led to the Homicide Division. She knew she was taking a backseat but it was only for the time being. She would assert herself when it counted, once they got inside the squad room. She wasn't the most experienced criminal defense attorney in the world, but she'd been involved in one or two murder cases, even one recently. She was no Bennie Rosato, but she could get the job done. She hoped.

She hurried down the corridor, which curved because the Roundhouse was three round sections put together, the source of its nickname. She was no longer surprised by the poor condition of the building: Fluorescent lights flickered, greenish floor tiles were grimy and broken, and the walls were of cheap paneling, circa 1960s. They passed the bathroom on the right, its door propped open by a trash can, and it smelled as bad as she remembered from last time. Every year, politicians talked about moving the department to a nicer building but it never happened, and Mary suspected the police needed a better lawyer. She would do it for free, for the public servants who kept her hometown safe.

The group reached the end of the hallway and went through a secured door next to a plaque that read simply HOMICIDE, then filled up the tiny entrance lobby, lined with rubbery black seats and wanted posters. Beyond the reception area was a front desk and a bustling, if cramped, squad room.

Detectives in short sleeves, their ties loosened, worked on ancient computers at battered desks, surrounded by mismatched gray file cabinets and bulletin boards with outdated memos, and bumper stickers for the Phillies and the Eagles. Windows with broken blinds lined the far side of the room and the air conditioners had a death rattle, so it was uncomfortably hot, and most of the detectives had little blue fans sitting on their desks, whirring away like so many toy airplane propellers.

Mary looked around for Detectives Randolph or Hilliard, whom she knew from Patrick's case, but they weren't in sight. She forced her way through the uniformed cops to Simon, putting a hand on his arm. Simon looked over, his mouth a tight line, and Mary knew him well enough to know that he was keeping a lid on his emotions. She never would have dreamed that he'd be a person of interest in a murder investigation and she knew he didn't kill Todd, but she had to find out why he'd been called in. The detectives hadn't told her anything more at the hospital and they had taken Simon in the squad car, so she hadn't been able to talk to him either.

"Detective Lindenhurst," Mary called out. "I'd like to meet with my client in an interview room before we talk."

"Do you really think that's necessary, Ms. DiNunzio?" Detective Lindenhurst turned around with a professional smile. "We're not going to keep him that long."

"I do think it's necessary, but thanks." Mary smiled back, equally professionally, then took a few steps forward with Simon toward the interview rooms on the right, a line of three doors cracked partway open. "Why don't I just take him in and I'll let you know when we're finished? We won't be long."

"Fine, this way." Detective Lindenhurst led them to interview room A and gestured them inside.

"I'm assuming this will be completely private," Mary said to him, just to be sure. "Last time I was here, the videocameras weren't working."

"It still isn't." Detective Lindenhurst smiled, more naturally. "And yes, it will be completely private. Can I get either of you a water or a coffee? We got vending machine coffee. It's better than it sounds."

Mary knew it wasn't. "No thank you."

Simon shook his head, glancing around as they entered the grimy white box of a room, and Mary closed the door behind them, following his gaze to the stainless-steel chair that was bolted to the floor, which had a pair of handcuffs hanging loosely from one arm. Next to that were two black-plastic chairs and one white, a rickety wooden table, blank Miranda forms, and an actual typewriter.

"Simon, sit down and try to relax. Everything is going to be okay. We're going to sort this out."

"Oh God, I hope so." Simon exhaled with a sigh, sinking into one of the chairs and putting his head in his hands.

"You're doing a great job staying calm."

"Thanks, I'm trying."

"I called your father on the way here, and he said he'll talk to your cousins."

"Oh no, he must've freaked out."

"He was upset, but he handled it, and he's going to stay at the hospital tonight. So he'll see you when we're finished here."

"Thank God Rachel was asleep when the cops came. I have no idea how I would explain it to her." Simon raked his hair back. "Did you see the nurses? Jenny? Susan? Even Dr. Linda, that's Rachel's oncologist. I can't imagine what they would be thinking. The cops searched me, patted me down, right in front of everyone."

"They're allowed to do that for their own safety."

"It was so embarrassing. At least they didn't handcuff me."

"Right." Mary sat down opposite him, pulling the chair over. "Okay, we don't have a lot of time, so let's get to the point. First, the possibility of suicide. Is that something that Todd would do? Do you know any reason he'd commit suicide?"

Simon shook his head, gravely. "It doesn't sound like him, to tell you the truth. He lets his emotions out. He's not the kind of guy to carry crap around. I just don't see him killing himself."

"Maybe something's wrong with his ex-wife or the kids. Was there a custody battle or anything? That's the kind of thing that makes people kill themselves."

"No, I don't think they had anything like that, and if so, they were over the hardest part of the divorce. It was all smooth. He has the visitation schedule. That much I know because we worked around it for a company retreat once."

Mary made a note on her phone. "So that brings us to murder. Somebody must've killed him, but why? Does he carry a lot of money on him? He had a Porsche, was he a flashy guy?"

"Totally, he always carried a lot of money. He had a nice Rolex, I know that. So maybe somebody killed him, but it sure as hell wasn't me."

"Does he have any enemies that you know of?"

"None that I know of."

"Okay, the cops must not think he killed himself either, because they brought you in for questioning. They didn't arrest you, but you're a person of interest. I'm assuming they called you in because they found out that he fired you, that you're suing each other, and they're thinking that's motive. The good news is that I guarantee you that's not enough to accuse somebody of murder and you were at the hospital—"

"Mary, there's something I need to tell you," Simon interrupted her.

"What?"

"That's not all they have. I saw Todd today. I talked with him at the country club, in his car."

Mary felt her mouth drop open. "What? When? How?"

"At the end of the day. I know I shouldn't've done it, I probably should've called you first." Simon's eyes turned pleading, his eyebrows sloped unhappily down. "But it just got to me. The lawsuit this morning, him making up those lies about me and the company suing me for two million. Maybe it was my breaking point."

Mary's throat went dry, but she didn't interrupt him.

"I thought, things got too complicated, involving lawyers. He and I are old friends, *were* old friends, and I thought that if we just talked to each other, we could hash it out man-to-man. I thought maybe we could settle it, since you or Bennie or whoever hadn't been able to."

Mary knew where he was coming from. Almost every client felt that a lawsuit could be settled if the lawyers just got out of the way, but it was rarely true. Once a lawsuit got filed, opposing sides invested in their side of the story. "So what happened?"

"Todd's a creature of habit, and it's Friday. Every Friday night in summer, Todd stops by the club. If it's a nice day he leaves work early, plays nine holes, and has a drink. If it's bad weather, like today, he has a drink with whoever's at the bar." Simon paused, running a tongue over parched lips. "So after we spoke this morning, I called him."

"Tell me exactly what you said." Mary pulled out her phone, scrolled to her notes app, and started a file.

"It wasn't a long conversation. I said, 'Todd, I got this lawsuit you filed against me for two million bucks and I think this is getting out of control. Let's try and settle this face-to-face.' He said, 'I'll give you ten minutes. Meet me at the club at five thirty. We'll talk in the car.'"

"That's it?"

"That's it." Mary was always surprised at how terse men could be. She needed fifteen minutes to say hello. Plus hugging time.

"So I left the hospital, got to the club, and went around the back, where he parks."

"You knew the club? You're not a member, are you?"

"No, but I've been with him and I know the drill. You drive in and the clubhouse is on the right, then the tennis courts and the bag drop, but he always parks in the farthest spot in the lot. He doesn't want anybody to mess up his Porsche."

Mary typed away. "So you drove there and met with him?"

"Yes."

"Was anybody else around?"

"No, not that I saw. It was raining like hell. Nobody was on the course or the driving range."

Mary guessed the club had security cameras, and they would have recorded Simon's car, including the license plate. "Okay, so then what happened? You got out of your car and got into his?"

"Yes."

"Was he there waiting for you or did you have to wait for him?"

"He was waiting for me."

"Was anybody else in his car?"

"No, he was completely alone and there were no witnesses, if that's why you're asking." Simon frowned, turning nervous. "But I swear to you, he was alive when I left him. He was alive."

"Okay, stay calm. Tell me the rest of the story."

"So I got in his car, and I said, 'Todd, what's the deal? What is going on? You know I didn't say those things about you, I would never run you down, and I get why you let me go, I know you're trying to save the company money.'"

"What was your tone like? Were you angry with him?"

"I was, but I didn't yell or anything. I was really trying to settle this. I didn't call him a liar. I was really trying to under-stand what happened." Simon opened his palms in appeal. Maybe I talked forcefully, like now, but I didn't raise my voice. I was trying to negotiate. I'm in sales, for God's sake. I knew what I wanted out of the meeting. A settlement. Like any deal, I wanted to close it."

"I understand," Mary said, hearing the ring of truth in his words. She couldn't understand how it had turned out so hor-ribly wrong. "So how did he react?"

"He got pissed. He started yelling. He said that it was bullshit that I sued him and he would be damned if he would settle it. He said he wanted his day in court. He wanted to clear his name. And he hoped I had to pay every penny of the two mil-lion bucks. Then I got mad."

"What happened?"

"When he said that, I saw red. I couldn't help it. He was vicious, vindictive, like he didn't care about Rachel at all. So I shoved him, and he shoved me back."

Mary's heart sank. "So it got physical?"

"Yes, we grappled."

"What do you mean by grappled?"

"Like we got into a shoving match. Look, I admit it, I wanted to hit him." Simon's face flushed. "But I'm not a violent guy. I'm not a fighter. I just shoved him and he shoved me back, then we grappled back and forth, then he shoved me against the car door and said get out."

"Then did you go?"

"Yes, I came to my senses. I knew fighting wouldn't solve anything. And he wouldn't listen to reason. So I got out of the car."

"How long were you in?"

"Fifteen minutes, tops."

"What did you do next?"

"I got in my car and drove back to the hospital."

"What time did you get there?"

Simon frowned in thought. "I'm not sure. Six o'clock, maybe. The traffic was horrible, rush hour in the rain. My dad was still there. Then he left with your father."

Mary thought a minute. "When you left the club, is there a gatehouse or anything? Was there a guard that would see you when you left?"

"Yes, they have a gatehouse, and you give your name and the member you're with or meeting. They don't write it down or anything. Or call. It's not that strict."

"But if you don't say a member's name?"

"They don't let you in, I'm sure."

"Did you see the guard when you left?"

"Yes."

"Talk to him?"

"No, I didn't. Just waved."

Mary tried to think of a question she hadn't asked. "So you drove away, and he was fine?"

"Absolutely." Simon's expression fell into grave lines again.

"Did you see anybody go to the car after you?" Mary was trying to puzzle out the timeline. "We don't know the time of death, but whoever killed him had to come pretty quickly after you left. Did you see any other cars in the lot?"

"Not that I remember. I didn't notice. It was pretty empty."

"Was it totally empty?"

"I don't think so, I don't remember." Simon licked his lips again. "As soon as I pulled into the lot, I drove to his car. That's all I was thinking about. Him and what I was going to say."

"Think a minute, try to remember."

"Remember what?"

"When you drove from the entrance of the lot to his car, did you make a direct line through rows of painted lines?"

"No, I didn't make a direct line. I drove around the perimeter to the farthest point where he parked."

"So you took the long way instead of going straight?"

"Yes, essentially I took the two legs of the triangle, not the hypotenuse."

Mary could visualize it, but didn't understand his actions. "So why didn't you just take the hypotenuse? Was it because there were cars in your way? Close your eyes and try to visualize it."

Simon closed his eyes, then opened them again. "I think it's force of habit, maybe I'm a creature of habit too. Either way, I drove around the perimeter of the lot. I didn't cut through directly, like on an angle. I'm not sure if there were cars there but if there were, there weren't many."

Mary didn't say what she was thinking, which was, *It only takes one.* "There's something else I don't understand. If there was nobody else in the lot, why did Todd park in the far corner? If nobody else was there, there's no danger of anybody bumping into his Porsche."

Simon shrugged. "I guess that's force of habit, too. That was his space. We all know it."

"Did he hold other meetings in the car?"

"Sometimes, like if we went for a drink and were going to talk about something confidential, we'd talk about it in the car before we went into the clubhouse."

"So you weren't surprised when he suggested the car, not the clubhouse."

"Right, I wasn't."

"So was this well known within the company, the talking in the car thing? And where he parks?"

"Not the whole company, but the people around Todd know."

Mary made a note on her phone. "Do you know if he told anybody that he was meeting you?"

"I don't know."

"Did he say?"

"No."

"If he told anybody, who would he tell? Who's his friend at the firm, er, I mean the company?"

"Nobody, really. He's a real glad-hander, like a typical sales guy. He has a lot of acquaintances but no good friend."

Mary couldn't relate. She had Judy. Or at least she used to. "What about outside the company?"

"Not that I know of, not since his divorce."

"Is he dating anybody?"

"Not seriously, that I know of. He doesn't have a problem getting dates. I think that might've been what happened between him and Cheryl but we never talked about it."

"You think he cheated on her?"

"I suspect it."

"Do you know with who?"

"I've no idea but there were one or two times when he wasn't where he said he'd be. I had my suspicions but I never said anything to him. Or anybody else. I don't run down my boss, no matter what anybody thinks."

"Okay, that's enough for now. I want to keep this short because they're waiting." Mary set her phone aside, meeting his worried gaze directly. "Here's what's going to happen next. Listen to me carefully."

"Okay," Simon said, leaning forward.

CHAPTER TWENTY

Bennie drove east in heavy traffic, encountering rain on the outskirts of Philadelphia. Drops pounded on the windshield, forcing her to slow down for safety's sake as she turned onto the expressway. She belonged in the city with so much going on, and the time with Declan had recharged her. She even felt better after the nap. She assumed Mary was at the Roundhouse and planned to let her know she was available as soon as she got to the office.

Suddenly her cell phone started ringing, and though she hated to talk on the phone while she was driving, especially in bad weather, she would take the call if it was Mary. She slipped the phone from her bag and checked the screen, surprised to see that it was Mike Bashir calling. She hadn't spoken with him since he'd become the president of OpenSpace, but his cell phone was still in her contacts because she used to work for him when he headed Joselton Ltd., another of Dumbarton subsidiaries. She had no idea why he was calling, especially since she had been fired, but given what was going on, there was no way she was going to pass up this call.

"Mike, how are you?" Bennie said, picking up.

"I've been better. I guess you heard that Todd was found

dead today." Mike sounded more tense than grief-stricken, and as far as Bennie remembered, he wasn't the kind of guy to tense up.

"I heard, I'm very sorry about that. It was really shocking."

"I know, it's awful, but I'm in Scottsdale at a trade show and I got a text from Ernie, our head of Security, that police showed up at OpenSpace. They have a search warrant and they want to look at everything. There's, like, six of them and they didn't even give us notice. Ernie told them to stand down while we checked it out."

Bennie let Mike talk, realizing that he didn't know she'd been fired, which wasn't that surprising. It had been between her and Nate, who was much higher up than Mike, plus Mike had been out of town. The right hand didn't know what the left was doing, a problem not unique to Dumbarton, in corporate America. Bennie considered filling him in, but her curiosity was piqued, so she kept her mouth shut.

"I mean, I understand why they want to look at Todd's personnel file or maybe look around his office, but from what Ernie's telling me, there's more than that. They want to search my office too. Can they do that? I don't like that idea, if I'm not there."

"Yes, as a general rule, the police can search the premises with the proper search warrant, and it makes sense that they would do that in connection with Todd's death. They don't know if it's a suicide or murder yet, do they?"

"I can tell you, it's not a suicide, that's not like Todd. I hear you met with him this morning. He didn't seem like he was on the verge of suicide, did he?"

"No, he didn't. So you think he was murdered. Who do you think did it? Was it random?" Bennie made a mental note, stockpiling information that she wasn't completely entitled to.

"No way, I'm sure Simon did it."

"Why would he?" Bennie steered ahead, dismayed.

"Because Todd fired him. It's obvious."

"But murder? That's an extreme response to a termination, don't you think?"

"Normally, but everybody knows that Simon has a sick kid and needed the money. We had a blood drive one day, I even gave. When Todd let him go, Simon snapped."

Bennie let it go for now. "Todd told me that Simon's sales were trending down and he had lost his edge. Did you agree?"

"I didn't know enough to agree or disagree. I delegate to my guys. Sales are Todd's problem. If the numbers aren't there, he answers to me. If they are, I don't interfere."

"But you approved the termination, right?"

"Yes. I always back up my guys. Todd told me he wanted to let Simon go, I backed him up."

"What do you think about the merits of the lawsuit, the one that Simon filed against Todd and the company? Do you believe that Todd made those statements about the daughter's medical expenses?"

"I have no idea."

"Did he ever say anything like that to you?"

"No. Anyway, you were saying, about the warrants?"

Bennie thought fast, forming a plan. "It sounds to me like you're right, in the point you were making. A warrant has to be specific in scope to be constitutional. In other words, a warrant gives the police permission to look only for documents or items that are reasonably related to their investigation."

"That's what I'm talking about! So why do they have to go in my office?"

"I agree with you, they don't." Bennie steered forward, reading the highway signs, their reflective numerals bright in the storm. "If the warrant seeks documents or seeks to search places that are irrelevant, it's overbroad in scope and invalid."

"So why did they ask then? And what are they looking for?"

"Evidence, in general. Most of the time, the cops get an over-broad warrant from a judge and it's boilerplate. Nobody calls them on it because they don't know the difference or have legal counsel. But you're right to do so, and I agree with you."

"Okay, so what do we do now? How do we know if this warrant is too broad or whatever you called it?"

"I have to read the warrant and make a judgment."

"I don't have it. Ernie has it at the plant. You want to call him and have him read it to you?"

"I have a better idea." Bennie put on her blinker and steered to the right, heading for the Blue Route. "I'm in the neighborhood, about fifteen minutes away. Why don't I go over to the plant myself? Read the warrant and see what's going on?"

"Good deal, thanks. I'll text Ernie. I gotta go."

"Thanks, safe travels." Bennie hung up the phone, feeling a twinge of guilt, but not much. Her motto had always been Don't ask permission, apologize later, and it had served her in good stead so far. Besides, it wasn't as if she had called Mike herself, misrepresenting her position. All she did was answer the phone and try to help a guy out. And all she wanted to do was peek around OpenSpace and see what she could see.

Bennie hit the gas, heading for Horsham.

Fifteen minutes later, she turned onto the road that led to OpenSpace, and though her visibility was poor, she could see a commotion in the parking lot, a marked change from earlier that day. Several police cruisers were parked idling in front of the building, and Bennie assumed the cops were inside, staying out of the rain. The administrative offices were lit up, and the factory was still running.

She turned in to the driveway, steered to the left through the downpour, giving the police cars and some other cars parked in front a wide berth. She wanted to get into the building, spook around, and then deal with the cops, not the reverse order. She parked around the left side of the building, cut the ignition, and braced herself to get rained on by grabbing her purse, putting it on her head, and bolting out of the car.

She ran for the entrance with her head down and under her purse, racing around the building. She splashed through puddles in the parking lot and bounded up the front steps in the downpour. She ran into the building and entered the lobby, which was empty except for three men standing in a circle. She recognized Ray Matewicz, the operations type who'd been in the meeting, but didn't know the other two. She wondered if one was Ernie Greeley, the director of Security named in the defamation complaint against Simon.

"Hello, Ray, hi, gentlemen," she began, brushing droplets off her khaki suit. She approached the two men she didn't know. "And you are?"

"Bennie, you don't need to meet anybody else." Ray broke from the group and strode toward her, unsmiling. "I assume you know that Simon killed Todd today."

"Well, I heard that Todd was murdered and I'm very sorry about that. My condolences—"

"You're not sorry." Ray folded his arms.

"Of course I am."

"Oh come on." Ray's eyes flashed with anger. "Why are you here?"

"I got a call from Mike Bashir about the police and I was in the neighborhood, so I came by."

"You were in the neighborhood?" Ray cocked his head skeptically.

"Yes." Bennie kept a straight face, a skill she had learned from telling lies to get to the truth.

"I don't believe for one minute that Mike called you. He's not even here."

"I know, he's in Scottsdale. In fact, hold on." Bennie got her phone out of her purse, scrolled to Recent Calls, and showed it to Ray. "See?"

Ray looked up from the phone screen, his mouth tight. "He called you because he didn't know you got fired. Oh yeah, we heard that, too. See, we called our *real* lawyer, Jason, when the cops came and Jason told us you got shit-canned. Did you tell Mike that?"

Busted. "Ray, look—"

"We saw Simon and his lawyer on the news. They said his lawyer is from Rosato & DiNunzio. We looked it up. You're the same Rosato. You're on the other side."

"There's no sides."

"There is to us. Todd is, was, our friend. You're here working for Simon."

"No, I came to help." Bennie held her head high. "You want the whole factory searched? Then I'll go."

"Go. Jason's on the way. Leave the premises, right now."

"Fine." Bennie turned away and headed for the door, her low heels clacking on the floor.

"And we want our documents back," Ray called after her.

"Which documents?" Bennie paused, turning around.

"When you interviewed Todd this morning, you asked for some documents. They got delivered to your office. We emailed you a digital file too. Those documents are ours, property of OpenSpace. We want them back tonight."

"The office is closed. Send a messenger in the morning." Bennie turned away. It was an odd thing to bring up, and her thoughts started to churn. She pushed open the exit door, covered her head with her purse, and sprinted to the car, reenergized. She couldn't explain why Ray would care about a bunch of personnel files and emails.

But she was going to find out.

CHAPTER TWENTY-ONE

Mary moved her chair over closer to Simon so he felt supported, as Detective Lindenhurst entered the room. He was a beefy blond and came off as older than he probably was, which was probably fortysomething. His face was so fleshy that his cheeks pressed against the bottom rims of his oversized aviator glasses, making little red marks on his face. The lines that traveled from his large, flat nose to the sides of his mouth were deep, as if he frowned a lot, which Mary suspected was an occupational hazard for a homicide detective.

"We're ready to get started if you are, Detective," Mary said, putting her legal pad and pen in her lap.

"I appreciate that. Can we hold on a sec for my partner, Detective Chang?"

"Sure."

"Thank you." Detective Lindenhurst smiled in a friendly way as he eased his large frame into the chair opposite her, looking from her to Simon. "Simon, you look like you could use a coffee or a bottled water. Are you sure I can't get you anything?"

"No thanks," Simon answered, his tone subdued.

"By the way, I didn't get to say this at the hospital, but I know

what it's like to have a sick child. My five-year-old niece had
bone cancer. She was at CHOP, too. It's hard to see a child go
through that kind of treatment. My wife used to say it was
harder on us than it was on my niece, but I didn't agree. At least
we understood what was happening and why. She didn't."

"How is your niece?" Simon asked, interested.

"Happily, she recovered. They're terrific at CHOP."

"Good to know," Mary interjected, breaking up Detective
Lindenhurst's attempt to connect with Simon. Being a person
of interest placed him in a legal purgatory, in that he wasn't
under arrest but he was nevertheless in custody. It wasn't completely to his benefit, since not all the constitutional protections
applied, and the police would try to make him feel relaxed,
as if nothing he could say would hurt him, when in fact the
opposite was true.

Suddenly the door opened, and Detective Chang came in
with a smile. He was younger, of compact build, and reserved.
His dark hair shone with gel, and his build looked slight in a
dark jacket. He sat down against the wall, ceding the floor to
Detective Lindenhurst. "Folks, sorry I'm late. Hope you didn't
wait for me."

Mary didn't bother to reply. "Detective Lindenhurst, can we
first clarify my client's status? I understand that he's a person
of interest, but why?"

"We're in possession of facts that lead us to believe he may
know something about the death of Todd Eddington. We'd
like to explore that with him. That's all." Detective Lindenhurst
shrugged his heavy shoulders, and Mary knew that he didn't
want to start the interview on this basis, which was why she
wanted to, to remind Simon that in this case, the policeman was
not his friend.

"But you're not arresting him. That means those facts must
fall short of probable cause to believe that he committed the
crime."

"Yes, exactly." Detective Lindenhurst pursed his lips, which were thick. "This is just an investigatory interview. You both are free to come and go at any time."

"But it is custodial interrogation."

"That's a harsh way to put it."

"But is it accurate? Will you Mirandize him, for example?"

"Yes, but only out of an abundance of caution. You understand."

"I do," Mary said, hearing that she had good reason to be concerned.

"And we will ask Simon to provide some samples before he leaves today."

"What sort of samples?" Mary asked, though she knew. She wanted it spelled out for Simon.

"A hair sample, blood, saliva, fingerprints, and a DNA sample. Only a mouth swab." Detective Lindenhurst turned to Simon. "This is standard operating procedure, as a point of information."

Mary interjected again, "You're not asking for his consent, are you? Because we're not consenting to a search for bodily evidence."

Detective Lindenhurst looked back at Mary. "We're not asking for consent. We have a warrant."

Mary masked her dismay. That meant the police had enough facts to raise probable cause to get a search warrant, but not yet an arrest warrant. "I'd like to see that before we produce the samples."

"Of course, after we speak." Detective Lindenhurst hesitated. "I suppose it makes sense to get these preliminaries out of the way first. In that vein, we would also appreciate him leaving his shirt and pants with us and we will provide him with a sweat suit to wear home."

"Fine," Mary said, having no choice but to agree. She had warned Simon that the police might make the request, so he knew not to overreact, and he didn't. The police lab would look for fibers from Simon's clothes in Todd's car and, given that there had been a fight, they would find some. For the same reason, they would probably find fibers and DNA from Todd's clothes and body in Simon's car. It would be strong physical evidence against Simon.

"We also have a search warrant for his home, office, and car. Just to verify, you reside at 2938 Holly Lane, Horsham, PA, correct?"

"Yes."

Mary let it go. The police were entitled to ask for basic information and there was no point in fighting when it didn't matter.

"And you are employed by OpenSpace, correct?"

"Until recently."

Detective Lindenhurst nodded. "The home and office are currently being searched, but we assume the car's in the parking lot at CHOP, correct?"

"Yes," Simon answered.

"And you drive a 2013 Ford Explorer, with the license plate TRAIN1."

"Yes." Simon smiled uncomfortably. "I collect trains."

Mary knew Simon collected trains, but she hadn't known about the vanity plate.

"And we have a warrant to search your phone, so I'd like to have that before you go."

"Fine," Mary nodded, and Simon didn't react, having been made aware.

"Bear with me a moment." Detective Lindenhurst turned to the rickety table, picked up some blank forms, and recited the Miranda rights to Simon, then took him through the standard form, acknowledging that he'd been read his rights. The detective had Simon sign it, then set the forms aside.

Mary went first. "Detective Lindenhurst, I don't want to

waste your time. My client is not going to answer any questions in this interview today."

"I haven't even asked one. Why don't you give it a chance?"

"I think a better way to proceed is for you to let us know why you called us in here."

"Okay, we'll do it your way." Detective Lindenhurst sighed heavily, leaning back in his chair. "As you know, Todd Eddington was employed before his death as sales manager at Open-Space and your client reported to him until Mr. Eddington terminated him a few days ago."

Mary noted he didn't emphasize the causal connection because he didn't have to.

"We are aware that your client has made clear he intends to sue, claiming that his termination was unlawful. His proof is certain statements he alleges were made by Mr. Eddington."

Mary didn't interrupt him, and he wasn't telling anything they didn't know already, which was the only reason he was telling it. It was way too soon for them to have made headway on their investigation.

"We are also aware that Simon was served today with the countersuit for defamation based on his alleged statements about Mr. Eddington, and that he became very upset when he was served."

Mary hadn't known that Simon had reacted badly, but she could've guessed it. Simon didn't move, listening quietly, his hands linked in his lap.

"As you may have heard, Todd Eddington was found dead in his car at approximately seven o'clock this evening. An autopsy is being conducted and until it is complete, we will not know the official manner of death. But the cause is a mortal stab wound to the chest. We think, three wounds, but that's not official."

"How do you know there were three?" Mary didn't know if he would answer, but you couldn't blame a girl for asking. Bennie would have.

"I was at the scene. I saw the body." Detective Lindenhurst's upper lip curled, and Mary guessed it had been a gruesome sight.

"Do you happen to know if he had his wallet or his watch?"

"He had both."

Mary drew the same conclusion that the police must have, that it wasn't a robbery. But for them, it made it more likely that Simon had done it. "Is it still an active crime scene?"

"Yes, until we close it."

"I'd like to go there, as soon as possible."

"We can arrange that."

"Have you found the knife that was used?" Mary took another shot. She was on a roll, probably because Detective Lindenhurst wanted to see if Simon would confess in return for a plea deal.

"No, we are actively looking for it. We expect to do better when the rain lets up."

Mary made a mental note. If the knife was disposed of outside, the rain might contaminate any physical evidence on the knife, like blood or DNA. "So obviously, you've ruled out suicide?"

"Yes." Detective Lindenhurst shook his head. "The medical examiner hasn't officially classified the death a homicide yet, as I say, but we saw no reason to delay talking with you and your client as soon as possible after Mr. Eddington's body was found."

"And why my client? Why call us in, as I asked before?"

"We have spoken with officials at the Tomahawk Country Club and we have determined that security camera footage shows your client's Ford Explorer entering the parking lot at 5:25 P.M. and leaving approximately twenty minutes later, at 5:50 P.M."

"How can you be sure it's his car? It's been a torrential downpour tonight. The visibility must be terrible."

"It's good enough to make out the vanity plate."

"So you have footage of the entrance and exit to the parking lot?"

"Yes."

"How about the parking lot itself?"

"We have most of the parking lot."

"Were there other cars in the lot?"

"Yes."

"How many?"

"Five."

"Have you questioned those drivers?" Mary said, though she had just gained a bit of valuable information.

"We're in the process of investigating." Detective Lindenhurst straightened in the chair, crossing his legs to reveal the leathery edge of an ankle holster. "However, the corner in which Mr. Eddington parked was out of range of the camera. He seemed to have parked at the farthermost point of the lot." The detective turned to Simon. "So where were you between five and eight o'clock today? Were you driving your car, or was somebody else?"

Mary interjected, "My client is not going to answer that or any other question."

Detective Lindenhurst continued, still facing Simon, "And if you were driving your car, did you meet Mr. Eddington and if so, what happened?"

Mary answered for Simon, "My client is not going to answer any of those questions. So you need to stop looking at him and start looking at me."

Detective Lindenhurst turned to her. "It would be in his benefit to talk to us," he said, keeping his tone light.

"Why is that?" Mary asked, keeping her tone light too.

"Let me explain to you how I see it, Mary." Detective Lindenhurst leaned over, his expression softening. "You practice civil law, and I happen to know that you tried to settle this case.

I admire that. I like when lawyers try to settle civil cases. Why do they do that, would you mind telling me?"

"Because it's easier than going to court." Mary knew where he was going, but it didn't make any difference. It wasn't going to change anything she did.

"That's what I thought. It saves everybody time. It saves the court's time too. The same thing applies here. I know you're with the Rosato firm and your combined experience in criminal defense is considerable. We can make a deal with your client and settle this matter, not unlike the deals that get made everyday in civil law, even the one you tried to make between your client and Todd Eddington."

"Correction. The dispute, and any settlement, would not have been between my client and Mr. Eddington. It was between my client and his former employer."

"That's a technical difference."

Mary thought of what Bennie had told her, borrowing the line: "I'm a lawyer, and the technicalities protect legal rights."

"But there was clearly resentment between your client and his boss, with accusations and cross-accusations over his termination."

"That seems argumentative, and I'm not here to argue."

"I don't want to argue either." Detective Lindenhurst gestured at the closed door. "We could step outside and talk about the terms of the deal. I wouldn't usually discuss that in front of your client."

"We're not interested in a deal, thank you." Mary thought a minute. "Detective Lindenhurst, let me ask you a question. You're telling me that you found Todd Eddington stabbed three times. That would suggest to me that whoever killed him probably got blood on their clothes and hands. Am I right?"

"Often, that's the case."

Mary gestured at Simon's hands, still linked in his lap. "You can see for yourself that my client doesn't have any blood on his hands or clothes."

"He could've washed up and changed his clothes at the hospital. Like many parents, he keeps a change of clothes there. They even have a shower for parents. I know from my sister, from when my niece was there."

"But he was wearing the same clothes this morning. I know because I met with him." Mary flashed on the scene at the hospital this morning, when she had been given the locket. So much had happened since then, the world had turned upside down. But she kept her head in the game. "As his lawyer, I can't be a fact witness, but I'm sure any nurse or doctor at the hospital could tell you that he had these clothes on, and so would their security cameras. Have you checked them?"

Detective Lindenhurst shook his head, his mouth a tight line. "Not yet, but we certainly will."

"In fact, when we give samples later, I'd like you to photograph my client's hands and clothes, to document that he had no blood on him."

"We intended to do that, that's standard operating procedure."

"And in addition, I know that when there's a stabbing, the killer can often wound himself, since blood can get slippery." Mary suppressed her revulsion at the thought to make her point. "Simon, turn your hands over and show Detective Lindenhurst."

"Okay." Simon raised his hands and flipped the palms up, and there were no wounds or cuts.

Mary asked, "See what I mean?"

"I didn't kill anybody, I didn't kill him!" Simon blurted out, and Mary shot him a warning glance, though it was so spontaneous that it rang true. She could only hope that Detective Lindenhurst remembered it when incriminating physical evidence began to roll in.

"Detective, if you don't have enough to arrest my client, and I don't believe you do, then we will give the required samples and leave." Mary stood up, cueing Simon to rise by touching his arm.

Detective Lindenhurst rose, with a frown. "So you're ending the interview."

"Yes."

"Well, then, I hope we'll be talking again, very soon." Detective Lindenhurst turned to Simon. "And of course, I'm asking you not to leave the jurisdiction for the near future."

Simon nodded, his expression shaken, but he didn't say anything.

Detective Lindenhurst looked down at Mary. "We'll go down the hallway to the nurse for the samples."

"I'll go with you," Mary said, then she and Simon left the room with the detectives, who opened a door and led them down a back hallway to the police lab.

Mary's thoughts raced, all the while. She worried it wouldn't be long before Simon was arrested, and if that happened, she didn't want to think about what would happen to Rachel. Murder wasn't a bailable offense, so Simon would go directly to jail, leaving Rachel without her one and only parent. Mary could only imagine the heartbreak it would cause Feet, Simon's cousins, and her own family.

Mary realized she had her work cut out for her. She had to find out who killed Todd, and the clock was ticking. While Simon was in the lab, she heard a text alert from her phone, so she reached into her purse and checked the screen. It was from Bennie:

at the office if you need me

CHAPTER TWENTY-TWO

Bennie got off the elevator, brushing raindrops off her suit as she made a beeline for the two cardboard boxes stacked on the floor, expecting them to contain the files that were in hard copy. She had already checked her email in the car to find that OpenSpace had emailed her Simon's emails for the past three years. She hadn't had the chance to read through them on the drive, but she had saved the entire file to Dropbox. It had been surprisingly large, but she remembered that Todd and Ray had called Simon the Mad Emailer.

Bennie went to the first box, checking that the mailing label read OpenSpace, then cut the masking tape with her car key, opened the top box, and looked inside. It contained a stack of purchase orders from earlier in the year, which had evidently been photocopied from the originals. She rifled through the rest of the papers in the box, and determined that they were all POs. She went to the second box, opened it, and they were full of POs too. She went to the third and the fourth, which contained call logs, then closed the box.

Bennie straightened up, reassessing the situation. She had hoped to be able to read the documents and copy them herself, but that wasn't going to work. She eyed the full boxes, estimating that it had taken the secretaries at OpenSpace a few hours to photocopy. Nate had said that he would send a courier to her office first thing tomorrow morning, and so there was only one thing to do: Call in reinforcements.

Fifteen minutes later, Bennie was standing at the Xerox machine outside her office, copying a purchase order, when Judy Carrier bopped down the hall, looking oddly energized for so late at night. Bennie turned slightly, but kept at her task. "Thanks for coming in."

"Not a problem." Judy smiled, reaching her, and the light from the Xerox machine flashed on her face like a corporate strobe. "Hey, you should close the cover when you photocopy things."

"I don't have time." Bennie took the PO off the glass, set it aside, and reached for the next email, pressing the button. The photocopier light went off again.

"It's bad for your eyes. Your skin, too. You could get photo-allergic dermatitis, I read that somewhere."

"I'll live."

"It also uses up the toner." Judy slid the photocopy out of the tray and placed it facedown on the pile, and Bennie placed the next PO on the glass, hitting the button.

"I'll buy more."

"It's bad for the environment."

Bennie looked over. "Why are you so wide-awake? Please tell me it's not cocaine."

"I've been weaving. It makes me happy. It's a natural high." Judy's eyes flared slightly. "I saw Mary on TV. I assume she's still at the Roundhouse. I texted her offering to help but she didn't text back."

"So did I."

"You did? That was nice of you." Judy slid the copy from the tray and placed it on the pile.

"I'm a nice person. I just get bad press." Bennie put another

PO on the machine and hit the button. "I'm copying the first box of documents, and there's four more in the reception area. If you could get started on a box, that would be great. They're going back to Dumbarton first thing in the morning."

"Because Nate fired you?" Judy slid the copy from the tray.

"Yes."

"Does he know you're copying them?"

"What do you think?" Bennie hit the button to photocopy another PO.

Judy smiled. "How did we get them in the first place?"

"Your basic corporate miscommunication."

"Why do we want them?"

"Because Nate doesn't want us to have them. I don't know if they're useful or meaningless. I'm hoping there's something in them that can help Mary."

Judy met Bennie's eye with hope. "Does this mean that you guys made up?"

"We weren't in a fight."

"You're getting a divorce." Judy slid the copy from the tray.

"I wanted to save the marriage, she didn't." Bennie started another photocopy.

"Maybe she will now."

"Let's worry about Pensiera. That's the priority. She's going to have her hands full with the murder case, and the other case is going to take a backseat."

"What other case?" Judy frowned. "I thought there was only the one case, the ADA case."

"They filed a retaliatory suit for defamation."

"Yikes!" Judy slid the copy from the tray. "How do you know that? I didn't even know that. It must have happened when I was out this afternoon. I had to be home for the loom delivery."

"I read the pleadings online. We can put our heads together when she gets here." Bennie hit the button on another PO.

"Can we order lo mein? We always order lo mein when we work late. It's our food reward."

"Yes, fine, whatever. Could you please go start Xeroxing? Use the copier in the coffee room. I really don't need you to help me Xerox. I have a J.D."

"Okay, but I'm closing the cover." Judy hustled off.

Half an hour later, Bennie was still feeding copies into the Xerox machine, with Judy doing the same thing in the coffee room, except that her ears were plugged with earphones while she listened to music. It meant that Bennie was the only one to hear the *ping* coming from the elevator lobby, signaling that Mary had arrived. Bennie turned from the machine and went to meet her, and Mary appeared at the head of the hallway, carrying her belongings and a big brown bag with grease spots in the bottom, the Chinese food.

"Hi, Mary." Bennie forced a smile. She felt awkward, which surprised her. Seeing her soon-to-be-ex-partner provoked emotions in her that she thought she had put away today. She briefly considered telling Mary that she'd been fired by Dumbarton, but that wouldn't have helped anything, as a legal matter. Bennie had worked for Dumbarton, so her being fired by them, especially for disloyalty, didn't cure her conflict of interest. Plus if Mary really wanted to leave the firm, Bennie didn't want to guilt her into staying. Besides, they had a murder case on their hands.

"Hi, Bennie," Mary called back, and to Bennie, her smile seemed equally forced. Mary looked around quickly. "Where's Judy?"

"She's in the coffee room." Bennie put her hands out for the Chinese food bag, which smelled like curry. "Here, I'll take that bag and I'll bring it in the conference room, so you can go get her."

"Sure, thanks." Mary handed her the bag, and Bennie accepted it, turned away, and entered the conference room.

She unpacked the white containers of rice, plastic tubs for the noodles and other entrees, chopsticks, and paper plates and napkins, then made place settings around the table, as she heard Judy and Mary talking excitedly in the coffee room.

Bennie stood around, waiting for them, and realized why she felt so awkward. It was disorienting, not knowing her role. She had a partner, but then again she didn't. She also had an associate, but the associate might become her partner. She was here to work on a murder case, but for the first time ever, the case was Mary's and she was working for Mary, like an associate. And she didn't even know if she was wanted. Maybe Declan had been right.

"Hey, guys, listen—" Bennie blurted out, as Judy and Mary came into the room together.

"Yes?" Mary asked.

"What is it?" Judy blinked.

"I just wanted to say, I guess to Mary, that I'm here to help. I don't know if you feel like you need my help, or if you want my help, but I'm here. If you don't, just say so, and I can just go." Bennie realized she was practically babbling, but Mary started smiling in a soft way.

"Bennie, no, don't go. Thank you so much for being here. I should've said something right off, but I was so touched when I got your text. This is really above and beyond, especially after, well, what I said about leaving the firm. I'm glad you're here and I can use the help."

"Good, because a murder defense takes some doing, and if he's just a person of interest, you only have a small window of time that you can work in. You need to move quickly and back them off"—Bennie caught herself taking charge, so she dialed it back—"anyway, that's why I'm here. I'm assuming it's all hands on deck."

"It is, that's exactly what it is." Mary nodded, looking

relieved. "I appreciate the help and I need help, I just didn't want to ask for it in the circumstances."

"So let's not even worry about our partnership right now. This time we really can agree to disagree." Bennie sensed it had to be said, and if so, it had to come from her. "Let's worry about the thing that really matters, your client, your friend Simon."

"That would be so great!" Mary brightened.

"And the thing is, I recognize this is your case, so I'm at your disposal. You run it and you're in charge. You tell me how you think I can help you best."

"That's so nice of you."

"Good." Bennie's chest felt oddly tight, but she ignored that too. Emotions could be such pesky things.

Judy smiled, then pulled up a chair. "So does this mean we can eat?"

"Yes," Bennie and Mary answered in unison.

Mary added, "Why don't you both start eating, and I'll bring you up to speed on everything that happened at the Roundhouse."

"Good. I'll get some coffee." Bennie went to the credenza and started brewing herself a cup.

"Mph," Judy said, her mouth full of noodles.

Bennie drank her coffee and Judy ate lo mein as Mary recounted the events of the day, starting with something about a locket and ending with the interview at the Roundhouse, after which Simon had given bodily samples and surrendered his phone to the police. Bennie listened carefully, and when Mary was finished, she seemed to look at Bennie across the table, with an uncertain smile.

"Well, Bennie? What do you think? I had to make a lot of decisions on the fly and I've never really represented a person of interest."

"I think you did terrific," Bennie said, meaning it. "I wouldn't have made any decision differently."

"That's good to hear." Mary sat straighter.

Judy paused between mouthfuls. "Bennie, what's the deal with a person of interest versus someone who was arrested for the crime?"

"There's differences in the rights accorded each of them, but for our purposes, that's not critical. The critical difference is that with someone already under arrest, the police, DA, and the entire law-enforcement mechanism has bought in. He's their guy and they're invested. They throw the full weight of the Commonwealth against him, all of their resources."

"Okay." Judy nodded, digging through the rice.

"But when you're representing a person of interest, you have a golden opportunity. The police are still gathering evidence and trying to make a decision. They want to do the right thing. They don't want to get the wrong guy, not only because they care, but because the DA wants a conviction. So as defense counsel, right from the beginning, I try to make them doubt their original theory. That's exactly why Mary did the right thing in pointing out the lack of blood on Simon's clothes and his hands." Bennie gestured to Mary. "Same thing going forward. Normally, we might not give them information as we learn it, but with a person of interest, I would funnel to them every single fact we uncover that suggests Simon is not guilty. It will make them think, slow them down, and force them to keep the scope of their investigation as broad as possible."

"That makes sense." Judy glanced up from her plate.

Mary brightened. "So what do you think about their case?"

"I think you're right to be concerned. They have a strong case against Simon, assuming the physical evidence comes in the way you think it's going to, which I think it will. When they look in his phone, they'll see that he called Todd. Given the surveillance video, any jury would believe that Simon initiated a meeting with Todd, met with him, and killed him."

"I know, right?" Mary's face fell again.

"Don't look that way. Buck up. Don't let a little opposition throw you." Bennie felt her juices start flowing, as if the battle had been joined. "Worst-case scenario, he's arrested, but not convicted. You have to fight to win, but we're going to win. He didn't do it."

"But his daughter's in the hospital, and she's waiting to get a transplant. He'll want to be there for her. She might, well, she might not survive."

Bennie hadn't thought of that. She felt the weight of the words in the conference room, which went suddenly silent. Mary swallowed hard, her Chinese food untouched. Judy even stopped chewing.

"Mary." Bennie met Mary's worried gaze. "Don't be upset. Everything is going to be all right. Let me tell you what Judy and I are up to, and what I learned today. But believe me, after we have gathered all of our information and understood every detail, we are going to fight and we are going to win."

"You think?"

"I know," Bennie answered, then filled her in. As she spoke, she could see Mary regain her emotional footing, nodding as she listened. When Bennie was finished, she reminded herself again that she wasn't in charge and had signed on to be second-chair to Mary's first. "So Mary, got any theories?"

"I think someone was trying to frame Simon. Todd's watch and wallet weren't taken, so it wasn't a random crime, and it wouldn't be if the killer was Simon. And I think somebody wanted Simon out of the company—the reduction in his territory, the eventual firing, it's like it was all part of a plan. Simon thought it was because of Rachel's medical expenses, so we sued. But what if it wasn't? What if Todd just said those things to cover up the real reason they wanted Simon out? And it culminates in framing him for murder."

"Then why deny the statements?"

"To provoke Simon to sue. They knew he couldn't take it lying down because of Rachel."

Bennie wasn't sure. "In that theory, Todd doesn't really matter. The target is Simon."

"Right. We just don't know why."

"The other possibility is that somebody had reason to want Todd dead, irrespective of Simon. The fact that these events are temporally connected doesn't mean that they're causally connected."

Judy plowed through her rice. "Huh? I can't think when I'm eating."

Bennie smiled. "The fact that they happen in the same time doesn't mean that there is a logical, causal relationship. It could be that the killer uses the litigation with Simon to his own ends and seizes the opportunity to kill Todd."

"I'm following," Mary said, nodding.

"We know that a lot of people knew about happy hour at the club and where Todd parked. So either somebody knew Todd would be there and they didn't know that Simon was coming, or somebody knew Simon was coming and they framed him. The question is, who would want Todd dead?"

"Do you have any guesses, Bennie?" Mary leaned forward. "You met Todd, at least. I know more about Simon than you do. We just have to put our information together."

Bennie mulled it over. "The framing theory is interesting, because motive is so clearly established with the lawsuits and Simon's termination. Simon looks like the typical disgruntled employee who snaps and kills his boss. Either way, the killer has to be somebody who knows that Todd parks in the same place and goes to happy hour on Friday, rain or shine. That means it's somebody in Todd's circle of friends, maybe at work. Or circle at the club."

Mary perked up. "To me, the logical place to start would be the two men who made allegations about Simon in the defamation complaint. Ernie and Ray. They were both willing to lie about Simon in the lawsuit and back each other up. That seems fishy, doesn't it?"

"Agree. I met Ray at the interview. Kind of a close-mouthed, no-nonsense operations guy. And Ernie called Mike Bashir about the cops and the search warrant."

Mary nodded, excited. "We should narrow in on them when we go through the documents and emails."

"Okay." Bennie got on the same page. "So what's the plan of action?"

"In the morning, we go to the crime scene. I set it up for ten o'clock and I'd like you to go with me."

"I will." Bennie felt pleased.

Mary turned to Judy. "You stay here, okay? You make sure all the docs are boxed and that courier gets them. Do you mind doing all the Xeroxing tonight?"

"Fine with me." Judy nodded, chewing away. "But I'm keeping the lid closed. I'm not a fan of radiation, unlike somebody we know."

Mary blinked. "What lid?"

"On the machine. I don't want a third ovary."

"Forget it," Bennie interjected. "Mary, you were saying?"

Mary faced Bennie. "I think you should take the sales info, and I should take the email. I'll eliminate the emails that are irrelevant, then make a document index like we do on any big civil case, classifying the relevant documents by subject, using a keyword, and making it searchable by subject."

"Right, do it down and dirty. Narrow it down to the past six months, for starters. I'll learn everything about Simon's sales and we can put our facts together."

"Yes." Mary rose with a smile. "I got a second wind!"

"Me, too." Bennie stood up, opposite her. "Let's get to work."

"Can I have the last spring roll?" Judy asked, but the others were already leaving.

CHAPTER TWENTY-THREE

Mary slipped into bed at five in the morning, her sheets cool and her bedroom dark. She felt exhausted and depressed, having barely made a dent in Simon's emails, and Bennie had felt the same way, since all she had managed to do was plot Simon's call logs, purchase orders, and other sales information on Excel spreadsheets. They had both left the office to sleep for an hour or so before they had to get up, shower, and leave for the crime scene. Poor Judy had stayed behind to Xerox her heart out, make the deadline for the courier, and then go home and sleep in.

Mary pulled the cotton blanket up slowly, not to wake up Anthony, and her eyes hadn't adjusted to the darkness yet, so she could only see the outline of his shoulders, his body turned away. He must've been as tired as she was, since he had been at her parents' house after the news broke about Simon's being taken in for questioning. She had texted him to go over and try to keep her parents' blood pressures in a normal range. She hoped he had succeeded. Otherwise she hadn't had a chance to catch him up on anything.

Anthony stirred, shifting around to face her in the darkness. "Honey?" he asked softly, running a hand lightly down her arm.

"Oh, hi. I thought you were asleep." Mary shifted closer to his chest, feeling the warmth coming off of his skin. She always said that he ran hot, like a furnace. "When did you get home?"

"About two hours ago."

"Oh no, later than I thought. Were they upset?"

"Yes. My mother was there too. It's a lot for them. I'm glad I went."

"I'm glad you did, too, thanks so much."

"You must be beat." Anthony rested his arm around her.

"Not a great day." Mary nestled closer to him, turning her head to the side.

"You want to fill me in? I can't sleep anyway. I feel terrible for Simon. He's the gentlest guy in the world. It's impossible to think that he would kill his boss, or even hurt his boss. He'd never hurt anybody."

"I know."

"Is he okay? How is he?"

"He's hanging in. He did well with the police. I left him at the hospital with his dad. They have each other. We went back to the office and Bennie and Judy helped with his defense. Right now he's just a person of interest, not really a suspect or even arrested, so we're going to do everything we can to make sure that doesn't happen, or at least delay it."

"I'm sure you will, you guys make a great team."

"Right." Mary realized that Anthony didn't even know about the disciplinary charges against her or that she was leaving the firm. Or *considering* leaving the firm. She felt a guilty twinge inside, because they had agreed to make big decisions jointly, since she had a tendency to operate like the single girl she used to be. "I guess I should mention that, well, it did come up today that I might have to think about leaving the firm."

Anthony chuckled softly. "That's funny."

"Anthony, I'm not kidding."

"What are you talking about?"

Mary braced herself. "It's kind of a long story."

"I have time. Are you serious? Tell me what's going on. How can you leave your own firm?" Anthony edged away, and Mary was beginning to discern his features in the dark, his eyes widening and his lips forming a disbelieving O.

"I don't have to make a decision yet. We're tabling the discussion for now."

"Who's we?"

"Bennie and me."

"You already discussed this with Bennie? What about me and you?" Anthony asked, sounding hurt. "Don't we get to discuss it?"

"Of course, it's just that everything happened so fast today. You and I will definitely discuss it, when the time comes."

"When will the time come? This is a huge decision."

"After we get over the hump with Simon. I'm trying to keep him out of jail." Mary kept her tone patient, but she felt too drained to discuss it now. All she wanted was some sleep, so she wouldn't be a wreck.

"How did this even come up? Mary, if you're serious, how will we support ourselves?"

"I would open my own firm."

"You would do what?" Anthony propped himself up on his elbow, fully awake. "When did this happen? What are you even talking about? How can you go out on your own?"

Mary stifled her irritability, which was growing. It wasn't necessarily directed at him because he had a right to ask everything he was asking, but just not now. "I think it can be done. If Simon's civil cases go forward, that's the only time it comes into play. But I do have a client base. I think they'll go with me."

"But it takes money. You have to rent an office. You have to pay overhead. You need start up costs."

"I know that—"

"—and I don't have a job right now."

"I know that too but—"

"—and we don't have the savings that we used to, not since we bought the house—"

"Anthony, I know all that," Mary shot back, more harshly than she intended.

"We've been talking about having a baby. Really trying. How would that work? We keep putting it off?"

"No, I want a baby, too."

"So how do you have a baby and start a new firm?"

"I don't know."

"You're not superwoman."

"No, I'm not. I'm just too tired to talk about it now, okay? I just am."

"Fine." Anthony turned over, facing away from her. "You and Bennie let me know when you want to talk about it."

"Anthony, really?"

"I'm going back to sleep."

CHAPTER TWENTY-FOUR

Bennie slipped into bed in the darkness, stretching out in the center of the mattress and breathing a relieved sigh. She remembered reading about the pleasures of the unshared bed and sometimes she felt that to her core. Sometimes it was good to have a whole bed to yourself. Like when you had worked all night on somebody else's case and secretly worried that an innocent man was about to be arrested for a crime that he didn't commit.

She reached for the night table for her phone, which was becoming her dirty little nighttime habit. She knew about the articles saying that you shouldn't check your phone before sleep, but some days it was the only time she could catch up on her email or the national news, and tonight her brain was in overdrive.

She looked at the phone screen, noticing for the first time that she had gotten a text from Declan, and she clicked through.

Call me when you get in, no matter how late. Love you.

Bennie felt herself smile. It was sweet of him. He was a thoughtful guy. She felt a rush of love, remembering that she had had sex earlier. She had almost forgotten. How can you forget that you had sex? This might've been the wackiest day she ever spent in her life. She pressed the number to call him back, and Declan answered after one ring.

"Woman, where you been?"

Bennie liked when he called her that, even though it was corny, vaguely sexist, or both. "Did we have sex today? Or was it my imagination?"

Declan chuckled softly. "Wait, was that you? Are you the blonde?"

Bennie laughed too. "What are you doing still up?"

"Thinking about you."

"Nice things?" Bennie snuggled down in the sheets, liking the sound of it. She didn't know if this call would lead to phone sex, but there were worse ways to blow off steam. And phone sex was the best of both worlds. You got the sex but didn't have to share the bed.

"I was thinking you should let Mary go out on her own."

"Way to kill the mood."

"Sorry but I'm on fire."

"So am I." Bennie chuckled, but Declan didn't.

"I've been thinking about it. What was it like when you went back? Did she need you?"

"I'm not sure that she needed me, but she was happy that I was there to help."

"How did she do at the Roundhouse by herself?"

"Very well. Great, in fact."

"That's my point. She's a fine lawyer. She has to find it out for herself."

"I know that, and she will. I'm just helping her." Bennie didn't get it. Declan usually didn't care about office politics. "What's gotten into you?"

"I'm bothered."

"Why?"

"I think she's too used to turning to you. She's used to you filling the gap. If she wants to go out on her own, let her go. You'll be fine."

"Do we have to talk about this now?"

"Why not? It's important."

"It's late at night." Bennie was trying to get her mojo back.

"I'm not sleepy."

"I'm not either."

"I don't like you being taken advantage of. Mary's taking advantage of you."

"No, she's not," Bennie said, defensive.

"Yes, she is. You like her, so you don't see it."

"I thought you liked her, too."

"I do. But I think you should let her move on. I wouldn't keep a partner who wasn't committed to me."

"She's committed to me."

"How can you say that?" Declan kept his tone even, but he sounded annoyed. "She junked the partnership to represent a friend."

"That's not true."

"Babe. What's the status of your partnership?"

"We tabled it for now."

"Junked."

"Tabled isn't the same as junked."

Declan snorted. "Same difference. Either way, you're left hanging. She just can't come and go when she pleases. One day she's in, one day she's not. On her terms. She should have to fish or cut bait. That's what you want in a partner. Commitment."

Suddenly Bennie wasn't sure they were talking about Mary anymore. "Declan, is this about us?"

"Maybe," Declan answered after a minute.

"Really?" Bennie felt a tug in her chest. "I thought everything was going so great. We had such a good day."

"You dropped in, out of the blue. You said you were staying the weekend, then you left. Maybe it was a good day for you. It wasn't such a good day for me."

"Wow, really." Bennie didn't know what to say. He was right, which made it worse.

"Long-distance gets old, babe. Today didn't help. I miss you. It was nice having you here. I'm unhappy you left. I don't like sleeping alone."

Sometimes I do, Bennie thought but didn't say. "Declan, do we really need to talk about our relationship now?"

"Why not? You said you weren't tired."

"I'm too tired to talk about our relationship. I'm not too tired to talk about anything else." Bennie was trying to lighten the mood.

"I guess it bugs me." Declan's tone softened. "I dropped everything when you said you were coming. Canceled two conference calls."

"I didn't know that. You said you weren't busy. You told me to come ahead."

"I thought you were staying."

Bennie sighed, suddenly exhausted. She'd thought she was kidding about being too tired to talk about their relationship, but now it was true. "Look, I'm sorry."

"Let's get some sleep."

"That's a good idea. Love you."

"You, too," Declan said, hanging up.

CHAPTER TWENTY-FIVE

TOMAHAWK COUNTRY CLUB read the bronze letters in a stone wall, and Mary drove onto the property with Bennie in the passenger seat. They were both in lightweight suits, which was the only thing they had in common. Boring clothes.

"People love golf," Bennie said idly.

"Have you ever played?"

"No, I row. It's the sport that's the most like work."

Mary smiled. She liked when Bennie was self-deprecating, which wasn't often. In contrast, Mary herself raised self-deprecation to an art form. And liked it that way, frankly. "I never golfed in my life. I'm from South Philly."

Bennie smiled, and they pulled up at a stone gatehouse, where an older guard opened a small window. "Good morning," he said with a smile.

Mary introduced them both, then said, "We're here to see the crime scene. The police are expecting us."

"Fine." The guard tsked-tsked. "Such a terrible shame about Mr. Eddington. We all liked him. Nothing like that ever happened here before. Everybody's upset. Members and muckety-mucks, you know."

"I'm sure. And I know Todd loved it here. Every Friday night he was here, no matter what, right?"

"Yes." The guard nodded. "Like clockwork."

"Did he usually come with anyone?"

"Usually alone. He met his foursome if he played in the morning."

"His usual foursome? Guys from the office?" Mary took a flyer. "Like Ernie or Ray Matewicz?"

"Don't know those names." The guard shook his head. "I think he golfed with customers mostly. Mr. Davis, Mr. Cullen, Mr. Nustrall. Mr. Gallagher used to join but not lately. That's who I remember. They'll miss him."

Mary made a mental note of the names. "Were you here last night, the night he was killed? Did you see him come in?"

"No, that's not my shift. I'm off at four."

"Oh, who's shift is it?"

"The police already asked me that." The guard frowned. "Hey, did you say you were with the police?"

"Not exactly, thanks," Mary said, hitting the gas. "Take care now."

"Well done." Bennie smiled as they drove off.

"Thanks. Can't blame a girl for asking, right?"

"Exactly." They both laughed, and Mary steered up a winding asphalt driveway that bisected an immense front lawn, its grass so uniformly short and green that it could've been Astroturf. It was a beautiful day, the sun climbing a cloudless blue sky and in another mood, she would've felt good. They approached a large putting green on the left, where golfers practiced in complete absorption, their heads down.

Bennie looked around. "This will be a different kind of crime scene."

"I know. It's hard to believe somebody was killed here." Mary drove them past a lovely Tudor mansion of gray stone with hatched windows and a gabled slate roof. A quaint wooden sign identified it as the clubhouse, and golfers were coming in and out in groups, talking and laughing.

"The parking lot's around the back," Bennie said.

"How do you know?"

"I Google-mapped it."

Mary looked over, surprised. "That was a good idea. I should've thought of that."

Bennie shrugged it off. "It had a street-view photo, but it was taken in winter. I think it will be different in summer. We'll see."

Mary felt guilty that Bennie was being so helpful and kept trying to put the partnership dispute to the back of her mind, but wasn't succeeding. Bennie had worked her butt off last night, digging into the case, organizing the files, and setting up a war room in the conference room. She had even taken orders from Mary, who was trying to get used to being the one giving orders. It felt strange to be the driver of a car in which Bennie Rosato was a passenger, both literally and figuratively.

Bennie pointed to the right. "Go that way, it's back there."

"Thanks." Mary slowed to let a golf cart go by, then followed the curve around the clubhouse. To her left was a set of tennis courts, already full of singles and doubles players, and beyond that, just ahead, on the left was a driving range that had golfers whacking the ball into the distance.

"This is the first parking lot," Bennie said, gesturing, and Mary looked around to see a large parking lot shaped like a square, mostly already full.

"I guess people get here early to avoid the heat."

"Probably."

"That's it, up ahead." Mary drove forward and pointed to a secondary parking lot beyond the large one, a smaller square that was completely empty and cordoned off by yellow crime-scene tape, a grisly note that was incongruous in the lovely, exclusive setting.

"I see."

Mary fell silent. A man had died here, horribly. The thought made her sick inside, even though Simon could be on the hook. Murder would always be more than a crime to her. It was a sin.

"You okay?" Bennie asked, cocking her head.

"Yes." Mary shook it off. A single police cruiser idled at the entrance to the secondary parking lot, and inside sat a uniformed policeman, probably running the air conditioner.

"Where does Todd park again?" Bennie asked. "In the very last spot?"

"Yes, in the farthest corner." Mary cruised around the perimeter of the first lot. "I'm approaching it the way Simon did, around the outside."

"I don't know if those other cars that were parked here will yield anything."

"Me neither. If the killer knew Todd parked at the far corner and wanted to get him, they'd wait for him in the second lot. No reason to risk being seen running from one car to the next." Mary eyed the empty spot where Todd would have parked, but noticed that on its far side was an expanse of grass, then thick bushes. Beyond that were oak trees. "Look at that, beyond the lot. That's interesting."

"I know what you're thinking. I noticed the same thing." Bennie craned her neck, as Mary pulled up behind the police cruiser.

"The killer could've come on foot, from behind those bushes."

"Yes, that's what I was thinking last night. On Google Maps, the bushes had died back because it was winter. Nobody would've been able to hide there because they would be seen. But in full bloom, those bushes would hide anybody behind them."

"Right." Mary felt her heart beat faster. She cut the ignition and reached for her purse. "We have to see what's on the other side of the bushes and trees. If there's access, then things are looking up."

"Bingo." Bennie and Mary got out of the car, and the uniformed officer emerged from the cruiser, leaving it idling.

"Good morning," the cop said, with a smile. He was older and stocky, with a silvery mustache and thick glasses that covered warm brown eyes. He held a clipboard, and his name tag read PATTERO.

"Officer, I'm Mary DiNunzio and this is my—" Mary stopped herself, then let it go. "My partner Bennie Rosato."

"Nice to meet you both." Officer Pattero handed Mary the clipboard, which held a crime-scene log and an attached ballpoint pen. "Please sign in, and include your address, phone number, and the time and date."

"Sure." Mary filled in the information, then handed it to Bennie, who did the same thing and handed it back.

"Ladies, thank you very much. You're free to look around and take any pictures or measurements you need." Officer Pattero gestured beyond the cordon. "I'll wait in the car and please touch base with me to sign out."

"Thank you," Mary said, ducking under the cordon, with Bennie right behind her.

"I brought a measuring tape."

"Good thinking," Mary said, looking over. "Again, I should've thought of that."

"It's just experience, Mary. Nothing else," Bennie said after a moment, and Mary looked away, touched. She took a few steps forward, then Bennie caught up with her, and both women looked around, taking in the surroundings. The secondary parking lot was completely out of the action. The driving range and tennis courts were way back beyond the other cars, and ahead to the right was the clubhouse in the distance.

Mary turned around and looked up at the metal stanchions that held covered lights, which were located in each aisle of the regular parking lot. "I'm looking for the security cameras."

Bennie turned around, squinting at the covered lights. "I think they're hidden in the lighting fixture. But you can see how the range wouldn't cover the far end of this lot, the secondary lot."

"Right, but it would get the entrance to the primary lot." Mary turned back again to the bushes. "Let's go look there. I'm dying to see what's on the other side."

"Me too. We can measure later." Bennie followed Mary and they fell into stride, walking across the parking lot, into the grass, and stopping at the fringe of the bushes, which automatically felt cooler.

"What kind of bushes are these?" Mary took out her phone and started taking pictures. The bushes were well established and had grown together, making a perfect screen from the parking lot. The photos would be for their own use back at the office, and she'd have to take some better ones later, for trial exhibits. Though she prayed it wouldn't get that far.

"We used to call them sticker bushes." Bennie reached in her purse and pulled out the measuring tape. "I want to see how wide this thicket is."

"Agree, I'll come with. You don't have to go it alone." Mary plunged into the thickets, turning sideways so she didn't disturb it completely. She felt little thorns scratch her legs, and catch her suit jacket, but she kept going. Bennie did the same thing two bushes away, measuring at the same time, and they arrived at the far side of the bushes at roughly the same time.

"Six feet!" Bennie called out, retracting the measuring tape. "These bushes are six feet wide. That's quite a barrier."

"And then there's these trees." Mary looked up, and the oaks were tall, leafed almost all the way down the trunk. There was a grove of them, and the underbrush was thick with weeds and tangled overgrowth. She made her way through the trees, and so did Bennie on the other side, and both women went forward until they cleared the woods.

They found themselves standing on unmowed grass that bordered what appeared to be a service road that led to a metal gate, which stood propped open. Outside the gate was a street, situated perpendicular to the service road, and traffic traveled on the street, which appeared to be public.

"That's good news," Bennie said, shielding her eyes from the sun.

"Agree." Mary squinted, then moved diagonally to get a parallax view and see the end of the service road. "Goes right off the property. It's like a service entrance."

"Nice. We'll double-check it after we leave."

"Could you see this road on Google Maps?"

"Yes."

"So the killer could've looked on Google Maps and seen the road too. At this time of year, he would've known the bushes and trees provided cover. He doesn't have to have come in a car, parked in any lot, or be a member of the club."

"Yes, exactly."

"And given that most people knew of Todd's habits, it broadens the possibilities of who is the killer."

"Agree." Bennie nodded. "I think this would play very well for us before a jury. They have the video of Simon's car, but they can't argue that the access is restricted by the gatehouse or main entrance. All we need to do is raise reasonable doubt."

"Yes. Not that we want to get that far."

"Understood. By the way, I measured and it's about thirty feet of trees. It's the perfect place to lie in wait for someone. And assuming the killer drove here, the bushes would hide his car too. Todd wouldn't see him coming."

"Right," Mary said, heartened.

"Let's go measure the lot and take some pictures."

"You know what I'm doing after that, don't you? I'm going to call Detective Lindenhurst and tell him about the service road. He must have noticed it, but I want him to know that we know. I'm going to be a bug in his ear. Call him every day and tell him something that favors the defense."

"Right." Bennie smiled. "You learned from the master."

Mary laughed, though she wasn't sure Bennie was kidding.

CHAPTER TWENTY-SIX

Bennie took her place beside the easel in the conference room, which she had converted into a war room, her favorite décor. She felt like their defense was getting into gear, her favorite thing. And she had a fresh cup of coffee, her favorite drink. All of her favorites were coming together, and she was in her element, fighting for an innocent defendant in a murder case.

"You ready?" Bennie asked, as Mary sat down, swiveling her chair to face the front. Mary's documents, notes, and laptop occupied the east side of the conference table, and Bennie's documents, notes, and laptop occupied the west. They had decided on the way back to the office that it made sense for them to give each other a progress report on their respective tasks.

"Go for it." Mary popped the top of her Diet Coke.

"Okay." Bennie consulted her notes. "I'll summarize what I learned rather than take you through the Excel spreadsheets and the source data. You can thank me anytime."

"Thank you." Mary smiled.

"Obviously, if we were looking at the defense of an employment discrimination action, I would have focused on Simon's sales performance and that's what I would be breaking down for you. Suffice it to say that the call logs, purchase orders, and sales figures support what Todd was saying, that Simon didn't make quota in his last month, which was June. In other words, the documents back up their claim in the employment discrimination case."

"Which we don't care about right now."

"Right." Bennie consulted her notes. "What I focused on is Todd. I was trying to learn as much as I could about Todd, his sales, and his clients, so we can figure out who or why anybody would want to kill him. I requested department-wide sales figures, which made absolute sense when this was an employment discrimination case, and that includes Todd, who still sells. So we have Todd's sales figures for the past year."

"I didn't realize." Mary perked up.

"Todd told me during our interview that he kept the big clients, he called them his bread-and-butter. Now that I've looked at his sales figures, I know what he meant. OpenSpace manufactures and sells cubicles, and that isn't a business that gets a lot of reorders from the same customers. Not like a paper company or a company that sells office supplies. Understand?"

"Yes."

"The only exception to this is Todd's five top clients, which are growing companies that are opening branches or franchises in the area. So they have the possibility of reorders." Bennie picked up a Sharpie and began writing on the easel paper as she spoke. "They are: Number one, Hartmann Insurance, an insurance brokerage in Wayne. Number two, Your Next Contractor, a call center in King of Prussia and referral service for area contractors. Number three, Anywhere Office in Jenkintown, which rents cubicles and workspaces to people who can't afford to rent an office."

Mary took notes on her laptop.

"Number four, SAT Academy, an SAT prep service out of Devon that's taking over the Main Line, and number five,

Jamison Mackleheeny, LLC, who we both know is a litigation support service that hires contract lawyers for document review in major multidistrict litigation. In other words, a life of indentured servitude."

"Lawyer hell."

"Yes." Bennie nodded. "Now. We learned something very interesting from the guard at the country club today, thanks to you. We learned who golfs in Todd's regular foursome. I wrote the names in my phone. Mr. Davis, Mr. Cullen, Mr. Nustrall, and previously, Mr. Gallagher."

"Right."

"And I looked them up on the way here, while you were on the phone with Detective Lindenhurst. They have LinkedIn accounts and they're in the white pages, and it turns out that two of them are with Todd's top clients. With one exception."

"What's the exception?"

"I'll tell you in a minute. We're going to do this in an orderly fashion." Bennie turned to the poster board and wrote as she spoke. "Rick Davis is the president of Hartmann Insurance, and Brandon Cullen is the owner of Anywhere Office. So who is Mo Nustrall?"

"Who?"

"I looked him up in the white pages online, which gave his last known address as Lansdale, PA. He lives there with his wife, and her maiden name is Linda Matewicz, which is a name you don't forget."

"Is she related to Ray Matewicz?"

"I bet she's his sister. There weren't any other families with that surname in the area."

"Whoa." Mary made a note on her laptop. "So Todd is tight with Ray's brother-in-law."

"That's interesting to me, especially considering that Ray Matewicz is high up at OpenSpace—and also one of the employees claiming that Simon defamed Todd and the company."

"Me, too."

"And if you look up Mo Nustrall, you'll find that he has a LinkedIn account and he's a VP of Sales at PowerPlus, which is another of Dumbarton's subsidiaries."

"Good to know." Mary nodded as she typed.

"That leaves Mr. Gallagher, whom the guard said used to be in the foursome. I looked him up online, but Gallagher is such a common last name and I don't know the first name. There were a lot of corporate and management types in the area named Gallagher, but I cross referenced it with Todd's clients and found Pollstar." Bennie went around the side of the table to her laptop and hit a few buttons. "I remembered something from the sales reports that didn't make sense at the time."

"What?"

"Last year, according to Todd's sales, his number two client was Pollstar, a call center in Willow Grove that conducts polls for political campaigns and business marketing. It struck me as strange that Pollstar was so high up in sales last year, but literally fell off the map this year. I remembered it because the guard said that Gallagher used to be in the foursome, but wasn't lately."

"I'm following."

"I assumed the sales dropped because Pollstar did political polls during the election and that was over. But then, I couldn't figure out why Todd would keep the client, since he prefers the clients that have repeat business." Bennie thought back to the interview with Todd at OpenSpace. "He strikes me as the kind of guy who networks, rather than makes friends."

"Right."

Bennie realized she was a little like that, too. She put it out of her mind. "So he must expect future business from them."

"Where did you say Pollstar was?"

"Willow Grove, why?"

"Hold on. I saw something like that in an email." Mary turned to her document index, reading down the email numbers. "He wrote so many emails and he writes a lot each time. I only got through about two hundred of them, and my document index was broken down into basic subjects."

"What were the subjects?"

"Well, his top clients each got their own subject, and he wrote to Todd about them a lot, and there had been some fussing. Not a big deal, but Simon has a lot of ideas about how the client should be dealt with." Mary spoke as she kept looking through the emails. "For example, when the clients had complaints about the quality, he always sides with the client."

"Not the kind of thing that endears you to bosses."

"No." Mary located the number of the email, then started going through the numbered stack. "In fact, I made a whole subject for quality control because that's what he put on the subject line. He had a lot of those emails to Todd."

"Can I see an example?" Bennie came around the side of the conference table.

"Okay, this is typical." Mary pulled an email from the stack and held it out to Bennie, who read it:

From Simon Pensiera

To Todd Eddington

Re Quality Control

Todd, I'm really concerned about the quality of the woven fabric on #7251, color Vulpine Gray. I know Pasture is bottom-of-the-line but that shouldn't matter. Jorge Jimenez at Neshaminy Business Solutions called me and gave me an earful about it, so I went over and saw what he was talking about. He is right. The weave on the fabric at the base on several of his cubicles is uneven and there is a pull in the fabric on one of them. The fabric wasn't even attached properly, so somebody must've been careless spraying the glue. I think the line is slacking and you should talk to Ray about it. I suggested an on-site repair to Jorge and he is willing to give it a try, but we both know that's not going to do the job.

Bennie handed it back. "I see what you mean. Did Todd write him back?"

"Yes. Hold on." Mary turned to the second stack, produced another email, and showed it to Bennie, who read:

From Todd Eddington
To Simon Pensiera
Re Quality Control

Simon, I'll talk to Ray.

"Does Todd always respond?" Bennie handed it back to Mary.

"No. Sometimes Todd responds to the emails and sometimes he doesn't. I'm assuming Todd also responds by calling Simon, too, and we can ask Simon about that if it matters." Mary gestured at five stacks of emails. "Those are quality control emails, and I divided them according to the nature of the complaint. So far I have fabric, metal, construction, wear and tear, and paper."

"What's paper on a cubicle?"

"There's paper that goes on top of the drywall. Sometimes it's not attached properly. It matters because it doesn't protect the gypsum from moisture loss. I think."

"Gypsum?"

"Gypsum is some type of stone that's in drywall."

"Look at you, learning the lingo."

"I did my homework last night." Mary returned her attention to the stack, thumbed through it, and pulled out another email. "Like this."

Bennie accepted the email, skimming it:

From Simon Pensiera
To Todd Eddington
Re Quality Control

Todd, I happened to walk through the factory floor yesterday on my way to a smoke break and I noticed the drywall on the top-of-the-line product looked funky. The paper was bubbling, which could signify that there was too much water in the drywall. The top-of-the-line product was supposed to be 5/8 inch and be appropriate for noise and firebreak barriers. You should probably talk to Ray and he can talk to the folks at OfficeSolutions. It's probably a mix-up and should be corrected before it gets fabricated. I mentioned it to Brian Mulcahy because he was on the line at the time but he didn't have any satisfactory answers.

Mary handed Bennie another email. "This is from Todd. He did respond to this one."

Bennie read the response:

From Todd Eddington
To Simon Pensiera
Re Quality Control

Simon, I'll talk to Ray.

Mary said, "A man of few words. Not to speak ill."

Bennie gave her back the email response. "But we were talking about Pollstar."

"Oh, right." Mary turned to one of the stacks and started flipping through it. "I think I read about a company in Willow Grove that had some electrical issue. Here we go." She turned around and gave Bennie the email.

Bennie read it:

From Simon Pensiera

To Todd Eddington

Re Quality Control

Todd,

I got a call from Michelle Botuzzi at Delaware Valley Deed & Title that the undercounter LED keeps flickering on their product, top-of-the-line, #9272. It effects two out of ten cubicles. Michelle says it gave the one employee a headache and can provoke a migraine. You should talk to Ray or somebody at PowerPlus. That shouldn't happen in top-of-the-line. It's embarrassing.

Bennie handed it back. "Did Todd respond?"

"No. I assume he couldn't. Simon writes a lot." Mary pursed her lips. "Simon's a really smart and wonderful guy. He works really hard and he expects everyone to do the same. He looks out for his accounts. It's not like he's being a jerk."

"I don't think he's being a jerk."

"He just cares. He's responsible. It's what makes him a great father, too."

"I'm sure. Don't worry about it. How about emails to or from Ernie, the head of security? Did you come across any of those?"

"Not so far."

"How about from Ray Matewicz?"

"Not yet. I don't think that Simon writes to Ray directly, or vice versa. Simon follows the chain of command, asking Todd to talk to Ray."

"Which makes sense because Todd and Ray are buddies." Bennie couldn't put it together. She felt like they were on the right track, but missing too much information. "Do you think that Simon knows that Todd is friendly with Ray's brother-in-law? That they play golf?"

"Probably. Simon is a family guy. He cares about families."

"Then we're reinventing the wheel, discovering information that Simon can supply. I know he's at the hospital, but we need him in the loop. We don't want to waste any time."

"Right." Mary frowned. "But I doubt we can get him here today. He can't leave Rachel."

"Then there's only one solution."

CHAPTER TWENTY-SEVEN

"This way." Mary led Bennie down the hospital hallway to the lounge, then went inside to find Feet sitting slumped in a chair, alone. His head was buried in his hands, and his back hunched over. "Feet?"

"Yo." Feet looked up, his eyes glistening with fresh tears behind his Mr. Potatohead glasses.

"What's the matter? Is Rachel okay?" Mary sat down beside him, followed by Bennie.

Feet heaved a hoarse sigh. "We lost the donor. She dropped out."

"Oh no. What do you mean?"

"The donor who was going to give the marrow. They say she got in some kind of accident. I think she changed her mind." Feet blinked his hooded eyes clear. His scraggly eyebrows sloped down, and his parched lips formed a heartbroken line. "I bet she got cold feet on account of, it hurts. The docs said it's like getting kicked by a horse."

"So what happens to Rachel now?"

"The docs gotta find another donor."

"She stays here in the hospital, right?"

"Yes. But we go back to square one. They gotta make sure

she stays in remission." Feet lifted his glasses to wipe his eyes from underneath, using his clubby fingers. "The longer it takes, the worse it gets. Every day she gets weaker."

"Don't worry, Feet." Mary patted his arm. "They know what they're doing. They'll take care of her. This is the best hospital in the country."

"I know." Feet recovered, sniffling. "Your father and them went to get take-out. The cousins were sick of the cafeteria. You know how real Italians are about food. Simon's with Rachel. Does he know you're comin'?"

"Yes, I texted him." Mary gestured to Bennie. "Feet, you remember Bennie, don't you?"

"Sure, hi, Bennie." Feet smoothed down his white shirt, extending a hand knobby with arthritis. "Nice to see you again."

"You too." Bennie smiled.

"Hey," said a weary voice from the door, and they all turned as Simon entered the lounge, letting his expression show the anguish he must be feeling, as if he'd slipped off a mask. His clothes looked lived in and his face grizzled, as if he hadn't shaved this morning. He pulled over a soft chair and flopped into it with a heavy sigh. "So you heard the bad news?"

Mary patted his arm as he sat down. "Yes, I'm so sorry."

"What a setback. God, as if she hasn't gone through enough. Now we have to start all over again."

"The poor thing. What does she understand?"

"Not much, luckily. She can't follow the countdown. She knows the date of her Transplant Day. You get a blue T-shirt and everything. But she'll forget by then." Simon rubbed his face, as stressed as Mary had ever seen him. "They're trying to find another donor. We have to keep her on track. We don't want to lose more time or our eligibility status."

"You mean she has to stay in remission."

"Right, and the chemo protocol is tough, she has to keep her strength up. Finding a new donor is prolonging the agony, literally." Simon tried to shake it off, shifting his attention to Bennie, and Mary realized they hadn't met.

"Oh, Simon, this is Bennie Rosato."

"Your partner?" Simon blinked, confused. "I thought you were—"

"She's helping on your case. We went to the crime scene together today."

"But what about the conflict of interest and all?"

Mary had wanted to gloss it over but Simon was owed an explanation. "We back-burnered that matter and also your civil cases for now. The criminal case takes front and center."

"Good." Simon leaned over and shook Bennie's hand. "Thank you, Bennie. I really appreciate you coming on board. This murder case scares the crap out of me. I can't believe it's even happening. It's like a nightmare, and I thought I had a high tolerance for nightmares."

"I bet." Bennie nodded. "I'm sorry to hear about the setback with your daughter's donor. In that regard, there's something we should talk about before we get to your case."

Mary hid her puzzlement. She had no idea what Bennie meant.

Bennie dug in her messenger bag. "Simon, I'm concerned that you need to assign someone your power-of-attorney, in case medical decisions need to be made for Rachel's care and you're arrested. I pulled some papers for you to look over."

Mary cringed. "Bennie, really? You drew up papers? Can't this wait?"

"No, it shouldn't. I had some form POAs in my file. I'm sure we can get them notarized in the hospital." Bennie handed the papers to Simon, who accepted them with a resigned nod.

"Thanks, I get it. Plan B. I was saying that to my father this morning. I'll give him my power-of-attorney." Simon handed Feet the papers. "Dad, will you hold on to these? We'll have to deal with them."

"Okay, I heard." Feet adjusted his glasses on his nose, beginning to read the POA forms.

Mary breathed an inward sigh, relieved that Simon hadn't been hurt or offended. "So, Simon, we need to talk to you about Todd's murder case. We have a few questions."

Bennie looked over with a slight frown. "Mary, should we do this all together?"

Mary didn't get it. "What do you mean? Do you need to leave?"

Bennie's gaze shifted to Feet and back to Mary. "No. I meant, shouldn't we have this conversation with Simon in private?"

Mary grimaced, hoping that Feet hadn't understood what Bennie meant, which was likely since his hearing was almost as bad as her father's. "No, this is fine."

"Go ahead." Simon glanced out the open door. "We don't have much time. Meanwhile, the nurses, our pediatric oncologist, and our social worker, they all know I was taken away yesterday. They're trying to be nice but I know what they're thinking. They think I'm a murderer."

Feet shook his head, still looking down at the forms. "My son would never kill nobody. Never. They can't arrest him. He didn't do it."

"Try not to think about it, Feet." Mary took out her laptop, fired it up, and turned to Simon. "To begin, did you know that Ray's brother-in-law plays golf with Todd? I think his name is Mo Nustrall."

"I didn't know they golfed together, but it doesn't surprise me. Todd was friendly with Mo."

"Do you know Mo?"

"I met him once or twice. He comes around the office sometimes. He's at PowerPlus."

"To see Todd?"

"Yes."

"Obviously, Ray, too."

"Yes."

"Did you ever play golf with them?"

"I can't remember the last time I played golf." Simon shook his head, pained. Feet paged through the power-of-attorney forms, slumped in the chair, and said nothing.

Mary continued, "Okay, so when I went through your emails, I saw a lot of email that you wrote on quality issues."

"I know, it drives them crazy. They roll their eyes. They call me The Mad Emailer. But it's important to keep the consistency of quality. It affects sales. They seem not to want to acknowledge that, but to me it's obvious." Simon frowned. "The interesting thing about cubicle manufacture is that there's no building code that applies to them if they're under sixty-seven inches like ours. There's no inspection like an office building. But for all intents and purposes, a cubicle becomes a wall not subject to code. It's the industry's dirty little secret. Now, I pitch the high quality of our units to my accounts. So I monitor it. It drives me nuts when production lets down. My word matters to me."

"So that's why you write emails about, like, the weave of the fabric?"

"Yes, the fabric matters, too. It's cosmetic but it's what accounts see. We have twelve colors. The accounts choose it carefully. They want to match the rug or the curtains. It's a thing. When the color dye is inconsistent or the fabric weave looks funky, they're not happy."

"And I saw you made a number of other complaints about even the things that are internal, like the metal, the lighting, and the drywall."

"Right, why are you asking me this?" Simon asked, mystified. "Why does this matter? I mean, you're trying to figure out who killed Todd, right?"

"I'm coming to that." Mary was working on a theory, just beginning to cohere. "Whose job is it to make sure that the quality on the production lines is consistent? Is that HR or Operations?"

"Operations. It's Ray's job."

"So you have all these complaints and you write to Todd about them, correct?"

"Yes."

"Why don't you write to Ray directly? Because that's not the chain of command?"

"Correct. I want to keep Todd in the loop and I know they're buddies, so I know Todd will talk to Ray."

Mary took a flyer. "This can't endear you to Ray, can it? You're pointing out problems that he's not noticing or not doing anything about. You're essentially saying that he's not doing his job."

Simon frowned. "It's not like that in business. Ray doesn't take it personally."

"Don't you think it makes Ray look bad?" Mary thought back to her conversation with Bennie, about business and personal not mixing.

"No, not really. Granted, it would make him look bad if I wrote to *his* boss, Mike Bashir, but I never did that. I only told my boss. Todd."

"Did Ray ever say anything to you about you pointing out all these errors?"

"No."

"Do you think Ray likes you?"

Simon shrugged. "I used to. Before those lies they put in the defamation suit. If he's going to say I made those statements, he's no friend of mine."

"Did you ever write to Ray directly on a quality issue or for another reason?"

Simon thought a minute. "Yes. From time to time, when an issue wasn't getting addressed."

"Like what?"

"I don't remember." Simon rubbed his face again. "Okay, yes, I do. The fabrication was sloppy on one of my accounts. It was Crowley's, a wholesaler for medical equipment. The metal frames of the units weren't plumb. They were out of whack. At first I thought it was the assembly, but it turned out that it was fabrication. I never got another order from that account. I remember I wrote Ray about that and we had some back and forth."

Mary made a mental note. "Were there other accounts as well, that you remember you wrote to Ray about?"

"Does this matter?"

"It might. Maybe Ray was more angry with you than you know. Maybe he had something to do with Todd's murder."

"You think *Ray* killed Todd?" Simon recoiled, aghast. "He was Todd's friend. He would never do that."

"Look at the facts, Simon. Ray is willing to lie for the company, saying that you defamed Todd. And somebody framed you for Todd's murder or is willing to let you go to jail for it."

Bennie interjected, "Simon, you should know that I spoke with Ray last night at OpenSpace. He told me he thinks you killed Todd, no question. Ask yourself why he would say that. The answer is, the best defense is a good offense."

Simon shook his head, nonplussed. "I have nothing against these guys. Nothing. I don't know why they're doing this. I don't know why they would kill Todd."

Mary touched his arm. "Look, it's only a working theory at this point, and we have to keep digging. I wish I had emails you'd written to Ray, but we don't. We only have emails between you and Todd."

Simon blinked. "I have my emails to Ray."

"How? They took your laptop."

"I keep copies of my emails in the cloud."

"You do?" Mary asked, surprised, and one look at Bennie's expression told her that she felt the same way. They could have just struck gold—or it could be a dry hole. "You have your emails?"

"Yes, I keep a copy of every email I have ever written or received. I like to keep a record, an archive. Those emails have so much valuable information. Sales, accounts, contacts, and quality issues like the ones we're talking about. My work email is company property, so I don't make a thing about it at work. I hardly ever consult it, but I like to know it's there."

"So how do we get it out of the cloud?" Mary spun her laptop around to face Simon. "You can access it from any laptop, can't you? It's stored in the ether."

"True, but . . ." Simon hesitated. "I don't remember the password. It's been years since I've used it."

"What are your go-to passwords?" Mary spun the laptop back. "Tell them to me. We can try a few."

"No, it's not a normal word like Rachel's name or our first dog. I use a password generator. It's nonsensical."

"Do you have it stored anywhere, like in your phone? I have one of those virtual wallets with my passwords stored." Mary didn't add that she had it only because Anthony had made her.

"I take no chances because it's the company phone. I don't want them to know about it. I write my passwords down on a sheet of paper at home."

"Have you even been home since yesterday?"

"No." Simon raked back his hair. "I've been wanting to go home and see what the house looks like if they searched it, but I haven't had a spare minute. It's just been too busy to leave here, with everything that's going on. Also I figured the cops impounded the car."

Mary's thoughts went into overdrive. "I'm assuming they searched your house. We should go check it out. Tell us where you keep your password, and we'll go right away."

"How does that work? Do they break in? Do they leave the

door open?" Simon rubbed his face. "I'd call the neighbors but they're on vacation. It's that time of year."

"It's okay, we're on it." Mary touched his arm. "Your password is where?"

"I always keep it in the same place. You know my home office, on the first floor? Desk drawers on the left, the top one. It's hidden in a Phillies schedule."

Suddenly Feet looked up, his eyes welling again. "Mare, you want me to sign this power-of-attorney in case they take Simon away? Do you really think they're gonna take him to jail?"

Mary touched his arm. "Feet, don't get upset. I don't think that's going to happen."

"But you brought the papers. You want me to sign the papers. Bennie does and so does Simon. That means you all think he's going to jail. The cops think he did it. His company thinks he did it. They think he killed his boss because he got fired." Feet held the papers in the air, his lips starting to tremble. "They're going to take my son away? They're going to put him in jail for a murder he didn't do? He didn't do it!"

"Feet, no," Mary said, trying to calm him.

"Dad, it's okay." Simon got up and went around Feet's other side. "It's just a formality. That's what I was saying to you this morning. It's like insurance. You get car insurance, it doesn't mean you're going to crash. It's just in case."

Just then, Bennie's phone started ringing, and she checked the screen, looking at Mary. "It's Nate."

"Who's Nate?" Simon asked, next to Feet.

"He's the president of Dumbarton Industries, the parent company."

"You mean he's the big boss?" Feet's lined face flushed with emotion. "The *capo di tutto capi*?"

"Excuse me." Bennie rose, answering the call, "Nate, what is it?"

Suddenly Feet jumped out of his seat. The POA papers

fluttered from his hand, and he lunged toward Bennie. "Gimme that phone!"

"Dad!" Simon shouted, going after him.

"Feet?" Mary called out, as Bennie whirled around in surprise and Feet grabbed the phone from her hand.

"You're the big *mahaf*, you bastard?" he shouted into the phone. "You never shoulda fired my son! He did a great job and he would never murder nobody! You're not gonna take him away! I won't let you! Mary and Bennie won't let you! My granddaughter needs her father—"

"Dad, stop!" Simon grabbed him, holding him around the shoulders. Mary arrived at Feet's other side and was about to take his arm when suddenly Feet let out an agonized cry, dropped the phone, and crumpled to the floor, clutching his chest.

Mary screamed. "He's having a heart attack!"

CHAPTER TWENTY-EIGHT

Bennie experienced what happened next as an awful blur. Mary screamed, loudspeakers barked. Simon knelt on the lounge floor, cradling his father, whose lined face had gone ashen. Nurses and doctors came running, racing into the lounge, performing CPR. A crash cart arrived, more personnel swarmed, and they brought the old man to life just as a stretcher arrived with even more personnel. Trained aides lifted him onto a gurney with an expert 1-2-3 count, taking his vitals all the while, then whisked him down the hallway to the emergency department of the University of Pennsylvania Hospital, which was just next door in the medical complex. A stricken Simon hurried behind the group, calling instructions to Mary to stay behind with Rachel.

Bennie remained on the periphery during the commotion, then accompanied Mary as they walked back to Rachel's room. They didn't talk because Mary was busy texting her father and mother to tell them to call her, and after they'd reached Rachel's room and ascertained that the child was sound asleep, Mary stood outside the room, kept an eye on Rachel, and called a slew of relatives and friends, informing them as calmly as possible of what happened and answering all their questions.

Bennie was amazed to see how calm Mary was in an emergency, and couldn't help but feel that the tables had turned, with Mary taking charge of the situation and Bennie standing numbly aside, her emotions churning within her chest. She remained outside the child's hospital room, struggling to control herself, looking through the window at the little girl.

She had never been in a children's hospital and couldn't get used to the incongruity of the Mylar balloons and plush animals next to the IV stalks and the blood pressure monitors. And little Rachel looked so frail, her bald head so like a baby bird's, with sparse flyaway hairs and dark circles under her eyes, even though her eyelids were closed. Her dimpled hand rested on her chest, showing a plastic IV port that sported a Monarch butterfly sticker.

Bennie kept replaying in her mind what had happened in the lounge, feeling a wave of guilt for having brought the power-of-attorney forms. She didn't know what she had been thinking. Well, she did, which was worse. She had thought she was being helpful, but she had failed miserably. She'd grabbed the papers just as she'd left the office, thinking that she had made a heads-up play, but she'd been horribly wrong.

Bennie watched Rachel's chest rise and fall, her thoughts turning. She didn't know Feet and had no idea of his emotional state. She didn't know how old he was or even why he was called Feet. She avoided using the nickname because it seemed so goofy, even disrespectful. Or maybe it was because she felt like such an outsider to Mary's South Philly community. Somehow, she didn't deserve to use the nicknames of people she hardly knew.

Bennie shook her head, only vaguely aware that she was doing so. Beyond Rachel's bed was a window that overlooked the atrium, and there were even more happy Mylar balloons, mobiles, and a massive staircase of families moving up and down, living their lives in a hospital while their child went through some of the hardest ordeals the planet had to offer.

And Bennie stood on the other side of the glass, wondering how she could not have realized what a mistake she had made.

Bennie felt tears come to her eyes, but kept her head turned from Mary as she blinked them away. She should have realized that showing Feet the papers and confronting him with the fact that his son was about to be arrested for murder could have provoked a heart attack. Especially since his grandchild was mortally ill. Worse, he had just learned that she had lost her marrow donor.

Bennie felt her chest tighten with fury at herself. How could she have been so stupid? How could she have been so blind, so thoughtless? Just because she didn't wear her emotions on her sleeve didn't mean she had none. She always tried to be professional, but she'd been so professional that she'd almost killed someone.

Bennie swallowed hard, trying to seal in the pressure building up inside. She prayed that Feet survived and she would never forgive herself if he didn't. She didn't know how Simon would survive it, with his daughter so sick and his father in an emergency department, an entire family in mortal jeopardy. And Bennie could finally understand what Mary had been talking about all these years, about how close she was to the South Philly community. As Mary made phone call after phone call, it became clearer and clearer to Bennie that Mary was as close to Simon, Feet, and his family as she was to any blood relative.

Listening to the phone calls, Bennie realized that her younger partner was at the center of a loving network, all of whom counted on her, relied upon her, and looked to her for guidance. Mary was completely in control, deserving of their respect, and Bennie wondered how she had missed all of this before and for so long. She had told Mary that she would be second-chair on the case and take orders, but had forgotten all about that with the power-of-attorney forms. She hadn't even thought to mention them to Mary, much less to ask her if it was okay to present them to Feet or Simon. She had simply reverted to form, functioning as if it were her case.

"Bennie?"

Bennie looked over, coming out of her reverie. "Oh."

"Are you okay?"

"No," Bennie blurted out, swallowing hard.

"You look upset. Simon always tells me, 'See the child, not the illness.'"

"It's not that, not only that."

"What do you mean?"

"I'm sorry I showed his father those forms. I never should've done that, I didn't know and I should've asked you—"

"Bennie, whoa, whoa, whoa. It's okay." Mary stepped back, surprised. "You couldn't have known. You didn't know him."

"That's the point, I couldn't have known and yet I acted. I didn't know him, and yet it was a terrible decision, Mary, he couldn't handle it, he was too upset, and it's all my fault—"

"Bennie, I'm as much at fault as you. You're the one who was right. He shouldn't have been in that meeting. *That's* what he couldn't handle. Being a part of the whole discussion about the murder case, it was all too much for him. We should have taken it outside—"

"No, that wasn't it, it was the papers."

"No, it was the murder case, that's why he grabbed the phone and yelled at Nate. Anyway, listen." Mary stopped, brightening. "Simon just called and he's stable."

"He is?" Bennie felt tears begin to well up, but she willed them back down. "What happened?"

"He had a heart attack. They're doing tests now. Simon is on his way back and then we can go."

"But he doesn't have to leave his father."

"The cousins are there, my father and mother are on their way."

"So? He can stay. We're here."

"What?"

"We can keep an eye on Rachel," Bennie heard herself say, which sounded uncharacteristic even to her, and Mary frowned slightly.

"We have to get going, Bennie. We have to get to Simon's house. I want to get those passwords. I want to get into the cloud. Simon can be arrested at any—"

"But Simon will need to talk to you when he comes back."

"He'll be fine."

"He might need to rest or eat or shower. We can stay here and watch Rachel, then go."

Mary smiled slightly. "Are you the real Bennie Rosato? Since when does work wait for anything?"

"Since now," Bennie said, inwardly stung. "I'm an old dog but I can learn new tricks."

Mary straightened up. "I'm a young dog and evidently I'm learning new tricks, too. Because as soon as Simon gets here, we're leaving."

"You sure? Because it's your call, and I really mean it this time. It should have been your call with the papers, too."

"Forget it."

"So we're going?"

"Totally. We have a job to do."

Bennie glanced at Rachel, uncertain.

"Bennie, we're *lawyers*. When it's time to go, we *go*."

CHAPTER TWENTY-NINE

It wasn't until seven o'clock at night that Mary and Bennie got to Chantilly Mews, the development where Simon lived. It had taken longer than everybody thought to get Feet situated in the main hospital, and Simon looked exhausted by the time he returned to Rachel's room at CHOP. He'd said he'd be fine, but Mary wondered how much a human being could take. She remembered the other day that Simon had talked about his breaking point, but she realized that CHOP was full of parents who were finding strength in themselves that they hadn't known they had. And so were their children.

Mary drove through the winding streets of the development in silence. Bennie hadn't said a word the entire trip, nor had she checked her phone or email, and Mary had never seen such a change in her. Bennie was never the type to be prone to guilt, and Mary had always thought she herself had won the office pool on that particular emotion. She didn't blame Bennie for showing Feet the power-of-attorney forms, and on the contrary, blamed herself for having the discussion in front of him. She had always believed that business was personal and family could be included anywhere, but she was starting to question the assumption. Bennie may not have known Feet, but Mary did. He was her father's best friend and the most intelligent, as well as the most sensitive, of The Tonys. Mary should've known that Feet was nearing his breaking point, and it made her more worried than ever about her father, who had been so depressed the other night in the lounge.

Mary steered through one street, then the next, almost at Simon's house, her fingers gripping the wheel. Something about the act of driving reminded her of her own power. She was in the driver's seat and she could do more than she thought she could, too. She had to keep the pressure on and find out who killed Todd and why. She knew that Simon was innocent, but the police were working around the clock to collect evidence against him. It was only a matter of time before they got the hair and fiber tests back, proving that Simon was in Todd's car.

Mary felt time ticking away on Simon's freedom, which was why she had made sure that the power-of-attorney forms were signed before they left the hospital. Simon had chosen her for power-of-attorney, so she was truly in charge and she wasn't about to let him down. She turned left onto his street, which was at the periphery of the development, with a forest of newly cultivated evergreens beyond, undoubtedly as per local zoning ordinance.

The sun had hidden behind the oddly regular treeline, and a purplish sky had fallen, dropping a final curtain on the day. Modest brick homes with attached garages and large front lawns lined the street, which seemed unusually quiet, with only a few kids playing. It could have been the heat, but Mary was guessing that families were away on vacation, since more than one garden needed weeding or the lawns looked especially dry.

Mary pulled in front of Simon's house and turned off the ignition, remembering when Simon had thrown a housewarming party here, years ago. His wife, Ellen, had been alive and Rachel was the adorable dark-haired infant they all believed was healthy. But even then, a deadly disease was lying in wait, written into the baby's DNA, which would darken to a poison that shared the same veins as her lifeblood, like a lethal best friend. Cancer was a murderer. Mary hated cancer, but working on Simon's case had brought her to the epiphany that cancer came in many forms—and even in allegedly healthy people. Murderers had a form of cancer, too. It was hate beneath the surface, waiting for its chance to strike and kill. And it had to be stopped.

"This it?" Bennie asked, looking out the window.

"Yes. Let's go." Mary came out of her reverie, slung her messenger bag on her shoulder, and got out of the car. Humidity saturated the air, even at this hour, but she fell into step beside Bennie as they walked up the front walk, scanning the house. The front door, which was black, was closed. "I wonder if the cops broke the lock to get inside?"

"They usually do. Sometimes they leave the door wide open, which sucks. I know a case where they left the door open and the resident was burglarized. But not in a nice neighborhood like this."

Mary got out the house keys that Simon had given her anyway, and they made their way up the walkway. Predictably the front yard looked unmowed and the house needed some maintenance. It was a brick colonial with traditional black shutters and a white portico over the front door, but the shutters looked faded and white paint peeled on the roof of the portico.

"Here we go." Bennie opened the door as they reached the front step, and it swung open, so they went inside.

"His home office is to the left," Mary said, remembering the layout, with the stairwell to the second floor directly ahead but the living room off to the left, then a kitchen, followed by the home office that led to the garage.

"Gotcha." Bennie flicked on a wall switch, and they both looked around with dismay. The police search had obviously been thorough because the cushions on the sectional couch in the living room had been upended, books and CDs had been taken from an entertainment center and scattered willy-nilly on the sisal rug, and artwork and family photos had been unhooked from the walls and stacked on the floor.

"They weren't kidding." Bennie frowned, looking around.

"Right." Mary looked away, pained. She had such nice memories of this house and she hated to see it this way. She picked her way through the living room and went to the kitchen, followed by Bennie, and it had been searched thoroughly as well. Every cabinet door hung open, exposing stacks of dishes and mugs with sayings on them, among them WORLD'S GREATEST MOM.

"Here's what they're looking for," Bennie said, standing in front of an open drawer that held kitchen knives in a long wooden block.

"The murder weapon, right?"

"Yes. Obviously they wouldn't expect to find it in the drawer. But we need to know more about it. Does Simon hunt?"

"No."

"Then I'm guessing it was a common kitchen knife. Whoever framed him would use a knife Simon would have owned."

"What if it's one of a set that he had? And that one could be missing? The killer could have made it look as if Simon had taken the knife from home." Mary looked through the knives in the drawer, and there were a few with black handles that appeared to be steak knives, possibly from a set. "But a steak knife wouldn't do it, would it?"

"No." Bennie looked up. "And anyway, I doubt Simon entertained much, agree? It's not as if people would be aware of what knives he had, or if he'd been given a set."

"I agree." Mary glanced around the kitchen, and for the first time noticed a black smudge of fingerprint dust on the white Corian of the counter. "They dusted for fingerprints."

"Yup." Bennie straightened up. "And they'll find Simon's

prints in Todd's car, too. On the door handle and on the inside. Where's the home office?"

"This way." Mary led her through the open doorway into a square, windowless office, which held a wood workstation in the corner with cubbies partway up the wall. A blue router remained connected, so the wireless was probably still active, though Simon's desktop computer was gone and must have been seized. Its mouse had been left behind, on top of a pad that was an enlarged photograph of Rachel as a baby.

"He said top drawer on the left. Look for the Phillies schedule."

"On it." Mary beelined for the drawers, which hung open, their contents having been dumped in a large messy pile on the dark rug. There was nothing left in the top drawer, so she crouched down and started sifting through the pile, and Bennie crouched down opposite her. They searched through packs of new checks, bills, pens and pencils, stale gum, gas receipts, and random business cards.

"I hope the cops didn't find the passwords." Bennie kept looking, and so did Mary, rooting through the paper, one bill after the next. If the police had dumped the drawers out in order, the contents of the first one would be on the bottom of the pile.

"They would have to be incredibly lucky to have found it. Who looks inside a Phillies schedule?"

"Phillies fans?" Bennie moved some papers aside, suddenly exposing a trifold Phillies schedule with slick graphics. "Go, Phils!"

"You got it! I hope the passwords are inside!" Mary scrambled over as Bennie opened the schedule, and they both cheered. Inside was a narrow piece of paper on which Simon had written twenty-five passwords in his characteristically neat printing. The passwords were incomprehensible and listed beside their respective websites. Mary skimmed the list quickly until she got to the tenth password, 8sj2s77Tuyx1, for PensieraNet.

"Bingo!" Bennie said excitedly.

"Let's get busy." Mary reached into her messenger bag, pulled out her laptop, and powered it on and sat cross-legged on the floor with it, firing it up. Her heart began to beat faster.

"Now we're cooking with gas." Bennie sat beside her, and Mary logged into settings, joined PensieraNet, and after a process of trial and error, used the password to open Simon's emails.

"Wow." Mary watched as thousands of emails piled onto the screen, organized by year. She narrowed the search to the current year, filtered them using the name Ray Matewicz, and still came up with a screenfull. "I guess there were more than Simon remembered."

"But I'm sure a lot of them won't be relevant."

"Right." Mary scanned the first one, which was about scheduling a meeting. "And it looks like some have Ray as a copy, which isn't all that helpful. I would refine the search further but I don't want to miss anything."

"Understood." Bennie read over Mary's shoulder. "We should divide the labor. I'll take the first six months and you take the last six months."

"Okay." Mary highlighted the first six months of the emails as Bennie reached into her messenger bag, pulled out her laptop, and powered it on. Mary forwarded Bennie the emails in sections since it was so large, but in time, they both had their six-month segments and were reading away.

Mary read through email after email, taking notes in her Word file, but even an hour later, she wasn't having any luck. Simon's emails to Ray were only technical in nature, confirming details of POs, product specifications, or changes in a line's production schedule, which affected delivery dates to Simon's clients. Mary scrutinized this last category for signs of anger against Simon on Ray's part, but there was nothing to support her theory and she was starting to worry that it was a dry hole. The only back-and-forth between Ray and Simon that was remotely fussy was over delays in deliveries.

Darkness fell outside the window, and Bennie turned on a chrome Luxor lamp on the worktable, which cast a conical pool of light on the two lawyers, their laptops, and the disarray of papers on the floor.

"You having any luck?" Bennie asked, before she resettled.

"Not yet." Mary glanced at the time on her computer screen, which read 9:15. "I worry about time."

"Me too. Keep going."

"There's no other choice, is there?" Mary opened the next email, heartened because its subject line was Quality Issues. She read:

> Ray, I emailed Todd about this but he hasn't gotten back to me and I need an answer for Susan at The Jarrat Organization, a call center for software support for their accounting program. She is unhappy with the lighting in her top-of-the-line units and she says it flickers. I've noticed this in another account and already brought it up with Todd because it's provoking migraines in employees. This could be a liability issue for the company and Todd said he would do something about it, but this is the second customer of mine who's complained. Susan is one of my biggest accounts and I would like not to lose another account over quality issues that don't get the attention they deserve. Please advise ASAP. Thanks. Simon

"Hey, look at this," Mary said, heartened, but not exactly sure why. "Here's something about a quality issue, concerning the wiring."

Bennie leaned over and skimmed the email. "What's interesting about it?"

"I don't remember seeing an email from Simon about quality issues at this account before. This suggests he's written to Todd about The Jarrat Organization, but I don't remember seeing any email about that."

"Maybe you forgot."

"Hold on, let me check." Mary went into the file of her notes from the previously sent emails, and her document index was organizing them in several different ways, one of which was by Simon's accounts. She scrolled the list of accounts, reading them aloud to Bennie. "Look, I don't see any mention of The Jarrat Organization."

"Maybe you didn't get that far. You hadn't read through all the emails yet, had you?"

"No, but this is referring to an email last month. I had gotten that far."

"What did Ray write back?"

"Let me see." Mary started scrolling through the emails, and the response appeared a week later, which was terse:

Simon, will do. Ray

"Keep going and see what else you can find." Bennie returned to her laptop, and Mary did the same, feeling a tingle of excitement. She didn't know if it meant anything but it did seem strange, and it gnawed at the back of her mind as she read through one email after the next, each one confirming technicalities of specifications, meetings, or purchase orders, most of which showed Ray as a copy but not a direct recipient. But only a month later she came upon another email about quality control, and her heart started to pound.

"Bennie, look at this." Mary skimmed the email, which was decidedly testier in tone:

Ray, I wrote you about these wiring issues before and I haven't heard anything from you or Todd. We tried to fix the flickering in the lighting on-site but it didn't repair the problem. You should know that some of the employees at Jarrat have physical handicaps like visual impairments and migraines. This is going to result in liability for the company or me losing a client if it doesn't get fixed by the end of this week. I assume the wiring is manufactured by PowerPlus and you should talk to Joe or somebody else over there in operations but this has to be dealt with. Susan is fit to be tied because one of her employees is talking about filing a complaint with the state human relations commission. This is a legal issue that needs to be attended to right away. Please get back to me by the end of the week.

"Interesting." Bennie shifted over. "See what Ray replied."

"Right." Mary was already scrolling through the emails, past one week, the next, then the week after that, but there was no response from Ray. "Ray didn't answer. Ray wouldn't ignore that, would he?"

"Possible, since you heard what Simon said, they roll their eyes at him. He's like the boy who cried wolf."

"I know but Simon wouldn't let them forget it."

"Maybe they talked about it but there was no email."

Mary didn't think so. "Simon told us he rarely talks to Ray. And you would think he would've remembered that, because it's what we were just asking him about, conversations with Ray over quality problems."

"So what are you thinking?"

"I'm not understanding why I didn't see any mention of Jarrat before." Mary searched her document index again, but there was no mention. "It's not there. This is a significant quality issue, clearly discussed with Todd and Ray, but it wasn't included in any of the email that the company sent us. So there's one obvious conclusion."

Bennie lifted an eyebrow. "You think it was intentionally omitted?"

"Honestly, yes." Mary felt her heartbeat quicken again.

"Think about it. They kitchen-sinked us with emails. They expect us to get snowed under reading them, but they don't realize that we have a way of checking if there's any missing. They don't know that Simon archives his email. It's only because I read the email they produced and compared it with Simon's email archive that we know that these were omitted from the production."

Bennie nodded, perking up. "So the question isn't what emails did they produce. The question is, what emails *didn't* they produce?"

"Exactly!" Mary almost cheered. They were finally getting to the bottom of something, but of what, she didn't know.

"So why did they leave them out?"

"To hide them. So the question is, what are they hiding?"

"And why?" Bennie asked, her blue eyes glittering.

CHAPTER THIRTY

Bennie kept reading the emails, but they were repetitive and technical, and a hunch was forming in the back of her mind. She turned to Mary. "I think there's something going on with quality control, so why don't we refine the search to only quality control."

"You feel confident enough to narrow it? What if we miss something?"

"Take a chance. We don't have a lot of time." Bennie set down her laptop and shifted over. "I don't think the answer is in my emails. I think it's in the recent stuff."

"Okay, I'm filtering the leftover emails now." Mary typed away, and in the next moment, the screen turned white except for a single email with the subject line Quality Control. "Whoa."

"Let me see." Bennie leaned over and read the email:

Ray, Did you talk to anybody at PowerPlus about the wiring yet? Susan at Jarrat keeps asking and I want to give her an answer. I know you're busy lately but can you please get back to me on this? Flickering in the wiring can be a real problem, not just for people with migraines. What if it sparked or started a fire? You can't negate those

possibilities, and Susan is already voicing concerns about that. So
please get back to me.

Mary frowned. "I never saw this email before, either. This
should have been included in the production. Todd is copied
on it."

"So it was also intentionally omitted. They hid it from us.
They never knew we'd compare." Bennie sensed that her hunch
was correct. "And we know there was no response because it
would've been filtered in."

"Right, but why?" Mary looked over. "So where are you
going with this?"

"Fire, like Simon said." Bennie was thinking out loud. "Let's
think about it logically. They took out the emails concerning
wiring issues and Jarrat. The fact that it's about Jarrat doesn't
matter, but what matters is the issue. The big problem with
bad wiring isn't that it causes migraines. That would be a
problem peculiar to Jarrat. The real problem with faulty wiring is that it causes fires."

"Right," Mary said slowly.

"So we know that they hid these emails from us. Simon was
telling Todd and Ray that there were wiring issues in the cubicles. He put them on notice that something bad could happen and the most likely thing that would happen is a fire."

"Oh my God, you're right." Mary's eyes flared open. "So
maybe Jarrat had a fire?"

"Not Jarrat because Simon would've known that. We
would've heard about that. But another account. All of the cubicles at OpenSpace contain wiring manufactured by Power-
Plus. Any one of the accounts could have had a fire and if any
of those accounts had a fire, OpenSpace was put on notice by
Simon."

"I get it!" Mary said excitedly. "He's a whistle-blower, but
he doesn't know it."

"Right, because he doesn't know about the fire. So there must've been a fire. Or at least it's a working theory."

Mary turned to her laptop, her fingers poised above the keyboard. "So what do we do? How do we find out?"

Bennie's thoughts raced. "You have a list of the accounts, right?"

"Right."

"We know it's not on Simon's accounts or we would've heard it. So start with Todd's."

"That would make the most sense!" Mary started typing away. "We should start looking in the file that has Todd's accounts, which they produced to you." She looked over with a slight frown. "What if they omit the account we're looking for from the list? That would be the thing to do if they were going to hide it, wouldn't they?"

"No, they would have no reason to do that. Remember they don't know we can compare, and also, at that point, they just wanted to show a complete listing of sales numbers."

"Here we go." Mary leaned back as a spreadsheet of Todd's current accounts filled the laptop screen, with the company names running down the left side. "Larkspur Graphics, LLC. Deal Town Dollar Stores. Bethlehem Bank. ITTemps. Swarthmore Senior Services. Quorum Public Relations . . ."

"Remember, Todd keeps the accounts that are repeat business or opening branches."

"Right, good point."

"So we have to see if there was a fire in any of those accounts. We could Google it or look on the company website."

"If we Google it, we can plug in 'fire' and the company name."

"But that might not get anything if it wasn't a fire, or if there was a fire but it didn't reach the newspapers. I would start with the company websites, see if there's a mention of any kind of any incident, whether it's fire or not, involving electrical wiring."

"Okay. You take the first ten accounts, I'll take the second ten."

"Go for it." Bennie navigated to the website for Larkspur Graphics, then the About Us page, which went on about the graphic design franchise that helped people create their own websites, now opening offices in Philadelphia, Wilmington, and Marlton, New Jersey.

"Nothing so far," Mary said, typing.

"Same." Bennie navigated to the next website, Deal Town Dollar Stores, which seemed equally innocuous, a line of dollar stores opening in Delaware and West Virginia. "Todd's territory extends pretty far."

"Agree, I'm seeing that too. Tot's Togs makes kid's clothes and it's in northern Virginia."

"Keep going." Bennie plugged in Bethlehem Bank, and as soon as the company website popped onto the screen, she sensed they had struck paydirt. "Mary, look at this."

"You got something?" Mary leaned over, and they read together:

> We at Bethlehem Bank are devastated by the fire which took place in our newest branch in Manassas last month. Our thoughts and prayers go out to the family of our Adele Watson, a bookkeeper who perished in the blaze. We thank God that there was no further loss of life. The cause of the fire is currently under investigation, and the branch will be closed for the near future. We hope to rebuild and reopen again soon, to serve the wonderful community of Manassas, Virginia.

"Oh no," Mary said, hushed. "It was a fatal fire. Somebody died."

"I know." Bennie scrolled down, and at the bottom of the

page was a small photo of a sweet-faced older woman with a funereal black frame around the picture, under which it said, ADELE WATSON.

"This is it." Mary met Bennie's eyes, her expression turning grave, the shadows harsh from the overhead light. "Let's spin it out together. Bethlehem Bank buys cubicles from Todd, who has been put on notice only a month before that the electrical wiring is faulty. And Ray is on notice too."

"So OpenSpace is liable, and not just for the damage to the building." Bennie felt the weight of her words. "They're liable for the death of the woman. It would've been broad civil *and* criminal exposure. Remember, Simon had problems with the wiring at Jarrat and also with Crowley Medical."

"Right, there's no telling how many other cubicles were affected. Once they were on notice, they covered it up. They didn't care if anybody died."

"At this point, the cause of the fire is unknown, but those investigations take a long time. I bet nobody from OpenSpace is volunteering the information about past problems in the electrical wiring. In fact, they hid it from us." Bennie felt anger glowing like a flame in her chest. "So they covered it up and the question is, how high up does it go. Does it stop at Ray or does it go to Mike Bashir? And is Mo Nustrall involved, too? He must be. He runs sales at PowerPlus. They play golf together."

"I agree. I bet Mo is involved, but not Mike because he's new."

"Right and it's not like he came from PowerPlus. So let's bet they keep it to those three."

"Ernie the security guy might be involved in the cover-up, too, since he was in the defamation complaint. They never should have done that. They overplayed their hand. But they're not professionals."

"I reserve judgment on Ernie." Bennie's instincts were telling her otherwise. "Criminal conspiracies are smaller than people think. Ernie doesn't know production details. He's a plant security guy and that's how they view him. Ernie could have lied in the complaint because his job was on the line. I say the bad guys are Todd, Mo, and Ray."

"But why would they kill Todd?"

"That's not a hard one. They find out about the fire and it's under investigation. It's one of Todd's clients, and they agree to cover it up in the beginning, but Todd starts to get nervous. Todd knows he can go to jail for this. This is a criminal act, so maybe he wanted to spill the beans."

"So they kill Todd to silence him. But what about Simon? Maybe that's why they fired Simon in the first place!" Mary answered her own question, shifting forward excitedly. "He probably doesn't know anything about the fire in Manassas, because it's far away and outside of his region. It certainly doesn't make any Philadelphia papers, and as soon as that happens, Todd keeps it quiet in the company."

"Right."

"But Todd and Ray are still worried that Simon has information about the faulty wiring, it's just information that he doesn't know the significance of. So they want to get rid of him but they don't want to raise alarm bells. They reduce his territory and fire him."

Bennie got it. "But Simon senses it's a pretext. He knows they're lying to him and he thinks the real reason they fired him was because of Rachel's medical expenses."

"He's half-right." Mary smiled, understanding. "He's right that they're not telling him the real reason they're firing him, but the real reason for firing him is that they don't want him to stay at OpenSpace. They don't want him to keep raising questions about the wiring issues. They don't want him around if or when there's another electrical fire. They don't want him to find out about the fire in Manassas."

"Right, but then he sues them, and we kick up a fuss, so they've got to improvise. At the same time Todd is making noises like he's going to come forward, so Ray kills him and frames Simon for the murder, and meanwhile—"

"Meanwhile, Simon is so preoccupied with Rachel and her need for a transplant, which happens just at the same time, that he's forgotten completely about this wiring thing. It gets lost in the shuffle."

"Oh my God, it's a perfect murder." Bennie shook her head.

"They just didn't count on us."

"Teamwork makes the dream work," Bennie wisecracked, ignoring the twinge she felt inside. It really was fun working with Mary, but this wasn't the time to say so, and the moment passed.

"I'm calling Detective Lindenhurst right now." Mary dug in her purse for her phone. "We need to tell him to pick up Ray for questioning."

"He's going to say it's speculation, so we need to collect all this information and bring it to him. Get our ducks in a row."

"Right." Mary pressed the number to call Detective Lindenhurst. "Can you make a separate file for this information, so we can email it to him in some understandable form? I want to have it in his hands right away. We don't have any time to lose."

"Understood." Bennie turned to her computer laptop and started organizing the file. "Can you put him on speaker?"

"Sure," Mary said, hitting a button. "Detective Lindenhurst, this is Mary DiNunzio."

"Yes, Mary," Detective Lindenhurst, his tone tense. "I was just about to call you. We just arrested Simon Pensiera for the murder of Todd Eddington."

Bennie recoiled, saying nothing. It felt like a body blow.

Mary had gone white in the face. "No, you can't, you have the wrong man, we were just about to call you, you need to get

Ray Matewicz in for questioning. He's the killer and we know why—"

"Mary, we have the right man. We have the autopsy. Todd Eddington's body has been released. Your client's hair, fiber, DNA, and fingerprints were found on the body and in Todd Eddington's car. And we found the murder weapon in your client's home—"

"But Ray must have planted it here!" Mary interrupted, frantic. "They know where Simon lives. It couldn't have been that hard to get in there, and Simon's away all the time at the hospital. Plus the street is practically deserted, since everybody's away on vacation."

Bennie could see Mary getting upset, but she didn't interrupt.

"Mary, your client is about to be booked. If you're smart, you'll advise him to make a deal. I can probably get him twenty years."

"But he didn't do it!" Mary shouted, then seemed to catch herself. "And he *can't* go to jail. He has a sick child who needs him. And his father—"

"I have to go. I'll be at the Roundhouse all night. Good-bye." Detective Lindenhurst ended the call.

"Wait, hold on!" Mary said anyway.

Bennie put a hand on her arm. "Mary, keep it together."

"I can't!" Mary hung up the phone, letting out an agonized groan. "Simon was arrested at the hospital! What if Rachel saw? What's going to happen when word gets back to Feet? I can't believe this! We were *so close*!"

"I know, and we still are." Bennie tried to calm Mary down, but she felt the same way. "The fact that Simon was arrested doesn't mean it's the end. It's just the beginning."

"But Bennie, this time he's *going to jail*!" Mary's eyes widened with fear. "What happens to Rachel now? To Feet? This is a *disaster*!"

"We can deal with this. We've been through worse."

"Not worse than this!" Mary began to tear up, and Bennie knew it was time to get her into motion.

"Pack up your laptop. Get your things. We need to get down to the Roundhouse." Bennie put her laptop away.

"But I need to call everybody, my parents, Anthony, the cousins. I have to tell them, and they have to go sit with Rachel."

"You do it on the way. I'll drive." Bennie pointed at Mary's laptop. "Get your stuff. Let's get going. The best way to help Simon is to be down there for him. Not up here whining."

"I'm not whining!" Mary knelt down, closed her laptop, and shoved it in the messenger bag. "Okay, maybe I am, but this is awful!"

"Let's go." Bennie turned out the light and headed out of the office, but the house had gone dark.

"Right behind you," Mary said, as they hustled into the kitchen, then into the living room.

They had reached the front door when Bennie heard an odd muffled sound behind her. Bennie turned around just in time to see a masked shadow in the darkness, clamping a gloved hand over Mary's mouth and dragging her backwards.

Bennie was about to scream when a blow to the head stunned her. She cried out in pain and felt herself falling.

The last sound she heard was a horrible guttural sound, barely human.

It must have been Mary.

CHAPTER THIRTY-ONE

Mary heard a man's voice yelling at her. The noise crashed through her skull. Her head exploded in pain. She couldn't make out what he was saying. Her head hurt so much. All she felt was pain. It paralyzed her. She couldn't think. She couldn't focus. She couldn't stay awake.

"Are you alive or not?"

Mary heard the question louder. The man was right at her ear. Her head hurt so much. Everything was dark. She couldn't see anything. She tried to open her eyes but something covered them.

She tried to speak but she couldn't talk. Something filled her mouth like a gag. She bit down. It was wet cloth. It tasted like blood. She realized that it was her own.

"Wake up!"

Mary tried to say something but her mouth was so dry. The words stuck in the back of her throat. She almost gagged and ended up coughing. She tried to pull the cloth out of her mouth but she couldn't move her arms. They felt wrenched behind her back. She felt pressure against her left side. She was lying down.

"Shut the hell up!"

A rough hand grabbed Mary's arm, shaking her. Agony

arced through her skull. Her head throbbed like a solid ball of pain. Reflexively she tried to talk. Only a weird ah-ah-ah came out.

She heard heavy footsteps on the floor. She felt the vibration with each tread. A door slammed close. The deadbolt was thrown. She was locked inside a room of some kind. Somewhere.

Mary didn't know what was going on. She couldn't think through the pain. She had never felt anything like it before. She tried to remember what had happened. She tried to shout but only the weird sound came out again.

She felt afraid but it was veiled. She was in a mental fog. It muffled everything. Feelings. Thoughts. She could barely put a sentence together in her head. There was too much pain to feel anything. So much pain that it numbed her. All she wanted to do was sleep to get away from it.

She closed her eyes and tried to go back to sleep. Lose consciousness. Then she heard voices, not far away. Something told her it was in another room. Not far away. It sounded echoey. She tried to listen.

"She still alive?" a man asked.

"Yes," another man answered.

"How's her head?"

"What do you think?"

"Is she conscious?"

"No."

"So she's still bleeding."

"Yes."

"How much?"

"What am I, a doctor? Go in and look for yourself."

"I'm doing something here. Can't you see? I asked you if she's bleeding."

Mary tried to stay awake. To listen. To understand. They were talking about her. She was bleeding. She couldn't remember how she got here. She couldn't remember why she was here.

She didn't know what was going on. She could barely stay awake. She wanted to go back to sleep but she didn't. Something inside her told her to stay awake and listen. Something was telling her to survive. Whatever was happening to her, it was something she had to survive.

"What's the difference? She bleeds now or she bleeds later? Who cares?"

"It's called evidence. I told you to put the tarp down."

"It wouldn't have helped."

"It would too. Now we gotta clean it up. It's not my cabin."

Mary struggled to stay awake. To try and understand. They were in a cabin. The two men had brought her there.

"It's not my fault. It's because her head hit the floor."

"You hit her too hard! Why didn't you tell me you had brass knuckles? Who the hell has brass knuckles?"

"How many times you gonna say that? I told you, I didn't want to take any chances. What if she screamed? Those houses are close together."

"That's why I told you to cover her mouth. No one saw us anyway. I was able to drive up the damn driveway and there wasn't anybody around."

"I did cover her mouth!"

"Then what were you worried about? She wasn't going to scream if you had your hand over her mouth."

"Get off my case, Ray."

Mary heard the name. *Ray.* It didn't mean anything to her. She couldn't even remember who she remembered. She didn't know who was in her life. Then she started to remember something. A driveway. A house. She had been in a house for some reason. She hadn't been alone. She had been with someone.

"We had a plan. I gave you the little one. How could you screw that up?"

Mary heard what he said. *The little one.* She must be the little one. She was little. She couldn't remember her height exactly.

She knew she was little. That meant there was a bigger one. She didn't know who the bigger one was. She must've been with somebody bigger. She tried to remember who was bigger. The answer was everybody.

"You and your plans! Your plans got us into this mess! Now what are we going to do?"

"I told you I'll figure it out."

"You better figure it out fast. Somebody is going to be looking for them. She's half-dead already."

Mary realized he meant her. She was half-dead. She felt half-dead. She felt warm and wet. She knew there was blood on her and it was hers. It was hard to breathe through her nose. She couldn't smell anything. She realized there was blood in her nose. She was congested with blood. She couldn't breathe through her mouth because of the cloth. She realized she was panting a little, trying to get air.

"We can't kill them until we figure out what they know and what they told the cops."

"You want me to go ask her? I have a way with the ladies." The man chuckled.

Mary shuddered, involuntarily. She realized what he meant. She didn't want to think about it. She felt a bolt of fear, less muffled. She was a little one. This was very bad. They were going to kill her. She didn't know why. She couldn't remember anything. Except that there was a big one. She remembered that she had been with somebody bigger when something had happened. She had been grabbed from behind. It was coming back to her now, in bits and pieces. It was a memory just out of reach.

"Is that supposed to be a joke?"

"Lighten up."

"Help me get into this laptop. They have everything under password. The phones too. I took the batteries out of their phones."

"Why do you wanna get in the laptops?"

"I wanna see if they sent that email they were talking about."

"How did you even get wireless up here? My cell gets no reception."

"You don't need wireless to check sent emails. Plus if we got wireless, then anybody could track these laptops. Without wireless, they can't."

Mary lost track of which man was speaking, Ray or not-Ray. But what they said made her remember something. A laptop. A phone. She had those things. She could almost visualize them but not quite. And there was an email. Something about an email. It was so hard to think. She couldn't summon up a single image in her head. She couldn't form a sentence. Maybe the bigger one was another woman. They had been together. Mary felt the answer just out of her grasp. She could almost see her hands reaching for it, her fingers trying to pull it from thin air.

"You heard 'em. They're onto us. We can't finish 'em until we know what they told the cops."

"Who's doing the honors?"

"You are, like before."

"Why me?"

"Why not you?"

"She's a woman. *Two* women."

"Oh please. They're not women. They're lawyers."

Mary could hear what they said but couldn't react. She was terrified but back in the fog. She couldn't feel her own fear. She started falling asleep again. The pain took over, obliterating everything. She wasn't strong enough to resist it. She tried to breathe, but her nose bubbled blood. She was losing consciousness.

She let it go. If the men were going to kill her, she couldn't stop them.

She was half-dead already.

CHAPTER THIRTY-TWO

Bennie figured out where she was, by smell. She'd been put in a small building that had to be a smokehouse. It reeked of smoked meat. She sensed it was primitive or very old. The floor was dirt, which felt cool against her cheek. The air was filtered with ashes from a dormant fire that smelled close by. She was alone and she didn't know where Mary was.

She lay on her side, blindfolded and gagged. Her hands were duct-taped behind her back, but her legs were not. She'd been too big to be carried like deadweight. They'd made her walk from the car to the smokehouse. She'd been beaten on the head and arms, but the pain was tolerable. She was keeping her emotions and her terror at bay. She had to be on top of her game to stay alive.

Bennie sensed she was in the country, not only because it was a smokehouse but because it was so quiet. She assumed there was a house or a cabin near the smokehouse, some distance apart. She knew there was a lot of deer hunting in central Pennsylvania. It would make sense to have a smokehouse to smoke venison near a hunting cabin. So either it was a cabin or house, but Bennie was praying that Mary was safe and alive.

Bennie swallowed hard, worried. She had been driven here

alone in the trunk of a car, filled with tools that jangled, so it wasn't Mary's car. There had to be at least two men since she and Mary had both been abducted at the same time. She had no idea if there was a third man here. Her working theory was that Ray and Ernie had taken her and Mary. Mo was an outside possibility. Either way, it was proof that she and Mary had been right. The conspiracy had killed Todd.

Bennie tried not to panic. She figured that they had driven Mary separately. She didn't know if Mary was here or in a different location. They couldn't risk leaving Mary's car in front of Simon's house. Sooner or later somebody would notice and call the cops.

Bennie prayed that Mary was still alive. That last horrifying cry echoed in Bennie's brain. Mary must've been struck hard on the head, with what Bennie didn't know. If they had taken Mary where Bennie was, they were in the middle of nowhere. She doubted Mary was getting medical help. It would take time to reach a hospital once this was all over. And it had to be over. They would survive. Bennie would make certain. She just didn't know how. Yet.

Bennie returned to her mental inventory. It was useful to review what she knew so she could figure out her next step. She estimated that the car trip here took about three hours. She had even managed to hear the directions coming through the car's interior, even though she'd been in the trunk. The driver had used GPS, which told her that he was unsure of the route. So it must not have been his place.

They had taken the expressway out of the city, then the northeast extension, but after that left the highway. The terrain had turned from smooth asphalt to bumpy back roads. The ambient traffic noise had lessened. She'd heard a horse neighing at one point. The elevation had gone from flat to hilly. The air in the trunk was close, but grew cooler.

She drew a mental circle in her mind that intersected towns

three hours away from Simon's. It would've encompassed farmlands, and even parts of the Poconos or the forest. She tried to remember the street names that she heard as they got closer to their destination. It was easy because they were all bird names. Bluebird Lane. Mockingbird Road. The destination had been Eagles Drive.

Bennie tried to estimate what time it was. She was going to say about eleven o'clock at night. It wasn't late enough for anyone to start worrying yet. Detective Lindenhurst might be surprised, but he wouldn't be alarmed. Nobody from the office would know. Declan would have no idea. Anthony might start to wonder, but he was at the hospital with Feet. There would be no cavalry coming. She and Mary were on their own. And it was all up to her. Which, oddly, felt familiar.

She reminded herself that she'd been in dire straits before. She had been buried underground, for God's sake. Left for dead. She had gotten out of that alive. She had stayed calm and cool and found a way out. She would have to do the same today. Tonight. Whenever. Now.

She rocked back and forth, trying to get enough momentum to start rolling. She wanted to see what the walls were made of and where the door was. She'd never been in a smokehouse but she knew it was a small building, usually of wood or stone. It smelled old and dusty. So there had to be a loose board she could break with her foot or a stone she could dislodge somehow. Something. Some way. She had to get out. She rolled over once and was about to roll over again, but froze.

She heard the jingle jangle of keys. Someone was coming. The sound came from over her shoulder, so she must've been facing away from the door. She didn't want them to know she was awake and alert. She had played possum in the car. Until she figured out what to do, she was going to take that tack. She rolled back to where they had left her.

She heard the *ca-chunk* of the key in a lock, then the drawing aside of some sort of bolt, and made it back just in time to hear the door open. It scraped along the dirt floor. It sounded like wood. She made herself focus on the details not to be afraid.

The door must have been ajar because the air stirred the ashes and the dirt, but it felt cooler, blowing her hair from behind. The man's shoes scuffed in the dirt. He must have a flashlight or phone light because she saw a sudden brightness through her blindfold, so he was shining it in her face.

"You and me have to have a little talk," a man said. His voice came from up above. He was standing above her, near her feet. He sounded tall.

"Where's my partner?"

"None of your business."

"Is she here? Is she alive? You better get her a doctor if she needs one. Who are you?"

"It doesn't matter who I am."

Bennie took a flyer. "Well, you're not Ray because I know his voice. So you're either Ernie or Mo. Which one are you?"

"None of your business."

"I say Ernie." Bennie kept her tone strong, though she felt anything but. She'd been a lawyer for a long time, so she knew a thing or two about criminals and the way their conspiracies worked. She would have to use all of her legal superpowers to manipulate these guys.

"Whatever. I'm not here to answer your questions."

"Please take my blindfold off, Ernie. Let's be real. I know who you are, and you're going to kill me anyway. But you're in a bigger jam than you know. And I can help you get out of it."

"Ha!" Ernie burst into derisive laughter. "They said you were somethin' and they weren't kiddin'."

"No, they weren't. I'm not something, I'm somebody. My

name is Bennie Rosato, and I'm one of the best criminal lawyers in the entire country. If you're smart, you'll hear me out. Most times I charge a fortune for what I'm about to tell you. You want some free legal advice?"

"Shut up and—"

"If you watch TV, you know the shows talk about somebody being guilty or innocent. But that's not true in real-life criminal law. The way it works in real life is that guilt is proportionate. In other words, there are degrees of guilt." Bennie kept going because he didn't stop her. "The person who killed Todd is the most guilty. He's going to jail for a long time. He might even get the death penalty. But the two guys who didn't kill Todd, they're not as culpable as the man who stabbed Todd— unless one of them solicited the killer to kill Todd. So you're either the actual killer or you got manipulated into killing Todd."

"You don't know jack."

"I know the law, and all you have to do is listen. Ray is the one who had the big bad problem and he's the one who wanted Todd dead. He's the one who wanted to cover up the electrical issues, in cahoots with his brother-in-law, Mo. They've been cutting corners at PowerPlus. They're the ones who benefit and get paid. I'm betting Ray solicited you, or Mo did. You're just the enforcer. You're the muscle. The one they send to do their dirty work."

"You have it all figured out."

"I kind of do. Because it's not that hard to figure out. It's just common sense. I've known a lot of security types in my day, and they fall into two categories. They're either former cops or former criminals. My boyfriend is a former state trooper. My firm investigator is a former cop. You're not a cop. I can tell."

"You're chatty." Ernie chuckled again, and Bennie realized it was a habit, when he was nervous.

"And that's why I make the big bucks. As I was saying, I don't think you're a criminal, but I bet you've been a bouncer. You can handle yourself. If trouble breaks out on the factory floor, you can handle that too. You make about sixty grand a year. They make a helluva lot more. They're higher-ups, relatives. They're taking advantage of you right now."

"And how's that?" Ernie's voice was heavy with sarcasm.

"Ray didn't come talk to me because he knows me. He doesn't want me to know that it's him. I haven't met you, so he sent you in. I'm betting that's the pattern. He keeps his hands clean. He sends you to do the bad things. But if he sent you to kill Todd and you did it, don't take the fall for him. And if he's telling you that killing me and my partner is going to make your legal problems go away, don't listen to him. Because the exact opposite is the law."

"Oh really?"

"Yes. You want my advice? Right now, you can just go. You have a car. You should drive it away. You should tell that genius Ray to do the same thing, and Mo too. Flee the jurisdiction. You'll be out of the country before they find you. Don't kill any more people, especially not me and my partner. Because if you kill three people, two of them very well-known lawyers, there's going to be hell to pay. And all three of you are going to pay it, equally."

"What's the password to your computer?"

"Ernie." Bennie tsk-tsked. "I'm worried you didn't listen to my lecture and it was a really good one. I laid it out for you. Completely, totally free."

"What's the password?"

Bennie didn't like the new anger in his tone. "Why do you want to know my password? What could possibly be in my laptop that you need? If you're in my computer, you're going to be bored to tears. It's full of legal briefs."

"Did you send that email to the cops or not?"

"You mean the email that Mary asked me to send? So you were listening to our conversation in the house. You overheard us."

"Did you send it?"

"Yes," Bennie lied. In fact, she hadn't sent the email to Detective Lindenhurst. She'd wanted to get Mary moving and she figured she'd send it from the car, but then she and Mary had been attacked. "We didn't want to waste any time getting it to Lindenhurst. We knew it was only a matter of time until they arrested Simon. We wanted to beat them to the punch. The cops know everything—"

"I don't believe you."

"The email told about the fire at Bethlehem Bank, and I attached Simon's emails warning about the wiring at Jarrat and Crowley's. Simon put you on notice. He knows all about it too." Bennie laid it on thick. "We told him at the hospital today. He probably told the cops already."

"What's your password?"

"The cops will charge Simon, but they're going to investigate what we told them, they have to. They know me personally. I'm a certified BFD. That's why I'm telling you. You should leave us and run—"

Suddenly Bennie felt a vicious kick to her stomach. She cried out instinctively, curling into a ball to protect herself. It was no use. Her hands were still behind her back. Ernie kicked her another time, on her hip. On her back. On her upper arm. She could hear him grunting with effort, then he stopped.

Bennie lay panting in agony. Her entire body ached. Adrenaline poured into her system, leaving her shaking. Dirt dug into her cheek. Her eyes watered reflexively from the pain. She hurt too much to regroup. She had to think of something. She had to work on him. She told herself he kicked her because she must have gotten to him.

"Now you gonna tell me your password? Or do I have to beat it out of you?"

Bennie mustered her strength to speak. "If you keep this up, I'm not going to help you anymore."

"Ha!" Ernie laughed abruptly, then kicked her again.

CHAPTER THIRTY-THREE

Mary regained consciousness only slowly, then forced herself to wake up. Something inside was telling her she had to stay awake. She couldn't give in yet. She couldn't sleep. She couldn't give in to hopelessness. If she gave up she would die. She had heard what they said. She was somewhere, and the two men would kill her. She started to wake up more and heard them talking in the other room. There were still two men, Ray and not-Ray.

"Why didn't you get the password?" one man asked. It was Ray.

"She wouldn't give it to me."

"You couldn't get her to give it to you?"

"She wouldn't."

"So smack her around."

"I did. She wouldn't give it up."

"But she told you the cops know everything? She said she sent the email to the cops?"

"Yes and she said they told Simon. Simon knows too."

"You're so stupid."

"Why am I stupid?"

"She told you she sent the email. So why wouldn't she give you the password then?"

"I don't understand."

"The reason she wouldn't give you the password is because you would find out that she didn't send the email."

Mary tried to make sense of what they were saying, but she couldn't. They were talking about an email of some sort. Whether it was sent to the police. She had no idea what they meant. She didn't know who the *she* was they were talking about. It must've been the bigger one. The woman she was with. She couldn't remember who that was. It was strange. If she was with another woman, they must have been friends. Why couldn't she remember? What was wrong with her brain? What have they done to her? She tried to keep listening to the men. They sounded angrier than before.

"Maybe she just didn't want to give me the password."

"No. That bitch lied to you. She didn't send the email. The cops don't know anything. They arrested Simon. It was already on the news."

"Simon knows. She told Simon."

Mary's head turned at the name *Simon*, as if her body knew something that her brain didn't. Simon was a name she should know. Simon was somebody she knew. She tried to think who. But she knew it was somebody. It came to her then, a little boy's face. Then a man's. It was Simon. She had known him when he was little. Simon was an old friend of hers.

"And so what?"

"Simon's going to tell the cops."

"And what are they going to do about it?"

"They're going to investigate it. They have to, don't they?"

"Of course they don't. They're not going to believe him. He won't have any proof. They know he's under arrest and he'll say anything. And anyway, he doesn't even have his lawyer anymore. Even if he gets a new lawyer, the lawyer's going to tell him not to talk to the cops. So he's not going to tell the cops anything."

"The new lawyer can tell the cops. They'll investigate it, they have to."

Ray scoffed. "No they don't. They're cops. They have their boy. They're not gonna look at anybody else. They think Simon did it. We set him up perfectly. It was a great plan and it worked."

Mary felt a tingling as she listened. The men were talking about Simon and about lawyers. Suddenly she realized that she was a lawyer. Simon was a friend. She was Simon's lawyer. She couldn't figure out which man was talking. They were talking so fast she couldn't follow. Or she just couldn't follow because they were saying so much. She couldn't process the information even though she understood the words. It was like a flood of words and back-and-forth that she couldn't understand all at once.

"They figured it out. It didn't work that great."

"It was just a fluke that they figured it out. It was a fluke that Simon went to the lawyer and a fluke that bitch acted like she was working for us when she was working against us. You should've seen her at the meeting, full of herself, bossing everybody around. She loves it. I can't stand bitches like that. Todd hated her too. She worked him over. I have half a mind to go in there and beat the shit out of her."

"So why don't you?"

"What do you mean?"

"Why don't you go in? Why do you send me in?"

"You know the answer to that. Because she knows who I am."

"So what's the difference if she knows who you are?" Not-Ray sounded angry again. "We're going to kill her anyway. That's what you said. You said I'm going to kill her anyway. And she figured out who I am."

"No she didn't."

"Yes she did. She knows my name."

"How?"

"She took a guess."

"She knows about me?"

Mary thought Ray said that. She was losing track of who was talking when. She tried to think of something to do to save herself. It hurt too much to move. She couldn't even string a thought together. Her face felt wet and stickier than before. She was bleeding into the blindfold. The cloth stuck to her eyes as the blood dried. She blinked and blinked but more blood ran in. The thought nauseated her.

"I don't know," not-Ray said. "We didn't talk about you. She knows it's me."

"Whatever. Why are you getting so paranoid lately?"

"I'm not paranoid."

"Yes you are. You're griping. You on your period?"

"It's just that with Todd we had a plan. We had it planned out. This isn't planned out. And now we get two new people. Women."

"Stop with that. They're lawyers." Ray was getting testy, too.

"She's a famous lawyer, isn't she? She's famous?"

"What are you talking about?"

"She's famous."

"She's not that famous if you didn't know who she was."

Not-Ray fell silent, and Mary could hear some walking around. She remembered they were in a cabin. The floor must be made of wood. But the cabin seemed small. They were right outside her door. They weren't worried about her hearing because they were going to kill her. She was going to die in some horrible way. She began to feel the emotion she hadn't before. Stark, cold terror.

"Did she tell you she was famous?" Ray asked. "Were you talking to her?"

"No."

"You were gone awhile. You were talking to her, weren't you? What did she tell you? That she's rich and famous? Did she offer you money?"

"Yeah, she offered me money."

"How much?"

"She didn't say. She just said that she'd pay if we let her go. Her and her partner."

"She said that?"

"Yes."

"Anything else?"

"She wanted to know how the partner was. She doesn't want us to hurt her."

Mary heard it clearly, more clearly than before. Wherever they had walked to was closer than it was before. They had said *her partner.* The other woman, the bigger woman, must've been Mary's partner. Mary remembered in a flash. Her partner was named Bennie Rosato. An image materialized instantly in her brain, an image attached to the name. Tall, blonde, athletic. Bennie Rosato was her partner. She knew Bennie Rosato. She had known her a long time. Not as long as Simon but she knew her.

"She asked about her partner? That's touching. She's probably gay for her."

"Why you gotta say that?"

"Say what?"

"That she's gay?"

"It's the way she acts. Bossy."

"My sister is gay."

"Is she bossy?"

"All sisters are bossy." Not-Ray chuckled.

"Whatever. Listen. Go in and take a picture of DiNunzio."

Mary knew that name. It was her name. She remembered that her name was Mary DiNunzio. She had a partner named

Bennie Rosato. She had an old friend named Simon Something. She was a person. She started to feel more and more human. She existed as a human being because she knew other people. Otherwise she was just a bloody mess that could barely breathe.

"Why do you want her picture?"

"Just go do it."

"Why? Why do I have to go take her picture? It's disgusting."

"That's the point."

"So why can't you do it? She doesn't know you. She won't recognize you. Why do I have to do all the dirty work?"

"What's gotten into you?" Ray raised his voice.

"I don't like the way things are going. I think we should get out of here. I think we just should go." Not-Ray raised his voice, too.

"And leave them here?"

"Yes. Just leave them. If they die, they die. But it's not like we killed them. I killed them."

"You're losing your nerve. Sack up."

"I'm being smart. We got away with Todd. We might not get away with these two. Why put ourselves back on the hook? We killed Todd to get off the hook."

Mary pricked up at the name *Todd*. She knew that name. She couldn't remember the details and something told her there were a lot more details. But Todd was connected to Simon. The police thought Simon killed Todd, but Ray and not-Ray had killed Todd. And they had been working with a third man whose name she didn't remember.

"We're not doing that. We wait for Mo. He's on the way. Then we kill them. He's going to help us get rid of the bodies. He's bringing lye and all. He knows a place in the woods where no one will find them."

Mary tried to breathe but she was starting to pant from fear. It was because Ray and not-Ray were talking about lye. About burying her. About her and Bennie's bodies. Suddenly she realized what upset her so much. It wasn't that she and Bennie would be dead. It was her family. She remembered she had a family. A mother, a father. A husband, Anthony. Their faces floated into her consciousness. She knew what they looked like. She knew what it felt like to hug them. To hug them back. She even knew the way they smelled. She had a *family*. They all loved each other. It would kill them if she died.

"I think people are going to find them," not-Ray said, louder. "We're gettin' greedy."

"Now you're being paranoid."

"It's not paranoid. I don't think it's a good plan. I think we should just go. DiNunzio's going to die. She's bleedin' out. Rosato's never going to get out of the smokehouse. She's going to die in there. No one will find them."

"What about Mo's hunting buddies? They own the cabin jointly. They're coming up when black powder season starts."

"That's not 'til fall."

"So?"

"So here's my plan. We leave now. Then we wait a month or two, then we come up and clean up the mess. Then it's all over with. By then, Simon will get convicted. We didn't have to kill anybody else."

Mary was remembering more and more. Bennie had helped her. They had worked together. They had figured out it was a conspiracy to kill Todd because he knew something. The men were going to kill her and Bennie because they had found them out. That was all she could remember. But it was enough.

Mary had to figure out a way to get out of here. She didn't know where they had Bennie. She had to see if she could save herself and Bennie. She couldn't just lie here and wait for them to kill her.

"You know what they're going to smell like in two months, over summer? You know what they're going to *look* like? Ernie, you up for that? I'm not."

Mary heard his name. *Ernie.* Not-Ray was Ernie. Ray, Ernie, Mo. She wasn't going to let them kill her or Bennie. She had to get out of here. She tried to move but it hurt too much. She had to think of another way.

"It's a better plan, Ray. It's easier. It's no-risk."

"Tell you what. We'll talk to Mo about it when he comes."

"Why wait? Call him off. Leave and tell him not to come up."

"I'm not gonna do it without Mo. I'm not gonna change the plan without talking to him."

"It's not a change in the plan. It's makin' the plan. We made the plan on the fly."

"Ernie, it's not you and me that make the plan. It's me and Mo that make the plan."

"Oh really?"

"Yes, really."

"Then you're goin' to take her photo."

"Fine. Give me your phone. It takes better pictures than mine."

Mary heard footsteps coming to the door, then the door opened but there was no locking sound. So they hadn't locked her in. Maybe there wasn't a lock on it. It must've been a bedroom door. The footsteps walked right to her side, vibrating the wooden floor, and she stayed very still, terrified. These men were capable of murder. It scared her to be this close to him. She reminded herself he was only going to take her picture.

Ray pulled up her blindfold, but the blood made it stick to her eyelids. "Ugh," he said, recoiling.

"I can't see," Mary said, weakly. She kept her eyes closed. She didn't even try to open them. She was starting to get an idea. "I can't see anything. I can't open my eyes. Can you just wipe them? There's so much stuff. I can't see anything."

"Shut up, you dumb bitch! I'm not touching you again!"

Mary heard the click of a smartphone camera, then the

tread of footsteps as Ray walked to the door and shut it behind him. She blinked her eyes again and again, shifting onto her side so the blood would run out. It hurt her eyeballs to move her lids but she kept it up. She cleared her eyes enough to look around the room.

Everything was fuzzy but she could make out the outlines. There was a bed and nightstand with a lamp and an old land-line phone. If she could get to the phone, she might be able to call 911.

Mary started to move.

CHAPTER THIRTY-FOUR

Bennie heard a rustling outside the smokehouse door and keys jangling, so she rolled back in place as fast as possible. Every movement hurt her ribs. She had just found the door with her feet but she had to stop. She knew it took three rolls to get back to her original position. The rustling sounded closer and closer. She prayed this wasn't the end, that someone wasn't coming to kill her. If it was Ernie, she had a new approach she was going to try. A last resort to save her life and Mary's.

Bennie completed the third roll, getting herself back in place, trying to suppress the aches. It even hurt her ribs to breathe. Her front was turned away from the door. She lay in dread in the darkness, listening to the key in the lock. She was running out of options.

She'd made her way around to see if there were any other ways out, but there weren't. The smokehouse was an eight-by-eight square, because it took about five rolls to get from either side. She'd kicked along the wall on her back and tried to suss out any weakness, but the wall felt like fieldstone under her shoes. The only weak spot was the door, which sounded like wood, but she had just started exploring it when she heard the keys jingling.

The door scraped open on the dirt floor, and there were footsteps behind her, right at her neck. She felt the cool air again at her back, which told her she was in the correct position. She curled into the fetal position involuntarily, a body memory of the beating earlier. She still ached in her ribs, which must have been broken. She tried to stay calm. "Ernie, that you?"

"I need to know your password." It was Ernie.

"No, you don't. I told you." Bennie tried to regain her former bravado. It was harder since the beating.

"You asked how your partner was."

"Yes, how is she? Tell me." Bennie felt a bolt of fear that was impossible to suppress.

"I have somethin' to show you."

Bennie felt herself being rolled over, wincing with rib pain. Her blindfold was yanked up. She squinted against the sudden light from a smartphone. She could only see a shadow behind it, a hulking silhouette.

"This is how she's doin'." Ernie held up a smartphone photo, and Bennie gasped, horrified. Mary was lying down in a pool of her own blood, her face bloody. Her eyes were closed. She looked lifeless.

"Is she alive?"

"Yes, but she's bleedin' out."

Bennie willed herself to stay calm. She told herself that head wounds could be bloody. Not all of them were fatal. Mary could survive this, but not much longer. There was so much blood on the floor. "Ernie, please, you need to get her to a doctor. You need to get her help. Can she talk? Is she sensate?"

"Sensate?"

"Can talk and think."

"Don't know about that."

"Why are you showing me this?" Bennie struggled for emotional footing. She couldn't bear to look at the picture any longer. She stole a peek at the door, directly behind him. She was facing it now. It only looked like one layer of wood and it was weathered.

"Tell me the password and I'll get your partner to a doctor. The only chance she has is if you tell me the password."

"How do I know you'll do it?" Bennie glanced up at him, recognizing him now that her eyes had adjusted to the light. "So is this what you look like, Ernie?' "

Ernie pulled her blindfold down. "Tell me the password and I'll save her life."

"I don't believe you. You're going to let her die."

"Tell me the password."

"I'll tell you the password, but I'm going to tell you something else first. Don't you see what's going on? I know Ray is here, but are you waiting for Mo? I bet you are. Let me tell you what's going to happen when Mo gets here. They're going to kill you."

"Bullshit!" Ernie blurted out.

"Ernie, they're using you. Mo is Ray's brother-in-law. You're the odd man out. What did they tell you is going to happen? What did they say the plan was? That you're going to kill me and Mary, and then you're all going to drive away? That's not happening in a million years. You're a loose end, just like Todd was a loose end. They're going to kill you, Ernie."

"You don't know what you're talkin' about."

"But before they leave, they're going to stage the scene. They're going to frame you for our murders the way they framed Simon for Todd's murder. Don't you see the pattern here?" Bennie kept talking because he didn't stop her. "It's Ray who makes the plan, isn't it? He tells you what to do. He's framing you for my murder and Mary's. He made you take the photo of Mary, didn't he?"

"Wrong again. He took it."

"Who's camera is it? It's your camera, isn't it?"

Ernie didn't answer.

"I'll take that as a yes. The photo's not on Snapchat, is it? Of course not. You can try to delete it but that doesn't work. The cops will still find it. It's in the ether now. It's in the cloud. Nothing you delete from a cell phone is ever deleted. You know that. You're in security." Bennie sensed she was making headway. He hadn't kicked her again. "Hell, it's probably a company phone, isn't it? Ray did that for a reason, Ernie. He's framing you for my murder and for Mary's. In fact, he's tricking you into framing yourself. You're going to be dead as soon as Mo gets here."

"This is crazy," Ernie said, chuckling again.

"You must have a gun. You probably have a carry permit. I bet the only gun Ray wants to use is yours. Mark my words. Even if he has a gun or Mo does, they're not gonna use theirs to kill me or Mary. Even if there's a hunting rifle around, they're not gonna use that either." Bennie ignored her rib pain. It even hurt to talk. "But your handgun, yes. So they're going to make up some story that makes it look like we killed you trying to get away. It's gonna be three dead bodies up here, and you're one of them. End of story."

"Tell me your password if you want to save your partner's life."

"Ernie, what I'm saying is true." Bennie bore down, terrified at the thought of losing Mary. "They're *family*. Brothers-in-law. They trust each other. They're not gonna take a risk that you'll break ranks. Framing you and killing you solves everything. You're going to be dead as soon as Mo—"

"Tell me your password or I'll go down there right now and kill your partner."

"You said you would take her to a doctor."

"All right, I'll take her to a doctor."

Bennie knew he was lying. He wasn't going to take Mary to a doctor, but she couldn't take the chance. She told him her password, which was BEARLY12, after her first golden retriever. "But Ernie, be smart. Take Mary to a doctor. If you get her out of here, you can save yourself. Use her as an excuse. Take her and go."

"Just like that. What a joke."

"It could work," Bennie said, desperate. "Tell Ray she needs to get to a doctor, then drop her off at the nearest hospital and keep going. You'll be free. She'll see a doctor."

"Why would Ray agree to that?"

"Because it fits the facts better for a staged scene." Bennie was making it up as she went along. She hadn't figured out that part. "If she dies wherever she is, they can't arrange the body or move it without someone knowing. Blood spatter. Blood evidence. You know how forensics works."

Bennie heard the sound of his footsteps, walking away. Panic rose in her throat. She couldn't let Mary die, so horribly.

"Ernie, please! It's the smartest move. It's your only chance. It's her only chance. You said you would. Ernie. Ernie!"

Bennie heard Ernie close the door and lock it, leaving her in the darkness. Tears welled in her eyes but she let the blindfold soak them up. She told herself to get her head back in the game. She couldn't save Mary lying here.

She tried to wrench her hands apart for the umpteenth time, ignoring her aches, but the duct tape wouldn't give. But now she knew where the door was and what it looked like. It was an old door with a bar across the middle. The lock hadn't been embedded into the door, so it must have been a padlock outside. Not hard to break open, and her legs were strong. The noise might be a problem, but she had to try. She might be able to kick out the bottom. It would hurt like hell but adrenaline flooded her system.

She started rolling toward the door.

CHAPTER THIRTY-FIVE

Mary finally caught a lucky break. She had been inching her way along the floor, fighting the pain in her head, but she'd been afraid to make noise. She'd had to stop every inch or so to make sure Ray couldn't hear her, in the room outside the bedroom. But the last time she stopped, she noticed the sound of snoring coming from the other side of the door.

Ray had fallen asleep. The snoring was loud and deep. She started moving faster, wriggling along the floor like a snake toward the phone. Her hands were still wrapped in duct tape behind her back, and no matter how hard she tried, she couldn't wrench them apart. Her ankles were duct-taped too, and she couldn't get them apart.

She writhed along the wood floor, closer and closer to the phone. There was no rug on the floor, and she inched farther and farther, slipping along. It struck her suddenly that she was sliding in her own blood.

The thought shook her to her very foundation, but she couldn't stop. She didn't know how long Ray would be asleep, she had to get to the phone. She might be able to knock it from the table without waking him up.

Suddenly she heard a sound outside the room and she froze,

only three feet from the night table. There were footsteps on the floorboards in the other room, and she guessed Ernie had come back. She had missed her chance. She didn't know if she'd get another one. She didn't want to die here. She didn't want Bennie to die here.

"Ray, get up! We need to talk."

"Okay, relax," Ray said, grumpy. "Did you get the password?"

"Yes."

"Good."

"What is it?"

"BEARLY12."

"Good job. Did you have to beat it out of her?"

"No, I did what you said. I showed her the picture and told her I'd kill her partner if she didn't tell me. It worked."

"Nice."

Listening, Mary felt a wave of guilt that Bennie was worried right now about whether she was alive or dead. She couldn't imagine how horrible that picture was of her, and it must have horrified Bennie no end. It killed Mary to think they were using her to hurt Bennie. It struck Mary then that Bennie was in her family too.

"Ray, we need to talk. I want to understand the plan you're making."

"Hold on, let me look in the laptop. I want to see if she sent that email."

"Fine, we can talk while you're lookin'. I want to understand how you expect me to kill these women, exactly."

"What do you mean?" Ray asked, sounding preoccupied.

"I mean, what's the plan? Exactly. Shoot them? Or stab them like Todd? How am I supposed to do this?"

"Hold on. Here we go, I'm into the computer. Now all I have to do is get to the email. Let's see. She uses Thunderbird."

"Ray, can't you talk while you look through her email?"

"What's your rush? Cool your jets. Here we go. I'm in her sent email."

"So did she send it?"

"No!" Ray shouted, triumphant. "I told you! That bitch *lied* to you!"

"But we don't have wireless. Maybe it didn't get it? Or download it? Whatever?"

"It should have been there. She lied straight out. That's why she didn't want to give you the password. She was bluffing."

"Okay, *whatever.* I want to talk about the plan."

Listening, Mary was starting to remember more. The email they were looking for was about evidence. It was coming back to her now. A fire at one of Todd's accounts, that they had found out about online. Mary had wanted to tell the police. She had hoped to get it to the detective before they arrested Simon. But she had been too late. She had asked Bennie to send it, but Bennie must have forgotten. She wasn't sure why it mattered.

Mary kept her eye on the phone, not daring to move. She prayed they didn't come into the bedroom right now. They would see exactly what she was up to, but they sounded busy. Ernie was more agitated than before. Mary didn't know why.

"Ernie, what do you want to know about the plan?"

"How do you want me to kill them?"

"Well, the way I see it, we're going to do what's quick and easy. We're going to shoot them."

"And why is that?"

"Why not? I'm not worried about the noise, like with Todd. There's no reason to stab them. It's more of a mess to clean up. No one is ever gonna find these bodies. So we don't have to be careful."

"So whose gun are we going to use? The only ones who have guns are me and Mo."

"We use yours."

Ernie hesitated. "Why mine?"

"Again, why not? What's with all the questions? What difference does it make what gun we use?"

Mary wriggled closer to the phone stand, sliding in her own blood. She tried not to think about it. Her head still hurt so much. The shouting, the stress. Her skull pounded. Her body was so weak. She couldn't breathe. Every motion was an effort. She was two feet away from the night table.

"If it doesn't make a difference, let's use Mo's."

Ray hesitated. "Come to think of it, we can't use his. You're the only one with a carry permit."

"So what difference does that make?"

"I don't know, I was gonna figure it out with Mo. We're going to discuss it. I don't have all the details down yet." Ray sounded exasperated. "It makes sense to use your gun because yours is registered and licensed. You're the director of Security, for God's sake."

"So what?" Ernie raised his voice. "I thought the plan was to shoot them, bury their bodies, and cover them with lye. What difference does it make if they get killed with a registered and licensed gun?"

"What's the big deal? Why don't you want to use your gun?"

"What if somebody finds the bodies in the woods? They could find my bullet. The bullet could be traced to my gun. The bodies are going to decompose but the bullet never will."

Mary shuddered at the very notion. It made her sick to her stomach to think of hers and Bennie's bodies decomposing. She couldn't believe that their murder was being discussed like a game plan. She had to do something. She was running out of time. She looked up to see how far the phone was away from her. She estimated a foot.

"Mo says nobody's gonna find these bodies. He knows exactly where to bury them. Nobody comes up here."

"What about hunters? Dogs? Somebody goes huntin' or hikin' with a dog in the woods and the dog finds the bodies.

And before you know it, somebody calls the cops and there's my bullet."

"You're worrying about nothing. This is what I'm telling you, you're getting paranoid."

"You think I'm paranoid?"

"Yes, I think you're paranoid."

"I don't care if you think I'm paranoid. Let's say I'm paranoid. If Mo is so damn sure that he knows where these bodies can be buried, let's use his gun."

"What? Why? What gives here? That's not the plan—"

"You just said you didn't know what the plan was. You hadn't figured it out yet! Now you're telling me it's not the plan to use Mo's gun? What the hell, Ray? Don't pee on my leg and tell me it's raining."

"I don't want to say yes without checking with him. I don't even know if he's bringing it."

"Call him and ask him to bring it."

"I can't, there's no cell reception."

"Use the landline. I saw one in the bedroom."

Mary felt a bolt of fear at the sound. If they came in here now, she was dead. She reached the base of the night table, lying at the leg. She was in so much pain she could barely think. She wasn't sure what to do next. She had to get the phone off the table. She tried to free her hands but the duct tape held tight.

"I don't want to call him. We'll talk when he gets here. What's the rush?"

"What time's he getting here then?"

"He had to stay late at work. Two hours."

"That was two hours ago. He should be here by now."

"Maybe he got hung up. Maybe there was traffic. What the *hell* is your problem?"

Mary had to get the phone off the table. She struggled to sit up, so she could knock the phone onto the floor with her shoulder, but she didn't have the strength to raise her upper body. She felt dizzy and weak. She slumped back down.

"Did he say he was bringin' his gun?"

"Of course he's bringing it."

"How do you know? Did you ask him? You're the master planner. Or did you make sure that mine was the only gun? So we had to use mine—"

"No, I didn't!"

"So, did you ask him if he was bringin' his gun?"

"No, I didn't have to! He keeps it in the truck!"

Mary heard the conversation go from tense to heated. Ernie and Ray were starting to yell at each other. She hoped the shouting would hide whatever noise she made if the phone dropped. She had to wait for the moment. She held her breath. She had to make the right move. If she blew it, they would come in and kill her. Her head pounded hard. So did her heart.

"Ernie, what the hell are you trying to say? What is your *problem*?"

"Okay, you want to know what I'm sayin'? I'm sayin' that I don't know if I trust you anymore, pal!"

"What are you talking about? We've worked together fifteen years!"

"But we never killed nobody! I'm startin' to see you using me! You're treatin' me like garbage! Like I do your dirty work and you're the puppet master!"

"How?"

"You and Mo are family, I'm on the outs! I started to think, what if I kill these women and we *don't* all drive home together? What if you two decide to off me and go your merry way?"

"Why would we do that?"

"It solves all your problems, doesn't it? Somehow you stage the scene so you frame me for murderin' the women and you guys are gone! You'll never have to worry about me spillin' the beans! You guys are brothers! Lookin' out for each other! You always have!"

"Since when?"

Mary lay on the floor, blinking her eyes, trying to keep them clear of blood. Suddenly she spotted a phone wire running down the side of the night table. It was only six inches away. She went toward it, dolphining to the side of the night table.

"Since forever! That's how we got into this in the first place! You and Mo usin' the cheap wiring! The cheap drywall, too. The units wouldn'ta burned so fast if you used the five-eighths of an inch! The burn rate's slower in the good stuff, but he's paddin' the bottom line at PowerPlus and you're gettin' a cut!"

"Don't get high and mighty! You kept your mouth shut! We paid you fair and square!"

"So *you* say! What's a fair cut? I don't know if what you're tellin' me is true! You and Mo are thick as thieves!"

"Ernie, calm down! What you're saying doesn't make any sense! Mo is on the way with the lye! We're going to shoot these bitches, bury the bodies, and be done with it! We're a yard from the end zone here!"

"How do *I* know he's bringin' lye? I don't think he's bringin' any *lye*! I think you're just waitin' for him! I think *that's* your plan! Then he comes up, you shoot me, and you leave DiNunzio's car in the driveway with my car! You two go home in his truck, after I'm *dead*!"

"Ernie, you're out of your mind! There's no way! We're in this together! He's bringing the lye! That much we planned! The details about which gun we use, fine, whatever, we'll use his gun if that's what you want!"

"That's what I want! I want to use his gun!"

"Fine, we will!"

Mary got her face right next to the wire and tried to grab it with her lips behind the gag. She got it on the third try, struggling to breathe. She waited for the right moment to pull the phone off the table. She remembered that landlines used to be heavy and noisy. If the shouting kept up, she had a fighting chance. Then all she had to do was press 911 with her nose. For the first time in her life, she thanked God she had a big nose.

"And I want *him* to shoot the women, Ray! I don't want to shoot the women! You say it doesn't matter? It matters to me! I don't shoot *women*!"

"Okay, he'll do it! Sheesh! Just sit down! Let's sit down! Get out of my face! I feel like you're coming at me!"

"I'm tellin' you, I don't like this, Ray! It stinks to high heaven!"

"Ernie, sit down. Let's sit down. You need to calm down. Cool down. You want a beer? I'll get you beer."

"No, I don't want a beer." Ernie huffed loudly.

"Good, sit down. Take a breath. Geez, this is getting out of control."

"Ray, don't tell me what's gettin' out of control. What's out of control is that we got away with killin' Todd and now you want me to kill two women. One is a famous lawyer. You think the cops are gonna let that go? I don't think so. And it's all on me. I won't do it. I've done enough. I'm out."

"Okay, you're out," Ray said flatly, and suddenly, there was a shout and a terrifying burst of gunfire, *pop pop pop pop!*

Mary tried not to think about the horror of what was happening in the next room. She'd only get one chance. She tugged the phone cord. The phone came tumbling down on her head. She managed not to cry out in pain. The phone landed on the rag rug. The receiver fell right near her face.

Pop, pop! came more gunfire, and then there was silence.

Mary had to act. Ray had killed Ernie. Ray was going to shoot her and Bennie next. She didn't have a moment to lose. She heard a dial tone from the receiver.

She wiggled into position to call 911.

CHAPTER THIRTY-SIX

Bennie lay on her back, her feet pushing against the bottom part of the door. She ignored her rib pain, her will to survive in charge. She wished she could kick the door open, but she was too weak and she worried about making noise. The bottom of the door was the weakest, it must have rotted where rain had collected and snow had piled up.

She kept pressing and pressing, making isometric pulses, like killer lunges against the door, one after the next. She had been an elite rower in her younger days, almost making the Olympic team, and her thunder thighs were coming in handy.

She grunted with pain, pushing against the bottom of the door, feeling the boards weaken and finally begin to creak beneath her feet. She kept the pressure on and heard them splinter, then pressed harder, listening for the tiny breaks in the wood fibers as they gave way, her sense of hearing more acute because she couldn't see anything.

Bennie's feet burst through the door, sticking out the other side, then she shifted down, breaking through the hole with her calves, then her knees, and finally her whole body, sliding out of the smokehouse on her back.

Bennie rolled over on her side, then partway up, and staggered to her feet, blindfolded and handcuffed behind her back with the duct tape. She was finally outside, breathing in a deep lungful of fresh night air, ignoring the aches and pains, masked by another surge of adrenaline. She had to get going.

She hurried forward, hearing twigs and old leaves under her feet. Thorns scratched her ankles. She was in some kind of underbrush, and sooner or later, she knew she would hit a tree. In fact, she needed a tree. She turned around, walking backwards to mitigate any injury to her face, and she finally walked into a tree, from behind.

She had to hurry. She rubbed her duct-taped wrist up and down against the tree, feeling its rough bark scratch and tear her skin. The duct tape was on tight. The only way to get it off was remove it along with her skin.

She rubbed and rubbed, ignoring the pain and the blood, flaying her own skin until she finally rubbed off a section of the duct tape and broke her hands free. Her fingers flew to her blindfold and she ripped it off, whirling around to get the lay of the land.

The smokehouse was behind her at the top of the hill, but down in the valley she could see a small clapboard cabin with a peaked roof. It had a yellow bug light out front, and the wood looked as weathered as the smokehouse. Some of the windows were open, and she heard voices coming from within, Ernie and Ray shouting.

Suddenly she heard a fusillade of gunfire, *pop pop pop pop!*

The horrific noise rattled her teeth and jolted her senses, galvanizing her into action. She hustled down the hill toward the cabin, darting from tree to tree to keep from view. She prayed that they hadn't shot Mary.

Bennie scanned the area as she ran. The woods were dark, and there were no lights from phones or flashlights. She didn't know if the shooting had been outside or inside. Ray and

Ernie could be outside. She didn't know where Mo was. She hadn't heard any cars but she wouldn't have necessarily.

She hurried downhill to the cabin, her head wheeling around the entire time. The cabin was small, maybe two-bedroom, with the front door on the far right side of the front wall under a rickety shed roof and a window. The bedrooms must have been to the left. Lights were on inside, and the ambient light lit the area around the house.

Bennie veered left as she scurried down the hill. She knew at some level that she was in pain from her ribs, but she didn't feel a thing. Two cars were parked to the right on a dirt driveway, Mary's and a dark sedan that Bennie must have been brought in.

She scurried around the bedroom side of the cabin, using the trees as cover, her heart in her throat. She gave the cabin a wide berth and got level with the window in the front bedroom, which was lit from within. Bennie looked inside. The bedroom was empty and the door was open.

Bennie kept running around the cabin and came to the second bedroom, which was also lit. The bed was empty but the door was closed, which told her that Mary must be inside. They wouldn't leave Mary in the bedroom with the door open. Bennie prayed she was still alive.

She wished she had a weapon, but there was nothing. She looked around for a rock but there wasn't one. None of the tree limbs was small enough for her to break off for a club. She was racking her brain when a pickup appeared, approaching the cabin from the driveway side. She jumped behind a tree just as the truck's high beams raced over her tree.

She held her breath, her heart thundering. The high beams swept away, leaving her in darkness. It had to be Mo. The pickup drove up the driveway and parked next to the other cars. The ignition shut off, and the big engine rattled into silence.

The driver's-side door opened and the interior dome light went on, illuminating the driver as he climbed out of the truck. He was a slim blond man who Bennie didn't recognize, probably Mo.

Mo walked around the cabin to the front, and Bennie lost sight of him, which was when she realized something. She had a weapon. It had just arrived. She scurried around the back of the cabin and raced for Mo's pickup. It was a big black one with a massive engine.

She reached the truck and crept to the passenger side, then around the back bumper so she wouldn't be seen from the cabin. She hustled to the driver's side, opening the door quietly. She slid into the driver's seat, relieved to see the keys were still in the ignition.

Straight ahead lay the sidewall of the cabin, which had two windows into the living room. She could see that Ernie had been shot to death in a chair. His chest leaked blood. His head hung backwards at a hideously unnatural angle.

Ray and Mo stood next to him, talking. Bennie didn't wait to hear what they were saying. Ray stood on the left and Mo on the right. She could get them both, with any luck. Mary's bedroom door was closed. If Mary wasn't dead already, she was going to be in the next five minutes.

Bennie slipped on the seat belt, visualizing the steps in her mind. She had to do it all at once before Ray and Mo had time to realize what was happening. If they got out of the cabin, she'd never be able to get them. They'd shoot her and Mary.

She twisted on the ignition and stomped on the gas pedal. The truck zoomed forward instantly, its high-volume engine roaring to life and its back tires spitting gravel and dirt. Bennie hung on tight, powered ahead, and drove the truck directly into the cabin.

The truck exploded through the wall with a deafening crash.

Bennie rocked but the seat belt held her. Clapboard busted. Windows shattered. Glass flew. Electrical wires got yanked out.

Bennie plowed all the way into the living room. The truck hit Mo, crushing his chest. The impact sent him flying backwards against the wall between the bedrooms. The sight horrified her but it was kill or be killed. Mary's door blew open.

Ray lunged out of the way, diving for the floor. A gun flew from his hand and went sailing into the air as he fell.

Bennie braked, tore off the seat belt, and leapt from the driver's seat to get the gun. Ray lunged for the gun at the same time. Bennie was there first. She had almost reached it when Ray grabbed her ankle and yanked her backwards. The gun slipped from her grasp.

"No!" Bennie screamed in pain and fear.

"You bitch!" Ray jumped on her, grabbed her hair, and slammed her face into the wood floor. Her forehead pounded but she stayed conscious. She kicked backwards, torqued her body, and flipped him behind her, so she was lying on top of him face-up.

Ray hooked his forearm around her throat. Bennie clawed his arm, trying to pry his fingers off, raking his skin. His grip got tighter. He grunted with effort and satisfaction. She gagged, coughing, momentarily helpless. He was going to strangle her. The gun was far away from them both.

Suddenly Bennie spotted Mary, her hands and feet bound with duct tape, wriggling on her stomach toward Mo's crumpled body. Mary was gagged, her features barely recognizable through the blood. Still Mary started making urgent noises in her throat, as if she were trying to tell Bennie something.

Then Bennie saw what Mary meant.

There was a gun lying on the floor next to Mo. Mo must have had a gun on him, tucked into the back of his waistband. It had come out when he'd fallen.

Bennie felt her head growing light. She gagged and coughed.

She couldn't breathe. Ray was choking her from behind. He was strangling her, squeezing her neck in the crook of his forearm.

Bennie looked directly at Mary. Their gazes connected. They both knew they had one last chance. Bennie knew what she had to do. And she knew it was the time to do it. So did Mary.

Bennie mustered every last bit of strength in her body, pulled down on Ray's forearm, and savagely kicked backwards at his ankles, again and again.

Ray's grip loosened, giving Bennie a split second of air. Gasping, she tore his arm off her neck, scrambled up, and lunged for Mo's gun. He caught her by the sleeve but it ripped off.

She grabbed the gun from the floor, whipped the barrel around, and started firing. Ray was already in motion, coming after her.

Pop pop pop, went the gun. Fire burst from the muzzle. The air filled with smoke and cordite.

Bennie kept firing, emptying the gun. Bullets struck Ray in the stomach and legs. He dropped to his knees. Blood burst like red blooms from every bullethole. He fell face-first to the floor. The wounds weren't fatal, but he was immobilized.

Bennie dropped the gun and whirled back to Mary. Mary lay motionless on the floor, her hands taped cruelly behind her. The back of her head was bloodied and her hair matted with dried blood.

"Mary!" Bennie knelt beside her, turned her over gently, and picked the bloody gag from her mouth. "Mary, are you okay?"

Mary nodded, coughing.

"Thank God!" Bennie looked frantically around. There were two phones on the ground, probably Mo's. One was the company smartphone, probably password-protected, and the other was a burner phone. She grabbed the burner with her free hand. "Don't worry, I'm calling 911!"

"I already did . . . on the landline," Mary said hoarsely, then resumed coughing. "I couldn't talk . . . but I think they can tell where we are . . ."

Bennie looked around for the landline, praying that Mary could stay alive until help got here.

CHAPTER THIRTY-SEVEN

Mary felt only dimly aware of what happened next. There was a lot of commotion with her at the center. Paramedics and police filled the cabin to bursting. They swarmed around her, taking her vital signs and putting her on a stretcher, then fitting an oxygen mask to her face and a stiff plastic collar around her neck. They placed orange foam blocks on either side of her head, then lifted her onto a gurney and wheeled her outside.

Red and blue lights flashed through the night. Sirens blared, making her head feel even worse. There were more cops, paramedics, and other people outside. Two paramedics rushed her to the back of an ambulance, loaded her inside, then slammed the doors closed after Bennie climbed in.

One paramedic shouted to the driver. The ambulance lurched off. The other paramedic started doing more things to Mary, hooking up an IV, wiping her face, and rattling off vital signs.

It got harder and harder for Mary to stay awake and she began to feel herself give up again. She hurt so much she didn't want to feel anything anymore. Every bump of the ambulance made her head hurt. She was dimly aware that the paramedics were talking to each other about her and answering questions from Bennie, but Mary didn't understand what they were saying.

She felt a calm rush over her, a certain peace that was telling her to let go. She was in God's hands now, and she had to keep her faith.

She kept her eyes closed, letting herself slip out of consciousness, and in time she felt herself floating away. She sensed she would have flown away completely, gone up to Heaven or out into space, if not for something anchoring her to the Earth, tethering her to the planet by the warmth of its very human grasp.

Somebody was holding her hand.

Somebody who wasn't letting go.

Mary didn't have to open her eyes to know who it was.

Her heart told her.

CHAPTER THIRTY-EIGHT

Bennie sat on the waxy paper of an examining table, still dressed in her bloody and torn clothes, having been examined by a doctor, a physician assistant, and a nurse. Mary had been taken to another examining room, and Bennie felt nervous and edgy, not knowing how she was doing. Mary had been unconscious when they got to the hospital, and nobody was giving Bennie any information, much less guarantees. She had cross-examined the paramedics in the ambulance, but they had kept their mouths professionally closed. They weren't about to give her medical information about Mary because Bennie had no legal standing vis-à-vis her. Under federal law, friends didn't count.

Bennie got off the table and started pacing, which always made her feel better, even though she had an array of aches and pains for which they'd given her megadoses of Advil. She heard that Ray was in surgery but expected to survive, which improved her mood. She didn't want him dead, she wanted him in jail. She herself was fine except for two cracked ribs, and they'd cleaned her up, bandaged her hands and wrists, and given her a butterfly stitch at her hairline, promising that the cut wouldn't scar. At this point, Bennie would wear any scar as a badge of honor.

"I'm back," said the nurse, pushing aside a patterned curtain, with a pleasant smile. Her name was Karen, and she was a middle-aged woman with short brown hair and rimless glasses that emphasized the roundness of her pretty face.

"Is there any news about my friend Mary?"

"No, nothing." Karen looked away, which Bennie took as a bad sign. Every time a jury returned with a losing verdict, they always looked away when they came back into the courtroom. Every lawyer knew it. It was a juror tell.

"Would you let me know if there's anything I should know?"

"Yes, of course." Karen handed her a smartphone. "You asked for a phone? You can use mine."

"Oh, thank you." Bennie accepted the smartphone, grateful. The screen had a picture of a corgi in a cart. "Poor little guy."

"She's fine. She drives better than most people."

"Thank you, I won't be long." Bennie wanted to call Declan and Detective Lindenhurst, but she wasn't sure whom to call first.

"Good, because there are a few policemen outside who want to speak with you."

"The local cops? I spoke with them already and I asked them to contact the Philadelphia police."

"They did but they just want to check one or two things with you."

"Okay, I need to make two calls. I'll keep it short."

"Sure, okay. Just come out when you're finished and I'll have your discharge papers ready."

"Thanks." Bennie scrolled to the phone function, hesitated, then made the first call.

"Babe, are you okay?" Declan asked, alarmed. "I've been calling and texting. Anthony's been calling Mary. We heard you left the hospital together. We're both worried. Her family—"

"I'm okay and so is Mary." Bennie felt so good to hear his voice. Emotions welled up from somewhere behind her cracked ribs, but she didn't want to give in to them right now, when she had so much to do. "This was as soon as I could get to a phone."

"Where are you? What happened?"

"I don't have time to fill you in now."

"Give me the headline."

"We figured out who killed Todd and framed Simon. It was a conspiracy."

"Are you serious?"

"They tried to kill us but they couldn't."

"*What?* Oh my God, are you hurt? Is Mary?"

"I'm fine. I'll keep you posted but I'm worried Mary has a head injury. She's in the examination room now."

"Oh no," Declan said, hushed. "Should I tell Anthony?"

"Yes, and I'll call as soon as I know more."

"Who killed Todd? Where are they? Were they arrested?"

"Two are dead, one survived." Bennie felt her stomach twist. She took no pleasure in killing Mo. She never would've done it but to defend herself and Mary.

"How did *that* happen?"

"I'll tell you another time." Bennie didn't want to elaborate now. "I have to call the Philly police, brief them, and try to convince them to release Simon."

"Okay, so where are you?"

"I'm at a hospital in the boondocks. If it had more activity, there would be reporters, so there's a silver lining." Bennie realized she couldn't wait to see Declan. She just wanted to bury her head in his chest and feel his arms around her. She wanted to feel safe again. "Where are you?"

"I'm outside Philly on my way to CHOP."

"You're not home?"

"No, I left as soon as Anthony called me. He can't reach Mary."

"Thanks," Bennie said, touched. She felt tightness in her chest again and chalked it up to recent injuries, if not true love.

"Do you want me to come to you?"

"No, thanks. I gotta go call the cops. I love you."

"Babe, I love you too. I'm sorry we fought."

"Me too. Call you later."

"Love you, bye." Declan ended the call, and so did Bennie. She exhaled, got her emotional act together, then dialed the number for the Homicide Division, which she unfortunately knew by heart.

"This is Bennie Rosato, can you put me through to Detective Lindenhurst?" she asked, and she was put through immediately.

"This is Lindenhurst. Bennie, I've been expecting your call."

"Did the local police contact you?"

"Yes, they did. They briefed me."

"Have you released Simon?"

"Not yet."

"Why not? The charges should be dropped. He didn't commit the murder."

"I can't do that without a statement from you and Mary, in addition to our own investigation. We understand one of the suspects, Ray Matewicz, is alive. We need to talk to him."

"You may have heard that Mary was very seriously injured. She's in no shape to give a statement. I can give a statement for us both."

"I'm sorry to hear that." Detective Lindenhurst's tone changed. "I like Mary very much."

"She'll be fine," Bennie said, unsure if she was trying to convince him or herself. "Detective, if you've spoken with the locals you have more than enough information to release Simon. You don't need to wait for Ray."

"I'm afraid that's not true. We have procedures to follow. I have to speak with the ADA and the DA."

"Simon has a sick child and he needs to be with her. She needs her father. Her grandfather had a heart attack. I'm not going to stand around while you drag your feet."

"I understand your position. We have to follow procedures and complete our investigation. We need you to come down and make a statement."

"I already gave it to the locals. I told them everything. Can't you get it from them?"

"No. We need one of our own. We need you to come down to the Roundhouse."

"Why? I'm staying with Mary. I'm not leaving her. If you really need a statement, I can give it now, by phone."

"We have procedures. After we have all our i's dotted—"

"Release him," Bennie said, beginning to get angry.

"We can't do that. We just can't open the door and let him out—"

"Yes you can, and you damn well better." Bennie felt her temper give way, even if it wasn't completely lawyerly. "Simon Pensiera is an innocent man. He was wrongly charged for murder by *you*. The men who killed Todd tried to kill me and Mary tonight. Is that enough for you? How much proof do you need?"

"Bennie, relax and—"

"Don't you dare tell me to relax!" Bennie had never interrupted anyone so much. She was turning into Mary and she liked it. "If anything happens to Simon's daughter while he's wrongly in your custody, I will sue you personally, I will sue everybody in the Homicide Division, and I will sue the city of Philadelphia!"

"Wait, hold on—"

"No, *you* hold on!" Bennie exploded, taking out all of her rage and frustration on Detective Lindenhurst, which was his own damn fault. "I will garnish every cent you make until the day you retire and then I'll take your pension! I will take your house and I will take your car! Do you hear me? I will not permit you to imprison my client when you know full well that he's innocent! What part of I-will-ruin-you don't you understand?"

"Bennie?" Karen called from the curtain, and Bennie didn't know how long she'd been standing there.

"Karen, sorry." Bennie covered the phone with her hand. "Was I making too much noise?"

"No, that's not it." Karen's face fell. "Mary's being Medevac'd to University of Penn Hospital in Philly."

"Why?" Bennie asked, her heart aching.

"They can run tests that we can't. They have a specialized trauma care unit, a neurological ICU."

"Does she need surgery?" Bennie's face twisted.

"I don't know. They just told me to get you."

"I want to go with her."

"Fine, but we have to hurry."

Bennie said into the phone, "Detective Lindenhurst, if you want a statement, I'll be at the University of Pennsylvania Hospital. Good-bye."

CHAPTER THIRTY-NINE

Mary couldn't seem to stay awake, she didn't know why. Her head was killing her. She knew only that she had been in a noisy helicopter with new medical personnel and Bennie still holding on to her hand. She'd been only dimly aware when the helicopter landed and was met by another group of medical personnel who hustled her on her gurney onto a windy rooftop, then rushed her through hospital corridors with everyone running alongside her shouting to one another, holding IV bags of blood and saline, and rolling equipment on stalks.

Bennie never let go. She ran faster than all of them.

They ended up in another examination room, where they examined her all over again, stitching up the back of her head. They gave her an ultrasound at her bedside, then swept her off to a CAT scan, after which they told her what was wrong. She had an epidural hematoma, a blood clot caused by blunt trauma. They were trying to decide if she needed surgery, evaluating as tests were performed.

Mary caught snippets of their conversation; "no coma," "no pupillary changes," "EDH volume less than thirty milliliters," "midline shift less than five millimeters," and "clot thickness less than fifteen millimeters."

Mary didn't know what the details meant, but she sent up a silent prayer.

She was lucky and blessed to have come this far.

She had a lot to live for.

Her family.

CHAPTER FORTY

While Mary was being examined, Bennie gave her statement to Detective Lindenhurst and two other detectives in a spare meeting room at the hospital. She started with the partnership dispute with Mary, the interview of Todd at OpenSpace, and how she came to obtain the company documents, compare them with Simon's emails, and discover the hidden emails, then the fatal fire at Bethlehem Bank. She finished by telling about the abduction, how Ernie had been murdered by Ray, then how she had hit Mo with his truck and shot Ray in self-defense.

Declan sat next to her during the entire account, and his presence didn't seem as unusual to her as it would have before. She never would've had a boyfriend with her in any legal proceeding, but she wanted him close. Before she'd met with Detective Lindenhurst, she'd told Anthony what happened to Mary, out of earshot of Mary's family, The Tonys, and two of Simon's cousins, all waiting for Mary in the lounge. Bennie couldn't wait to rejoin them, another new feeling, but she was going with the flow. Feet was in stable condition in the very same hospital, and Rachel was next door at CHOP, watched over by Simon's third cousin.

Bennie finished her statement. "So Detective Lindenhurst, I assume that covers everything."

"You might be right." Detective Lindenhurst closed his skinny notebook, looking up. "I don't have any further questions."

"I don't see how you could." Bennie reined in her temper but it wasn't easy. "When are you going to release my client? He needs to be with his daughter and father right now, not sitting in a jail cell for a crime he didn't commit."

"I understand your position. We're in the beginning stages of our investigation."

"What have you done?"

"We've spoken with Mike Bashir, the company president. He's returned from Scottsdale. We don't believe he has any knowledge of what Ray and Ernie were up to, so the conspiracy doesn't go any higher."

"Agree, but he was concerned about the police searching his office."

"We discussed that with him and we cleared him. We're waiting on Ray Matewicz, who's in stable condition. We've begun to liaise with the local police, since it's outside of our jurisdiction to get the bodies autopsied and examined—"

"What difference does that make?" Bennie interrupted, even though she was trying not to interrupt. "What more could you need?"

"Bennie, you know these things are complicated when you're liaising with other jurisdictions. They don't work as fast as Philly. They don't have the personnel or the access to the labs." Detective Lindenhurst checked his watch. "And it's two thirty in the morning."

"What are you talking about? I'm awake, you're awake, judges are on call twenty-four/seven, and so are district attorneys."

"Not out there. I can't raise anybody."

Declan frowned. "We're talking about Clearfield County?"

Detective Lindenhurst nodded. "Yes, the cabin was in the town of Hobart in Clearfield County. Todd Eddington was killed in Philadelphia County, but Ernie Greeley and Mo Nustrall were killed in Clearfield County. As such, Clearfield County has complete jurisdiction over those cases, though they're related cases. I have to coordinate with them before I can release Simon."

Declan blinked. "I know the district attorney in Clearfield County. Walker Severn."

"Yes, that's his name," Detective Lindenhurst said, surprised. "How do you know him?"

"I was a state trooper for over a decade. Clearfield County may be the boondocks to you city folk, but it was in my district. I know the players. Why don't I call Walker? See if I can light a fire under everybody?"

"Yes!" Bennie perked up. "Call him."

Detective Lindenhurst hesitated. "It's not standard procedure—"

"*What?*" Bennie wasn't having any. "Since when is the old boy network *not* standard procedure? Please, I've been on the outside of it my entire legal career. Don't tell me that Declan can't call some guy who can call some other guy to pull some strings! We're only asking them to speed things up!"

Detective Lindenhurst raised a hand. "I was about to say that even though it is not standard procedure, I'm not against Declan making a call to expedite this matter, given the circumstances."

"I'll do it right now." Declan took his cell phone from his back pocket, and Bennie reconsidered the merits of bringing her boyfriend to a legal proceeding, especially when he proved useful.

Declan put the call on speakerphone after he reached Walker Whoever and together they hashed out the steps required to gain Simon's release. It took another half hour and when the conference call was finished, Declan met her eye in a meaningful way, telegraphing that he was satisfied but he knew enough not to say so, in case she didn't agree. She was falling more and more in love with him every minute, but that would have to wait.

Bennie turned to Detective Lindenhurst. "So let's nail this down. When are you releasing Simon?"

"If Walker comes through with the information we requested, I'm hoping I'll be able to release Simon by tomorrow afternoon."

"Or nine o'clock."

Detective Lindenhurst smiled slightly. "Noon is a possibility."

"How about ten o'clock? I'll settle for ten o'clock."

"I'll see what I can do." Detective Lindenhurst chuckled, rising, and everybody behind him stood up, getting ready to leave.

"Thank you." Bennie stood up, too. Her ribs were hurting again but she ignored it. "I'm sorry I yelled at you before."

"It's okay. It happens." Detective Lindenhurst's smile widened.

Declan burst into laughter. "At least she apologized to you. I think she likes you better than me."

Bennie laughed too. "I don't like anybody better than you right now. You're golden!"

They all laughed again, said their good-byes, and walked to the door of the meeting room. Detective Lindenhurst and the others went left, heading for the elevators, and Bennie and Declan turned right, toward the lounge. Just then, she spotted a familiar figure midway down the hall, coming toward them. Nate, wearing a blue sweater, pressed jeans, and a contrite expression.

"That's Nate Lence," Bennie said under her breath.

"*The* Nate Lence?" Declan focused on Nate like a police dog. "Am I allowed to take him outside? We're already at the hospital. He won't have to go far to get stitches. Or crutches. It's convenient for all parties."

"No." Bennie smiled. "Just be nice and civil."

"Is hand-to-hand combat civil?"

"Please be nice, for Mary's sake. She's what matters now."

"Fine," Declan said, resigned.

Nate reached them in the hallway. "Bennie, I heard what happened and I came to say how sorry I am. About Mary, about you, and everything."

"Thank you. Nate, meet Declan Mitchell."

"Nice to meet you, Declan." Nate pursed his lips, extending a hand to Declan, who shook it without breaking it off.

"Hello, Nate."

Nate turned to Bennie. "I was just in the lounge. I met Simon's family and Mary's. I'm going to get to the bottom of what happened at OpenSpace. I'll find a way to make it right. First thing in the morning, I'm going to speak to Corporate Giving at CHOP. I'm sure the Blood and Marrow Unit could use a contribution."

Declan interrupted, "Does money excuse what you did? Firing Bennie? Accusing Mary of disciplinary violations?"

Bennie rushed to say, "Nate, I'm sure CHOP would appreciate that. Now, we have to go. We want to be with Mary's family as well."

Nate avoided Declan's eye. "I truly am sorry. We can talk later."

"We don't have anything to talk about, Nate. Good-bye." Bennie started to walk away, taking Declan's hand before he used it to commit bodily harm.

"But Bennie," Nate called after her, turning. "We do have cases coming in, and I'd like for you to represent Dumbarton again. We need you in your former role."

"No, thank you," Bennie called back, taking Declan away. "We have to go. Good-bye."

They left Nate behind, and Declan looked over. "Nice burn, babe."

"Wasn't it? And you behaved yourself. Sort of."

"That's because I love you."

"I love you, too." Bennie smiled, but it faded as they reached the lounge. She could see Mary's teary family through the glass window. "I hope she's going to be okay."

"Me too," Declan said quietly, opening the door.

CHAPTER FORTY-ONE

Mary didn't open her eyes, though her head felt better. They'd told her that she wouldn't need surgery but had to be monitored, with "neuro checks" and "serial CT scans" administered at regular intervals. She couldn't eat in case she had to go to surgery, but she wasn't hungry anyway.

She was so tired, but she could hear all of the people she loved around her, and she listened to their quiet voices as if it were the most beautiful music she had ever heard. Anthony was talking to her mother-in-law El Virus, her mother was praying softly, and her father was whispering for the first time in her life. Mary heard Bennie, Declan, and Judy too.

Mary waited to hear Simon's voice, but she didn't, and it nagged at her as she drifted in and out of sleep. She worried about Feet and Rachel, wondering how they were. She assumed The Tonys were with Feet.

Mary knew it must be daytime because she felt a warm square of sunlight on her bed, though she didn't know what time it was. Her head felt heavy and her throat hurt. She could feel the oxygen tube lying against her cheek and a plastic clip around her index finger. She knew she would look horrible, but luckily she was among family, which was best defined as people who love you no matter what you look like.

She drifted back to sleep to the lullaby of everyone talking, and the next time she woke up, she recognized another voice: Simon's. Mary worried that Simon wouldn't be in the room long, since he had Rachel and Feet to take care of, so she tried to wake herself up to talk to him.

"How's Rachel?" Mary opened her eyes enough to see them clustering around her. But no one answered her question about Rachel. She felt a tingle of concern that there was bad news and they were keeping it from her.

"Simon, how's Rachel?" Mary asked again, dry-mouthed.

"She's fine," Simon answered, materializing at Mary's side and giving her arm a reassuring squeeze.

"For real?"

"Yes, absolutely. They think they might have found a new donor. We have only one more test to go, then we'll know for sure."

"That's wonderful." Mary felt the news suffuse her with joy. "And your father?"

"Dad's still stable. He might get a stent. He's worried about you."

"We're all worried about each other."

"That's love."

"Yes, it is." Mary felt a familiar grasp on her hand, but this time it felt different than before. It was Anthony. "Anthony, you okay?"

Everybody smiled, and Anthony answered, "Now I am."

"Good. Love you." Mary let herself drift back to sleep. She didn't need to hear Anthony tell her he loved her. She already knew.

She was lucky and blessed in him and all of them, and when she finally succumbed to sleep, she felt in a state of grace, even on Earth.

Because Heaven was right here.

CHAPTER FORTY-TWO

Bennie and Declan didn't get back to her house until dawn, and Bennie shut the door behind them, exhausted and in some pain. The Advil and adrenaline had finally worn off, as if her body knew it was finally time to let down, and as she turned away from the door, she felt a deep ache from her broken ribs.

"Hurting?" Declan asked, concerned. "Why don't you go upstairs and lie down? I can make you some eggs and bring them up."

"No thanks, I'm not hungry." Bennie trundled to the staircase. "All I want is to get out of these disgusting clothes, take a shower, and sleep for a month."

"Go right ahead. I'll be up in a minute. I'll make you a cup of tea."

"That would be nice." Bennie kicked off her shoes and trudged up the stairs, feeling achy with each step, holding on to the banister for support. She reached the top, headed into the bathroom, and closed the door behind her. She flipped on the light and avoided the mirror, knowing it would give her nightmares.

She took off her blazer, which was stained with blood that had dried in stiff patches. She was about to drop it on the tile floor when she noticed that one side of the blazer was heavier than the other. She realized something was in the pocket and she put her hand inside, surprised to find Mo's burner phone still in her pocket. She must've left it there.

She pulled it out, shuddering at the bloody fingerprint on the phone cover. It was her print from when she thought she needed to call 911. She flashed on the two cell phones that had been on the floor next to Mo's body, his company-issued smartphone and his burner phone. Mo must've kept the burner for his machinations with Ray and Ernie. It would probably hold evidence that would support her statement, so she made a mental note to turn it in to the police. But she felt curious about what was inside.

Bennie flipped it open and scrolled to the text function, but there were no texts, which probably meant that they had been deleted. She didn't know if the burner phone supported encryption apps or the like and she was too tired to care. She flipped to the phone call function to check the recent calls. A list of recent calls popped onto the screen.

Bennie recognized the first number, which appeared twice. She didn't know if it mattered, but it didn't make sense. She needed her new favorite sounding board.

"Declan, can you come up?" Bennie called downstairs, getting her second wind.

CHAPTER FORTY-THREE

Sunday morning was insanely humid, and Bennie felt the relief of air-conditioning as she opened the door to Vetri's, the same fancy restaurant that she'd met Nate in before. She acknowledged the maître d' and made her way through tables packed with people having brunch. The air was filled with happy chatter and grinding espresso machines. It smelled like fresh coffee and artisanal rolls.

"So we've come full circle," Bennie said, pulling out her chair when she reached the table.

"We have." Nate rose while she sat down, looking fresh in a linen sportcoat, blue T-shirt, and jeans.

"Do you have an entire rich-guy wardrobe?"

"There's a reason for that." Nate took his seat. "I was so glad when you called."

"Well, I thought it over. I changed my mind."

"How so?" Nate leaned over the table with a warm smile. "Is this where you tell me you like me better than Declan?"

"No." Bennie shot him a warning look. "And no more talk like that."

"Got it." Nate put up a hand. "Limit-setting. This far and no further. I got it. For the time being."

"I mean it," Bennie said sternly. "Declan didn't agree with me being here today, but I don't want to throw the baby out with the bathwater. I've done a lot of great work for Dumbarton, and we've been friends a long time."

"Truth," Nate said, in an encouraging tone. "So does this mean you're working for me again? Please?"

"Yes, but with a few conditions."

"Terrific!" Nate brightened. "What are they?"

"You write to the disciplinary boards and withdraw your complaint about Mary. You dismiss your defamation lawsuit against Simon. And you settle Simon's suit against OpenSpace for whatever Mary asked, because we have you dead to rights."

"We?" Nate lifted an eyebrow.

"Yes, and I'm not finished yet. You apologize to Mary when she gets out of the hospital for what you put her through. And you better make a contribution to CHOP. You want to buy your way back into Heaven, it's going to cost you."

"And if I do it all? We start over?"

"Yes, I was angry with you, but it's not fair to blame you for what happened. You didn't know what was going on. You didn't even know those guys."

"Not at all. Thank you." Nate nodded. "How's Mary?"

"Recovering, thanks. She lucked out."

"I'm so sorry she went through that. And you, too."

"It was pretty awful." Bennie didn't want to elaborate, not with him. She was here doing what she had to do. "What are you going to do about what happened? Todd, Mo, Ray, and Ernie were cutting corners on the electrical. A woman died at Bethlehem Bank. They may have been cutting other corners, and how are you going to get to the bottom of it?"

"I turned it over to Jason to investigate and he's great. He'll follow the facts and if we need to fire or even charge anyone else, we will." Nate's expression turned grave. "And down the line, I'm selling OpenSpace, PowerPlus, and the other subs involved in cubicle manufacturing. I'm getting out of the business entirely."

"Really?" Bennie asked, surprised.

"Yes, you can work on the deals. It might make you feel better."

"I'm never happy when people lose jobs, Nate."

"I'm not closing the companies, I'll sell them. I'll lose money, given what those knuckleheads did to the brand, but I want to be done with it. I assume you saw the media. The PR is terrible."

"What would you expect?" Bennie had seen the headlines and knew that it would bother him. Appearances were everything to Nate.

"Whatever. Now that you're back on board, I'll buy another coat company. Do some good in the world. Get into the social justice business."

"I don't think social justice is a business, Nate."

"You know what I mean." Nate chuckled.

"I do. I know exactly what you mean. In fact, I thought I knew you better than I did, but it turns out I was wrong."

"What about?"

"I thought you were totally surprised that those guys were up to no good."

"I was."

"I thought you didn't know any of them. Not Todd, not Ray, not Mo, and not Ernie."

"I didn't know them. I don't know them."

"You disappoint me, Nate. For the last time."

"What do you mean?" Nate frowned, and Bennie dug in her purse, pulled out Mo's cell phone, and set it on the table between them, bloody fingerprint and all.

"This is Mo Nustrall's burner. The blood belongs to me."

Nate glanced at the phone. He pursed his lips but said nothing.

"Nate, if you didn't know Mo Nustrall, why did you call him? I looked at his call log. Your number is there twice. The second time you called him was an hour before he tried to kill me."

Nate's expression changed, his eyes hardening as he met her gaze directly. "So I take it you're wearing a wire?"

"Bingo. I just wanted to be the one to tell you that you got caught. I told the cops you would never admit anything to me." Bennie smiled. "Once the cops showed Ray the phone, he flipped on you. It gave him a bargaining chip, and he served you right up. You knew everything, all the corner-cutting to pad your margins. You found out about it at PowerPlus on one of your factory tours, when you overheard Mo on the phone. But you didn't fire him, you covered it up and expanded the operation. It turned criminal when Adele Watson died in that fire at Bethlehem Bank, and it was a slippery slope. You conspired to kill Todd, Ernie, then even Mary and me. I'm trying not to take it personally."

Nate glanced around the dining room, newly edgy. "So there's undercover cops here?"

"Right again. You're going to jail for a very, very long time." Bennie rose, standing aside because undercover police were already in motion, jumping up from their tables and coming toward them. Uniformed police had burst into the restaurant and charged toward the table. They all swarmed Nate, who looked wildly around but realized he had no escape. One cop frisked him, and another slapped a pair of steel handcuffs on his wrists.

Nate looked at Bennie, stricken. "I need a lawyer."

"You're kidding, right?" Bennie snorted.

A third cop said, "Mr. Lence, you are being arrested for conspiracy to commit murder and criminal conspiracy. You have the right to remain silent, and if you cannot afford an attorney, one will be appointed for you . . ."

Nate tried to hide his face as the police escorted him past the stunned gaze of the other patrons, some of whom raised their phones, taking pictures and filming.

Bennie watched him go with grim satisfaction. She flashed on the picture of Adele Watson from the Bethlehem Bank website. Nothing could bring Adele back, but justice was still the best consolation prize going.

Bennie left the table, grabbing Mo's phone. Her work here was done, and she had to get to the hospital.

CHAPTER FORTY-FOUR

By Wednesday, Mary itched to go home. She had been moved off of the neurology floor, ostensibly because her condition had improved, but probably because she had too many visitors. Anthony had slept over every night, and Mary's mother, father, and El Virus stayed all day. Judy, Bennie, and Declan came in and out, fitting in visits around work. The Tonys stayed with Feet, and Simon and his cousins stayed with Rachel, who was still waiting for a donor, the only dark note in an otherwise happy ending.

"When are you getting out of here, Mary?" Judy asked, which was the question of the moment.

"As soon as they can get rid of us."

Anthony patted her leg on top of the coverlet. "I saw Dr. Drinkwater in the hallway. He said you might be discharged today, but he'd come in and let us know."

Mary glanced out the window to a sunny sky. "It's already afternoon, and I don't want to spend another night here. I'm ready to go."

"You sure you feel well enough?" Bennie asked, from the foot of the bed. She was back in her khaki power suit, and the bruise on her cheek and butterfly stitches at her hairline only made her look more badass. Her picture and Mary's blanketed the news, but the TV stayed off in the hospital room. Mary didn't need the reminder, and her parents didn't need the cardiac.

"Yes, I'm tired, but that'll go away."

"YOU GOTTA TAKE IT EASY, HONEY. DON'T PUSH IT. DO WHAT THE DOCTOR SAYS."

"I will, Pop." Mary didn't have the heart to tell him that the doctor told her to avoid loud noise, stimulation, and excitement, which was the DiNunzio trifecta.

"Sì, Maria, è vero," her mother said, looking over from the windowsill, where she was arranging yet another vase of flowers. Mary's clients had turned out in force, bringing flowers, biscotti, and balloons, and her mother had arranged the gifts around the room to make it homey, which even she couldn't accomplish.

Declan nodded. "You should take the rest of the week off. Just rest."

Mary shrugged it off. "I don't think it'll take that long. I'll be back sooner than that."

Judy perked up. "So does that mean you're coming back, Mary? Like you're *coming back*? Mommy and Daddy aren't breaking up after all? Rosato & DiNunzio forever?"

Bennie shot Judy a look. "That decision is up to Mary. She doesn't have to make it now. She should think it over and come back only when, and if, she wants to."

Mary swallowed hard, meeting Bennie's eye. She remembered that the last time she had met Bennie's eye so directly, they had been in mortal danger. Bennie had saved her life, risking her own. Mary felt tears welling, but she didn't want to cry in front of everybody. She didn't know why she would cry anyway. Everything had turned out okay. She had no reason to cry.

Mary cleared her throat. "Bennie, I'm very sorry that I

considered leaving the firm. I can't imagine a more loyal partner, and friend. I would love to come back, if you would have me."

"There's no apology necessary." Bennie's expression softened. "And of course, I'd love to have you back. Hell, you're already on the sign."

"Thank you!" Mary felt a rush of gratitude.

"That's a relief!" Anthony said, grinning.

Mary noticed Judy hesitate, but didn't know why. "Judy, what's up?

Bennie smiled slyly. "I'll tell you what's up, Mary. Judy is joining the partnership. If it's okay with you."

Judy's head whirled around. "Bennie, are you serious? You would still make me a partner?"

"Absolutely!" Bennie patted her on the back. "It's the right result. Let's do it!"

"OF COURSE, YOU GIRLS ARE A TEAM! ALL OF YOU'S!"

Mary didn't get it, happily confused. "Awesome! But when did this happen?"

Bennie looked vaguely sheepish. "When you told me you were leaving the firm, I didn't want to lose Carrier, so I offered her a partnership to keep her. She told me she had to make up her mind, but now it's easy. It'll be the three of us."

"The three of us!" Judy repeated, excited. "Yay!"

"The three of us!" Mary laughed, delighted.

Bennie joined her, laughing. "This will be an adventure!"

Declan rolled his eyes. "That it will."

Just then the door opened, and Simon entered the crowded room with a broad grin. "Mary, you're up and at 'em! You look great!"

"I am, I feel great. We're about to hear when I get to go home. How's Rachel?"

"She's doing well, and so is my father. The Tonys and my

cousins have everybody covered, so I could come over and see how you are."

"Did the new donor come through?" Mary asked, sensing that his mood was too good for it to be otherwise.

"As a matter of fact, yes. It's official now. Rachel is back on the countdown." Simon grinned, and so did everybody else, but a funny undercurrent left Mary feeling as if they knew something she didn't.

"What's going on?" Mary scanned their faces and they started looking at each other and smiling. "You guys are the worst poker faces in the world."

Simon answered, "Mary, ask who the donor is."

"Who?" Mary asked, mystified.

"Bennie." Simon gestured at Bennie, who waved him off, flushing.

"Really?" Mary gasped, touched. "Bennie, I can't believe you! That's amazing! When did *that* happen?"

Bennie shrugged it off. "I did the cheek swab and I was a match. Please don't make it a big thing."

Anthony looked over with a smile. "It *is* a big thing! It's a wonderful thing to do."

Declan put his arm around Bennie. "He's right, babe. Now your secret's out. You really do have a heart."

"And more importantly, marrow," Judy interjected.

There was a knock on the door and they all looked over to see Dr. Drinkwater stick his bald head in the door. He was short, chubby, and African-American, with a good sense of humor. "Whoa, do you have room for me in there? It doesn't look that way."

"Come on in," Mary answered, and everybody moved aside as Dr. Drinkwater approached the bed with a warm smile.

"How are you feeling, Mary?"

"Good, thanks. Am I going home today?"

"I'd like to take a few minutes to examine you, then ask a

few questions." Dr. Drinkwater hesitated, glancing around. "Would you rather do that in private?"

Mary smiled. "No, don't worry about it. Everybody here is family."

"Everybody?" Dr. Drinkwater asked, his dark eyes bright with amusement behind his tortoiseshell glasses.

"Everybody," they all answered in unison, then started laughing.

"EVEN YOU, DOC!"

Everybody laughed again, including Dr. Drinkwater, who turned to Mary, getting down to business. "So how's the headache?"

"Comes and goes. Less often than before."

"How's the pain, scale of one to ten?"

"One."

"Any dizziness?"

"No."

"Nausea?"

"All gone. Can I leave today?"

"Yes, and your discharge papers will explain your wound care. You got twelve staples back there, so follow the directions."

"Okay." Mary smiled, happy to be leaving. They'd shaved a bald spot into the back of her head, but she had a new perspective on the importance of hair. She almost thought her head bandages looked cute, like that injured emoji.

"If you experience nausea, vomiting, seizures, loss of consciousness, or any change in mental status, go to the ER right away."

"Will do."

"Take it easy for the next two weeks. No reading, no TV. No work, no excessive exercise."

"Not a problem."

"In addition, you'll have to return for a follow-up CT scan

in two weeks, and don't worry, it won't affect the baby. None of the tests we ran will affect the baby."

Mary must have heard him wrong. "What baby?"

Anthony looked over. "*What* baby?"

"MARE, DID HE SAY 'BABY'?"

Dr. Drinkwater looked from Anthony to Mary, with a smile. "Oh my. Did you not know, Mary? You're pregnant."

ACKNOWLEDGMENTS

Here's where I get to say thank you to those experts who helped me with this book, which contains information beyond my ken.

The ethical quandary at the heart of this book is actually a cutting-edge question in legal ethics. I didn't intend it that way, it just happened, which doesn't sound impressive but is absolutely true. As soon as I thought of the question and didn't know the answer, I consulted one of the foremost experts in legal ethics in the country, who just happened to be an old friend of mine, Lawrence Fox, Esq.

Larry heads the Ethics Bureau at Yale Law School, and as soon as I posed my question to him, he said that would make an excellent question for the class, and to make a long story short, I ended up on a conference call with twenty legal geniuses at Yale Law, who undertook this legal issue as part of their course. I won't tell you how they all came out, because there is a clear divide of authority that I exploited ruthlessly for this novel, but suffice it to say that I think they all deserve an A+. I thank them here for their support, especially to Larry, who gave me the benefit of his scholarly wisdom as well as his decades of practice as a Philadelphia lawyer, and that's saying something. If you are interested in legal ethics, you should read his wonderful and enlightening book, *Red Flags: A Lawyer's Handbook on Legal Ethics.*

Another group who deserves major thanks here is the incredible group of physicians, nurses, and staff at the Children's Hospital of Philadelphia, whom I admire so much that I dedicated the book to them. I knew that I couldn't write this novel without their medical expertise, and I wanted to honor what is a difficult experience for the families of critically ill children.

So I contacted Amy Burkholder, who runs communications for CHOP, and she put me in touch with the amazing Stephanie Fooks-Parker, Anne Wohlschlaeger, Megan Atkinson, and Patricia Hankins. This powerhouse hosted my assistant/best friend, Laura Leonard, and me for an entire day at CHOP, giving us a careful tour of the Blood & Marrow Transplant Unit and giving us the same orientation that a parent whose child was about to receive a bone marrow transplant would be given. We learned more than I could have hoped, and we even met Dr. Stephan Grupp, director of CHOP's Cancer Immunotherapy Program, an amazing doctor who's using his considerable superpowers to try to save the lives of children every day.

Thank you to everyone at CHOP for everything they do for children all around the world. I saw firsthand how much they care about their young patients, and I am deeply grateful to them for taking the time to explain their work to me, down to the smallest detail. And my hat is off to the parents and siblings with family members being treated at CHOP. You exemplify strength, devotion, and the true meaning of love.

For criminal law answers, thanks so much and a great big hug to my dear friend, the brilliant public servant Nicholas Casenta, Esq., chief of the Chester County District Attorney's Office. Thank you (again) to Detective Thomas Gaul of the Homicide Division of the Philadelphia Police Department.

Thank you to my genius editor, Jennifer Enderlin, who is also the senior vice president and publisher of St. Martin's Press, yet she still finds the time to improve every one of my manuscripts, including this one. Thank you so much, Coach Jen! And big love and thanks to everyone at St. Martin's Press and Macmillan, starting with the terrific John Sargent, Don Weisberg, and Sally Richardson, plus Jeff Dodes, Lisa Senz, Brian Heller, Jeff Capshew, Brant Janeway, Erica Martirano, Jordan Hanley, Tom Thompson, John Karle, Sara Goodman, Samantha Davis, Anne-Marie Tallberg, Kerry Nordling, Elizabeth Wildman, Caitlin Dareff, Talia Sheer, Kim Ludlum, and all the wonderful sales reps. Big thanks to Michael Storrings, for outstanding cover design for the series. Also thanks to Mary Beth Roche, Laura Wilson, Samantha Edelson, and the great people in audiobooks. I love and appreciate all of you!

Thanks and love to my agent, Robert Gottlieb of Trident Media Group, whose dedication guided this novel into publication, and to Nicole Robson, Emily Ross, and Trident's digital media team, who help me get the word out on social media.

Many thanks and much love and hugs to the amazing Laura Leonard. She's invaluable in every way, every day, and has been for over twenty years. Laura, I love you! Thanks, too, to the great Nan Daley and to George Davidson, for doing everything else, so that I can be free to write!

Finally, thank you to my amazing daughter, Francesca, for all the support, laughter, and love.